The Scandalous Summer
of Sissy LeBlanc

The Scandalous Summer of Sissy LeBlanc

A Novel

Loraine Despres

wm

WILLIAM MORROW   75 YEARS OF PUBLISHING

An Imprint of HarperCollins*Publishers*

HarperCollins books may be purchased for educational, business, or sales promotional use. For information please write: Special Markets Department, HarperCollins Publishers Inc., 10 East 53rd Street, New York, NY 10022.

FIRST EDITION

Printed on acid-free paper

Library of Congress Cataloging-in-Publication Data
Despres, Loraine.
    The scandalous summer of Sissy LeBlanc / Loraine Despres.— 1st ed.
        p. cm.
    ISBN 0-688-17389-6 (alk. paper)
    1. Women—Louisiana—Fiction. 2. Louisiana—Fiction. 3. Scandals—Fiction. I. Title.

PS3604.E76 S38 2001
813'.6—dc21

2001016260

01 02 03 04 05 QW 10 9 8 7 6 5 4 3 2 1

*To my husband, Carleton Eastlake, who fifteen
years ago succumbed to the charms of a southern belle
and proves every day that marriage is definitely
not the root of all suffering*

Love is the crocodile in the river of desire.

—Bhartrihari, *The Vairagya Sataka,* c. A.D. 625

When you get to be a certain age, you realize that the only

thing you have time for is doing exactly what you want.

Rule Number Fifty-six

THE SOUTHERN BELLE'S HANDBOOK

Prologue

SISSY STEPPED INTO the main terminal of the New Orleans airport and was captured by that Louisiana aroma that encircled her memory and swept her back in time. On the flight from Washington, she thought she'd been prepared. But she'd forgotten the smell of bourbon and Coca-Cola that permeated the airport even at ten in the morning. In the recycled air, it mixed with the dank, sensual smell of oysters on the half-shell and invaded her very pores. The scent carried her back to that summer almost fifty years ago that ended when Peewee LeBlanc walked into the Paradise Lost and saw her sitting on Parker Davidson's lap and went out to buy himself a gun.

It had been a real hot morning.

But that's already redundant. If you know anything about summer in Louisiana you know that the heat, moist and heavy, presses down on the pavement until it sends up shimmering mirages, and lovers, looking for a little noontime solace, stick to one another in high-ceilinged bedrooms. But the bar was cool, especially after a couple of tall glasses of bourbon and Coke over cracked ice.

She remembered how she'd jumped up off Parker's lap and smoothed down her skirt. "Peewee . . ."

Beads of sweat dripped into her husband's eyes. He wiped a tar-stained hand across his forehead.

"Mama, over here!"

The sight of her daughter running through the airport snapped Sissy out of her reverie. Marilee LeBlanc was thin, tense, and perpetually in a hurry. She wore the uniform of the East Coast career woman—black. They all wore it.

Sissy wondered what they were in mourning for, their lives probably, because they sure didn't seem to have much fun these days. Not that Sissy had had that much fun when she was young, but at least she'd had the concept.

She introduced her daughter to the gentleman who had been kind enough to help her with her carry-on bag. He was Marilee's age and handsome, Sissy thought, in a beefy, Southern way.

Marilee took the bag, but there were no smiles over fluttering eyelashes. "We have to hurry. The senator is waiting."

Sissy shook hands with the gallant stranger and thanked him warmly. She watched him walk toward the escalator with a bounce in his step. Men love to rescue damsels in distress, as long as it doesn't take too much time or effort, Sissy thought. *To get a man to feel good about himself—and you—ask him do something for you and thank him sweetly.* That was Rule Number Forty-eight in Sissy's Southern Belle's Handbook, a rule she'd been using with great success for years.

"I don't know why you're always picking up men," Marilee said.

"And I don't know why you aren't," said the older woman, pushing her daughter's hair off her face.

As Marilee drove over the causeway that shot straight through the swamp, Sissy looked out of the window. Lovely white water lilies floated in the gray water next to the freeway, choking the life out of the wetlands. The merciless romance of Southern decay.

She didn't want to go home. And then she caught herself. It had been half a century since she thought of Gentry as home. Where did that come from? God, she needed a cigarette, but she didn't dare light up in her diet-obsessed, health-regimented daughter's car. Besides, she'd given up smoking five years ago, after dire warnings from those Doctor DoRights who're so set on keeping you alive, they take away all reason to live.

Marilee was talking about the campaign. "We could have used you down here with the older demographics."

"We've been through all that. Small-town people have long memories."

"But I still don't get it. Daddy was the one who committed the murder."

"I know, sugar, but a lot of people thought I drove him to it. Of course," she added with a sigh and a stab of guilt, "they were right."

WHEN THEY ROLLED into Gentry, Sissy asked her daughter to swing by their old house. Marilee groaned, but turned the car up Church Street. Memories were dive-bombing at Sissy from the roofs of old houses, slipping through the slits in the windows with the long poisonous fingers of oleander leaves. She began to feel queasy.

"Stop here for a minute, will you?"

Marilee protested, but stopped the car in front of their old house, which had been renovated and restored to its nineteenth-century glory. The gardens had been professionally landscaped, the honeysuckle had been cut away from the square columns, and the whole house gleamed with fresh, white paint. The for-sale sign in the front yard said it was a "Heritage Home." Sissy wondered how many other families had lived there, and what kind of heritage they'd found after she'd left those familiar walls in scandal.

She popped the door open and got out. "Mother, we don't have time!" Marilee wailed.

"Sugar, when you get to be a certain age, you realize that the only thing you do have time for is doing exactly what you want. Rule Number Fifty-six in the Southern Belle's Handbook."

"Spare me," said Marilee, who'd heard about the Southern Belle's Handbook her entire life. "You know I have no intention of ever becoming a southern belle."

"I know, dear," Sissy said, wishing she could help her daughter, who was recovering from yet another miserable love affair. She turned toward the house.

Marilee pounded on her horn. "Mama! We'll be late for the victory celebration." But when Sissy didn't stop, Marilee jumped out of the car and followed her. "The senator . . ."

Sissy cut her off. "I'm sure a United States senator will be able to get along without me for five more minutes. Don't you want to see where you grew up?" She picked up the shining brass knocker and let it drop.

They waited a minute. "Okay, nobody's home. Can we go now?" Marilee asked.

But Sissy, who was always so solid and filled with energy, seemed to sag and stumble.

"Are you okay?" Marilee reached out and steadied the old woman.

"Just let me rest for a moment." Dizzying impressions, not reality, but the reality of memory swirled in her head. She staggered and reached for the reproduction of her old porch swing . . .

"Mama!"

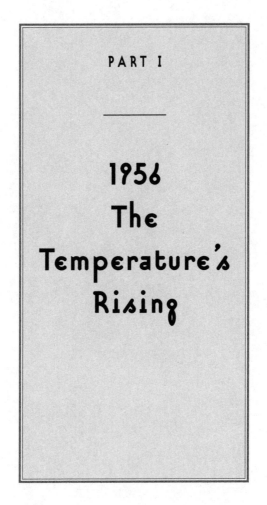

PART I

1956
The
Temperature's
Rising

A girl has to find out if there's life before death.

Rule Number Forty-seven

THE SOUTHERN BELLE'S HANDBOOK

Chapter 1

SISSY LEBLANC SANK down on her porch swing and heard its old chains groan. She threw back her head and rubbed a cut lemon over her hair to bleach it a little in the sun, all the while wondering if you could really kill yourself with aspirin and Coca-Cola. Of course, she wasn't seriously considering suicide. Sissy never seriously considered suicide. Besides, only a teenager would try to poison herself with aspirin and Coke. She figured a bottle of a hundred would do it. Along with that six-pack of Cokes in her kitchen pantry. God, it was breathless today.

She ran her fingers through her hair. She'd just washed it and had hoped that letting it dry out here in what passed for a breeze would give her some relief. It didn't. She was too restless to do anything much in this heat, not that housework had ever been one of Sissy's priorities.

She'd been restless for days, feeling as if she'd burst if something didn't happen. Of course that was crazy, because nothing ever hap-

pened here in Gentry. Except she'd heard Parker Davidson was
back. Parker Davidson, her high school sweetheart.

She flipped her wet hair over her face and leaned her chest on her
knees. The honeysuckle growing wild along one of the six square
columns that held up the porch roof was making another assault on
the house, sending tendrils through the cracks in the warped planks
under the swing. She'd have to crawl under the porch and do something about it. Soon.

Parker hadn't even called. Not that there was any reason why he
should after all these years. She wasn't sure she wanted to see him
anyway. He was probably fat and full of himself now. God, this
heat was making her crazy.

She sat up and saw a telephone truck had stopped across the
street in front of a scarlet oleander bush on the side of the Methodist
church. A lineman had already stepped out. She didn't get a good
look at his face, but he was big like Parker. That boy was sure
traipsing through her mind today. If she went into town, she'd
probably see his likeness in half the men who turned a corner or
walked in front of her on the street.

As the lineman worked his way up the telephone pole, she saw
his suntanned arms glisten with sweat. She watched his back muscles bunch up and smooth out under his wet work shirt.

Memories of old feelings crept over her. She reached for a spray
of honeysuckle and wound it in her hair.

Lighting a cigarette, she found herself staring up at the lineman's
thighs. She couldn't help but notice how his shrink-to-fit jeans had
shrunk just right. She lifted her skirt a tad to let in the breeze.

The lineman pulled himself onto the top crossbar and bent forward to cut the wisteria vines that had twisted around the wires.

Sissy fanned away the smoke hovering in the still air in front
of her.

Then he bent backward under the wires. He hung upside down
by his knees and leaned way out.

She held her breath.

Reaching his arms above his head, he sheared away the vines. Clumps of wisteria fell through the damp air.

Suddenly, Sissy saw him begin to slip off the crossbar. The ground beneath him was littered with broken cement and covered with gnarled roots. She imagined him falling head first. Dying right there in front of her. Instead he tossed his clippers, jack-knifed up, grabbed hold of the crossbar. And waved.

Jesus! Sissy blew out a column of smoke. Of course he'd reminded her of Parker Davidson. He was Parker Davidson! And he was showing off just like he'd done in high school.

She stood up and waved back. Why'd he have to see her today of all days, when she looked like a drowned cat? As he made his way down the telephone pole, she slipped inside.

Sissy wasn't really beautiful, but men never noticed. With her deep green eyes, her shoulder-length auburn hair that swung when she moved, and the way she moved as if she enjoyed just being inside her body, men had always paid her lots of attention. Although after fourteen years of marriage to Peewee LeBlanc, she'd begun to need reassurance. Leaning into the little round mirror she'd hung by the kitchen door, she freshened her lipstick and grimaced. She took her hair and the eyes for granted. She was worrying about the almost imperceptible lines at the corners of her mouth and the tiny fleshy places that seemed to have dropped overnight from the edge of her chin.

But then, Sissy thought, it's not what a girl looks like that captivates a man. It's how hard he has to work for her. *A smart girl makes a man sweat.* She decided to make that Rule Number Sixteen in The Southern Belle's Handbook, which was what Sissy had ironically titled that compendium of helpful hints and rules her mother and grandmother had tried so hard to instill in her. Her mother had wanted her to grow up a gracious Southern lady. Her grandmother just didn't want the bastards to grind her down. Sissy had added to it over the years, until the Southern Belle's Handbook became her personal credo. She kept it in her head, assigning numbers at random, but then Sissy always had a random relationship with numbers.

Through the screen door, she saw Parker walk across the street. She filled two tall glasses with ice and grabbed a couple of Cokes from the pantry. All thought of mixing them with aspirin had vanished.

Then she strolled onto the front porch and found Parker standing on the sidewalk. His tool belt was slung on his hips like a holster. Out in the country, the afternoon freight blew its warning whistle.

"Steal any police cars lately?" he asked.

Sissy shook her head. "Crime just hasn't been the same without you, Parker." She remembered the night after he'd scored five touchdowns against Gentry's biggest rival, they'd stolen the sheriff's car and ridden all over town with the siren blaring in celebration. Until they were arrested. The sheriff had chased them halfway to Hammond in a commandeered pickup.

Her parents had been upset. Parker's had been beside themselves. "We have a business to run in this town," Mr. Davidson growled when he had Parker by the arm and was heading out of the police station.

Mrs. Davidson whispered to Parker, "Sugar, you just can't embarrass us like this in front of the gentiles."

But the Davidsons didn't have to worry. Nobody blamed Gentry's star football player. The teachers. The coach. The other kids. Nobody blamed him at all. They blamed Sissy. Rule Number Six, Southern Belle's Handbook: *Whatever happens, they always blame the girl.*

Parker tried to make everyone believe it had been all his idea, that he'd talked her into it, but everyone knew he was just being a gentleman and taking up for her.

The truth was they'd gotten into trouble together. The decision had been mutual, made in a flash. They'd raced each other to that empty patrol car.

Parker took the stairs two at a time. "God, Sissy, you're all grown up."

She set the Cokes on a wicker table. Her hand fluttered up to her hair. "Fourteen years will do that," she said and wondered if he meant she looked old.

"I think you're even prettier than you were in high school."

Was he serious or just putting her on?

They moved toward one another until they were standing so close, she felt engulfed by his physical presence. Overwhelmed. She'd forgotten how tall he was, well over six feet. She lifted her face to kiss his cheek and then thought better of it. His shirt and hands were covered in creosote, the dark brown tar they painted on the telephone poles to preserve them. She stepped back. "Parker, what in the world were you doing on that telephone pole?"

She caught the blush even on Parker's dark skin. She saw the color rise up his neck and over his cheeks. "Have to clean the debris away from the lines before it takes out the power."

From the sheepish way he said it, Sissy had a sudden insight. No one had actually sent him to cut down the wisteria across from her house. She'd bet Parker had thought that up on his own when he saw her sitting on her porch. Was he just showing off for her? She examined the pole and realized that when he'd leaned way out, he could look directly into her backyard. He wanted to see if Peewee's truck was parked there. He was spying on her. Damn! Nobody had gone to that much trouble for her in years.

She wondered why he was working for the phone company in the first place, but she felt it would be rude to come right out and ask. Rule Number Nineteen, *A lady never embarrasses a man with direct questions*. That had come from her mother, but Sissy being Sissy had embellished it with an addendum all her own: *There are plenty of other ways a smart girl can find out what she wants to know*.

She fell back on her teasing ways. "I don't know why I'm even talking to you, Parker Davidson. I know for a fact you've been in town over a week. And you haven't even called." She tossed her wet hair.

Parker licked a droplet of water that had been whipped off her hair and onto his lips. "I tried. Three, four times."

She thought he must be lying. Then she remembered the phone had rung several times that week, but when Peewee or one of the boys had picked it up, no one was there.

As if reading her mind he asked, "How is old Peewee?"

"Fine, just fine. He works for the parish."

"Sounds like a real steady job."

"It is."

The freight train rumbled through town. They felt the house tremble. Sissy searched the man for clues of the boy she had known. He had the same strong features, the same dark brown hair and heavy eyebrows, the same dark eyes. But now, their corners were crinkled. She felt an irrational envy. He'd gotten those lines without her. His skin was tanned tight across his high cheekbones. With his athletic grace and dark skin and prominent nose, he looked like an Indian. Not a real Indian with their round faces, flat noses, and slightly oriental eyes. But the movie version: Jeff Chandler playing Cochise. Tall, dark, and Jewish. She caught an earthy smell of musk mixed with the creosote.

The ladies' choir began to file into the Southern Methodist Church of Gentry on the opposite corner. They wore starched cotton dresses with sleeves and collars so as not to give offense in the House of the Lord. Some of them waved to Sissy, standing barefooted on her porch in her low-cut, yellow sundress. Parker and Sissy parted self-consciously and waved back. She saw Amy Lou Hopper—who always prided herself on dressing appropriately—adjust her pointy blue glasses before entering the church. Poor Amy Lou, Sissy thought.

She took a seat on the far corner of the swing and smoothed her circle skirt demurely over her knees. Underneath, she felt her legs stick together.

Parker took off his heavy tool belt and sat down so hard the swing jumped and whined. They turned to one another, but fourteen years of silence came between them.

Sissy took a Coke off the wicker table and offered it to him. She heard the ice clink and felt the glass sweat. For the first time in fourteen years their hands touched. Sissy was shocked at the sensation that rushed through her body. It was as if he had reached his big, hairy hand down her dress.

"Thanks," he said and took the glass, leaving Sissy's hand wet and empty.

She touched the tips of her fingers to her cheek and felt where his hand had touched hers. She started to speak, thought better of it, offered him a cigarette and took one for herself. He cupped his hand and leaned forward to light hers.

A hummingbird fluttered inches from the honeysuckle on the porch post. It hovered in space, lusting for the nectar.

The silence between them became charged and dangerous. Sissy had to fill it, but she didn't want to sound strained, or worse, stupid. But she felt stupid and he looked strained. And then she remembered Rule Number Eleven. *Men find themselves the most fascinating subject of any conversation. When in doubt, let him talk about himself.*

"Sammy showed me some of those postcards you sent." Parker hadn't sent many, but the ones he'd sent had pictures of golden Buddhas, elephants, Chinese junks. "Did you really see all that stuff?"

He was flattered by her interest, as she knew he would be, and launched into the story of his travels. "You'd love it, Sissy. Temples a thousand years old next to skyscrapers." He told her how he'd sailed the South China Sea, trekked through the mountains of Thailand on elephants, swum in the Bay of Bengal.

"It must be something to be wild and free," she said, and there was naked longing in her voice.

"It's something, all right."

Sissy flashed back to that last year in high school, when her future was wide open. Anything seemed possible then. Anything, except that she'd spend the rest of her life trapped in the little town she was born in. While Parker roamed the world. Oh well, like her grandmother said, *Don't jump off the roof if you don't expect to hit the ground*. Rule Number Sixty-two.

He asked about old friends. Sissy answered mechanically, but she was listening to the sound of his voice, not his words. The air was breathless, heavy, the way it gets before a storm. She felt they were wrapped together in the late afternoon heat. She rubbed the cold, wet glass against her neck and rolled it over her chest.

Parker watched and stopped talking. He gulped down his icy drink.

The organist across the street played the first chord. Sissy felt anxious. "You want another Coke?" she asked. Her voice was strained.

"If it's not too much trouble," he answered softly, still watching her.

"No trouble at all."

She stood up, threw her cigarette butt on the concrete porch step, and ground it out with her bare foot. She'd read about ballet dancers whose feet were that tough and was proud to find hers were too, after summers of climbing barefooted over the rocks at the creek with her kids. But she hadn't meant to put out a burning cigarette in front of Parker. She caught him staring at her. She felt like a damn fool. He was going to think she'd turned into some kind of a redneck hick. She practically flew off the porch and into the kitchen.

Sissy had always been a flirt. She'd tried out a lot of rules on how to do it, and discarded most of them, but Rule Number Five was always with her: *Boys will squirm and grown men will pull on their collars when a girl tosses her hair and looks at up them through her eyelashes, or even better, over her shoulder*. Through the years, she'd learned that this was more than a rule, it was a law of nature, immutable and very reassuring. But Sissy always did it for fun, just fun. She wasn't going to actually do anything.

When she married Peewee, she'd promised to be a good and faithful wife. And Sissy never went back on her word.

Of course, it hadn't been so hard to resist temptation. There hadn't been a lot of it around.

But here was Parker, back after all these years.

The strap of her sundress had slipped down over her shoulder. She hitched it up and reached her long, freckled fingers into the ice bucket. Empty.

She pried a gray metal tray up out of the little freezer section, but the lever was frozen tight. So she picked up the ice tray and smashed it hard against the sink, which gave her some relief, but didn't help much in getting at the ice. She turned on the tap. Pretty soon the cubes were floating.

What was wrong with her today?

A shadow fell across her body. Parker leaned against the doorway. She didn't turn. Nothing would make her turn or look at him over her shoulder.

"Anything I can do to help?" he asked. She felt the weight of his shadow on top of her. She shut off the tap.

A calloused hand reached over her shoulder and picked up a dripping cube. He rubbed the ice over her shoulders as she stood paralyzed. He ran it under her hair, under the strap of her sundress and over her chest. His hard calluses scraped gently as they slid across her freckled skin. She started to say something, but he ran the ice cube over her lips. She tried to tell him to stop. He gently pushed the melting cube, hardly more than a wafer now, into her mouth.

He bent down—and without touching her body—kissed her lips, tasting their cold wetness, licking her lips until Sissy shivered. She touched his chest and found heat radiating from it.

"Open my eyes so I may see . . ." Choir practice had begun and Sissy snapped out of her fantasy. Parker was still leaning in the doorway. "Need any help?" he asked again.

"Here." She gave him the Cokes to open. She threw the ice cubes into the glasses and poured the rest, water and all, into the ice bucket.

Parker handed her the opened bottles. She turned and knocked over the bucket with her elbow.

"I don't know what's come over me today," she said as ice and water spilled all over the peeling linoleum with its faded yellow and orange flowers.

Parker bent down as Sissy grabbed a dish towel. "No harm done," he said, cupping the ice cubes in his big hands and throwing them into the sink.

Sissy was mopping up the water under his work boots, when Parker bent and gave her his hand. The pungent scents of musk and creosote rose around her. She felt disoriented, confused.

Inhaling deeply, she could actually feel the heat radiating from him. It was real. Her lacquered fingernails were shaking. She thought about releasing the buttons on Parker's work shirt. When the blue denim fabric fell away, would she see the brown hair, just as she remembered it, curling softly over his chest? She wanted to bury her head in it. She imagined his big suntanned hands sliding around her. Those big rough thumbs caressing her small breasts. Rubbing them. Sissy felt her nipples harden. Her body came alive. She wanted to run her hands over those wonderful thighs. She could almost feel the bulge under those metal buttons on his shrink-to-fit jeans. Feel him bunching up her skirt, sliding his hand under her pants. She groaned softly.

"Sissy, are you okay?" he asked, still holding her hand.

Reality returned. But she didn't want any part of it. Then she realized his hand was trembling, too.

"Place in my hands the wonderful key/That shall unclasp and set me free," the ladies sang across the street.

The Southern Belle's Handbook chattered away in her head, reminding her of all the sensible reasons she should stay away from this man. To hell with the Southern Belle's Handbook. To hell with the creosote. Sissy stood on her tiptoes and raised her lips to his. And with the flash of mutual decision that had gotten them into trouble all those years ago, they were in each other's arms. He kissed her gently. She closed her eyes and felt the roughness of his sunburned lips and his cold, hard hands play on the wings of her back.

Sissy usually went through her life as through a tunnel, never touching the walls. But today the walls were crashing in on her. For the first time in years she wanted something.

As the sun lit up the stained glass window over the stove, Parker began to bunch up her full skirt. She felt his jeans rub against the bare skin of her thighs. He groaned softly. His right hand stroked her underpants, while his left hand reached into her sundress. She could hear the material rip, but she didn't care because he was working one breast out of her strapless bra. She sucked in her breath as he touched her nipple. She touched his jeans and felt the material around his buttons strain and pull tight and take on a life of its own. Parker lifted her up and pushed her against the sink. Breathing hard, he hooked her underpants and their lips came together as he slowly slid them off.

"Open my eyes, illumine me . . ." the choir sang.

"I can't, Parker," she said, and they were the hardest words she'd ever had to say. Pushing him away, she opened her eyes and saw the faces of her children pressed against the screen door.

"Oh my God!" she whispered, straightening her dress and pulling up her panties as best she could as the choir echoed, ". . . Spirit Divine."

"Sissy . . ." Parker began, and then he saw the children's faces, too.

She unlocked the screen door. "What are you all doing here? I thought you were at a baseball game! I said I'd pick you up at six.

How'd you get home?" She knew how stupid she sounded, how guilty, but she couldn't help herself.

"Hickey got mad and took the ball home. So Mr. Fletcher gave us a ride," Billy Joe, her twelve-year-old, said. He stared up at Parker.

The three children crept in together.

Chip, thirteen and surly, said nothing. His face was shut down, but his eyes cut back and forth between his mother and the stranger. He saw the wine-red lipstick smeared across Parker's lips and on his work shirt. And smiled.

Sissy pulled up the strap of her sundress and began to babble. "Children, this is Parker Davidson. He was captain of the football team when your mama was a cheerleader. I must have told you about him. Parker, this is Chip, my oldest, and Billy Joe, and Marilee, my baby." She put her hand on the little girl's shoulder. The six-year-old wrapped her arms around her mother's hip and eyed the stranger from the folds of her mother's skirt.

"Hey there, partners," Parker said, more coolheaded than she would have imagined possible. And then with a catch in his voice, he asked, "You got any more?"

"This is it," Sissy said brightly, too brightly.

Chip turned away in disgust. So Parker bent over slightly and held out his hand to Billy Joe. But the children weren't looking at his hand or their mother's wet hair, which she was trying to tie up in a prim knot on the back of her head. What they were staring at was closer to Marilee's eye level. Then Sissy saw it, too.

"Parker, for God's sake," she hissed, "turn around!" He did and saw the metal buttons on his jeans were straining to burst free. He tried to adjust his pants and caught the lipstick stain on his shirt. The children took off giggling, slamming the screen door behind them.

The ladies of the Southern Methodist Church of Gentry raised their voices once again. "You have a friend in Jesus," they trilled.

It's a good thing, thought Sissy as she ran down the stairs after her children. I'm gonna need all the friends I can get. "Get out of here!" she called back to Parker.

HE WATCHED HER haunches work under her yellow sundress as she ran across the grassy yard, through the laundry hanging out on the line to dry, past the wilderness of white and scarlet oleanders growing along the fence. His heart was keeping time with the choir as they sang and clapped. He tucked in his shirt and tugged on his jeans, but there was nothing he could do about the bulge that had risen again as he watched her. Jesus. He'd had no idea she could still do that to him. He had to wait. He couldn't risk running into some stray Methodist and ruining Sissy's reputation once again. That was the last thing he wanted. He already felt terrible about the kids.

He focused his breathing. Pretty soon he was able to head for the door. He glanced into the mirror and spotted the indelible lipstick on his face. He had grabbed a towel and begun to rub his mouth when he heard a truck drive up on the gravel and a door slam.

"Sissy!" a male voice yelled. Peewee LeBlanc had come home.

SISSY RAN AFTER her children. She wasn't so worried about Marilee. She was still a baby, but the boys were different. She could imagine the smirks and dirty jokes.

"Sissy!" Peewee yelled.

She saw the kids hightail it over a fence and disappear. Maybe it was for the best. It would give her time to figure out what she should say to them. But what could she say? Neither the Southern Belle's Handbook nor all those books on child rearing she'd read over the years, and she'd read them all, dealt with what to tell adolescent boys who catch their mother kissing a strange man next to the kitchen sink.

Peewee stopped on the top step of the front porch and kicked the

mud from his boots. He saw Amy Lou Hopper come out the side
door of the Methodist church.

She whisked off her pointy blue glasses and waved a plump
white arm.

Peewee turned. "Hey, Amy Lou, you seen Sissy?"

"Why, yes," she said, and smoothed the stiff wave of blond hair
that dipped over one side of her forehead. "Yes, I have."

Storm clouds hunched together over the house.

THE KITCHEN DOOR faced the church. Parker cracked open the
screen and spotted some of the women he'd known as a boy growing up. They were walking along the sidewalk, singing in two-part
harmony as they headed for the parking lot. Then he saw Amy Lou
Hopper standing on the curb and heard Peewee's voice coming from
the front porch! Parker slowly eased himself back into the kitchen.

Peewee saw Amy Lou hesitate and then walk out into the middle
of Hope Street. He felt like a jackass. Of course she wasn't going to
stand out in front of the church and holler. It wouldn't be ladylike.
Peewee knew that, unlike his wife, Amy Lou always acted like a
lady. "She was sitting right out here in front of God and everyone,"
she said in a pleased voice as she placed a white, pointed-toe linen
pump up onto the curb.

Amy Lou waited impatiently for Peewee to ask her what Sissy
was doing in front of God and everyone. She prided herself on the
fact that she was not a gossip, but of course if Peewee came right
out and asked, she'd be bound as a Christian to tell the truth. After
all, a man had a right to know what his wife was up to. She was
crossing the sidewalk to enlighten him when Peewee spotted the
tool belt lying next to the swing on the front porch. He picked it up
and saw the name on it, Parker Davidson. And then he didn't want
to talk to anyone. He turned abruptly, leaving Amy Lou striding
across the broken concrete.

Parker was checking the window next to the pantry when he

heard the front door slam. Would he have time to get the screen off? The only other door led through the dining room, and Peewee was entering it now.

Peewee walked around the old walnut dining table and straight into the kitchen. "Sissy!" He made his voice deep. He was the man of the house, after all. He had a right to know what was going on. "Sissy!" He heard his voice crack on the upswing.

The sun, dying behind the stained glass window, cast its red glow, but the room was empty. Peewee glanced through the pass-through into the pantry. Nothing. The kitchen window was open; its screen securely in place.

"Sissy!" Peewee yelled, not caring if his voice cracked this time, setting the tool belt down on a chair and throwing open the screen door.

The ladies in the parking lot turned to see what the commotion was all about just as Sissy, her mouth full of clothespins, pushed her head through the sheets hanging out to dry in the backyard.

"You want me, Peewee, or are you practicing for the parish hog calling contest?" She gave him an exasperated look and hefted a wicker basket filled with damp clothes onto her hip. "Don't just stand there, give me a hand before it starts to rain."

Storm clouds were closing in fast.

Peewee went out to his wife, who was jerking sheets off the line and dropping them into the basket. Under the eager eyes of the Methodists, she gave him a quick kiss on the cheek, grimacing at the pungent odor of tar and stale sweat rising from his body. Her nose twitched as her lips brushed his blond stubble. "I thought you were working in the office today."

"No such luck," he answered as he pulled the clothespins off the sheets still on the line. "Norbert called in sick again. We was patching that stretch over by Raceland, so guess who had to go out there?" He dragged the last of the sheets down and waved to the ladies heading home before the storm.

Sissy knew that *so much of the unpleasantness in a marriage is a direct result of the husband feeling underappreciated.* Rule Number Fifty-five. What she could never understand was how a smart woman let that happen, especially since it was so easy to remedy. "You poor thing. You don't mean you were working all day on the road in this heat?"

Peewee nodded.

"Come on, you need a beer." Sympathy and understanding oozed out of her words. Peewee didn't exactly smile, but he did look grateful and he took the towering laundry basket from her.

She followed him into the house. His sandy-blond hair was cropped so short, she could see his pink scalp showing through and the place where his glasses made dark marks on the back of his ears. His otherwise trim figure was beginning to spread out softly in the middle and roll over the top of his slacks.

Peewee put the laundry on the kitchen table, and as he caught sight of her full on, his blue eyes narrowed. "What the hell have you been up to?"

"I can't imagine what you mean." She picked up a pack of cigarettes and slapped her pockets in vain for a match.

Then she noticed an ice cube on the linoleum. She curled her bare toes over it.

"Look at yourself, woman."

Sissy looked down and saw creosote stains down the front of her sundress. It was not the afternoon attire recommended in the Southern Belle's Handbook.

"What's been going on around here?"

Rule Number Twenty-three popped into Sissy's mind. *When a train heads straight at you, a smart girl derails it.* She looked her husband in the eye and said, "Peewee, I have spent the day chasing after a bunch of kids, cleaning up your mess, and taking care of this big old house. Who do you expect me to look like, Dinah Shore?"

It didn't work. Peewee pulled the chair out from under the kitchen table and held up the tool belt. "What's this doing here?"

"How should I know?" She kicked what was left of the ice cube under the sink and picked up the laundry basket. Finding no matches under it, she slammed it back down and started opening drawers. God, she needed a smoke.

"Says it belongs to Parker Davidson."

Sissy froze mid-drawer and then, with as much nonchalance as she could muster, said, "Oh, yeah. Parker's back." She heard the rumble of distant thunder.

"What was he doing here?"

Sissy didn't hesitate. "He came over to make indecent advances. In his spare time, he fixed the telephone line." She grabbed the box of kitchen matches from the stove and shook them, but she came up empty.

"What are you talking about?"

"He's working for the phone company."

"Come on." He sounded shocked.

"True." Sissy didn't understand it either.

Peewee was silent for a moment, taking it in. Then a smile spread across his face. "The great Parker Davidson, Gentry's biggest football star and war hero, is stringing phone lines? The Jew boy that was gonna bring back fame and glory?"

"Peewee! Stop it! You know I can't stand it when you talk like that."

"Damn!" Peewee said, ignoring her reproach. He couldn't remember when he'd felt so good. And then a nagging thought curled around his brain. "What was he doing on our front porch?"

Sissy wanted to explode, but forced a teasing smile. Rule Number Eighteen, *Fools and husbands fall for flattery.* "Oh, Peewee, I just love it when you're jealous."

"I'm not jealous, I just want to know what's going on."

"I saw him working in the hot sun and offered him a Coke. Is that okay?"

He didn't say anything. He pressed his lips together and after some thought nodded as if the whole issue wasn't worth much consideration.

"Good. Now stop being so silly. I married you, not him. Remember?" She ruffled his blond crew cut, knocking his two-toned glasses askew, and kissed the air near his cheek. Desperate for a match, she sashayed into the pantry, a cigarette dangling from her lips.

And then she dropped her cigarette.

Parker Davidson was crouched on top of a shelf, partially hidden from the little window, displacing paper bags, a carton of matches, and four jars of Sissy's pickled watermelon rinds, which he was holding in both hands. The shelf was made of good, strong cypress, but it was bowed under Parker's considerable weight. He shrugged and grinned.

Sissy was furious. He thinks this is some kind of a damned adventure. She backed out of the pantry, closing the door behind her.

Stretching her mouth into an imitation of a smile, she said to her husband, "Why don't you go on over to the telephone company and drop off the belt?"

"Why should I?" He wiped off his two-toned glasses, which Sissy had smudged.

"Well, Parker just started working there. He could get into a lot of trouble."

"No skin off mine," Peewee said, taking a beer from the icebox and crossing to the pantry door.

Sissy heard the first drops of rain hit the roof and saw the sky flash white.

A small face peered through the kitchen window.

Sissy put her arms around her husband. "I'm sorry I blew up at you, sugar, but you know how I hate it when you ask me all those questions. I mean, I already have a daddy. I never expected to marry one." She kissed him and then made a face. His skin was greasy. "Why don't you run a nice bath and I'll come in and wash your back." She did her best to make it sound suggestive and it worked because Peewee said:

"For God's sake, woman, we haven't even had supper yet." He took a swig of beer and pushed her aside. His hand was on the pantry door. Sissy blocked his way. Her heart was pounding. She had to think of something. She took the beer out of his hand and sipped it. Then she handed it back. "I wasn't making an indecent suggestion. I just thought you'd feel better after a nice, cool bath."

Peewee wavered, and then turned the doorknob. "Just as soon as I get me some of your pickled watermelon rinds."

"Why, sugar, I got a plate of them, nice and cold in the fridge. Tell you what, you just go and lie down in that tub and I'll bring them to you on a tray with another beer. What do you say?" She was proud of how casual she sounded.

Peewee let go of the pantry door. "You mean it?" There was surprise in his voice. She knew he felt she should wait on him more, the way women were supposed to wait on their men, but with three kids and a big house she could never work up the energy.

"Course I do. You deserve a little attention after spending the day in this hot sun."

That did it. "Sounds good to me." He turned toward the door, slapping her on the butt as he passed, when Billy Joe rushed into the kitchen, breathing hard. "You all gotta come . . ."

"Billy Joe, you're sopping wet!" Sissy said,

Sounding just like his own father, Peewee took his son by the arm and said, "Young man, you know better than to stand there dripping all over your mother's linoleum. Now, march!"

He pushed the boy toward the bathroom, but Billy Joe stood his ground. "Marilee fell into the gravel pit."

Sissy saw the lightning splinter down the middle of the sky.

"I told you kids to stay away from there, didn't I, didn't I!" Sissy cried, clutching her son. Hysteria tightened around her voice. Sissy's brother Norman, the big brother she'd spent her childhood trailing after, the reason she was nicknamed Sissy—he couldn't pronounce Cecile—dove into the gravel pit the day he came home from college. And drowned.

She was surrounded by the thunder.

*   *   *

RAIN SHEETED OVER the windshield when Peewee skidded to a stop in the mud. Layers of clouds shrouded the late afternoon sun. Before Sissy and Billy Joe could get their doors open, Peewee jumped out of the pickup and ran to the edge of the water.

He knew his little girl could hardly swim. He'd never found the time in all her six years to teach her. He'd left that to Sissy, and that wasn't good enough, not nearly good enough.

Rain obscured his sight behind his two-tone plastic glasses. He took them off and wiped them on his shirt when a flash of lightning lit up the man-made lake and Peewee saw Chip, his oldest son, with his shirt off, staring into the far side of the pit. Then Peewee spotted a lump of pink caught up in a bunch of branches. Was that Marilee wrapped around a fallen tree?

He yelled. Chip looked up through the pelting rain, pointed into the pit, and yelled back, but Peewee couldn't hear him. Peewee bent down to untie his boots. He handed his glasses to Sissy, who'd run up behind him.

"Wait a minute," she said. "We've got to find out where she went . . ." But the rest of her words were smothered by the roar of thunder that seemed to shake the pond. Billy Joe was screaming something, too. He grasped his father's arm, but Peewee pushed them both aside and plunged into the deep water of the pit.

"Peewee, don't!" Sissy screamed.

But he didn't hear. He tried to strike a bargain with God. Don't take Marilee, not yet. Please. Let us have her a little longer and I'll . . .

Lightning zippered across the sky. The pit lit up. Peewee froze in the water. But no electricity charged through his body. He wordlessly thanked God for saving him this time and began to count the seconds before he heard the thunder. One and . . . He splashed wildly toward the mound of pink. Two and . . . His arms and legs were working like pistons. Please just let her hold on. Just let her hold on until I get there. Three and . . . He lifted his head up and yelled in Chip's direction, but he got no response. Four and . . . Peewee was swimming as fast as he could, but not nearly fast enough. His legs were getting heavy in his waterlogged slacks, which were riding up on him. Five and . . . Thunder shook the pit. God, he wished he were out of here. He tried to think about John Wayne. What would the Duke do? He wouldn't let a little lightning stop him. Finally Peewee reached the floating tree. Branches tore his arms as he fought through their tangle, but he hardly felt them. He snatched up the pink mound. And came away with Marilee's shirt.

His little girl wasn't in it. He put his face into the murky water and opened his eyes, hoping he wouldn't see her floating naked in the dark. The darkness went on forever. He'd heard the pit went down a hundred feet in some places. He'd never be able to dive that far. Lightning flashed through the water and then the thunder. Oh God. Anyplace but here.

SISSY RAN BAREFOOTED through the dunes of gravel piled up next to the pit. The thunder crashed around her. She wrapped Chip in her arms. "When did you lose sight of her?"

But Chip wiggled away. "First you gotta promise, I get that chemistry set at Rubinstein's, the big one, and oh, yeah, Billy Joe wants a red Schwinn."

"What?" Sissy couldn't make out what he was saying. She pushed him away from her and looked into his face. He was grinning. Billy Joe, his tears totally gone, was shaking his head. Lightning crackled above them. Sissy screamed through the thunder. "Where is she?"

Chip didn't budge. "First you gotta promise."

"The only thing I'm going to promise, young man, is to let you live . . . maybe. Now, where's my baby?"

"She's not in the water, Mama."

"Shut up!" Chip hit his brother on the shoulder. "You'll ruin everything." Billy Joe swung around, ready to give as good as he got.

And then as the lightning flashed, Sissy saw Parker against the darkened sky, lashed by the wind and rain, standing on top of a tall gravel dune. In front of him was a small girl in a big T-shirt. She waved at her mother.

Sissy ran down to the edge of the pit. The boys ran with her. "Oh my God, Peewee, get out of there!" She screamed, but her husband didn't hear her. He had disappeared beneath the surface. The rain beat on the water, hiding all traces of him.

Sissy looked up and saw Marilee alone on the hilltop. She called for her to come down, but her voice was drowned out by the thunder.

"I'll get him." Billy Joe took off toward the edge of the pit.

Sissy ran after Billy Joe and pulled him back. "You don't have the sense God gave crawfish. You know you can't swim in an electric storm." She waved at Peewee when he came up for air, but he ignored her and dove again.

She turned back to Chip. "Get Marilee." Chip didn't budge, so Sissy started up after her daughter, sinking into the gravel with every step. The boys trailed behind her. "Your daddy's gonna whip the pants off you when he finds out."

"No he won't," Chip said with smug assurance as he came up next to her. " 'Cause you're not gonna tell him nothing." Sissy glanced at her firstborn and began to shiver, but it wasn't from the rain and the wind. She turned back and kept on climbing, barefoot in the slippery gravel. She recognized that tight smile, the squint of those pale blue eyes.

"We was trying to rescue you, Mama," Billy Joe said on her other side. The twelve-year-old put on the tragic face he had worn in the kitchen and then broke into a self-conscious grin. "We just wanted to give Mr. Parker time to get away."

But he didn't get a chance to finish. Chip ran around her and punched him. "Shut up, I'll handle this." Then he said to his mother, "We saved you. Now you owe us. Deal?"

Sissy didn't want to believe what she was hearing. Chip pursued her up the hill. "A chemistry set would be very educational. Okay? Okay?" When he wanted something, he wanted it bad.

Sissy picked up her daughter and ran with her, sliding through the gravel. The little girl giggled. "Did Chip tell you what I want? A movie star doll with her own suitcase. Did he?" It was all a big game to her.

Lightning sizzled through the sky immediately above them. Thunder shook the water. Sissy began throwing gravel. When Peewee came up, she pointed to Marilee, who waved to her daddy and then ran up the embankment to her big brother.

"Is she gonna do it?" the little girl asked, panting.

"Course she is," said Chip. And then, "She better."

Sissy bent over to pull Peewee out of the pit. And as the folds of her skirt fell away, Chip spotted a creosote handprint. A mean smile spread across his face. "Don't worry. She'll do it."

Chapter 2

PARKER DAVIDSON DROVE slowly down the muddy service road that surrounded the gravel pit. Piles of rock cast phantom shadows through the rain. Every few seconds when the windshield wipers cleared away the sheets of water, he could see the landscape of mud and pebbles and it looked like a landscape on the moon.

He knew he hadn't heard that note of terror in the boy's voice. Not the terror he'd heard during the war, when boys, not much older than Billy Joe, looked into the grimace of death. But he had to be sure.

He rolled down his side window. The cold rain beat on his face, but he had to see. He drove almost all the way around the pit, before in a flash of lightning he spotted the little girl hiding, pressed like an angel into a hill of gravel in somebody's big white T-shirt. Kids.

He got out of the car and spoke to her softly as the rain lashed them. But she was skittish of him, which was only right, he figured.

She started to run up the gravel dune. He followed her to be sure she wouldn't veer off, run somewhere else. As soon as he was certain Sissy had seen her daughter, he disappeared. He thought about sticking around, but decided he'd gotten her into enough trouble.

The truck lurched in the gravel and mud. Then it caught and leaped ahead. He was surrounded by thunder.

He rolled up the window so the rain no longer pounded on his face, turned down the feeder road, and headed back to town away from the dreary landscape of the strip mine. Raindrops beat a tattoo on the roof of the cab.

"Jew boy," echoed through the raindrops.

Parker tried to shake it off as he turned onto the blacktop lined with tall loblolly pines. He'd run into that sort of thing a couple of times in grammar school when one of the country boys called him "nothing but a dirty Jew." And a minister's daughter explained politely how he was going to hell because he'd gone to her daddy's Bible school and knew about Jesus and still didn't believe. But he'd hardly ever run into it since then. He wasn't so naive as to think anti-Semitism was dead. The war made that clear. But people who didn't like Jews tended to stay away from him. Or at least they didn't insult him to his face. Peewee's offhand remark had thrown him. Is that the way they all talked behind his back? he wondered as he drove down the leafy residential street, slowing for the stop sign in front of the Methodist church. He looked at Sissy's house across the street, where he used to take her after movies. They used to kiss good night on that same front porch.

When he'd first heard Sissy was going to marry Peewee, Parker had kicked a hole through his bedroom wall right into the living room. It had taken three tall glasses of Scotch and water to calm his father down enough to inspect the damage. Finally he walked into Parker's room and said, "You're just going to have to face it, son. Girls like Sissy will date Jewish boys, but when they get married, they generally find themselves a nice gentile."

Parker hadn't believed it. He didn't know why Sissy had dumped him for the toad, but he didn't want to believe that.

Steam was forming on the inside of the windshield. He rolled the window back down and hit the gas pedal, splashing parked cars with muddy water on the rain-slick street. But he couldn't go very fast, not with the speed bumps and stop signs and cross traffic. He rubbed his hand on the steering wheel. He could still feel the curve of Sissy's waist under his palm. And the way her flesh yielded to his fingers when he slid them down her body.

He'd missed his last call, and now it was nearly six, past time to close up. Calvin Merkin, his supervisor, would be hopping mad at having to wait for him. Parker had blown into town without much money. He'd never liked to save for tomorrow what he could spend today. Calvin, who'd been in Parker's class, but whom Parker barely remembered, had taken him on right away, made a job for him. Parker had tried to hold out for something better. But this was about the only job in town.

Suddenly, a rickety pickup packed with crates of chickens swung out in front of him. Parker fluttered his brakes as he came into the intersection. The telephone truck skidded sideways. Lightning flashed on an old hearse full of high school kids coming straight at him, paying no attention to the stop sign. Parker threw his weight on the wheel, turned into the skid, and managed to get the truck out of their way. The teenagers were safe, but he couldn't get around the chicken farmer, who was going fifteen miles an hour. He heard the thunder growl in the distance.

Parker pounded on the steering wheel with his fist and then forced himself to relax. He inhaled the dark, woody smells of the rainy summer evening and thought about the auburn-haired cheerleader who'd jumped into the air and yelled for him every time he made a touchdown. And then leaped into his sweaty arms when the game was done.

He'd tried to put her out of his head at first, but over the years he'd found memories of her helped. He'd thought about her during the war, when the wet heat of the South Pacific nights and the buzzing of the flies made him think about Gentry.

He thought about her after the war, too. He was just twenty-one in 1945 when it ended, and he hadn't a clue what he wanted to be when he "grew up."

He'd always expected he'd get a football scholarship and then turn pro. Everyone did. But that dream ended on some no-name island when he caught a load of shrapnel while building a bridge under enemy shelling. A bridge that in the end was never used. He got the Silver Star for leading his men on that fool's mission. Nobody in his right mind would have done it. But then, during the war, nobody ever accused Parker of being in his right mind. He was just young and wild.

Sissy's father gave him a big write-up in *The Weekly Avenger*. GENTRY'S GREATEST FOOTBALL STAR BECOMES GENTRY'S MOST GALLANT WAR HERO. Schoolchildren from all over the parish wrote him fan letters. He read a couple and threw the rest away. Too many of his men had died.

The chicken truck headed toward the intersection at Church and Grand Avenue. The light was green. Come on, come on, Parker willed. He sure as hell didn't want to be fired his first day on the job. It would be like flunking your high school reunion. But here he was, caught in the Gentry rush minute, behind a shipment of poultry that slowed for oncoming traffic.

Lightning shot across the sky. A car pulled out of the courthouse parking lot and the poultry truck stopped politely. And missed the green light. Parker shook with the thunder.

He wished he were back in Asia where you could nudge frightened farmers right through country intersections.

He'd taken his discharge overseas. With no career and nobody waiting for him, he'd set out to see the world. Somewhere there had to be something that made him feel as good as running ninety-five yards for a touchdown with Sissy leaping up in the air and the whole town standing up and cheering for him.

He bummed all over Asia. He never worried about money. With his training in the engineering corps, he knew he could always pick up something.

Of course his parents were desperate for him to come back and go to college on the G.I. Bill and then take over the shoe store. But Parker wasn't ready to settle for that.

The chicken truck turned left on Grand. The town was founded in 1870, shortly after the Civil War, but the streets were named in 1910 in a fit of civic boosterism: Grand Avenue, Progress Street, Commerce Street, Education Drive, Church Street, and of course Hope. All that naming hadn't helped much. The population hardly grew at all. Parker shot straight across the tracks, hung a right, and drove through the two-story stucco business district that ran for five blocks on Grand along both sides of the railroad tracks. His father's shoe store was gone. The neon sign he'd helped hoist over the entrance had been replaced by a wooden plaque with "Nettie's Knits" burned into it.

All those years of worrying about "the business." All those entreaties to set a good example and become a pride to his race, while of course never mentioning or calling any attention to his Jewishness. All that fear of "waving the flag." In the end, what difference did it make? They called him a Jew boy behind his back and bought their shoes down the street at Rubinstein's.

A red-and-green neon sign outlined the department store on the corner of Grand and Progress, where he turned. Golden letters flashed on: RUBINSTEIN'S SERVING GENTRY SINCE 1875. The raindrops on his windshield lit up in a splatter of color, the colors of the temples of Thailand.

He'd landed there in 1948 and felt an affinity for the steamy, underdeveloped country with its temples of gold and red and green. He acquired a real taste for the spicy Thai food and the lissome women who cooked it.

He found a job with Jim Thompson, an American G.I. who was revolutionizing Thai silk, changing it from a cottage industry into a major export. But Parker didn't much like textiles or working for the fastidious, fussy Thompson.

He was more comfortable with a former Seabee captain, who was starting up a construction business and promised to teach him anything he didn't already know about building.

They took an influential Thai businessman in as a partner and began to build downtown Bangkok. Parker was on a roll again, as his company moved into the spotlight. His partners took care of the contracts, the bribes, the business. Parker stayed at the job site. He liked being out there in the heat with the other men, building something he could see, something he could lay his hands on.

One of Thompson's pretty weavers moved in with him and Parker settled down, as much as he could settle down. As soon as the actual construction slowed, he'd be off by himself trekking through the mountains on elephants or wandering around the jungles of Burma on foot. Once he disappeared into a Buddhist monastery and didn't come out for two months. At first he thought he'd found what he was looking for. There the monks in their saffron robes tended rows of golden Buddhas and taught him that this life was just one small step in the eternal journey. They showed him how to take away the pain of living. But after a couple of months, he realized they were so focused on the pain, they'd given up on the joy. He couldn't stay. The river of desire was too strong in him.

Then in 1954, when a big contract they were counting on didn't come through, his American partner skipped town with all their money. Parker managed to pay off his men. He knew they'd have starved if he hadn't. But it wiped him out. And he wasn't able to repay their big suppliers. He remembered his father telling him, "A man has to stand behind his word." Parker felt he'd had his shot and he'd dropped the ball. He was humiliated.

His Thai partner suspected Parker was in league with the thief. All Americans looked the same to him. With an Asian prison looming over his future, Parker, who was carving out a place for himself as an international businessman, was forced to slip out of the country at night, in an old fishing boat that belonged to one of his laborers.

The girl cried. She wanted him to marry her and take her back with him. He considered it. She was strong and sweet and when she'd throw her long black hair around and look at him from the corner of her eye, he found her hard to resist. But he knew it would be wrong. He didn't love her.

By then he'd had more women than he could count, in every color and hue. And some of them meant a lot to him. But he always held back. Something indescribable was missing.

He slunk back to the United States with the bitter taste of defeat on his tongue. He felt like a stranger in San Francisco, where nobody cared that he claimed to have been part owner of a construction company in some godforsaken underdeveloped country.

He returned home to his mother, now living in Miami, and his sense of humiliation was complete. The only work he could find was on nonunion construction crews. His mother lied about his occupation.

He met a girl in Miami, this time Southern and Jewish. She was smart and sarcastic, and had wonderful curly red hair. Her father owned a big Cadillac dealership and was willing to take Parker into the business.

"Perfect," his mother said.

The date was set. Parker went with his fiancée to pick out their silver. As he watched her agonize over the pattern, arrange knives and spoons on different place mats, he envisioned their life together and he couldn't make himself go through with it. He couldn't spend the rest of his life living off his father-in-law's dole. Besides, that indescribable something wasn't there.

His mother said he'd find any excuse not to get tied down. "You're thirty-two and you don't have anything to show for it. No family. No education. No business. Nothing. It's time you built yourself a life, boy, or life's going to pass you by." He knew she was right.

In the middle of his life, Parker's vision of himself was shrinking.

He decided to go back to Gentry, where, once upon a time, crowds cheered and called him the great Parker Davidson. Besides he wanted to see how Sissy was doing.

He'd half hoped she was settled and fat, so he could reject her as she had once rejected him. He intended to close the door on that painful adolescent fantasy. So the last thing he'd expected was the heat their encounter had generated. But there it was. Maybe that's what he'd really been hoping for all along.

He swung the telephone truck into the rutted gravel parking lot. Calvin Merkin, his supervisor, was standing in the doorway looking pissed.

Parker jumped out and went inside to face him. As the lightning flashed and the thunder boomed, Calvin did his duty and chewed him out for a good five minutes, until he noticed the lipstick on Parker's shirt. "I should fire your ass, boy," he said. "Who you been catting around with? Some housewife with a bad phone?" But his eyes didn't show anger. Instead they gleamed with eager admiration. "You SOB."

Parker said nothing.

"Come on," Calvin said. "I'll let you buy me a drink."

They went out into the parking lot together. Calvin watched Parker grab a jar of homemade pickled watermelon rinds from the telephone truck and toss it into his MG.

"Damn!" said Calvin. "Damn! She gave you a souvenir!"

"I'll see you at the Paradise," Parker said, and peeled away from the curb.

He'd fallen in love with Sissy in the days of his youth, when he was struggling to remain pure at heart. He'd never even tried to make love to her. Now he ranked that as one of the stupider decisions.

As he pulled up to the bar, he thought about the bigoted toad she'd married. But he didn't know what to do about it.

Chapter 3

SISSY STOOD IN the bathroom window, her hand on the creased, yellowing shade. She heard the voices of Frankie Lymon and the Teenagers floating down the empty street singing "Why Do Fools Fall in Love." Good question, she thought as she saw the second-hand hearse filled with high school kids round the corner under the streetlight.

She remembered what it was like when she was in high school looking for trouble on a hot summer night and her biggest problem was she might not find any.

The storm had blown over, leaving the town breathless and muggy. She pulled the shade down and hung her green chenille robe on the hook in back of the door. The wet clothes everyone had thrown into a heap and left for Mother were lying in a puddle on the black-and-white tile.

Balancing an ashtray on the edge of the old, claw-footed tub, she sank wearily into the water. It was barely tepid now that she'd got-

ten the rest of her family bathed. She closed her eyes, too tired even
to pick up the soap.

After a while she sat up and took a drag on her cigarette. As the
nicotine curled through her system, the horrors of the afternoon
came back to taunt her. Peewee had been so brave. Foolish but
brave. He could have died in that damned gravel pit like Sissy's
brother Norman had all those years ago. Guilt crawled up and
down her stomach. Okay, that did it, enough. *She was going to
remain a good and faithful wife just as she'd always been.* She
decided to make that Rule . . . she searched for an appropriate
number . . . Fifty seemed about right.

She ran the pink bar of soap along her arms and around back of
her neck where her auburn hair was more or less pinned up. No
more yielding to temptation, she swore to herself. What does it get
you, anyway? A different man. Big deal.

A memory flashed through her body of another man, a long time
ago, a short powerful man in a hunting jacket. She reached for her
cigarette. Southern Belle's Handbook Rule Number Seventeen: *A
lady doesn't waste her precious time on bad memories.* She inhaled
shakily. Ashes fell into her bath. Shit. She tried to grind out the
butt, only to knock the ashtray onto the floor.

Love is like cigarettes, Sissy thought as she leaned over the edge
of the tub and shoveled up the dead butts and old cellophane wrap-
pers. It gives you a little pleasure while you're at it, but it leaves you
with a bad taste in your mouth and a pain in your chest.

She picked up her still burning butt and tried to take one last
drag, but it fell apart in her ash-wet hand.

She stretched her chin to her chest, working the kinks out of her
neck, and wondered what she was going to do when she saw Parker
again. Nothing, she assured herself, wallowing in soapy water and
rectitude. She was finished with love. From now on, she was determined to be a good and faithful wife. And love had nothing to do
with that.

She stepped out of the tub, rubbing herself dry with the last clean towel, a thin, flowered thing she'd gotten in a box of detergent, and then she slipped into her green chenille robe. She unpinned her hair. It fell around her face as she bent down to pick up the wet clothes.

As her sundress unfolded, she saw to her horror the creosote hand imprinted into the folds of her circle skirt. My God, had it been there all the time? She was pretty sure Peewee hadn't noticed. He would have said something. She brushed her hand over her skirt. She couldn't resist letting her fingers play over the sticky handprint one last time. Her body remembered what Parker's big hand had felt like when he put his dark mark on her behind, and then, in spite of her newfound probity, her nipples hardened. *One man's as good as another*, Rule Number Twenty-one, she reminded herself with as much conviction as she could muster. But her nipples didn't pay any attention. She wadded the dress into a ball.

As she passed the bedroom door, she heard Chip explaining to his father how Marilee had crawled out of the water when no one was looking. "Guess my little girl's a better swimmer than any of us thought." Peewee sounded pleased. Sissy glanced into the room and saw the little girl snuggled up next to her father in the big four-poster bed. What more do I want? she asked herself. She wondered if she should make up something appropriate for the Southern Belle's Handbook, but she was too tired.

She threw all the wet clothes except her dress into the washing machine and turned it on. Then she opened the broom closet and almost threw the crumpled dress into the rag bag. But remembering the look on Chip's face, she took it outside and threw it straight into the garbage, which was scheduled for pickup the next day. Something was happening to Chip. He was changing in front of her, not that he'd ever been easy. Maybe he needed more attention, more encouragement. She decided to buy him the chemistry set he wanted. He was right. It would be educational.

* * *

"TIME FOR BED," Sissy announced when she stepped into the bedroom. As she expected, this announcement set off much moaning and gnashing of teeth. Marilee whined. Billy Joe threw himself on the mercy of his father and tried to plea-bargain.

"Bedtime," Sissy repeated, ruffling her middle child's hair.

"You heard your mother," said the patriarch. Sissy smiled at her husband gratefully.

Forty-five minutes later, when all three children's heads had at least touched their pillows, Sissy returned to the bedroom. Peewee lay on top of the white sheets in his boxer shorts and T-shirt, reading *Popular Mechanics*. She switched on the radio to a down-and-dirty jazz station and felt her body respond to its beat. She swung her hips and did a slow grind. Peewee didn't even look up.

Locking the door behind her, she untied the sash of her green chenille robe. She let it fall to the floor at her feet and walked naked to the bed.

"Sissy, for God's sake!" Peewee jumped up. "What do you think you're doing, parading around for the whole neighborhood to see?"

"Don't worry, sugar, the curtains are drawn."

"But the shades aren't." He raced from window to window.

"You expect some late-night Methodist to stand in the yard, just waiting to get a peek at me?" Sissy was tickled at the thought and wondered, not for the first time, why men set such a store by a woman's modesty, while to women it was only a passing inconvenience.

Peewee filled the air with angry silence. So Sissy sat down on the bed and said, "I'm sorry, sugar, I really do appreciate your protecting my chastity and all."

She picked up the magazine he had laid across his pillow and tossed it to the floor.

"You just lost my place."

"I have faith you'll find it again." She held his eyes as she spread herself out across his side of the bed. "You were a real hero today." He didn't say anything, so she added, "And now, I think you deserve a reward."

"Oh, for God's sake, is that all you can think about?"

Sissy shot up. She felt as if she'd been slapped. "No, that's not all I can think about, but I do think about it. Don't you? Don't you think about it anymore, Peewee?"

"Course I do. You know I do. I'm just real tired, that's all. I had a hell of a day, or didn't you notice?" He sat down on the bed, careful not to touch her as he retrieved his magazine. He looked at her for some sign of assent. "Men are different from girls, Sissy. All you have to do is lay there and smile, but a man has to perform."

Sissy wanted to ask him why he wasn't up to some kind of performance, when she was sure at least half the men of Gentry would have been ready and willing the minute she slipped out of her robe. At least she hoped they would. Sometimes Peewee made her feel like a female reject. She reviewed the Southern Belle's Handbook in her head, but she knew it wouldn't be able to help her tonight. She imagined it with its binding cracked, gathering dust on a high shelf as she cracked and gathered dust, faithfully married to Peewee.

She didn't know why he was so peculiar about sex. In high school he'd been grateful that she was willing to do it with him at all. But after Marilee's birth, when her father had given them the family home and gone to live over the newspaper, Peewee had lost interest. She wondered if he had felt a loss of his manhood by agreeing to live in her old house. But the five of them couldn't very well go on living in that two-bedroom duplex without any yard for the children to pay in. Or maybe it wasn't that at all. Maybe by siring three children he'd proved himself a man and didn't have to work at it anymore. Or maybe it was just marriage. *If you want a man to "Abstain from fleshly lusts, which war against the soul," just marry him.* That should be Rule Number Seventy.

Snap out of it, said her practical voice. There's nothing in the marriage vows about a husband having to service his wife whenever she wants it. Except maybe that part about to have and to hold. She hadn't been had or held in a long, long time. Maybe that would explain what happened in the kitchen this afternoon. And then there was also that part about love, honor, and obey. Stop it, she told herself firmly. She ought to respect Peewee's feelings. He jumped into the gravel pit to save their daughter and if he didn't feel up to making love tonight, well, so what? That shouldn't shake her resolve to be a good and faithful wife.

She switched off the radio and walked over to the closet, where she slipped into an ugly cotton nightgown her mother-in-law had bought the last time she'd lost fifty pounds and had given away when she gained them back. She was always giving Sissy "perfectly good" nightclothes suitable for protecting her virtue from any and all assaults.

"Ah, come on, don't be like that," Peewee said.

"Like what?" Sissy lay down next to him, her body rigid. Good and faithful didn't necessarily mean happy. She pulled the sheet up to her neck.

Peewee didn't know what to do. He leaned over and kissed her, but when she began to respond, he pulled away, leaving her alone to stare at the brown water stain in the shape of a weasel that decorated the ceiling above her head.

The soft, honey-scented smell of night-blooming jasmine crawled over the windowsill and curled around her bed. And her hand strayed under her nightgown.

She breathed in the seductive sweetness of the jasmine. She felt her ribs and thought about how funny it was that Eve came from Adam's rib, but that women had had to give birth ever since. She tried to imagine little babies being cut out of men's bones. After giving birth three times she figured she'd be pleased to let the men have the experience.

Her hand wandered on down the smooth, flat skin over her belly.

Was she too skinny? Would Peewee be more interested if she had some meat on her bones? Is that what he wanted? She wondered if Parker liked big-busted women. But she knew the answer. She'd known it in high school. All men do. She wished she had bosoms like Marilyn Monroe and wondered what their marriage would be like if Peewee were more attentive. "If you were more of a woman, he'd be more of a man," prattled the Voice of Guilt. Come on, how could I be more of a woman? the voice she preferred asked.

She caressed the rough triangle of hair and let her hand stray further down. Peewee would have a conniption fit if he caught her. But Parker had awakened something inside her she thought had died. Awakened it and left it to lick her body without satisfaction.

She secretly began to stroke herself. But it didn't work. Peewee's leaden presence next to her made too great an impression on the bed. Even when she pinched her breasts, which usually got her going, she couldn't get her concentration up. Not with him lying there, reading *Popular Mechanics* and flossing his teeth.

She remembered when she was a child eavesdropping on her grandmother and her friend Selma Martin. "Every time he finishes plowing a row, he wants to come inside and fool around," Selma had complained.

"You'd better keep that to yourself," her grandmother had said, "or every woman in Gentry'll be after him."

But Mrs. Martin had continued to complain. "Saturday night, he wouldn't get off me for seven hours."

Sissy hadn't understood exactly what they were talking about at the time, but now she thought the preservation society should forget about the Martins' antebellum house and declare old man Martin a national treasure.

She wondered if all over Gentry there were couples doing it for seven hours, only the wives weren't letting on. And then she wondered what in the world a man did for seven hours. She guessed she'd never find out, since she'd taken the vow to remain good and faithful to Peewee. Hell, she'd be happy to find out what they did for seven minutes.

She looked at him, his lips moving as he studied. What? She leaned on her elbow to see what was so fascinating: a picture of a car engine. A car engine! When he had a perfectly good naked woman lying beside him. Well, if not naked now, willing to get naked in a flash.

Why was it that the men she wasn't married to always wanted to get into her pants, and the one man she was married to didn't? At least, not often.

THE HONEYED SCENT of night-blooming jasmine crawled through the window of the room the brothers shared. Chip inhaled and vague distorted images filled his brain. His mother's legs. The stranger. The way he had his hands on her. All over her.

Chip would soon be fourteen, but he was small like his father had been at that age and slow to mature physically. Puberty was just beginning to bedevil his body and give rise to new and troubling, but creative, ideas.

He slicked back his hair like the young hoods who rode motorcycles and kept their cigarettes rolled in the sleeve of their T-shirts. He adopted their grammar too. "It don't make no difference" was a favorite. But the hoods weren't fooled; neither were the wheels. Nobody wanted to have anything to do with him. He was forced to hang out with his younger brother and sister.

But when a subject like science took hold, he so far outdistanced his classmates, he could have been in another solar system.

He'd made a tent of his sheet and was studying the latest *Scientific American*. The beam of his flashlight shone through the white cotton and suffused the room with its soft glow. Sissy had caught him reading in bed over a year ago. She'd made a deal. He could continue, as long as he didn't keep his brother awake. She said she knew how hard it was to lie sleepless in the dark. But as far as Chip was concerned, she didn't know nothing. She'd never understand the mind of a scientist.

While Billy Joe slept, Chip was lost in a universe of spinning electrons, protons, neutrons, and chemical reactions. He pulled down the plaid sheet and looked around the familiar room, trying to see it as it really was. He stared at his brother, reducing him to ninety-eight cents' worth of chemicals. Less than a dollar. He wondered how he'd change if other chemicals were added. Which chemicals?

Then he saw the big live oak tree in the middle of the yard go dark. The light from his parents' room had been switched off. It was time for his midnight rambles.

Chip carefully placed a paper clip to mark his place and folded the magazine neatly next to his bed. Then he turned off his flashlight.

Feeling the boards with his bare toes and counting each one, he silently made his way through the hall and the dining room and into the kitchen. He ignored the icebox stuffed with Cokes and the cookies and went straight for the broom closet, where he turned his flashlight on and rooted around in the rag bag. When he didn't find what he was looking for, he crept into the bathroom and searched the dirty clothes hamper. Sweat and mildew filled his nostrils. Nothing. Then he remembered his mother's footsteps slapping against the cement.

Sneaking back through the hall he forgot to count and stepped on the third board from the bathroom door.

"Who's there?" Sissy called.

Chip froze.

"Chip, is that you?"

He heard her footstep and dove back into the bathroom, closing the door behind him.

"You okay?"

"I'm fine." And he reminded himself he was talking to fats, proteins, and sugars.

"Go on to bed when you're finished and put down the toilet seat, you hear?"

"Yes, ma'am."

Chip waited patiently, sitting on the toilet, until the house was still, and then he flushed, just to be sure. Counting carefully this time, the boy stole out to the front yard and pulled the yellow sundress with the creosote handprint out of the trash.

Chapter 4

PARKER AND CALVIN Merkin sat at a table at the Paradise Lost where Calvin drank beer after beer and complained about his wife. The light over the pine-paneled bar shone through Calvin's wispy brown hair, which he grew long on the sides and carefully brushed over the top of his head. He said he wanted Parker's advice, as a man of the world. But after a few minutes, Parker realized all Calvin really wanted was sympathy.

Parker nodded and made noncommittal sounds of solidarity as he looked around. His picture in his high school football uniform was displayed behind the bar along with the article calling him a war hero. But most of the guys he'd hung out with in high school had left town. They'd gone to college on the G.I. Bill and never returned or they'd found new opportunities in the city.

But a few remained to take over the family farm or run a small business. A couple of his old teammates spotted him and came over. One was tall and gaunt, with an unhealthy pallor and a heavy five o'clock shadow prickling over his cheeks. He had small black eyes with pouches hanging from them. Parker remembered they called him Plurb something. The other man Parker recognized as Sammy Rutledge, whose family owned Parish Motors. Sammy had been heavy when he played tackle. Now he looked as if he'd been stuffed into his skin like a German sausage. They'd been sophomores when Parker had had his famous senior year. Sammy slapped him on the shoulder. "What you doing back, boy?"

"It's about time, don't you think?" Parker said, motioning for them to sit down.

"Hell, yes," said Sammy, pulling out a chair. It creaked with his weight. Plurb hooked an empty from the next table. Sammy waved to Rosalie behind the bar and said, "Tell the truth. There's no place like Gentry, is there?"

"Damn straight," said Parker.

Sammy nodded to Plurb with approval. Plurb said nothing.

"Parker's working with me," Calvin said with obvious pride. He downed his fourth beer. Even though he was the supervisor, Calvin had the grace not to say Parker Davidson's working *for* me, but it was there anyway, hanging in the air.

Parker shifted in his chair. "It keeps me outdoors."

His former teammates nodded and said nothing, but they looked betrayed. Peewee was right. Parker was supposed to come back bringing them fame and glory they could bask in. Parker recognized the look. He knew he should have saved up enough money in Miami so he could just sit around Gentry and look important. But he'd go nuts doing that, so he said, "I never was one to settle down."

He saw Plurb's eyes shine with a dream of freedom—a man's freedom.

"Same ol' Parker," Sammy said.

"Gotta be wild and free," said Parker.

When Rosalie arrived to take their order, they fought over who'd buy the drinks. Parker slapped a five on the table, but Sammy pushed it away and handed Rosalie a ten. "This boy's been consorting with Yankees and worse. His money's no good down here."

Rosalie smiled and took Sammy's bill. "You all want some potato chips?" she asked, slipping her pencil behind her ear into her curly black hair. The gold was peeling from her drop earrings. She looked tired.

"Sure do, honey," said Calvin, patting her once voluptuous hips, now beginning to sag. "We just love your potatoes." Rosalie swatted at him like at a pesky fly. Sammy and Plurb laughed. Parker said nothing.

"Hey," Sammy yelled after her. "Bring three, four bags of pork cracklin', too." He brushed his pale crew cut with his palm in eager anticipation.

When Rosalie came back with the order, Calvin waited until she leaned over the table with a tray of drinks and rubbed his palm over her spreading rear. This time Rosalie jumped. Parker had to move fast to catch the tray before the beers turned over and landed on their laps.

"Hey, woman, you gotta be more careful," Calvin said.

Sammy and Plurb thought that was hilarious.

"Cut it out, Calvin," Parker said, handing the tray back to Rosalie.

"What's eating you, boy?" Calvin asked, his voice filled with the injured innocence of the intoxicated.

"Can't you see she doesn't appreciate it?"

"Sure she does. You love me, don't you, honey?" Calvin said, trying to pinch her.

"Course I do," Rosalie said, jumping back and moving around Parker for protection. She set out the last of the drinks, warily eyeing Sammy Rutledge, who was on Parker's right.

Sammy appraised the waitress with a crooked smile. Then he saw Parker's expression and decided to go with the winners. "Leave her alone, Calvin. You're drunk."

"Damn right," said Calvin. "And proud of it."

Everyone laughed at that.

When Rosalie was gone, the men relaxed. Sammy started to reminisce about Parker's famous ninety-five-yard touchdown against Hammond. While Calvin amiably downed his fifth beer, the three ex-teammates went over the game, play by play. Parker could almost hear the cheering as they relived that great afternoon. He felt better than he had in ages. He told them about the opposition tackle who'd tried to step on his face. "That's right. He did fall," said Sammy. "I remember thinking he wasn't real coordinated."

"Right," said Parker. "Lost all his coordination when I yanked on his shoe." Everybody laughed and Parker was glad he'd come home where he could find friends to share his memories.

"Why didn't you get the rest of us to beat the shit out of him on the next play?" Plurb asked. It was the first time he'd spoken.

"That would be playing his game," said Parker. "I didn't want to do that."

Plurb squinted at Parker. "I remember, you always was clean cut." He picked up his beer and sniffed it.

"Nothing wrong with that," said Calvin. His voice was loud.

Sammy agreed there was nothing wrong with that at all. Plurb said nothing.

"You never did get hurt, did you?" asked Sammy, tearing into the potato chips.

"Once, sophomore year." Parker described the game against Amite. "Doctor benched me for a month." He started to tell them about it, but they weren't listening. It was before their time.

"Remember the barf party we had after we beat Hammond!" said Sammy, washing his potato chips down with beer and opening a bag of pork cracklin'. "Man oh man, did I get sick." They ordered another round and moved on to the great barf parties of their youth. When the drinks came, Calvin kept his hands to himself.

After that, talk turned to the war. But pretty soon Calvin and Sammy were doing the talking, because all Parker would say about his Silver Star was "I guess I was in the wrong place at the wrong time." He never said any more.

"Tell these boys about some of them places you was living in. He was shacked up with one of them Thailand cuties," Calvin said, pulling on his eyes so they'd slant.

"No shit!" Pork cracklin' fell out of Sammy's open mouth.

But when Parker started talking about something besides cuties, Sammy cut him off. "Hell, Parker, me and Plurb was stationed over in the Pacific. We couldn't wait to get home. Them places are filled to busting with little brown people, don't even speak English." He passed the pork cracklin' around the table. "And the things they eat. Shit, that stuff ain't fit for a dog."

Plurb spoke for the third time that evening. "They eat the dogs, too."

A silence descended on the table after that. Parker searched for some way to fill it. He'd been the captain of the team and still felt it incumbent upon him to keep up their spirits. A muscle in his neck started to ache. Before he could think of anything, the others reached for their wallets and pulled out pictures of their families. Sammy showed off his plump wife and two plump sons. Plurb, with quiet pride, passed around a snapshot of his sweet-faced wife and six little girls in matching dresses and Mary Jane shoes. Calvin pulled out a snapshot of Thelma, who turned out to be blond and perky. Parker admired all the pictures, but didn't pull out any of his own.

Finally Parker's teammates wandered off, shaking their heads. Gentry's greatest football star and war hero stringing phone lines for Calvin Merkin. A satisfied smile played around Plurb's slack cheeks. Parker felt humiliated. He knew the most satisfying thing about other people's fame is seeing them brought down to your level of everyday disappointment, but that's not what he'd come home for.

"You still got family here?" Calvin asked, hoping to solve the mystery of why Parker had returned.

But Parker shook his head. "You know my father died."

"I always wondered why you didn't come back for the funeral."

"I was trekking through the jungles of Burma. By the time I found out, my mother had already moved to Florida." The two men looked at one another in silence. "She visited me in Bangkok that Christmas, but she didn't like it."

"Was you living with your Thailand cutie?"

Parker nodded and twisted his head to stretch the tense muscle.

"Your mama find out?"

"My girlfriend didn't have any other place to go. I couldn't throw her into the street."

"Jesus, Parker." Calvin wiped his head and then carefully arranged his hairs. There was admiration in his voice, but Parker heard anxiety, too. *He's afraid I'll get him in trouble.* Parker didn't know how to reassure him. This afternoon with Sissy had ignited a spark he wasn't sure he could snuff out. He wasn't sure he wanted to.

They drank in silence. Calvin began complaining again about his wife, Thelma, his ball and chain. Parker tried to match his description to the perky blond in the picture. Maybe she wasn't so perky anymore. Finally, she called and Calvin had to stagger on home for dinner. "Dammit, Parker, you're one lucky bastard. You're free to do anything. Anything you want."

"Yeah," said Parker. "Anything I want." He stayed at the Paradise until most of the crowd had gone home to their wives. He talked to Rosalie behind the bar for a while. Then he began to feel queasy. He decided to go on home and get himself some supper.

He got into his car with a grinding sense of futility. Nothing was working out. He should have known. He thought about Sissy and how he'd had to hide in the pantry because of that bigoted toad she'd married.

He heard the *Panama Limited* in the distance hurtling toward Chicago. The luxury express had roared through town twice a day, every day of his youth.

Red lights flashed at the crossing.

Suddenly Parker was back in high school and in the grip of a crazed adrenaline rush. He downshifted and charged the tracks. He could beat the old *Panama Limited*. He could still do it. The MG was caught in the blinding light of the oncoming train as it rushed toward him. The warning bell clanged as he floored the gas pedal.

The diesel screamed.

Parker white-knuckled across the intersection.

"Yowee!" he yelled into the night as the gates closed down behind him. The adrenaline had knocked out the grinding in his stomach.

And then as the train blasted and rumbled, he heard his saner voice. That was a damned fool thing to do! You almost killed yourself and all those innocent people. For what? For nothing.

Parker began to shake and had to wipe his palms on his jeans. As a kid he'd spent hours watching the trains. He'd been fascinated by them and the tales of heroes who'd given their lives to pull innocent victims from the tracks. When he was ten years old, he'd tried to strike a deal with God. As long as I've got to die anyway, let me do it saving a life.

So far, fortunately, the Lord hadn't seen fit to answer.

He crossed the tracks again at Education Drive and drove through the quiet to the high school. Nothing had changed. It was the same two-story brick building set back in the pines. The same broad steps where Sissy and the other cheerleaders used to sit with their legs bent under their skirts. The same double entrance doors, flanked by cement pilasters and surrounded by curlicues. *Mens sana in corpore sano* was engraved in the cement. He wondered if they were still engraving Latin above the doors of American schools. He doubted it.

He stopped the car and got out. He wanted to run those ninety-five yards one more time. His work boots made a crunching sound in the dried pine needles under his feet. The scent of pine was strong in his nostrils. He began to sprint. His face took on the wind. He rounded the corner of the school and kept on running.

The field was there as it had always been. The lights, the scoreboard, the cement stadium, in front of which Sissy had leaped into the air and led the cheers.

But they'd put up a chain-link fence.

He stood panting. He went over to the gate and shook it. It was padlocked. Damn. For a brief moment he considered climbing over it. He fit the toe of his work boot into a hole in the chain link. He grabbed the fence and looked up. Running around the top were two rows of barbed wire.

He got into his MG and slammed the door hard behind him. He switched on the engine, let it roar, and drove straight to the furnished house he was renting.

As soon as he opened the front door, Sid, his Brittany spaniel, exploded through it and threw himself onto his master's chest. Parker had rescued the dog in Florida after his former owner had abandoned him. Parker had renamed the dog for Sid Luckman, the famous Bears quarterback and hero of his youth. The beast barked and tried to lick his face.

"Cool it, Sid," Parker said as he pushed the dog down. "We gotta have a talk about gender. Not to mention species." He walked into the kitchen and heard his work boots make a hollow sound.

He opened a can of all-meat dog food and scooped it out into Sid's dish. Parker watched the big orange and white spaniel sniff it expectantly. Then, discovering it was only dog food, the animal lumbered over to the door, where he cast reproachful looks at his inadequate master.

"Starve," said Parker. But after a long canine stare and a few whines, Parker reached into the cabinet, took out a large dog biscuit, and tossed it. Sid caught it in his teeth.

Parker switched the radio to a country station. The cheerful voice of Gene Autry was singing "I've Got Spurs That Jingle, Jangle, Jingle." Parker opened a can of corned-beef hash. The aroma that wafted up around him reminded him of the food in Sid's dish, but he threw it into the skillet anyway. It would taste better once it was cooked.

Then when Gene extolled the joy of being single, Parker switched off the radio. A man could stand just so much cheer.

He paced the warped plank floor, waiting for the hash to heat up. He wondered what Sissy had fixed Peewee for supper and he wished she'd fixed it for him. He tried to imagine her here, in his kitchen, leaning over the stove, the strap of her sundress falling off her shoulder as she stirred her special stew or fried chicken for him.

The canned hash sizzled. He dumped the soft, greasy mess onto a plate. It didn't smell like dog food out of the can anymore. Now it smelled like hot dog food. Parker smothered it with American cheese and catsup. He started to add some of Sissy's pickled water-melon rinds, but thought better of it. He'd keep the jar as a sou-venir.

He took the plate and a glass of milk into the living room and set them down in front of the TV. Surrounding the Naugahyde lounger and TV table were the crumbs and stains of other meals.

A cockroach darted out from under the couch and made a run for an old potato chip. Parker watched it. He figured he was still fast enough to grab it, but what the hell, everybody's got to make a living. Just as long as he doesn't bring his friends. He patted his chair and got Sid to stand guard as he switched on the TV.

On top of the console his old football trophy—"Most Valuable Player, Gentry High School, 1941–42"—gathered dust. Most Valu-able Player. That was him, Parker Davidson. Most Valuable. Most Locked Out. He remembered a sliver of poetry he'd had to learn for senior English class: "And that one talent which is death to hide/ Lodged with me useless." He rubbed some of the dust off the tro-phy with his shirttail, wondering who wrote that. Milton? Then he realized his shirt was caked in creosote.

The Most Valuable Player of Gentry High sat down and spooned a gob of corned-beef hash onto a piece of white bread. He considered it for a moment. Then he pushed the greasy mess, dripping with catsup and cheese, into his mouth as Ralph Edwards appeared on the screen and said with jovial excitement, "This is your life."

Chapter 5

THE MEN IN Buster Rubinstein's glass-enclosed office at the top of the store were finishing up their noontime poker game. Sissy's father-in-law, Bourrée LeBlanc, laid down his final hand and pulled a pile of bills across the table. "Nice doing business with you all," he said.

"What I can't figure out, Bourrée, are you the luckiest white man in the parish or the biggest cheat?" That was Tibor Thompson, the district attorney and Sissy's uncle.

"Hell, Tibor, I ain't never heard of a politician *getting* cheated. Not in Louisiana, anyway. It's them that does the cheating, isn't it?" Bourrée accompanied these remarks with a bland smile.

Tibor's handsome, avuncular face froze. His brown eyes blinked a couple of times like a calculating machine counting up insults. Then he slapped Bourrée on the back. "What's that they say about Cajuns? If you know one that's rich and honest, you don't know him well."

The men laughed. Bourrée kept the smile on his lips, but his eyes narrowed. He was a timber manager who managed to pocket most of the profits as he clear-cut the land he was paid to take care of. He specialized in rich widows from New Orleans. His steel-blue eyes, which spoke of danger, and jet-black hair streaked with gray were an irresistible combination. Each widow recommended him to a friend. And Bourrée took care of them all.

His real name was Beauregard LeBlanc, but everyone called him Bourrée after a fast-paced, high-stakes Cajun card game, at which he was a master. Bourrée had always loved to gamble. He stood up to transfer the money from the table to his pocket and saw his grandchildren run into the toy department. Then he spotted Sissy following them. She was wearing a pair of khaki shorts and a wine-colored halter. His eyes narrowed as he watched all the men in the hardware department turn and stare at those long freckled legs.

He saw Chip take an elaborate chemistry set off the shelf and Billy Joe climb onto a new bike. As Bourrée carefully folded his winnings into his gold money clip, he figured he'd ask Sissy just what those children had done to deserve such expensive presents.

WHILE THE KIDS were making up their minds, Sissy wandered into the dress department. Above her, chipped mannequins in bad wigs perched on pillars, making even the latest fashion from New York look dowdy. She tried to tell herself she wasn't really giving in to Chip's blackmail. She was simply expiating her guilt, like when she made the boys mow the lawn after they'd done something naughty. Of course she knew better, but in a little town like this, with everybody minding everybody else's business, Rule Number Twelve of the Southern Belle's Handbook applied. *A lady must develop the knack of finding a noble motivation for doing what she wants, or she'll never get a chance to do what she wants at all.* Besides, she was always coming down on Chip. Maybe giving in to him this once would build up his self-esteem and he'd start acting like everyone else.

She idly went through the dress rack. She had no intention of buying anything, she assured herself, even though she'd had to throw away her favorite sundress. She couldn't. Peewee would have a fit, especially when he found out about all the stuff she was getting for the kids. She pulled out a green linen number and held it up to her, studying her refection in the mirror.

"It matches your eyes."

She swung around and saw Parker Davidson emerging from the hardware department with a new tool belt.

"I've been thinking about your eyes . . ." He was so close, she could feel his breath on her cheek. "And the rest of you."

"Go away, Parker," she hissed.

"You don't mean that."

"Oh yes I do." She stepped back against the dress rack. Her heart was pounding, but she couldn't be seen like this with him. "I'm a married woman!"

"I remember."

"Go away!" she said again. But he didn't go away. "Look, even if I wanted to see you again, which I don't . . ." She paused. She hadn't forgotten her vow to be good and faithful, but her breath was getting short just standing next to him like this and for a moment she lost her train of thought. "Even if I wanted to see you again, I couldn't. I've got to think about my children." She saw Amy Lou Hopper eyeing her from the hardware. Oh God, that's all I need, the fifty-thousand-watt voice of the Southern Methodist Auxiliary. Amy Lou squinted and then slipped on her pointy glasses to get a better look.

Sissy slid out of Amy Lou's sight. "Dammit, Parker, you know it's impossible." Her back was against the wall.

"I know. That's why I had this made." He pressed a house key into her hand. His address was wrapped around it.

"I can't take this!" Her voice was low, urgent. She tried to open her hand, but he had it in both of his and his hands felt so warm. "I mean it. I'll never use it," she said, but all she wanted to do was stand there with her hand in his.

"Just come over and talk. We haven't talked for years," he said softly.

"Hey, Sissy."

She jerked around and faced Uncle Tibor, the D.A. He was smiling his politician's smile, only inches away. The other men from Buster Rubinstein's noontime card game were coming down the stairs. What am I going to do now? she wondered, holding up her cheek for a kiss. She introduced her uncle to Parker. "We went to school together." She hoped he didn't remember they went together in school.

"I remember this boy," Tibor said in his hearty voice, the one he reserved for voters. "The best quarterback Gentry ever had." Sissy relaxed. "When you were playing, you were the best in the state."

"Thank you, sir." The two men shook hands and Sissy realized she still had Parker's key.

"I heard something about your running for the U.S. Congress," Parker said.

Tibor's face became very somber. "They need me, boy. They need me now more than ever . . ."

Oh no, Sissy thought, don't get him started.

But it was too late. Tibor threw back his wavy white mane, and like a racehorse who knows the course, he was off and running. He left the gate "protecting our way of life," galloped into the first turn "upholding states' rights," and hit his stride "getting rid of the Communists on the Supreme Court."

Sissy turned away in disgust. Ever since the Supreme Court decided to desegregate the schools, the poor, the ignorant, and the brutal had found a cause and were looking for a leader. So the politicians, like her uncle, were falling all over themselves trying to out-bigot each other. But Parker seemed fascinated. How could he be fascinated? *Let a man out of your sight for fourteen years, and you never know what he'll turn into.* Sissy decided to make that Rule Twenty-five of the Southern Belle's Handbook. Well, she hadn't exactly engaged him in a political conversation yesterday. She didn't have much time to think about it, though, because Buster Rubinstein and her father-in-law, Bourrée LeBlanc, were bearing down on her.

"Hey, Sissy." Buster held out his hand, but Sissy couldn't shake it. Her right hand still held Parker's key. She kissed Buster instead, using his considerable girth to drop the key into her purse. She hoped her father-in-law wouldn't notice.

As she expected, Buster became flustered by her kiss. Sissy had never kissed him before. As she put her lips next to his sagging white cheek, she caught a whiff of sweetness emanating from his skin. Was Buster using cologne? she wondered as she pulled away from him. She didn't know any other men who did. Maybe they all use it in the city. It was about time.

Buster adjusted his tie. He always wore a suit and tie at his place of business even on damp summer days like today. The fluorescent lights reflected on his bald head fringed with white curls. "Haven't seen you in a while. How're Peewee and the kids?"

"Peewee's fine. Just fine. And the kids are in your toy department right now, buying you out."

"That's what I like to hear," he said with a wide grin, rubbing his hands in front of his belly.

Sissy turned from Buster and offered a chaste cheek to Bourrée. He ignored it. His eyes switched from his daughter-in-law to Parker and back. "What you been up to, Sissy?" He knew who Sissy had gone with before she'd married his son.

Her heart was racing, but she managed to shrug. "Just taking the children shopping. These long summer vacations make them crazy."

"Makes a lot of people crazy," he said, eyeing Parker. I can't believe I got myself into this, Sissy berated herself as Tibor crossed the finish line, "protecting both races from mongrelization." Parker looked dumbfounded, which comforted Sissy, but surprised her too. She figured her uncle was just your garden variety bigot. Parker ought to be used to them by now.

Parker turned to say hello to Buster Rubinstein. The Davidsons and the Rubinsteins were the only Jewish families in Gentry when she and Parker were growing up, and subject to endless speculation among the kids, especially in seventh grade after a visiting evangelist had proclaimed amid an orgy of foot stomping and speaking in tongues that to get into heaven you had to save at least three souls and bring those benighted heathens to Jesus.

Suddenly, Parker became a hot commodity. He was the only kid anybody knew who wasn't already a Christian. Sissy would see him in intense conversations around the school yard with different boys and girls. She'd watch them press literature into his hands and watch him read it. But in the end he was a great disappointment to the faithful. He withstood their most fervent spiritual assaults.

They then turned their attention to the senior Davidsons and Rubinsteins, filling their mailboxes and covering their lawns with religious tracts.

Sissy's father warned her not to join the general harassment, although until that moment the idea had never entered her head. Then he gave her a little lecture in comparative religions. The upshot was that neither Jews nor Muslims were heathens. She dutifully brought these pearls to school, but the kids didn't care. Jews were going to hell and it was their duty to save them.

But resistance to conversion was about all the Rubinsteins and the Davidsons had in common. With their department store, the Rubinsteins were busy with the movers and shakers. Sissy had heard that Buster contributed heavily to her uncle's campaign. But she didn't know if it was out of friendship or because Buster was afraid of Tibor and his constituency of bigots.

She knew a gang had tried to run Buster's family out of the parish during the early years of the century. The shoot-out between the Rubinsteins and the J.O.C.s (Just Our Crowd) was part of Gentry's legend, as was old man Rubinstein's declaration, "Nobody runs me out of my home."

Nobody ever did. The old man got richer and richer. When he died, he left Buster half the business property in Gentry and controlling interest in the bank.

At first, all Buster wanted to do was enjoy his inheritance. When she was a little girl, Sissy heard her parents talk about the wild parties and all-night drunks, with people dancing on ice cubes at the Rubinsteins' big old house with the white columns out front and over an acre of lawns and gardens. Politicians, sportsmen, and even an urbane Catholic priest were rumored to have attended. But since Buster's wife had taken ill, the house parties stopped. Buster's entertaining had diminished to card games in his office with his buddies.

The Davidsons, Parker's parents, were quieter, not to mention poorer. They kept to themselves. She wondered if both families were trying to prove that Jews weren't as clannish as some people said. If so, it worked.

Her father-in-law told her that Buster, as a leading citizen of the town, had been approached to join the newly formed Ku Klux Klan. Bourrée thought that was a killer. "Those fools don't have the sense to know who they're organized to hate."

Buster had declined, of course, but there was talk that he got some of his employees to join and keep the lid on things.

Parker started to ask Buster about his wife when Tibor reared up again, promoting the "values of the American family." Sissy wondered which would go first, her uncle's bigotry or his friendship with Buster. And then she wondered if friendship wasn't too big a word.

But she didn't have much time to speculate, because Bourrée took her bare arm and pulled her aside. "You bribing my grandchildren, chère?"

She had to remind herself to breathe. People called Bourrée LeBlanc a lot of names, but stupid wasn't one of them. "Why, whatever gave you that idea?"

"It's not their birthday, and it's too hot for Christmas."

Southern Belle's Handbook Rule Number Three: *When caught red-handed, lie through your teeth.* "Why, Bourrée, you have the most astonishing imagination." She fluffed up her hair with her long freckled fingers and then sighed, "Of course I'm not bribing them, but I've just got to find some way to keep them busy this summer. That's all."

He seemed to buy that. Sissy began to breathe automatically again. Men are so easy.

Then Bourrée smiled a tight, mean smile and, with her arm still in his grip, cast an eye toward Parker and asked, "What you doing this summer that's so important?"

Sissy would have gladly strangled him, and to make matters worse, that was the moment Chip chose to come strutting in with his chemistry set, piled high with additional beakers and chemicals from the hardware department. "We're ready!" He saw his grandfather and went to him for a hug. "Hey, Pawpaw. You gonna take me shooting this Saturday?"

Bourrée let go of Sissy. "Sure am, boy. We gotta try out my new shotgun."

Chip grinned, looked around, and recognized Parker. He hesitated for what seemed to Sissy an awfully long time, and then he smiled his grandfather's tight, mean smile. "This should keep me quiet all summer long."

Parker turned on him and gave the boy a hard look. Chip stumbled back into his grandfather. Bourrée squinted from one to the other, which was when Sissy decided her best position was out. "Excuse me, gentlemen. But I've got to see to my children." She started to put the dress away.

"Take it, Sissy," Buster said.

"Oh no, I couldn't . . ."

"Go on, try it on at home. If you don't like it, just bring it back. You know your credit's always good here." In spite of the chipped mannequins, Buster hadn't kept Rubinstein's the biggest store in the parish for nothing. "Tell you what, the merchandise looks so good on you, I'll let you have it for twenty percent off." He smiled expectantly.

"Buster, you are a devil. You know how I hate to pass up a bargain."

He just laughed.

Sissy wanted their attention off Chip and Parker, so she held the dress up and turned, gauging her effect on her admirers. "What do you all think? Can you all imagine me in this dress?" She glanced at her father-in-law and realized with disdain, and a little pride, that the son of a bitch was imagining her without it.

"It'll look real good on you," said Buster. "What do you think, Tibor?"

"Real good."

"Well, then, if you all insist."She folded the dress over her arm and quoted Rule Number Twenty-four: "*A girl has to look her best while she's still young enough to look real good.* Don't you think?" And with that, she put her other arm around her son's shoulder and turned to go. "Come on, honey," she said.

Chip pushed her arm off and led the way past the hardware into the children's department.

The children wandered off while Sissy waited at the cash register. She pulled her wallet out of her purse. Parker's key dropped to the floor just as Bourrée came up behind her. They bent down together, but he scooped it up. "Is this an invitation, chère?" He dangled the key just out of her reach.

Sissy's heart was pounding. She straightened up and managed a weak smile and made her voice purr. "Why, Bourrée, are you angling for an invitation?"

"Why would I want to do that?" His eyes were blank, but there was amusement playing around the corners of his lips.

Sissy looked at the guns laid out in the display case. It wasn't the first time she'd wanted to shoot him. Instead she grabbed the key out of his hand and snapped it in her purse. Then, gathering her children around her, she herded them out to the car.

Bourrée stepped onto the sidewalk and called after her, "I'd put that key on a chain, if I was you, chère. Somebody get ahold of it and anything could happen."

"You're right," said Sissy. Then her eyes flashed over to Parker getting into the telephone truck. "You're right, cher, anything could happen."

Marriage is the root of all suffering.

Rule Number Thirty-seven

The Southern Belle's Handbook

Chapter 6

Bourrée LeBlanc sat at the round dining table, with his back to the wall, sharpening his carving knife. The roses in the cut-glass vase on the middle of the table trembled. In back of him, hunters and dogs chased helpless foxes all over the wallpaper. He contemplated his son and his three grandchildren and wondered why, when he'd raised three sons of his own, only Peewee, the runt of the litter, was around for Sunday dinner. The others had left town long ago.

Miss Lily, his wife, waddled in carrying an enormous bowl of mashed potatoes. She set it down and took off its flowered lid. Steam rose up and hit her in her pretty face, now swaddled in mounds of fat.

Bourrée watched with distaste as a drop of sweat ran down his wife's cheek, over her multiplicity of chins, to lodge between her ample breasts. He turned his head, trying not to see her dab those big, soft breasts with her napkin as Sissy came into the dining room bearing a platter of snap beans.

She blew a lock of auburn hair off her forehead and felt her peasant blouse cling to her. There was no air conditioning unit in the kitchen where she'd been working with her mother-in-law, and her whole body glowed damply from the heat. She wished she could throw off all her clothes and jump into the river, feel the water eddying over her, caressing her body, cooling off all her hidden crevices. Instead, she had to spend the day all trussed up like the Sunday chicken.

She bent over the table and put the platter on Miss Lily's lace tablecloth. Before she even looked up, she could feel her father-in-law's eyes searching beneath her scoop-necked peasant blouse. She slowly hiked up the neck of her blouse and sensually fluffed out the ruffles. Then she licked her lips with her little pink tongue. Eat your heart out, you old coot.

A tight little smile spread across Bourrée's face. Here it comes, Sissy thought. But she was caught off balance when he turned to his son and said, "Sissy tell you what she picked up at Rubinstein's on Thursday?" Peewee shook his head. Sissy glared at her father-in-law, but he just smiled back. "That broken-down football player, what's his name?"

"Parker Davidson?" Peewee's voice came out thin and high.

Just then Chip rushed in. "Pawpaw, you promised to show me your shotgun. When you gonna do it?" Bourrée ignored him, but Chip kept pressing with the same urgency that Sissy had heard when he was following her around the gravel pit demanding a chemistry set. "When, Pawpaw?"

"When I get good and ready," said Bourrée, not taking his eyes off Sissy.

For a moment Sissy felt grateful to Chip for trying to change the subject. But then she realized he wasn't protecting her. He was protecting a good thing. Did the boy expect to blackmail her forever?

"You didn't tell me you saw Parker Davidson," Peewee said.

Sissy shrugged. "Must have slipped my mind." She set her jaw and gave Bourrée a look to tell him to lay off. But Bourrée, with a satisfied expression on his face, handed his carving implements to

Chip so he could practice sharpening them. And Sissy made a tactical error. She forgot Rule Number Twenty-nine: *When a lady's actions are not beyond reproach, she never refers to them.* "I mean, when you live in a town of twenty-five hundred people, you're bound to run into everybody all the time. So don't you all let your minds run rampant. I went with Parker before I started going out with Peewee. We were just children then."

"I remember what kind of child you was," Bourrée said under his breath.

Peewee's head shot around. He stared at his father. Sissy waited for her husband to defend her, but then she saw he couldn't make himself say anything, not while he was sitting in the same chair he'd sat in during all those humiliating meals of his childhood.

"What kind of child was she, Pawpaw?" Billy Joe asked.

Peewee managed to tell his own son to sit up straight and mind his business.

"What did I say?" demanded Billy Joe.

Miss Lily pursed her lips. She adjusted the venetian blinds, which were caught in her new lace curtains. Light like prison bars fell across the room. "It was real sweet of you to bring the kids to children's services at our church this morning, Sissy. Real sweet. I mean, your being Episcopalian and all."

"One's as good as another, I expect," said Sissy, wiping up some milk Marilee had spilled. But when she stood up and saw Miss Lily's horrified stare, she hurried to add, "I mean, when you praise the Lord it doesn't matter whose house you do it in."

Miss Lily nodded. Bourrée caught Sissy's eye, a tight smile on his face.

Sissy ignored him, told her mother-in-law to sit down, and headed back into the kitchen. Sissy didn't mind hypocrites so much, she was used to them. What she hated was the way they had of getting you to join them.

She pushed through the swinging door into the kitchen and inhaled the rich smell of roast chicken. She had decided on church as a means to strengthen her resolve to remain good and faithful. She'd sat through the service in a reverie, enjoying the flowers and the music and the rich vibrations of Brother Junior's voice, hardly noticing that she was planning Peewee's funeral—after he died in a tragic accident, of course, due to no fault of hers. It wasn't that she wanted him out of the way. She was just imagining herself in black, simple and dignified, wearing her grandmother's pearls.

She bent down and opened the oven door. A blast of heat hit her in the face. All the time she was in church, Parker Davidson was walking the streets of Gentry.

She took the chicken out of the oven and set it on Miss Lily's heirloom silverplate platter. Being good and faithful sure wasn't all it was cracked up to be. She wondered what Parker was doing right now. She knew she wasn't being rational, but she felt abandoned.

She was thinking of Parker as she carried in the platter of chicken, but she snapped out of it when she heard Bourrée ask Peewee, "They give you that promotion you been angling for, boy?"

Peewee's ears went red and the blush spread up through his blond crew cut. He scrutinized his plate and shook his head.

Sissy's eyes blazed as she set the platter in front of her father-in-law. Bourrée knew Peewee had been passed over. She and Miss Lily had discussed it the week before. She rushed in to rescue her husband. "The only reason Daryl Morrison got that job is his family owns half the parish. Everybody knows that. He's got the IQ of swamp gas. And the personal charm to match." The children giggled. Peewee looked at his wife with gratitude. She sat down next to him and patted his hand. She never could stand to see him suffer.

Then at Miss Lily's urging, they joined hands and Marilee said grace. As the child thanked God for all His blessings, Sissy listened to the heavy, machine-made lace curtain flapping in the breeze from the air conditioner. It sounded like a man walking.

As soon as the prayer was done, Bourrée was at it again. "They still got you working on the highway with the niggers?"

"Bourrée!" said Miss Lily.

"I'll thank you not to use that word in front of my children," Sissy said.

But Bourrée just smiled.

Peewee looked up at his father. Sissy was reminded of a rabbit trapped in a hunter's flashlight. "Only when Norbert isn't around," he mumbled. "Road work's his job."

"Looks like it's your job, too."

Sissy couldn't stand it. She knew Bourrée was bored at these family gatherings, but she'd be damned if she'd let him take it out on her husband. Rule Number Fourteen, Southern Belle's Handbook: *The best defense is a diversion.* She kissed her husband on the cheek and entwined her long, thin fingers through his. "Peewee works so hard for me and the children. Don't you, sugar?" She ruffled his crew cut. Then she glanced over at her father-in-law to see if her diversion was working. She wasn't disappointed.

Bourrée growled softly as her long, freckled fingers caressed Peewee's fingernails, blackened with tar.

"What do you want, Sissy?" Bourrée asked as he raised the carving knife.

To make you suffer. But she said, leaning over toward the bird until her scoop-necked blouse slipped off her shoulder, "I'll take a thigh."

Their eyes locked. Bourrée laughed.

"One thigh coming up. What about you, Peewee? You want the drumstick?"

Sissy saw Peewee wince. He was a child again, a child who had grown up in a family of five and had taken what was plunked on his plate. "Sure, Daddy, anything will be just fine."

"I get dibs on the other!" yelled Chip.

"No, me!" cried Marilee.

"I said it first, didn't I, Pawpaw? I said it first!" insisted Chip.

Bourrée nodded to Chip, his favorite. "That's right, son. You said it first."

"But I'm the girl," whined Marilee.

"Give them both to the children," Peewee said.

"Yay!"

"You sure, boy?"

"Please," said Peewee. He pulled his hand away from Sissy's.

Miss Lily passed around the plates of snap beans and mashed potatoes. Bourrée carved off a piece of what looked like mostly skin and bone and put it on his son's plate.

"Look, Daddy," said Marilee. "Pawpaw gave you the wishbone."

"He sure did." Peewee turned to his father, a pleased expression spreading across his face. "Thanks."

Bourrée paused and, giving his son a bland look in return, said to his granddaughter, "I figure your daddy needs all the help he can get."

PEEWEE LEFT HIS parents' home with a vague but nagging sense of humiliation churning around in his stomach. He tried to wash it away with Dixie Beer, six-pack after six-pack of Dixie Beer, while helping Chip figure out ever more ingenious ways to combine hazardous chemicals. Sissy had been at him for weeks to spend more time with the boy. By suppertime, Peewee had managed to smooth off the rough edges of the afternoon. Of course, he was also walking into the doorjambs, and Chip wouldn't let him near his test tubes.

Peewee opened the bedroom window. It had cooled down a little. He adjusted the fan and lay down in the direct path of the breeze, but his mind heated up as he bumped against the affronts his dignity had suffered that afternoon.

His nickname, Peewee, had been given to him at just such a Sunday dinner. He stood a perfectly ordinary five feet eight inches now, if he stood up straight, but his growth had come late. His father had called him Peewee when he was only six years old and the smallest boy in first grade, the smallest boy in the whole school. Miss Lily had reproached her husband, but Bourrée had just laughed and warned her to stop babying the boy. Let him take care of himself. But Peewee couldn't. And for the rest of his life, the embarrassing nickname stuck to him like tar.

Most people didn't even know his real name was Peter. Every year, the first day of class, he'd tell the teacher, "Call me Pete." Nobody ever did. But then nobody ever paid him any attention at all, until Sissy.

"Don't let it worry you. Just remember small men do great deeds," his mother had said more than once. He'd believed her and had always meant to do great deeds—to show them all. But, somehow, life got in the way.

Peewee drifted off. Thoughts of his parents gnawed on him through his dreams. It was only natural, he guessed, for them to keep on seeing their youngest as a kid, but why'd they have to see him as such a dumb kid? He knew his father had been partial to his oldest son, which was understandable, and Miss Lily had always doted on the second. Peewee had come upon them as a surprise, the product of one of his father's drunken nights on the town. Bourrée had referred to it more than once. "There's love children and there's liquor children." He'd even introduced him as "the mistake of the litter." Peewee had spent the rest of his life trying to make it up to them, to please them, especially Bourrée, but he never succeeded.

To hell with them, he thought. He was a man now, with a family of his own. But nobody seemed to appreciate that. Not even Sissy. Especially not Sissy. He didn't understand why she and his father were at each other's throats all the time. He guessed they just naturally didn't like one another. And he couldn't blame either one of them. But then why was she always telling him the children needed to see their grandparents?

A woman is a mystery, he decided. He remembered somebody famous had said that once, or something like it. Well, it was true. And dammit, it was time she started appreciating him for the man he was and started treating him with respect. After all, he busted his butt all week, standing in the sun with a bunch of niggers just so she could put food on the table. It might not be his house, but he was the man around here. He had his rights.

AFTER THE CHILDREN were put to bed, Sissy went into her closet for her nightgown. When she came out Peewee jumped her. She turned, laughing.

He kissed her hard, pushing her against the door. She stumbled back.

"Cut it out, Peewee!" She tried to move away.

His arm came out and stopped her. His breath was stale with the beers he'd drunk before and after supper. "Why can't you just relax and enjoy it?"

"Because you're pushing me into the doorknob."

"Oh." He eased up so she could slide along the wall. He stayed right in front of her, though, and began rubbing up against her like a goat in rut.

Sissy thought it made for a nice change.

Besides, it would take her mind off Parker. Maybe for good and all. She remembered how she felt when she saw Parker again, when he was pushing her up against the sink. She could feel that way about Peewee. She knew she could. Rule Number Twenty-one: *One man's as good as another*, she reminded herself. But when Peewee unzipped his pants, she had to push him away. "What's the matter," he taunted, "you turning frigid on me?"

"Now, sugar, you know I've never told you no. And I'm not gonna turn you down tonight."

Dammit! There she goes again! That's not what he wanted. He wanted to take her. To force her to do his will. He didn't want her to do her damned duty.

"I've got to get myself ready," she said.

"You look ready to me." He was pulling up her skirt.

She kissed him on the cheek and tried to push his hands down.

"Sugar, hold on!" He didn't stop. "I just can't handle another pregnancy." That didn't seem to bother him at all. Southern Belle Handbook Rule Number Four: *When a man gets hot, all the blood rushes from his head, taking his brain cells along for the ride.*

He had her skirt all bunched up and was working on her panties. "Okay, if you want another baby, just go ahead." He was going ahead. "But you'll have to take a second job, 'cause otherwise we just won't make it." That stopped him for a moment, and a moment was long enough for Sissy to make a run for the bathroom.

She locked the door and stood looking around her, stunned, as if she'd forgotten what she was there for. Then she pulled out the drawer where she kept her diaphragm hidden from her children and from Peewee. He knew she wore it, but didn't want to see it, saying the mechanics took away the thrill. A lot of things took away the thrill for Peewee. She was sure the Southern Belle's Handbook had something to say about that. But she didn't have time to think about it.

She heard him at the door. She knew he hated being locked out. He wanted her to touch him, to keep up his interest. He put his head to the door. "Sissy," Peewee called in a gentle singsong, "I'm waiting."

"And I'm hurrying." She had to race against time. She grabbed a tube of jelly and spread a big gob of it all around the rubber disk, coating the edges so it would seal. Then she took off her panties and braced one leg on the edge of the tub.

Peewee was pacing around the bedroom. He picked up a beer that was getting warm by the side of the bed and chugged it down. What was taking her so long? He stroked himself to keep himself up. Dammit, this was her job. A man shouldn't have to do this to himself. Stories came floating into his head about going blind. Of course he knew they weren't true. She was just mocking him.

Sissy carefully squeezed the slippery diaphragm into an oval just as . . .

Peewee smacked the door. "Time to come out!"

She jumped. The diaphragm shot up in the air and stuck to the ceiling over the tub.

Peewee was pounding now. Sissy watched the rubber disk vibrate with every blow. Saw the rim quiver. Keep on pounding, Peewee, she willed. Keep it up. But he didn't.

"Sissy, what the hell's going on in there?"

"You wouldn't believe it."

She climbed up onto the rim of the old claw-footed tub, trying to grip its curved edge as best she could with her bare feet, and batted at the sloping ceiling with her fingertips. She thought maybe the rubber disk shuddered a little with the breeze, but it was still inches beyond her reach.

She grabbed a towel off the rack, flicked it in the air, and fell— hitting her head, scraping her knee against the faucet and her elbow on the side of the tub. The diaphragm, however, remained securely in place.

"What happened?" Peewee wondered if he should break down the door.

"Don't worry, honey, I'm just fine. I won't be but a minute." She turned on the tap to wash off her scraped knee.

Peewee sunk down on the bed, his head buried between his hands. She was taking a bath!

Then as if reading his mind, her voice purred through the closed door, "Now, sugar, don't get discouraged. Just go on and take off your clothes and lie down on the bed and I'll be in there as soon as I can."

SISSY STOOD IN the center of the water-slick tub flicking a towel up at the diaphragm, which held on to the ceiling with the determination of glue. But she was even more determined. She raised herself to her tiptoes and gave the towel a mighty bat. Close. The next strike was closer. Then Bingo! The tip of the towel swept across the sloping ceiling and knocked the diaphragm down behind the claw-footed tub.

When Sissy finally emerged from the bathroom, ready for action, smelling of White Shoulders cologne, Peewee was lying in bed with his eyes closed. She saw he was a little limp. But he was also naked. The Southern Belle's Handbook would say that's a good sign. "Peewee," she whispered, planning to give him a strip tease. She ran the palm of her hand over the soft bristles of his crew cut. "Peewee."

He opened his eyes, grabbed her, pulled her down onto the bed, and rolled over her. "It's about time."

She wound her arms around his neck and licked his ear, feeling his body come to attention. She waited for hers to respond, but before she could get going, he had her skirt up and was jabbing, desperate to enter her.

"Cut it out, Peewee, you're not digging a hole."

He stopped.

She smiled and began to stroke him. "I'm a girl, remember? You've got to take your time with girls."

Peewee sighed. Why couldn't he ever do what he wanted? Why were people always telling him what *they* wanted?

He pulled down her peasant blouse, gave one breast a resentful kiss, and then tickled her "down there." He stuck in his finger and wiggled it around. He remembered a marital guide advising the husband to think of it as an inkwell. He got a little "ink" on his finger, spread it around, and then popped right in with the next jab. At last.

Sissy closed her eyes and tried to remind herself, This is my husband. The man who married me and gave me his name. The man whom I promised to love, honor, and obey. But the weasel in the stain above her bed seemed to slide down from the ceiling. It crawled over her, panting and sweating. She blinked her eyes open to banish it from her imagination.

"That was real fine," Peewee said with a contented sigh, sprawled on top of her now. "Just right." He rolled off the bed and went into the bathroom to wash off.

Too bad speed sex isn't an Olympic event, he'd win the gold hands down, Sissy thought as she stared up at the ceiling. The weasel had slipped back into its place in the water stain above their marital bed.

Peewee returned with a satisfied smile. He tumbled into his side of the bed, turned over, and began to snore away all those beers.

Listening to him, Sissy traced the weasel's grin in the brown stain and felt her resolve flow out of her like tap water.

Chapter 7

SISSY SHIFTED HER weight in the hard wooden seat. She was back in her grade school auditorium listening to Amy Lou Hopper present the candidates for next year's PTA executive board. That woman exercised her jaw more than most people exercised their whole bodies. Sissy had heard that the girl Amy Lou's husband ran off with was a student from the Training School for the Deaf. Couldn't blame him.

Sissy shifted again and tried discreetly to pull out the little metal end of her garter belt, which had given up on her stocking and had embedded itself firmly in the flesh of her thigh. She'd like to meet the man who invented nylon stockings: hot in summer, cold in winter, and ripped before you got them out of the package. She was sure it was a man. No woman would have inflicted so much suffering on herself in the name of decency. He probably thought they looked sexy. Why do men think women are their most attractive when they're cramped, pinched, and constrained? she wondered. We don't ask guys to wrap themselves in nylon and totter around on high heels to attract us. Maybe it's that little overlay of pain we have to endure that gets their sadistic juices going. Rule Number Forty-nine: *What men find sexy is what women find uncomfortable.*

The applause snapped her out of her reverie. Amy Lou was introducing Carmalina Sangebina, candidate for PTA president. Besides being an outstanding mother of six, a loving daughter, and an enthusiastic wife, Amy Lou assured them that Carmalina was a woman of sterling character, with the courage to do the right thing in the face of adversity, and yet Carmalina was a team player, a consensus builder, and a brilliant negotiator. Hell, Sissy thought, Carmalina is wasting her time in Gentry. She ought to go directly to Washington and take care of the Communist threat, before lunch.

Carmalina took the mike from Amy Lou. They looked so proper and serious in their pastel summer dresses and their lacquered hair, like two big Buicks parked side by side. The candidate spread her lips into a smile that would bring pride to any Buick grille and began talking about the threat comic books posed to the morals of our youth.

All Sissy had wanted was to get out into the cool of the evening, away from the house, away from the kids, away from Peewee. But her only excuse was this stupid PTA meeting, where the stifling air was being fouled by the high-minded exhaust from Amy Lou Hopper and the grinning Carmalina.

The woman next to her fanned herself with her purse, filling Sissy's nostrils with the sickening mixture of Evening in Paris cologne and sweat. Sissy wished she were in Paris this evening. Hell, she'd settle for Shreveport. Anywhere but home or this mildewing auditorium filled with perspiring mothers, who must be as bored as she was. She wished she had their knack of not letting on. Southern Belle's Handbook Rule Number Forty-eight: *A proper Southern belle never lets others know how bored she is.* Well, it's something we can all aspire to, Sissy thought with a sigh. The woman next to her caught her sigh and smiled sympathetically.

Amy Lou recaptured the mike and waxed lyrical about the next candidate. Sissy's heart was beating, her breath was getting short, and her garter belt was killing her.

The next candidate was not smiling when she rolled up to the podium. She was much too worried about the younger generation, "who are our hope and our future, but who are beset by a myriad of temptations which can only lead them down that slippery slope with its inevitable slide into . . ." and she paused for effect, "juvenile delinquency!" That was it for Sissy. The trouble with this group was there wasn't enough delinquency—juvenile or otherwise. She looked over at her co-conspirator and found she'd disappeared.

Sissy stood up. She wanted to scream, run for the exit. Instead, she excused herself politely as she climbed over acres of laps and ran up the aisle.

Outside, the evening air was warm and moist and made her skin feel soft and sinful. The night-blooming jasmine crawled all along the fence and exhaled sweet, pungent odors, filling her body with an inarticulate longing. An owl called to her.

She walked across the parking lot and opened the door of the secondhand red convertible that Peewee had so adamantly opposed.

He'd explained that since they already had a pickup, a convertible would be an extravagance they didn't need. He'd also explained how a sedan was safer and much more practical for a family of five. Sissy should start acting her age, take on the responsibilities of motherhood, and accept Miss Lily's used Oldsmobile.

Sissy had set her jaw and was actually making up a bed for herself on the living room couch when she remembered the advice her mother had given her while she was cleaning her wounds after a knock-down-drag-out fight Sissy had had with one of the neighborhood boys. She was eight years old, beaten and bloody, but unbowed. "Sugar," her mother had said, "I know you were right and you know you were right, *but a lady shouldn't have to fight to get what she wants.*" Years later, Sissy had made that Rule Number Twenty.

So she'd crawled back into their conjugal bed, kissed her husband, and asked him not to pay her any mind. Women get funny around that time of the month. She'd be pleased to have Miss Lily's Oldsmobile, as long as it was in her name. She wanted something of her own.

The day after the papers were signed, Sissy drove her very first car over to Parish Motors and told Sammy Rutledge she wanted to trade it for a convertible. When Sammy asked what kind, Sissy told him: red.

The test drive was more than satisfactory. Sissy was ready to close the deal. Sammy offered her a chocolate doughnut. She set it in front of her on his desk and watched him pick up the phone. Was this how it was done? She'd never bought a car before. Who was he calling? He dialed the Department of Roads. He wanted to check with her husband. "Standard operating procedure," he told her.

Sissy put her hand on his. "Sammy, we grew up together," she said, leaning over until he could imagine he might be able to see right down her shirtwaist dress. Doughnut crumbs fell out of his mouth. Then she added in a low, conspiratorial voice, "I want it to be a surprise for Peewee, when he gets home from work."

It was.

He nearly had a fit. It was the wrong make or model or something. He got out old copies of *Car and Driver* and *Popular Mechanics* and showed her a whole bunch of statistics. Horsepower, turning ratio, 0 to 60. Sissy put on her most serious face and studied all the pages he thrust at her. And then when he was finished she said, "Sugar, I'm sure you're right, but you know, you can't pay too much attention to numbers when you're talking about a red convertible."

Sissy reached into her purse for the car key and found the other key still there. Well, she wasn't going to do anything about it, not tonight. She was going straight home. But as she pulled out of the parking lot, a vague feeling of anxiety began to surface. Even though she was driving with the top down, her hair blowing in the wind, she had trouble catching her breath.

She drove past the high school, turned down Hope Street, and saw Peewee through the window surrounded by the kids watching television. She meant to stop. She would stop just as soon as she could catch her breath. No sense in going home until she'd calmed down. Peewee would want to know what was the matter, why was she home so early, and she didn't have anything to tell him. Nothing was the matter!

She drove slowly around the block. The silent houses and carefully tended gardens made dark silhouettes against the star-lit sky. Here and there a porch lamp shone upon rosebushes, a child's tricycle left in the yard, a pink wrought-iron flamingo.

Inside those silent houses people slept or prepared to sleep. People who voted in the elections, ran businesses, paid their taxes, and thought they owned the town.

Suddenly Sissy had a revelation. The real owners of these houses never paid taxes. They didn't care who was elected or whether business failed. And they numbered in the millions. They came out on hot, muggy nights like this. They were the cockroaches that swarmed over summer sidewalks wiggling their antennae and slipping through tiny cracks in the floorboards to march across silent rooms into kitchens, where they ate the grease above the stove and invaded the cereal in open boxes. They shared their dominion with the snakes slithering up from the damp earth through knotholes, crawling around the bedposts into carefully laid-out slippers. But the majority was held by the termites who built whole colonies inside the walls themselves, excavating chambers for their queen, producing thirty thousand eggs a day, every day, hatching nymphs and warriors to undermine the antebellum mansions and simple three-room shacks that held their sleeping humans.

Sissy didn't turn back into her own street. She couldn't face the thought of putting the children to bed, kissing her husband.

She turned right on New Century Boulevard and crossed the tracks on Grand. The stores in the business district were dark and empty. Only Buster Rubinstein's office was lit up. She caught a glimpse of Bourrée and Uncle Tibor and some other men playing poker. She pulled up next to the tracks. The light was shining on Bourrée's back, darkening his already dark and cynical features. He cast a giant shadow as he pulled in the pot and finished up a joke at the same time. She heard some raunchy laughter followed by cries of "Pass the damn whiskey!"

There was life in that bright room. Sissy longed to join them. She saw herself sashaying right up to the table, pulling up a chair, and saying in a deep, rich voice, "Deal me in, boys." That would knock the Southern Belle's Handbook all to hell. It wasn't fair that men could go out and drink and gamble and raise all kinds of hell without hurting their reputations, and the only place a woman could go at night was to church or the PTA and listen to Amy Lou Hopper and Carmalina Sangebina honk their horns. Of course that was Rule Number Fifty-one: *Life's always harder for a woman. That's why we have to give it a bunch of little shoves and shakes, always taking care the buzzer doesn't ring and the lights don't come on screaming Tilt!*

She saw Bourrée get up and stretch. Tibor's voice came through the window. "Did you all hear the one about the nigger who wanted to be President." A chorus erupted: "That's an old one." "Well, I haven't heard it." "It's as old as Methuselah." "Why don't you just shut up and let the man tell his story?" Bourrée peered into the darkness and looked in Sissy's direction. She couldn't tell if he recognized her or not, but she stepped on the gas and lit out of there anyway.

She really should go on home. She had responsibilities. *But some nights your responsibilities are the last things you want to face.* She decided to make that Rule Number Fifty-seven.

She'd cross the tracks and go on over to Vista Drive, not that there was anything to look at, but it was a little higher and the air was scented with pine trees. She'd only sit for a minute, just until she caught her breath.

And that's how she found herself putting on her lipstick in the starlight, across the street from Parker Davidson's.

She switched off the engine. Fireflies flickered and danced in front of her windshield. The piping of the cicadas filled the night. When she was a child she thought their shrill call was the stars singing.

She took a deep breath and the clean scent of pine filled her head. She was beginning to feel better. She lit a cigarette. As long as she was here, she might as well return Parker's key. She wasn't going to use it.

But the house was dark and closed up. Where was he? She laid her head on the back of the seat and tried to blow smoke rings. He might be over at the Paradise, but she couldn't exactly go looking for him there. Not to give him back his key.

She got out of the convertible and threw her cigarette down on the cement, grinding it under her high-heeled sandal. The fireflies took off and danced across the street to Parker's. She drummed her long fingers on the side of the car. Maybe she should go on home. The PTA meeting would be breaking up soon, if Amy Lou had any compassion on those afflicted with a sense of civic duty, an affliction Sissy felt fortunate not to share.

An old Chevy with HOPPER'S DRUGS painted on the door wheezed around the corner under the streetlight. Oh, holy flaming shit! She'd forgotten Amy Lou's parents lived on Vista Drive. That's all she needed was for one of them to find her standing across from Parker's house, like some hormone-crazed teenager.

Sissy stepped onto the curb and ducked down behind the car. The old Chevy wheezed right by. She started to stand up when a porch light went on.

"Hello? Who's there?" Betty Ruth Bodine stumbled onto her front porch in a fuzzy robe, her hair in big curlers. "Get away from me, you hear?" Her words were slurred.

Sissy remembered how Betty Ruth had loved her whiskey in high school. But she'd taken the pledge when she married Brother Junior Bodine. Brother Junior was dead set against drinking, dancing, and going to the picture show on Sundays.

But Amy Lou Hopper—who, besides being president of the PTA, helped out in her father's drugstore—had let it be known that Sister Bodine was partial to the calming effects of a new kind of pill some doctor in Baton Rouge prescribed to rid her of her anxiety attacks. From the look of the way she was stumbling around, Sissy guessed Betty Ruth was real partial to those pills.

"Get going, you hear. Get out of here," Betty Ruth called, holding on to the porch rail to keep from falling down the stairs.

Sissy didn't know which was worse: she could stand up, identify herself, and kiss the last shred of her already shredded reputation good-bye, or she could remain crouched next to the car and risk Betty Ruth confusing her with a prowler and calling the sheriff.

But it wasn't prowlers that worried Betty Ruth. It was Satan. She'd worried about him ever since that hot afternoon when Brother Junior had led her, dressed in white, into the river to save her immortal soul. In her heart, Sister Betty Ruth had never been convinced the baptism had taken. And recently, as Brother Bodine's ministry had thrown them in the limelight—a radio show was in the offing, where she'd have to sing—she'd become convinced that Satan could read her heart, knew about her fake conversion, and lay in wait for her day and night.

Anxiety staged sneak attacks at Betty Ruth from every corner and rooftop and she needed more and more of those bitter white pills to fend them off. For Betty Ruth the price of eternal vigilance had become exhaustion.

Suddenly Betty Ruth dropped to her knees. "Lord have mercy on me!" she cried into the night, before starting a rousing chorus of "Onward Christian Soldiers."

The next day she would proudly tell everyone who would listen about her personal encounter with Satan, and how calling out the

Lord's name had sent him scurrying across the street. It was true she hadn't gotten a good look at him, but she'd distinctly heard his cloven hooves going clickety click against the pavement.

A SMART GIRL *can't just sit on the porch and wait for her life to start,* Sissy thought as she ran through the fireflies in Parker's yard. She'd make that Rule Number Forty-four. The scent of jasmine was everywhere. As the pungent white flowers swayed in the breeze, she began to think maybe she wouldn't give Parker back his key tonight. There was something so ungrateful about returning a gift.

She started up the old wooden stairs when suddenly a large dog exploded through a dog door onto the screen porch growling and barking. Sissy jumped down into the front yard and began backing out until she realized that the dog making all that racket was a big orange and white Brittany spaniel. She had never seen a killer spaniel. "Good boy, come on, that's a good dog," she said, clapping her hands. He calmed right down and started beating his tail, which seemed like a real good sign, until she tried to go up the steps again, which set off another chorus of snarls and much gnashing of teeth. Sissy had come too far to let a spaniel stop her.

She picked up a big stick, swung open the screen door, and yelled, "Fetch!"

The big dog pointed at the stick sailing out toward the street. He bounded off the screen porch and scooped it up. Proud of his enormous accomplishment, he returned and leaped at Sissy, who slammed the screen door in his face. The dog pressed his nose against the screen and let out a little moan, wagging his tail like crazy. "Okay, okay, come on." Sissy opened the door and scratched his head. They entered the house together.

She'd never been in any man's house alone before. A delicious sense of sin surged through her body. She walked around the living room, looking at the haphazard collection of rented furniture, feeling her skin move under her silky nylon dress.

She searched for pictures of women, but found none. In fact Parker had no pictures at all, except of his mama and daddy. There were no knickknacks from his travels, no profusion of possessions that marked a house a home. Except for his dog, Parker traveled light. Wild and free. Sissy experienced a sinking feeling. He was all set to drift away. "Good," she said and was surprised she'd said it out loud. She didn't want anything permanent anyway. She just wanted an adventure. God knows she needed one.

She wandered into his bedroom with its manly decor of wall-to-wall mess and sat down on the bed. Maybe she'd wait for him under the covers. Just imagining the look on his face made her giddy with excitement. She pulled back the spread, but the sheets were so gray and disgusting Sissy didn't want to venture into them, at least not alone.

She went back into the living room and flopped down on his brown Naugahyde lounger. The pungent odor of creosote surrounded her, bringing back memories that made her skin damp in her hot little nylon dress. She fanned herself with her skirt, but the sleeves were sticking to her arms. And then Sissy was possessed with a wonderfully wicked idea. Don't you do it, said her sensible voice. But even as the voice played in her head, a naughty smile drifted over her lips. She unzipped a navy blue zipper and pulled her little PTA dress over her head and threw it in back of her on the green pile carpet.

The dog was making such a racket, she didn't hear Parker's car door slam, but she heard him making crunching sounds in the gravel driveway. The Naugahyde against her bare skin felt like a great big sticky hand. She couldn't believe she was doing this. She was actually going to have an adventure after all these years. She arranged herself in her black lace push-up bra and slung one leg decorously over the arm of the chair, so her black garter belt would peek through the slit in her half slip.

She looked up at the door as he entered, sort of over her shoulder. She was gratified to see the surprise on his face.

"My God, Sissy!" But the delight she'd expected to accompany his surprise didn't materialize.

And then she saw why.

Following him through the door, actually holding his hand, was a redheaded mulatto whore.

The two women stared at each other.

The mulatto snatched her hand away and said, "I don't know what you had in your mind, Parker Davidson, but I don't do things like this!" Her voice was filled with the fury of betrayal.

Southern Belle Handbook Rule Number Seven: *When humiliated a lady should always fall back on her pretensions.* "You all don't have to worry about me," Sissy said, pulling herself up with the dignity of a great lady. "I don't want any part of your . . ." she paused, "shameless activities." So saying, she bent over to pick up her modest PTA dress and felt her stocking pop right out of her black lace garter belt. She grabbed her clothes and raced into the bedroom. The dog raced with her, panting, but Sissy slammed the door on the lot of them.

"Wait a minute, Sissy, I can explain," came Parker's muffled voice through the door.

"How?"

"Yeah, Parker, how you gonna do that?" Sissy heard the other woman ask.

Sissy was trying not to cry. Dammit, she wouldn't give them the satisfaction. How dare he give me a key and then come home with a whore. She went into the bathroom and splashed cold water on her face over and over until she cooled down—well, cooled down a little. Let's face it, she wasn't cool. All she was, was wet. She looked into the mirror and saw black rivulets of mascara running down her cheeks and felt the tears of mortification rising again. What was she doing standing around in her underwear in Parker Davidson's squalid little bathroom rubbing her face with his mangy towel? Southern belles didn't do things like this. That's what the handbook and ladylike behavior are all about, to save you from humiliation.

She'd make that Rule Number—oh hell, she was in no mood for numbers.

She emerged from the bedroom with her head held high like a queen. And tripped over the dog. Parker caught her. "Sissy, I know this isn't what you expected . . ."

She cut him off. Wrenching herself out of his hands and slapping the key on his oak coffee table, she said, "It's really none of my business if you want to consort with prostitutes!"

The other woman, who looked hardly older than a teenager, had been staring with unconcealed curiosity. Now she advanced on her. "What did you call me?"

There was something very familiar about her. Sissy couldn't place her, but she was sure she'd seen her before. Well, she wasn't going to let some teenage hooker intimidate her. "Excuse me, I didn't know you'd be so touchy. What do you want to be called? A good-time girl? A lady of the night?"

The younger woman swung back and would have landed a punch if Parker hadn't grabbed her arm. But Sissy was mad enough to take on both of them. So Parker grabbed her arm, too.

"Ladies!"

They struggled for a moment and then the girl dropped it. "You're not worth fighting over, Parker Davidson. Just drive me home like a gentleman and I won't bother you again."

"Clara's no prostitute," Parker said to Sissy, and introduced her to Clara Conners.

Sissy eyed her warily. She sure doesn't sound a prostitute. Doesn't look like one either with those prim white gloves. But that could only mean one thing, Parker's having an affair with a colored girl. And maybe that's worse. Maybe that's a whole lot worse! "It's really none of my business," Sissy said, heading for the door. The girl was staring at her again, making Sissy uncomfortable.

"Dammit, Sissy, don't take on like that," Parker said, reaching for her shoulder, turning her to him. "When you married Peewee, I didn't take a vow of chastity."

Sissy jerked out of his grasp. She saw the logic in what he said, but logical was the last thing she was feeling. "You're right. You're absolutely right. I'll let you all go to it, then."

Sissy had her hand on the doorknob when she heard the girl say, "Wait a minute. You don't have no . . . I mean you don't have any cause to be so stuck up. Don't you recognize me yet?"

"Clara, I don't think this is the place," Parker said.

But Sissy ignored him. She was staring into the entry mirror. "My God!"

"It took you long enough," Clara said. "You still think I'm a whore?"

"I hope not." Sissy's voice was soft and earnest. She took the young girl's hand and brought her next to her. They stood together staring into the brown, speckled glass. The resemblance was remarkable: They had the same bone structure, the same brazen tilt of the head, practically the same fine nose. But Clara's skin was a soft honey color and her naturally wavy hair wasn't actually red—it was dyed auburn and cut like Sissy's. And she was wearing a yellow sundress with a circle skirt!

Sissy couldn't catch hold of her voice. Her father had been widowed a long time, and before that, her mother had been sick for years. He'd never had any public love affairs, and he'd lived alone a long time, so it stood to reason. But still. She guessed it would take some getting used to.

Finally Sissy managed to ask the question, but to her chagrin it came out in a rough whisper. "Are you my sister?"

Parker groaned.

"Are you?" Sissy's voice took on an urgent note.

The girl hesitated and then said, "No, ma'am, we're just first cousins."

Parker shook his head. He knew he shouldn't have risked bringing Clara home after he'd given Sissy the key. But it hadn't looked like Sissy was going to use it. So when Clara called him, where else was he going to take her? Mixed couples weren't exactly welcome in the local bars and restaurants. He remembered running across a mine field on an island in the Pacific while Japanese gunners shot at him. He wished he could go back there now. "Clara, maybe you're right. Maybe I'd better take you on home."

But the women ignored him. "I only have one uncle," Sissy said.

Clara nodded, "I know. He's my daddy."

Sissy was stunned. "Uncle Tibor! The defender of racial purity?"

"Not around my mama, he's not."

"But he's campaigning to uphold our glorious Southern traditions!" Her delight was clear in her voice. It was too delicious.

"I believe that's one Southern tradition as old as slavery," Clara responded coolly.

Sissy examined her cousin again. Only the tone of her skin and the width of her lips marked her as Negro and even these features could be explained away. She might be from South America or even Italy, maybe. In a logical society she wouldn't be identified as colored. Sissy would bet she wasn't technically mulatto—quadroon or octoroon was more like it. There were lots of white daddies in her family tree. "I'm sorry I called you a prostitute. It was horrid of me."

The girl shrugged. "It's okay," she mumbled.

But Sissy knew it wasn't okay. It wasn't okay at all. She hated to think of herself as one of those Southerners who assume any pretty young colored girl with a white man is automatically a prostitute. "It's just that I didn't think Parker was in a . . ." She hesitated and then added, "A relationship."

Parker broke in then. "Clara lost her job today. She was working for old man Fletcher at the funeral home. She thought I might know someone who needed summer help."

"Is that right?" Sissy asked.

Clara didn't answer directly. She looked down at her white gloves and said, "I do need a job until September."

"She's going to the University of Chicago in the fall," Parker said with pride in his voice, moving in between the two women and leading them over to the sitting area.

"No kidding!" Sissy was impressed.

Clara nodded and sat primly on the couch next to the Naugahyde lounger. She crossed her legs at the ankles. Like a Catholic schoolgirl, Sissy thought. Or someone practicing for her debut.

"She won a full scholarship."

He sounds so happy for her, Sissy thought as she prowled around the room, maybe I've misjudged him. Maybe his interest in this girl isn't prurient after all. Maybe it's philanthropic. Well, anything's possible. She began to feel a warm glow toward her newfound cousin.

She moved over to the couch and ran her hand over the nubby orange upholstery. "Parker, would you get me a beer? And one for my cousin, too?"

"Sure," he said. But he didn't move.

Sissy knew he didn't want to leave them alone together. "If you don't have beer, Coke will be fine. Or Dr Pepper. Even Nehi."

"I have beer," he said grimly as he got up.

Sissy waited until he'd gone into the kitchen; then she perched on the arm of the couch next to Clara and asked, "How'd you know who I was?"

"Seen you . . . I mean, I've seen you and your kids around town. I've got lots of white relatives. More than colored," Clara said with a certain pride.

"And none of us ever knew." Sissy was so tickled. She had never heard a white person boast, "Got more colored relatives than white," but it must be true a lot of the time. It might even be true for her. It amazed her how invisible the children living in Butlertown were to all white people living on the other side of the tracks. Colored people in general were invisible, unless of course they worked for you. I've been passing this girl in Rubinstein's and at the drugstore for years and never really looked at her. Her delight turned to shame. "You're the spitting image of me when I was in high school," she said. Except, Sissy reflected, she'd never managed to look quite that neat.

Just then Parker came back into the room with three mismatched glasses full of beer. "Look, Clara, I've been thinking," he said, offering the beer around. "I know you need money for books and warm clothes and things. So why don't you let me handle the bus fare?"

The two women stared at him.

A philanthropist, Sissy decided. Her heart warmed.

Clara shook her head. "I can't take money from a man I've been sleeping with. Especially not a white man."

Parker, the philanthropist, crumbled right in front of Sissy's eyes and the dirty old man returned. She should have known. When he was in my kitchen trying to get into my pants, he was already getting into hers. Son of a bitch! He'd only been in town, what? A week, two?

Parker looked shaken. He turned to Sissy and saw her disgust. He turned back to Clara. "I'm not trying to pay for . . ."

Clara cut him off. "I know, but that's how my mama got started." Her voice softened. "When the time comes, I want to be able to say good-bye, clean, okay?"

As Sissy listened to them talk, a jumble of emotions and thoughts assaulted her. She'd believed that the real reason Parker had come back was to see her. Why else? He'd always loved her, hadn't he? Was he turned off by her vow to be faithful to her husband, or was he just catting around? He still wants to be wild and free, she thought. Maybe all that happened to them that afternoon in the kitchen was opportunity. A wave of terrible sadness broke over her. What did she care anyway? His peccadillo with this girl saved her from sin. Not that she'd been overly worried about sin when she took off her clothes and lounged about in black lace underwear. She looked at Clara with her soft young skin and tiny waist and wondered, Does he like her better than me? Am I too old for him now?

And then a thoroughly wicked idea occurred to her. It would put her right in the center of this triangle, help Clara get into that Yankee college and at the same time drive this two-timer crazy. "I could sure use some help with the kids this summer, I mean if that wouldn't be too much of a comedown for a University of Chicago coed."

"That would be terrific. I mean after washing corpses, nothing's a comedown."

"Then it's settled?" Sissy asked, excited. She loved getting in the middle of things and stirring them up.

"Oh, I don't think that's such a good idea," Parker said, trying to sound like the voice of reason. "What'll Peewee say? Won't you have to talk this over with him?"

Sissy smiled a slow smile and said in an intimate voice, "Why, sugar, you didn't seem all that concerned about my husband when you were all over me in my kitchen last Wednesday. But I know he'll appreciate the thought."

"You SOB," hissed Clara. "What do you do, just use me when your little housewife can't get out of the house?" Then she turned to Sissy. "I didn't mean . . ."

"That's okay," said Sissy, enjoying the fight.

"Clara . . ." Parker put his hand on her arm. She jerked back.

Sissy tried to hide her grin. Serves him right, she thought. She wondered if Clara would go for his throat, but she couldn't stick around. "That husband you're so concerned about must be wondering what's become of me," said the young matron in the navy blue and white dress. Then Sissy made up Rule Number Thirty: *Never leave any man you are even slightly interested in alone with the Other Woman.* "Can I give you a lift?" she asked Clara.

"I'd appreciate that," said Clara, moving away from Parker. "I live over by Butlertown."

Sissy said that would be no trouble at all, but as they opened the screen door, Parker pulled Sissy aside. "Don't do this."

"Are you worried we'll talk about you?" She turned to Clara. "What do you think? Is he worth risking my marriage for?"

Clara hesitated a minute and said, "I don't think he's worth any risk at all."

"Clara!" But they were gone. Together.

Sid ran after them, only to have the screen door bang shut before he could get through it. He crouched down against it and howled. Then he slouched back and nudged Parker into the kitchen.

Parker opened a can for the dog and a can for himself. When his hash was hot, he took it into the living room and sat down on the Naugahyde chair Sissy had lain in.

Less than fifteen minutes ago, she had been waiting for him, half naked, in this very chair waiting for him . . . when he'd walked in with Clara. But how could a man have resisted Clara when she called him from that pay phone with tears in her voice? She was so young and eager to please, with that fresh smell of youth.

He rubbed his hand along the arm where Sissy's legs had rested. He thought about her crazy courage, using his key, waiting for him in her underwear. And her delight at finding she had a Negro cousin. Most white women would have had a fit of shame and indignation at the very thought. Not Sissy.

A sweet sadness like an old song swept over him. Was that indescribable something that he'd been searching for, over so many miles, for so many years, been merely Sissy? Or was she just some impossible high school dream that wouldn't stand up to the test of reality? And if she was what he'd been longing for, then what? She had a home and children. What did he have to offer her or any woman?

He set his plate on the floor. Sid slunk into the living room, sniffed the hash, and then with his foot planted firmly in the plate, put his head on Parker's knees and moaned.

Chapter 8

PEEWEE HAD OBJECTED, of course. He didn't think they needed a maid this summer. "What are you, the queen? You can't do a little housework?"

That had been so easy, Sissy was ashamed of herself. After a contemptuous enumeration of all her duties taking care of their big old house, cooking and shopping for the family, looking after the children, mixed with less than an hour of anguished silence, Peewee was hers. Besides, everyone in Gentry knew that a man who couldn't provide his wife with help wasn't much of a man. No white lady should have to perform menial work.

Chip wasn't so easy. "I don't need nobody to take care of me."

"You don't need anybody," said his father.

"And I don't want nobody, neither," he declared firmly.

"Is that so?" asked his mother. "You planning to spend the rest of the summer doing the laundry? You all run through a lot of clothes in hot weather."

Chip admitted that wasn't part of his plans.

"You going to mop the floors every time one of you kids tracks mud into the kitchen?"

Chip admitted that wasn't how he had planned to spend his summer vacation either.

"Then you don't get a vote," said Sissy.

Chip glared at his mother.

"I'll talk to Hester Lee," said Peewee. Hester Lee had been with Peewee's mother off and on since he was born.

"That's okay, sugar, I'll find somebody."

"What's wrong with Hester Lee? She's real good with children!"

That's all Sissy needed, a spy carrying tales to Miss Lily. "If I had that old lady around here telling me about all her aches and pains, I'd end up working for her. I'll get me someone a little younger if it's all the same with you."

"You know a girl?" he asked.

Sissy nodded. "I do. And I've known her family for years."

"Well, she'd better be a good worker. I don't want to squander my hard-earned money if she's not willing to work."

"She's a lot neater than I am," Sissy said.

Peewee gave in. He didn't care anything about housework as long as somebody else did it.

SISSY WOKE UP at six forty-five and lay in bed enjoying that delicious time between sleep and real life. She was reveling in her coup. *Doing good can be so delightfully bad.* She decided to number that Rule Number Seventy-five. Parker must be going through the agonies of hell. Serves him right.

Clara was awake too, although she wasn't hanging around in bed. She'd set her alarm for five-thirty. Most teenage girls like to fool with their hair and nails, but for Clara they were an obsession. Because in spite of having the highest IQ ever tested by the Gentry school system, white or Negro, her real identity, the one she cared about, was all tied up with the way she looked. And although she always protested when the other kids called her stuck up, she couldn't help feeling deep down that her light skin did make her superior. Her earliest memory was sitting in church with her mother and having old dark-skinned ladies stroke her silky hair with envy, telling her mother what a pretty daughter she had.

So she'd set out to look white. She used Sissy as a role model, but kept herself better pressed. She protected her hands at all times and wore white gloves whenever she could. And she couldn't imagine why her cousin, who could afford to buy shoes, would want to go around barefooted.

She'd already taken out her curlers, brushed her hair two hundred strokes, taken a bath, and given herself a complete manicure. Now she was starching and ironing one of her few skirts and blouses that didn't match an outfit of Sissy's. "You always said, you've got to press to impress," she told her mother, who was leaning against the doorway and eyeing her with disgust.

Anyone seeing Denise Conners Johnson pull her lavender wrapper over her big, soft breasts would understand why a man as obsessed with race as Tibor Thompson would have trouble letting her go. With her café-au-lait skin and her slow, sensuous smile, she was his ultimate nightmare of racial mongrelization and his ultimate fantasy in a woman. As had happened with Sissy, Denise's beauty had trapped her and kept her locked in a half-life in Gentry.

"I didn't bring you up to work in no white folks' kitchen. Especially those white folks."

"Oh, Mama, don't get all shook up." Clara slipped into her freshly ironed outfit.

"Don't you sass me, neither!"

"I'm not sassing you, Mama," the girl said innocently. She knew how her mother hated to hear white slang coming from her mouth. She pulled her hair into a ponytail. She didn't want to look too much like Sissy today. What if Mr. LeBlanc noticed? She saw her mother shake her head and look out the window. Clara knew ever since she'd cut her hair, her mother couldn't stand to see her working it. Her long, wavy hair was her mother's pride and joy. Clara had had the longest hair of any little girl in the colored school.

But her mother didn't say anything about her hair today. "What you gonna do if your daddy comes over for a visit?"

Clara shrugged and tied a ribbon around her ponytail. She'd watched her white family for years. That's our cousin in her new car, she'd said to her brother when they first saw Sissy drive by in her red convertible. And they'd ponder on just what it was that entitled white folks to live so much better than they did. And now finally, she'd have a chance to observe them close up, and ferret out their secrets.

It was just in time too, because Clara had an agonizing and thrilling secret of her own. What nobody knew—not her mother, who'd been so proud of her for getting into the University of Chicago, not her teacher, who said they'd all be looking up to her, not her principal, who admonished her to apply herself and become a credit to her race—was that when Clara filled out her scholarship application, she'd decided not to check the box that said Negro. She'd checked the box that said Caucasian instead. Once she got there, she planned to say she was Creole. Nobody agreed on exactly what that was anyway.

SHORTLY BEFORE CLARA was due to arrive, Chip assembled his brother and sister on the roof of the house for a science lesson. Military science. From their sunny height, they surveyed the area and stood watch, straining with excitement. Finally they spotted Clara walking up to the back door, fastidious in her freshly starched skirt and blouse. Then they saw the white gloves and had to hold their giggles. They waited until she knocked on the screen door.

PLOP! Clara felt a dull blow to the top of her head. She reached up and to her horror came away with something wet, and colorless, tacky between her white cotton fingers. What had happened to her? She heard the whispers. Looking up, she knocked what was left of an apple onto the sidewalk. Somebody was throwing fruit at her! As she bent over to inspect it, a green-and-white-striped water-melon was rolled to the edge of the roof. Six little hands held it poised in the rain gutter. They took careful aim.

"Clara!" Sissy said, opening the screen door.

SPLAT. The large green-and-white biotic projectile crashed into the top of the door, knocking it cockeyed on its hinges.

The watermelon split into irregular pieces, bombarding the women with wet pink pulp. It finished with a salvo to their open sandals, covering them with vegetable matter and wedging tough black seeds under their straps and between their bare toes.

"I quit," Clara said.

"You haven't even started."

"That's right," Clara said, picking a chunk of watermelon pulp out of her auburn hair. "And I'm still alive. If it's all the same with you, I'd like to keep it that way." She turned and headed for the street, away from the war zone.

"Hold on." Sissy stepped out onto the pavement and called, "Chip! Chip! You get your butt down here. I know you're up there." Then to Clara, "You said you needed a job."

"Not this bad." And for the first time Clara wondered what in heaven's name she was getting herself into, going up north to a white college. Maybe they were all insane when you saw them up close. That would explain why the world was in such a mess. "At least at the funeral home, they drew a line between the living and the dead. They didn't try to bury the ones walking and talking." But Clara knew she couldn't go back to the funeral home. Not after what had happened with old man Fletcher. She hadn't been able to banish the memory of the undertaker's stinking breath when he grabbed her as she was dusting a table near the big walnut casket with Miss Mardee laid out in it. Clara could still see the glint of his gold tooth next to those rotting brown ones when he'd tried to stick his nasty old tongue into her mouth. She'd brought her knee up hard and fast, like her brother had taught her. Fletcher howled, stumbled back, and knocked Miss Mardee right out of her casket. She lay spread-eagled on the floor, formaldehyde running out of her mouth, smelling up the family viewing room something awful. That was the moment the old lady's grandson chose to walk in the door.

Fletcher fired Clara.

But she'd taken it personally. She hadn't held what happened to her against the whole white race. On second thought, maybe she should have.

"Nobody's trying to bury you, Clara."

"You could have fooled me," the teenager said, ignoring Sissy's attempt at Southern charm.

Sissy turned to the roof with a yell worthy of a long distance trucker. "Chip, if you don't get your butt down here by the time I count to three, you're not gonna be able to sit on it for a week. One . . ." She saw a flash of red overalls. "Marilee? Chip, if you've got your baby sister on the roof, you are in deep shit, boy."

AMY LOU HOPPER and Rowena Weaver, the relief organist and supervisor at the telephone company, were climbing the steps to the church across the street when they heard a four-letter word that never would have crossed the lips of any lady worthy of that name.

Amy Lou turned her ankle in her high-heeled blue-and-white spectator pumps. She was sweating and out of breath from the heat and the climb. However, she managed to say, "Can you imagine, in front of her children."

Rowena reached into her large basket purse and said nothing. Amy Lou continued, "As you know, I would never speak ill of any of God's creatures, but in Sissy's case"—she paused to pant—"I'll make an exception. Trash is trash."

"That's real Christian of you, Amy Lou," the relief organist said as she unlocked the big, church doors.

*   *   *

"MARILEE," SISSY CALLED. "Marilee, come on over to the edge of the roof, honey."

A face, bursting with giggles, peeked down at her.

"How'd your brother get you up there?"

"We climbed," said the little girl, pointing to an old magnolia tree shading the master bedroom.

"Well, you just climb on down. You, too, Billy Joe." There was no further acknowledgment. "I know you're up there. If your brother and Marilee are there, you are, too. Now come on down."

As the two children crawled across the roof to the magnolia tree, Sissy apologized to Clara. "They're not always like this. They were just having fun."

Clara nodded. "What's it like when they're having a real bad day?"

Sissy looked at the younger woman and looked up toward the roof where Chip was hiding. "You have every right to ask that question."

When Billy Joe and Marilee stood in front of her, Sissy introduced them to Clara and asked if they weren't ashamed of themselves.

Billy Joe hung his head and muttered. Sissy couldn't hear him. But when he saw his mother brush watermelon pulp from her cutoffs and pick a seed from between her toes, he said in a rush, "I didn't mean to hurt you, Mama."

"Me, neither," said Marilee, staring up at Clara.

"You all can't keep following after Chip. One of these days he's going to get you in real trouble, bad trouble," Sissy said, putting her arm around the little girl's shoulder.

"We was learning about science," Marilee said as if that explained it. "It was an experiment just like Icing . . . Fig Newton, or . . . something." She lapsed into confusion. "The one who hit people on the head with apples!" Marilee grinned, proud to get it right. Sissy shook her head and tried to bite back a smile. "That's what Chip said," the little girl insisted.

"My brother's gonna be a scientist," Billy Joe said.

"What's he studying, atomic bombs?" Clara asked.

Sissy made the two younger children clean up the sidewalk and then sent them to their rooms with orders to clean them up, too. "No reading comics until you're done."

"What about Chip?" Billy Joe wanted to know.

"I'll take care of him. You just worry about Billy Joe, you hear?" Then turning to Clara she said, "Come on, I've got coffee on the stove."

"Can't. I gotta go home and take me a bath. I mean I have to go home and take a bath," Clara said.

"No you don't," said Sissy.

Clara picked a chunk of watermelon out of her ponytail.

Sissy saw her point. "You can take one here."

"Where?"

"In the bathroom. Where do you think?"

"Your bathroom?"

Sissy had never shared her bathtub with a colored girl and she knew Peewee would have a fit. But my God, she thought, the girl's cleaner than any of us. "Of course," she said nonchalantly as if this were something she did all the time. "Where else?"

Clara entered the house warily. So far this white family didn't have much to recommend it. But she couldn't pass up a chance to take a bath in Sissy's bathtub and see what kind of soap and powders her white cousin used.

CHIP SAT ON the roof until the noon sun and the smell of fresh corn bread and collard greens lured him down. He slipped in the screen door.

He saw a woman who looked like his mother leaning into the oven. Smelled like his mama, too. But when she stood up, with a pan of corn bread in her carefully mitted hands, he saw she wasn't his mother at all.

"You the future scientist?"

Chip stared at her and then without a word he backed out the door. It bounced shut.

He was down the stairs when Sissy, who'd spotted him from her bedroom window, caught up to him. "Where do you think you're going?"

"Out," he mumbled.

"You march right back inside this minute and face the music," Sissy didn't know what tune she was going to play, but she was a firm believer in inspired improvisation. "First, I want you to apologize to Clara."

The boy stood in the middle of the kitchen with his head bowed.

"Well, young man, what do you say?"

The young man said nothing.

"We're waiting."

"I didn't do nothing," he mumbled.

"What?"

"I didn't do nothing," he insisted, "but hit a nigger with an apple." And then he snickered.

Sissy had never hit one of her children before, but she slapped Chip across the face. "I never want to hear a child of mine use that word!" The other kids shuffled into the kitchen to be on hand for the excitement, so Sissy turned to them. "You all hear me?"

"Yes, ma'am." Billy Joe said. And Marilee echoed him.

"Everybody says nigger," Chip mumbled, his eyes narrowed in righteous indignation.

And then Sissy knew what she had to do. She grabbed her oldest son by his T-shirt and dragged him over to the sink.

"And you say a lot worse," protested the boy, trying to pull away.

"There isn't any worse." Sissy picked up a bar of Ivory soap. She had used the word once in front of her mother and had gotten her own mouth washed out. To this day, she could swear like a long-shoreman—hell, she enjoyed that—but she couldn't say the "N" word. And no child of hers was going to use it either!

Clara watched them struggle at the sink and something moved inside her. Just when she'd given up any expectation that something good could come from these people, this white woman was taking up for her against her own child.

"You don't have to do that," Clara said as Sissy managed to shove some soap suds into Chip's mouth before he wrenched away, and knocking his mother in the stomach with his elbow, bolted out of the house.

Sissy turned and leaned on the sink. She blew a ringlet of hair off her forehead. Then both women laughed. And something solidified between the two of them, something even stronger than blood.

PARKER DAVIDSON DROVE by Sissy's house several times that morning.

He didn't see the boy on the roof watching him. But Chip saw Parker. The boy watched the telephone truck creep down the street in front of the house and then speed up, turn the corner, go around the block, and creep back. He smiled to himself. Knowledge was power.

It wasn't that Chip was intentionally malign, he just wanted what he wanted. Just as some people are born color blind, Chip had no ability to empathize with the subtle feelings of others. So although he wished he were popular at school, wanted to have a bunch of guys at his beck and call, making him feel important, he didn't have a clue how to make friends. All he had was his brother and sister and he'd learned early that Marilee would follow Billy Joe anywhere and Billy Joe loved to please: his mother, his father, his big brother. Chip saw that as a weakness—one that he was happy to exploit.

AFTER LUNCH, PARKER had worked out his strategy. He was going to be open with Sissy, direct and honest. He drove back to the house and saw the red convertible still parked on the street. He straightened his shirt and checked his hair in the mirror.

In his room, Chip was conducting an experiment to find out the effect on inanimate objects of an acid he'd just invented. He discovered two effects: one on the object itself and one on his lungs. It felt as if someone had taken a knife and scraped the inside of his chest. He flung up the window, gulped fresh air, and saw that the telephone truck was back. When he stopped coughing, Chip took out his lab book and noted the results of his experiment. Then he found a clean page, drew a line across the top, and wrote Parker Davidson. He recorded the time and date.

PARKER OPENED THE door of the truck when he saw Sissy come out of the house with a basket of laundry. The rusting hinges mewled. Perfect. He took a deep breath, and saw Clara step out behind her.

Already? They'd gotten together already? The two women were acting like old friends!

"Will you look who the cat dragged in," said Clara.

Sissy turned and felt a shock to her groin, but she said in her softest, sweetest, most malicious voice, "That two-timing SOB. Which one of us you think he's after?"

Clara rose to Sissy's sweet maliciousness with a voice that registered pure disgust. "Both."

Feeding off the disgust in Clara's voice, Sissy said, "He deserves to suffer."

"He sure does," said Clara.

The two women turned as one and walked back toward the house, swinging their hips and giggling like teenagers.

Parker slammed the truck door. What was he doing in this two-bit town anyway? He didn't come all this way to be made a fool of. He ought to leave tomorrow. Except then he'd never see Sissy again. No, this time he had to go the whole nine yards. Hell, he could do that. It was just a question of developing the right strategy. He gunned the motor and shot away from the curb.

"WHO WAS THAT!" asked Rowena Weaver as she and Amy Lou Hopper came out of the Methodist church. Rowena was tall and thin and favored print dresses with small flowers. Her brown hair was short and straight.

Amy Lou compressed her lips. She was carrying a round church fan with a smeared picture of a rosy-cheeked young Jesus, surrounded by rosy-cheeked angels. She fanned herself vigorously and carefully placed one high-heeled pump in front of the other as she made her way down the stairs. "Parker Davidson, I expect. He's been catting around Sissy when poor Peewee's at work."

Rowena looked at her friend. "What are you up to, Amy Lou?"

"Why, I don't know whatever you mean. I just feel sorry for Peewee, that's all."

MEANWHILE, SISSY AND Clara had forgotten all about the laundry slowly collecting spots of mold in the yard. With the venetian blinds shut tight against the blazing sun, they'd just found out that they both followed the same soap opera. Sissy was sitting on the couch and Clara was leaning against the wall behind her. They shared an ashtray.

The curly-haired heroine, suffering from amnesia, had wandered away from the safety of her small town, into the unknown perils of the big city, where she was beginning to fall in love with a dangerous man. You could tell he was dangerous, because he always wore T-shirts under his black leather jacket and drove a big, shiny motorcycle. His long dark hair was combed back into a duck's ass.

"What I wouldn't give to lose my memory and wake up with a stud like that." Sissy ground out her cigarette. "I'll tell you one thing, I'd never go back to sleep."

Clara leaned over and flicked an ash into the big ceramic ashtray. "If I see one like him in Chicago, I'll give you a call."

Sissy tried to picture herself roaring down the streets of Chicago on the back of a motorcycle. "Come on over here and sit down next to me."

Clara hesitated. She knew the rules.

"Come on." Sissy patted the pillow next to her. She'd never been comfortable with servants hovering over her. It was so unnatural. "Sit down. We're family."

PARKER KICKED THE truck into second, but he wasn't thinking about the ruts and bumps he was bouncing over, he was mapping out his strategy. He couldn't see Sissy at night when Peewee was there, of course. And he couldn't drop over during the day with the children and the Methodists on the lookout. And Clara.

Dammit, he'd really dropped the ball this time. He'd first seen Clara at a memorial service for his old high school coach, the day he hit town. She was serving coffee. For a moment he thought he'd found Sissy again. Sissy at eighteen. He couldn't take his eyes off her: the way her auburn hair bounced when she moved. He hadn't planned to take up with any other women in Gentry, but after the service the sky opened up and Clara was on foot. At first she didn't want to get into the car with a strange man, especially a strange white man. But as she told him later, she had on new shoes, which were getting ruined in the mud. So in the struggle between new shoes and safety, the shoes won. Besides, she said she had a good feeling about Parker.

They talked on the way home and Parker was impressed with her intelligence and drive. But what touched him was her voice, Sissy's voice.

The next evening, after trying in vain to reach Sissy, he stopped by the funeral home again. They drove to the gravel pit and parked in the moonlight. He told her he'd lived in Asia.

"I'd like to see that," she said.

Her eyes opened wide when he described riding elephants through the mountains during a monsoon, and wider still when he told her about vacationing in Hong Kong and getting caught in the Kowloon riots. He felt glamorous and powerful again.

He didn't tell her about his business in Bangkok and his humiliating failure. He hadn't told anyone in Gentry about that. Instead he asked about her plans for college. As she spun out her dreams and fears, Parker remembered what it felt like to be young with the whole world spread out in front of you, before the defeats of real life bludgeoned you into submission.

He slid his hand into hers, but he didn't make a move on her. It didn't seem right. She was just eighteen, for God's sake. He was thirty-two and only in town temporarily. He didn't want her to get hurt. But he needed the company of women. He felt more relaxed with them, less on guard. And he was constantly fascinated by the way they smelled, the way they played with their hair, crossed their legs.

He picked her up the next night and the next, until Clara got tired of his gentleman routine and made her move on him. Parker didn't say no. How could he, when that lovely young body was climbing into his lap, straddling him?

But after that, he stayed home nights or went to the Paradise. Until she called.

Now, even if he wanted to, he couldn't get at her, either. Not at work. Not at home, where her brother wouldn't let her to go out with a white man. He'd really screwed himself.

He stopped his truck out in the country. The telephone pole was planted away from the trees, standing alone at the side of the road, under the blazing sun. The iron grips would be too hot to touch with his bare hands. He pulled on his creosote-soaked gloves. They made his hands sweat and slip as he swung to the top of the truck. Then he grabbed the iron grips and climbed hand over slippery hand into the stifling air. By the time he reached the top, his shirt was covered with sweat. He unstrapped his headset and hooked onto a line. And dialed.

The two women sat side by side in the cool dark room, their eyes on the television. The leather-jacketed stud had found the heroine alone in her apartment, dressed for bed. He threw open the door. "I've been waiting all my life for this night." And then the telephone rang.

Clara picked it up, her eyes fixed on the screen, "LeBlanc residence."

Parker hung up. What was he doing? He was a grown man. He dialed again.

Clara turned to Sissy and without even bothering to put her hand over the mouthpiece said, "It's Parker. He wants to talk to you." Her voice sounded hurt.

Sissy reached for the phone, but one look at her cousin made her back off. She silently repeated Rule Number Thirteen: *A smart girl makes a man sweat.*

"There's nobody home . . ." Clara said into the mouthpiece. "I said there's nobody home, Parker, that means white or colored." She hung up.

As the pictures of the bare-chested stud taking the heroine into his arms flickered in front of them, each woman sank back into her own private world—and thought about Parker.

PARKER CLIMBED DOWN off the blistering telephone pole and kicked it.

It's okay for a woman to know her place. She just shouldn't

stay there.

Rule Number Fifty-nine

THE SOUTHERN BELLE'S HANDBOOK

Chapter 9

PEEWEE HAD THE windows of the truck rolled down, but he still felt stifled. He'd been working in the sun, with half a crew, when he wasn't supposed to be on the roads at all. And to make matters worse, they'd had trouble with some of the equipment, so he'd had to stay and work overtime. He'd been on the roads most of the month of June. If Norbert would kindly get over his damn summer flu, Peewee could go back to the office where he belonged. The smell of the tar was thick in his nostrils. A steel band of a headache was stretched around his forehead.

On the radio, Tennessee Ernie Ford was singing "Sixteen Tons." About getting older with nothing to show for it. The steel band tightened a good inch.

Peewee was headed for home when the song came to an end and a moronically cheerful chorus burst into the "Hadacol Boogie." He swung the truck around and headed down Grand Avenue for Hopper's Drugs. A tonic was just what he needed.

Amy Lou Hopper was standing in front of the prescription

counter with Rowena Weaver, talking about what had become her favorite topic. "She had a bad reputation back in high school, you remember?"

"I remember she was real pretty," said Rowena.

"I feel sorry for her daddy, trying to run a newspaper with a daughter like that," Amy Lou said. "Her poor mother, you remember Miss Cady, don't you? Well, she'd turn over in her grave. I swear, somebody ought to tell Peewee."

Lester Hopper, Amy Lou's father, looked up from behind the counter and shook his head. He was heavyset like his daughter, with a florid complexion and dark brown hair that had refused to turn gray.

Rowena said, "I don't think Peewee would take real kindly to the news."

Just then sleigh bells chimed over the front door. "Well, what do you know," said Amy Lou, whisking off her blue pointy glasses. Peewee LeBlanc had come for his tonic.

"Amy Lou, you keep your big mouth shut," warned her father.

Amy Lou tossed her head, pocketed her glasses and swept down the aisle.

In her white cotton blouse, she looked like a ship in full sail. Peewee watched her. He always did admire a woman with an ample prow, and for his money, Amy Lou had the best prow in the parish. He had to inhale sharply as it heaved to in front of him, all squeezed together under the prim white blouse, with a single drop of sweat shining like a diamond in the cleavage.

"Hey, Peewee." Amy Lou slipped behind the counter and smiled, looking really glad to see him, "What can I do for you?"

Peewee could think of a lot of things, but he asked for a bottle of Hadacol.

"Feeling a little peaked?"

Peewee nodded. "Must be the heat."

"I'll bet you want the king size, right?" she asked as she pulled a rolling stool over to her.

"Sounds right to me," said Peewee, feeling king-sized, watching her flanks as she mounted the step stool. Her tight navy blue skirt cupped her broad behind with each step. Peewee's hands began to sweat. He marveled at how she could balance all that weight on those little bitty high-heeled shoes. When she reached up to the top shelf for the bottle, he could see the outline of her big brassiere squeeze her back into mounds of flesh and he had to rub his hands on his pants to dry them off.

She climbed down. "This should do it," she said, holding out the big bottle.

"Yeah, it should." Peewee reached for the sixteen-ounce bottle and brushed the tips of her breasts by mistake. He looked at her, startled.

But instead of being offended she asked, "Anything else?"

Oh yes, but Peewee said only, "You got some of that Lava soap?"

"Sure do." She reached down for it and Peewee watched almost in pain as her chest brushed the top of the counter. When she came up, both of their faces were flushed. She pushed aside a stray hair that had come loose from her lacquered, blond upsweep and presented him with a bar of soap and a little tube.

"What's this?"

"A free sample." Their eyes met. "It's for a man who works with his hands."

Peewee pulled his hands down and hid them behind the counter.

"It's supposed to get under your fingernails and get them real clean. It's a problem for all my customers who work hard," and she said "work hard" as if that were something to be proud of. Peewee felt a wave of gratitude and the band around his forehead loosened. They stood there looking at one another. Peewee watched a little rivulet of perspiration find its way in between these two mounds that made up her wonderful prow.

"How's Sissy?" Rowena Weaver asked, coming up behind him.

Peewee swung around, feeling like he'd been caught at something. "She's fine, doing real fine."

"Be sure to say hello for me," Rowena said.

"I surely will." Peewee tried to remember the woman's name.

"Speaking of Sissy . . ." Amy Lou began.

"In the old days, they used to shoot the messenger," said her father.

"What?" asked Peewee, but Lester had moved on to fix a display in the back of the store. Peewee turned to Amy Lou and saw her eyes were shining.

There was an eager insistence in her words. "You know the other afternoon, oh, it must have been six weeks ago, you remember? When we was coming out of choir practice and you asked if I'd seen Sissy, well, I seen her all right."

Peewee didn't remember asking Amy Lou anything and he didn't want to hear this. He'd been hearing innuendos all over town, but he didn't put any stock in them. He couldn't. Because if they were true, it would mean that Sissy didn't love him and maybe never had. And that would mean nobody had ever loved him in his whole life.

"As you know, I am not one to carry tales, but I couldn't help see-ing the two of them. We open the church window for the breeze. I mean they was sitting there drinking in front of God and everyone."

"Drinking?" asked Peewee.

Amy Lou nodded sympathetically. "I hate to be the one to tell you this, but she was sitting out there on your front porch half-naked in some skimpy little dress, drinking in the middle of the afternoon with Parker Davidson. Did you know he was back?"

Peewee nodded. "She told me it was Cokes." Sissy had explained about Parker's tool belt and he believed her. He knew she was a flirt, but he also knew she'd never actually been with another man, not that they weren't after her. They were after her, they were after her all the time, and like she said, she chose him. Well, that was something to be proud of. Hell, all you had to do was look at the kids to know she'd never messed around. They were LeBlancs though and through. Of course they hadn't had a kid for six years, but what was he thinking? She was too eager for the connubial bliss he provided. No, he'd worry when she started getting headaches. But if she was drinking while he was at work, well, that was something else. One thing Peewee couldn't stand was a female drunk. "She said they were just drinking Cokes," he repeated.

Amy Lou tucked up her stray hair with her long, polished talons and leaned toward him, her breasts floating centimeters above the counter and inches away from his burning fingers. "Well, it must have been. Far be it for me to call your wife a liar, Peewee. All I saw was a couple of glasses filled with a dark liquid and . . . two people, Sissy and Parker." She lowered her voice and said confidentially, "They were having a real good time, drinking whatever was in those glasses. It could very well have been Cokes," she said with no conviction whatsoever in her voice.

The front door chimed. "I'd keep it down," said Rowena meaningfully to Amy Lou, because Parker Davidson had just walked in the door. The two women watched silently as the ex-football star strode through the drugstore. The floor shook beneath his feet. This was the first time Peewee had actually seen Parker since he'd come back to town and he looked a lot bigger than Peewee had remembered. The band around his forehead tightened.

"You look like you could use some of that tonic right now, Peewee," Rowena said.

Peewee nodded. Amy Lou reached under the counter for a little beaker that could be mistaken for a shot glass. He broke open the bottle of Hadacol and Amy Lou poured him a two-ounce dose of the patented secret formula: sugar syrup, a smattering of vitamins, iron, and one-hundred-proof alcohol.

Peewee was thirsty after a day on the roads, and he could feel the warmth of the liquid as it flowed into his chest. He was breathing easier now. He took another dose and felt the band pop right off his forehead. To hell with Parker. He was no threat. Like Sissy said, she dumped him in high school.

"You want another?" Amy Lou asked.

"Think I should?"

"Half a dose couldn't hurt; it's tonic." Amy Lou poured him an ounce and went over to the soda fountain and brought him back a glass of water over cracked ice.

Peewee downed it. The drugstore became a warm and friendly place. The smells of the sweet syrups and ice cream mixed with the smells of dark oiled woods and medicinal agents brought back layers of memories. His eyes made another foray at the spectacular prow displayed before him. Inches away. His fingertips were itching to brush it once more.

"Can I do anything else for you?" Amy Lou asked.

Peewee's eyes shot up. Could she read his mind? "No, thanks, this will be fine." But he was contemplating what she could do for him when the door chimed again.

A voice called cheerfully, "Yoohoo, Amy Lou." Wobbling a bit in her ankle-strapped spike heels was Sister Betty Ruth Bodine, her full skirt aflutter with ruffles, her hair done up in a blue bow.

Amy Lou sighed and climbed back up on the stool and reached for another bottle of Hadacol.

"Make it the giant economy size, sugar," said Sister Betty Ruth.

"How's Brother Junior? I heard something about a radio show," said Amy Lou, without turning around.

"You heard right. He's gonna be spreading the word of the Lord far and wide. 'Speak forth the words of truth and soberness,' Acts 23, verse 25," she said. "And while you're up there, sugar, make it two bottles, I don't want to risk running out. I can't tell you what a blessing a dose is now and then."

The tonic was making Peewee feel gregarious and belligerent at the same time. He left the ladies and headed over to the prescription counter. The more he thought about it, the more pissed he was that Gentry's greatest football star and war hero hadn't even bothered to say hello. Maybe they hadn't been exactly friends, but they had gone to high school together. The least he could have done was wave. "Hey, Parker," said Peewee when he got close enough, and added for conversation's sake, "What you doing here?"

Parker hadn't noticed Peewee.

"Here you go," said Lester, handing him a package of Trojans. But Parker, frozen at the sight of Peewee coming at him, shook his head and Lester slid the condoms right back under the counter.

"What're you getting?" asked Peewee.

Parker didn't even flinch. "Aspirin," he said in a deep, sure voice. The way things were going with Sissy—or not going, he hadn't even seen her in three weeks—aspirin would be more useful anyway.

"Here you are, boy, double strength. I figured you'll need it." The pharmacist handed him a big bottle.

"Thanks, Lester." Parker took out his wallet.

Peewee picked up the bottle of aspirin, pretended to study it, and said, as if it were an afterthought, "Found your tool belt."

This time Parker flinched; in fact he positively winced. Lester watched them, fascinated.

"Did you?" asked Parker trying to recover his composure, but his voice was no longer deep. It cracked.

"Sure did." Peewee felt great. And he was taking such pleasure in making his high school nemesis, the Big Man on Campus, squirm.

Parker had no idea what Sissy had done with his tool belt and was afraid to ask. Peewee wasn't about to give anything away. Lester was all ears and wished they'd hurry up and get on with it.

Finally, Parker said, "Thanks, Peewee." His voice was deep and resonant again. "Couldn't remember where it had got to."

"My front porch," said Peewee.

"Right," said Parker, "I remember now. I was working right out-side your house and your wife was kind enough to offer me a glass of water. I must have forgotten it. It was a real hot day."

"I heard it was a Coke."

"Uh?"

"The way I heard it, you and she were sitting on the porch drink-ing Cokes." His eyes were tight and suspicious.

"Could be," said Parker, wondering what else Peewee had heard. He pulled out a bill to pay the druggist when a tattered picture cut from an old high school yearbook fell out. Parker slapped his hand down over it and tried to cover with a large theatrical cough. Lester brought him a glass of water and a knowing look.

"What was it?"

"Oh, just an old . . ." Suddenly Parker stopped himself. Peewee hadn't seen the picture, he was still talking about what he and Sissy were drinking over two weeks ago. As if anyone cared. And then Parker had an idea, an idea that would solve his immediate problems, an idea so good he began to feel giddy. Palming the picture and putting it behind Peewee's back with an affectionate arm on his shoulder, he said, "Tell you what, let's go on over to your house and ask Sissy. Maybe she'll remember."

Peewee started. "I don't know, Parker, Sissy doesn't like me bringing people home at the last minute."

"Oh hell, boy, I wouldn't stay for dinner. I'll just say hello and pick up my tool belt. I'll even pick up a six-pack. What do you say?"

"Watch out for Satan!" Sister Betty Ruth had just consumed a couple or three shot glasses of tonic and was wobbling over to the prescription counter.

"We will," Peewee said.

"We'll make it our constant concern," said Parker gaily, trying to get his mouth straight.

"Don't you laugh, Parker Davidson. Satan is walking abroad on the streets of Gentry. I've seen him going toward your house and heard his cloven heels."

Parker remembered what a terror Betty Ruth had been in high school and was filled with sadness at what she'd become. "Go easy on the tonic, Betty Ruth," he said as Lester brought out a bottle of Miltown and put it in the bag with her Hadacol. Betty Ruth looked up at him and the ghost of the girl she'd been drifted across her face. But only for a moment.

"He's right," said Lester, his freckled hands resting in the pockets of his white pharmacist's jacket. "I'd be seeing the devil, too, if I were mixing this stuff with alcohol."

"Lester Hopper, you take that back. You know as well as I do that I haven't touched a drop of liquor since I took the pledge and I won't listen to your lies about my tonic. The formula's a secret, so there! Satan is putting those ideas into your head. Why, this stuff is as sweet as baby syrup." She turned to Peewee. "I told you Satan was abroad."

"Come on, Peewee," said Parker with his best good ol' boy aplomb.

Peewee still hesitated. "I don't think tonight's such a good idea."

"Well, at least let me pick up my tool belt."

Peewee didn't know how he could deny him that, especially since he'd brought it up.

Parker put his arm around Peewee's shoulder and said confidentially, "Besides, when you get a chance to save an old schoolmate from Satan, you gotta take it. Sister Betty Ruth says he's stalking my house at this very minute."

Without realizing it, Peewee had slipped back into the boy he was in high school, the boy who would have done anything to be accepted by Parker Davidson and the crowd he hung around with. And now this same Parker Davidson had his arm around him and was begging for an invitation to his house. What the hell, might be a good thing to let him see him in the bosom of his family. Once he saw how happy they were, he'd quit sniffing around Sissy.

SISSY SHOOK A couple of drops of Tabasco sauce into a bowl of beaten eggs and then tossed in as many pieces of chicken as would fit. A cigarette dangled out of her mouth and moved around as she talked. Clara, her hands protected by yellow rubber gloves, stood at the sink washing iceberg lettuce and drying each lettuce leaf separately on a clean dish towel. They were discussing Yankee men.

Clara wasn't supposed to be working this late, but she'd stayed, as she'd done for the past two weeks. Sissy suspected she was practicing her "white folks" speech and was glad to have her.

Sissy hadn't realized how lonely she'd been. People had always called her a man's woman. At first, when she was in high school, she'd been proud of that. It sounded cool. But who's a man's woman supposed to hang out with once she's married? If she hangs out with men they call her a lot of other names, and she sure didn't crave the company of those church ladies from hell—Amy Lou Hopper or Sister Betty Ruth Bodine.

Sissy spooned flour into a brown paper bag and shook salt and pepper into it. It was more than loneliness that made Clara important to her. Clara bustled around the house with a zest for life Sissy had almost forgotten. She was always up on a ladder, cleaning the molding around the high ceilings, washing the ceiling fans, or polishing the brass chandelier that hung over the dining room table. She made the scuffed hardwood floors shine and never tired of waxing and oiling the dark Victorian furniture. Coming from nothing, she was experiencing her first chance to care for beautiful things. Clara's constant caressing of her furniture, arranging the antimacassars, smoothing out the flowered slipcovers, stirred in Sissy a desire to fix up her home, which had suffered from her long malaise. During Clara's second week, they took all the oriental rugs outside, hung them on the line, and beat them. Marilee and Billy Joe joined them in a frenzy of satisfying swatting and whacking and smacking until they all felt empty and giddy and were covered in a rich layer of dust.

Best of all, Clara asked Sissy for advice. Except for her children, nobody ever asked Sissy's advice anymore. It made her feel smart.

And they shared a daydream. Sissy thought of it as the Great Chicago Fantasy.

It had started the morning Clara brought the University of Chicago catalog to work and asked Sissy what some of the courses were: Advanced Semantics, Beginning Etymology, Epistemology. Sissy hadn't had a clue, except she'd thought semantics had something to do with Jews. But a course on Advanced Jews hadn't made much sense.

A moldy dictionary, holding up a leg of the couch, had not elucidated: "Pert. to a study of meaning. A branch of semiotics dealing with relationships of signs and symbols to the things to which they denote. See semasiology."

"I know I've always wanted to learn about that," Clara had said.

Then Sissy remembered her father had given the children an old set of encyclopedias. With Marilee looking on, the two women pulled them down from a high shelf in the boys' room, wiped off the dust, and looked up semantics. Or rather Clara had. Sissy, with Marilee in her lap, had been busy with Volume C—Chicago—and then Clara had wanted to see that, too.

But the encyclopedia had been written in the thirties, so when Sissy took Marilee to see the story lady at the library, she checked out everything she could find on Chicago. The public library was open to all, but only whites could check out books.

Together Sissy and Clara pored over pictures of sailboats on Lake Michigan, concerts in Grant Park, and skyscrapers on Lake Shore Drive with smartly dressed people streaming out of them. Sissy imagined Clara riding along the shore of Lake Michigan on the back of a motorcycle driven by the stud in the soap opera. And then she put herself in Clara's place and felt her auburn hair flying in the wind. But when she wrapped her arms around him, he always had Parker's back and Parker's shoulders and Parker's waist.

They argued endlessly about what courses Clara should take, how to spend her weekends, and what to wear in the snow. Mysterious adventures in smoky jazz clubs beckoned.

Sissy dropped chicken parts coated with egg into the paper bag with flour in it, and shook it as she free-associated about all the Yankee men Clara would soon meet.

But that made Clara anxious. "I just hope I don't make a fool of myself."

"Oh, don't worry." And then without knowing why, she quoted

Rule Number Eleven: *Men find themselves the most fascinating subject of any conversation. When in doubt, let him talk about himself.* It was the first time she'd ever told anyone about the Southern Belle's Handbook or spoken a rule out loud.

"Handbook?"

"Well, it's my own rules of behavior. You know, how to attract men and get them to do what you want. And most important, once you've got them, how to stop them from stepping on you. Seems like that's been my curse since I was seventeen. I thought calling it the Southern Belle's Handbook was sort of humorous. I guess most girls carry something like it around with them in their heads."

"I don't," said Clara.

"Really? And you've done so well." Sissy paused for a moment and thought about it. "What do you turn to when you get in trouble?"

Clara shook her head.

"Gosh. I've been making up rules since before I was your age." She peered into the paper bag to check the chicken and then shook it some more. "It's gotten to be second nature. For example, Rule Number Three: *When caught red-handed, lie through your teeth.*" She dropped the coated chicken into the sizzling lard.

Clara didn't say anything. Then seeing Sissy watching her, she smiled and mumbled something noncommittal and patted each lettuce leaf with another clean towel. It wasn't until Sissy pressed her that she said, "It sounds kind of devious."

"Well, of course," said Sissy, dropping some more chicken into the brown paper bag. "That's the beauty of it."

Clara turned the tap on hard and rinsed out the sink. Then she took a box of cleanser and began scrubbing away at an old stain.

Sissy regretted having told her about the handbook. Now she felt she had to justify herself. She dropped the freshly coated chicken into the skillet and jumped back as the oil popped around her. "It's sort of like being colored. I mean colored people have their devious ways, don't they?"

Clara didn't look up from her work, but Sissy could see her lips were pressed together. "No, ma'am."

"Come on, when a white man calls you a bad name, well, I've never heard a colored person say"—Sissy pulled herself up and did an imitation of her grandmother—"I will not have you use that language in my presence."

Clara couldn't help giggling.

"And when a white woman asks you to do something you don't want to do, you all don't look her straight in the eye and refuse. No, you just get mumbly and you know"—Sissy searched for the right word—"colored."

"That's just self-protection." Clara's eyes blazed.

"Exactly."

"White women aren't treated like coloreds." Clara ran her gloved hands under the tap. "It's not the same thing at all."

"Maybe not," said Sissy. "But it's still a man's world. And *any woman who thinks she can get a man to do anything by going at him head-on is a fool*. Rule Number Ten. My mama always said, *A smart woman never lets a man know how smart she is*. That's Rule Number Twenty-eight." But Sissy thought she might drop that one. It just attracted dumb men.

Clara didn't say anything for a few moments. She peeled off her gloves and laid them out on the drainboard to dry.

"It's just something I do to keep myself occupied. You know advice I give myself." Sissy felt uncomfortable.

"You say you remember all the rules?" Clara asked.

"A lot of them."

"Why don't you write them down?"

Sissy stopped. Her cigarette felt overcharged. She took it out of her mouth. "Whatever for?"

"To help other girls."

"And give away all my secrets?" Sissy asked, flicking her cigarette. But she was flattered that someone thought she had something to write about.

"I know a lot of girls who could use them."

"Really?"

Clara nodded.

"I'll think about it."

"If you need any help with the writing, I made real good grades in English."

There was a hopeful, almost pleading note in Clara's voice. Sissy was surprised to hear it. Her face was hot with excitement. But then the voice she took for reality nagged in her head. Who're you kidding? Look at your life.

Clara turned on the oven. "You want me to make you some of my grandmama's shortenin' bread?"

"I always wondered what that was. I mean, I know the song." Sissy's voice was flat.

"Biscuits."

"Sure, go ahead." She was silent as she watched Clara scoop two cups of flour out of the chipped blue and white canister and add a pinch of sugar and salt.

Maybe someone would benefit from reading the handbook after all. There are a lot of women out there who are hopeless when it comes to men. But the handbook's mostly common sense. *Everyone likes to feel good about themselves. Especially men. You just kind of help them along. And when they feel good about themselves, they naturally feel good about you.* Damned if she hadn't thought of another rule. She'd number it One hundred and one. She wondered why men didn't have these strategies to make women feel good. They don't have to. It's a man's world. They get to earn the money. We get to stand around with our hands out. They get to make the calls. We get to wait by the phone. And without noticing when she started, Sissy found herself turning the chicken and thinking about Parker.

It seemed so unnatural for him to be right here in Gentry and never to see her. Not that she wanted to see him exactly. Okay, who was she kidding? She made up another rule, *A girl has to be honest with herself or she'll never get anything out of life but a palace of lies.* She liked that, it was almost poetic. She remembered a play on educational television where the heroine kept talking about castles in the clouds, or were they castles in Spain? Anyway, a palace of lies was worth writing down. And it wasn't even devious. Clara would like that. She wondered if Rule Number Sixteen was free. Maybe she ought to write them down just to keep track. She thought about telling Clara when she remembered, To thine own self be true. That was Shakespeare, wasn't it? Okay, so she wasn't original, but at least she was in good company.

Clara came out of the pantry with a box of baking powder. Sissy watched her measure out two and a half teaspoonfuls. What exactly do I want from Parker, anyway? I wouldn't even take his last call. Of course I never expected it to be his last.

You want him here, a voice in her head whispered. But not really here, not now, not in the kitchen with Clara. That wouldn't make any sense. Here, said the voice loud and clear. "You never told me why you took up with Parker," Sissy said aloud.

Clara reached into a cabinet and searched around until she found Sissy's aluminum sifter with the red wooden ball on its handle. She made a big production out of sifting the flour and baking powder into a pottery mixing bowl. Finally she spoke. "I told you he was waiting for me when I came out of the funeral home."

"Yes, but why'd you have anything to do with him?"

Clara shrugged and took a stick of margarine out of the icebox. Sissy watched her chop it into the flour with two knives until the dough was the consistency of coarse meal. "It gets real lonesome, when all your friends are getting married and having babies and you're just waiting for your life to start."

"What about the boys from your high school?" Sissy turned the crackling chicken with a fork.

"It's not easy for me."

"Because you're so light-skinned?" Sissy asked, hoping Clara would take her into her secret world.

"Because I'm smart. Besides, I don't want to mess with some boy telling me how much he loves me and asking me all the time if I love him and begging me to forget about college. I'm getting out of here. You know, some of the boys in my school are smart, too, but none of them are going anywhere." She made a hole in the center of the dough and poured in milk.

"You still haven't told me, why Parker?"

Clara stirred the batter with a big slotted spoon. "I don't know. Because he was nice to me. He listened like he was really interested in what I had to say. And well, why do you like one man instead of another? It wasn't because he was white, if that's what you're thinking. The last thing I want is to repeat my mama's life." She set out a pastry board and sprinkled it with flour.

Sissy wondered if she simply couldn't help herself. Or maybe she was looking for a sweeter version of her daddy. She didn't have time to explore this thought, though, because Marilee crawled into the kitchen, barking at them like a dog. Sissy told her to hush, so the little girl picked up a rubber ball with her teeth.

"You don't want to put that dirty old thing in your mouth, honey," Clara said. She looked relieved at the interruption.

Marilee crawled across the floor away from Clara, who caught up with the child in the corner and took away the ball. It was covered in drool. The child snapped at her and growled. Then she scooted around the room, barking and howling until Sissy flicked her cigarette in the general direction of an ashtray and said, "For Lord's sake, let her have it. My grandma always said a little good, clean dirt is nature's own homeopathic medicine."

Marilee panted in agreement. Clara went back to the sink and washed her hands. She shook her head at the white folks' foolishness, but she wiped off the ball and threw it across the kitchen where Peewee caught it as he opened the door.

"Hey, Peewee." Sissy moved her cigarette-filled lips to the side so he could kiss her cheek as she dropped fresh pieces of chicken into the pan of hot, sizzling lard.

Peewee turned to Clara. She was letting her hair color grow out to minimize the resemblance, but Sissy suspected Peewee wouldn't notice anyway. When a man believes it's only right and natural for physical characteristics to determine every aspect of a person's life, from where he goes to school to where he's buried, this same man is not likely to acknowledge, even to himself, that his wife looks like their Negro maid. "Think you could stay and serve tonight?" he asked Clara and then added with pride, "We're having company for dinner."

"Thanks for giving me so much warning," Sissy said indignantly. "Would it be too much for me to ask how many you invited or what you expect them to eat?"

But before he could tell her, Marilee set up a terrible racket, barking and growling as she ran into the living room.

PARKER WALKED ACROSS the front porch. Anxiety was churning in the pit of his stomach. What was he going to say when the children recognized him? This was insane, but he'd run out of strategies. He'd never actually gone after a woman before. They'd always come to him. Even Sissy. Especially Sissy. He smiled as he remembered her setting her sights on him, looking at him out of the corner of her eye, arranging to bump into him accidentally on purpose, books spilling in the hall between classes, dropping by the shoe store when he was working there. Not that he hadn't had his eye on her all along, but he'd appreciated the encouragement. He'd never had anything to do with a married woman, but this seemed different. He'd known her before. If she's happy, I'm gone, he promised himself as Peewee opened the door.

"Come on in, boy."

Parker handed him a six-pack of beer and slapped him on the shoulder, but what he said was drowned out by Marilee.

"Arf, arf, arf!" she shrilled, when she saw the way this dangerous man was looking at her mother. And then she saw her mother run her tongue over her lips and straighten her halter.

Peewee saw it too, but he didn't let it register.

"Arf, arf, arf!" Marilee screamed. All the fear she'd felt when she saw this enormous man with his arms around her mother came back to her. She looked up along his legs, up to his crotch where the material of his light summer slacks was bunching above her. Her barks, mixed with growls, were edged with hysteria.

Parker didn't know what to do. He wanted to pick up this little girl and soothe her, but of course he didn't dare. Still he had to do something before the whole purpose of the visit flew apart on him.

And then he saw Clara come out of the kitchen wiping her hands on her apron. Oh shit, what's she doing here? He thought she'd have gone home by now! Was this going to be another squeeze play? He nodded. She didn't respond. Instead she checked the button at the round collar of her crisp white blouse.

"Grrr," the little girl growled.

"Cut it out, Marilee." Peewee's voice was authoritative and loud and did absolutely no good. He grabbed at her, but she was too fast. She sunk her sharp little teeth right through Parker's light summer slacks and into his shin.

He let out a high-pitched howl, startling the child, but she hung on. His automatic response was to kick her right across the room, but he restrained himself. What can a six-foot-two-inch man do when a six-year-old child has him in her teeth? He can't yank her back by her hair.

He heard Clara mutter, "These white folks sure do know how to entertain company," as she walked back into the kitchen.

"Marilee, what the Sam Hill do you think you're doing?" Peewee yelled, yanking the little girl off Parker.

Marilee, shocked at her father's tone, began to weep. Sissy sat down on the floor, took her baby into her arms, and rocked her. Her eyes caught Parker's. She could see he felt foolish, but he managed to smile and refrain from rubbing his shin, which must have been smarting like crazy.

"I don't know what came over her," Peewee said. "She's not usually like this." Sissy heard an angry edge to his voice. He wants to be proud of his family, wants to show us off, and let a bachelor like Parker see what he's missing, she thought.

"No damage done." Parker was back in control. The two men squared off. Sissy could hear the testosterone buzz around the room.

When she was young she was thrilled when men fought over her, but now she knew that fighting was just something they did naturally. Women were only an excuse. If a man really loved you, he'd want you to be happy. He'd share. Of course, that man had yet to be born.

Parker knelt down on one knee and said gently, "I'm sorry I frightened you." He spoke to Marilee, but Sissy could feel the nearness of his body reach out to her and beg her to give him another chance.

The little girl wrapped her arms around her mother. Sissy held her, but didn't move away from Parker so the child would know she wasn't afraid.

"What you need is a real dog to play with," Parker said.

The little girl nodded. Sissy caught the calculating look on the child's face. The little girl twisted away from her mother and looked at Parker. "I like dogs," she said.

"You look like a girl who'd take real good care of one," Parker said, standing up.

Marilee nodded enthusiastically. Suddenly she grabbed her mother, hid her head, and began to scream again. Sissy stroked her daughter's head. "What's wrong, sugar? Tell Mommy."

That did it for Peewee. He went to his wife and yelled, "For Pete's sake, Sissy, don't encourage her. You've spoiled these kids rotten. Marilee, you stop that crying this minute or I'll give you something to cry about!"

Marilee must have figured she already had something to cry

about. Clutching her mother, she sobbed for all she was worth. Peewee grabbed the little girl and shook her, stopping her sobs. They
were replaced by hiccupping screams.

Clara came back into the living room to see who'd been bitten
this time. "Parker, look at your leg!" Blood was seeping through his
summer slacks.

Peewee wondered why the colored girl had said Parker, not Mr.
Parker. He'd never heard a Nigra make that mistake before, unless . . . Peewee smiled a man-of-the-world smile. The BMOC, Gentry's greatest Jew-boy jock, wasn't after Sissy, dark meat was more
to his taste. He was after a high yeller! And his servant to boot. If
Sissy only knew. Of course it wasn't the sort of thing a man should
tell a woman, but Sissy was his wife. She had a right to know. It
would do her good. He'd tell her that very evening as soon as they
were alone. Feeling sophisticated as hell, Peewee went into the back
to get Parker's tool belt.

SISSY WALKED INTO the kitchen with a bottle of hydrogen peroxide and found Clara with Parker's leg in her lap gently bathing it.
She also saw how much Parker was enjoying her ministrations.
They were talking softly and laughing. Damn him, damn him to
hell. He didn't come to see me at all. He came to see her! The man
has no shame. She looked at Peewee coming back with Parker's tool
belt and silently renewed her marriage vows. Trying to commit
adultery is just too tacky.

She slipped back into the bathroom, put the peroxide away, and
came out with a bottle of rubbing alcohol. "This is going to hurt,"
she said with easy confidence.

"Sissy," Parker protested, "you don't have to . . ."

"Oh, but I do," she said pouring the alcohol straight into the
open wound. Parker inhaled sharply and bit his lip to keep from
calling out in pain. Sissy poured on a little more alcohol. "I
wouldn't want you to get an infection."

Sissy caught Peewee watching them, chuckling to himself. He threw out his chest. "Clara, you want to bring us a couple of beers and set an extra place for dinner. We'll eat in the dining room tonight."

"That's okay, Peewee, I don't want to be any trouble," said Parker, who looked as if he were planning a strategic retreat to some safe place like a rattlesnake farm.

"No trouble at all, boy," Peewee said. And taking Parker by one arm and his wife by the other, he led them both out of the kitchen.

Clara went to the icebox. It was one thing to hang around helping Sissy. She did that for her own mama, and she'd taken care of kids all her life. But this was different. She looked into the living room and saw the white folks laughing in the breeze from the ceiling fan. She studied the man she thought had cared for her sitting with them. They'd put her in "her place," all right. Well, she wasn't staying there.

Sissy came out to the kitchen to see what was keeping Clara and found her putting on her white gloves. "What are you doing?"

"I gotta go."

"I thought you were going to help me with dinner."

Clara just stared at her and pressed her lips together. "The biscuits are in the oven. You can take them out in five minutes."

Clara checked her hair in the mirror by the door. Her face was closed down.

"Go on then," Sissy said, remembering with what pleasure she'd bathed Parker's leg.

WHEN PEEWEE CAME into the kitchen for another beer, he found Sissy looking out the door. "You paying her good money and she just walks out when we're having company? I told you to hire Hester Lee. But you wouldn't listen. Oh no, nothing would do, but you had to have that piece of high yeller trash. I knew it was a mistake from the start. There's none of them know how to work. I hope you've learned your lesson."

Sissy turned to her husband. "She's day help, Peewee. Lincoln freed the slaves."

Meanwhile, Parker had stepped out on the front porch to stretch his legs and figure out what to do next. He lit a cigarette and saw Clara walking down the street. Thank God. Maybe he could get Sissy alone yet, and somehow convince her to meet him.

Suddenly he knew how to do it. Simple. With Clara gone, he'd offer to help Sissy with the dishes. He imagined the two of them standing together at the sink. Again. Only this time he'd control himself. Peewee won't be a problem. Hell, if he keeps on guzzling beer, he won't be able to find the kitchen. Parker's confidence had returned. All he had to do was encourage Peewee on the path he'd already chosen. He could be as good a drinking buddy as the next guy. He saw Clara turn and look at him. He waved.

TEARS WELLED UP in Clara's eyes. It wasn't fair. The white girls always get it all. It's not a man's world. It's a white world. Well, she'd get hers just as soon as she hit Chicago. She'd be as white as any of them.

Then she saw Parker wave. He still cared about her after all. He wasn't just sniffing around Sissy. Maybe he'd even come out on the porch to signal her. She turned under the streetlight and waved back. She felt a little bounce return to her step.

Coming into the living room, Sissy saw them waving and saw Clara's bounce. She spun back to the kitchen. The fried chicken was crackling in the pan. She was wondering how she could coat Parker's with ground glass when Billy Joe banged into the kitchen. He gave his mother a squeeze. She kissed the top of his head.

"Wipe your feet," his father said, opening another bottle of beer, "and come on into the living room. There's someone I want you to meet."

Sissy turned back to the chicken. She thought of herself as brave, but not brave enough to be there when Billy Joe saw Parker again, although she didn't think Billy Joe would betray her. She threw a couple of chicken breasts into the sizzling fat. Splatters of blistering oil popped around her face. She jumped back into Chip, who'd slipped soundlessly through the screen door. Then she knocked the handle of the skillet and splashed boiling grease all over the floor.

"Oh, my God, Chip, are you all right? I didn't burn you, did I?" She searched his bare legs.

"I'm okay."

"You shouldn't sneak up on people. Someone could get hurt."

Chip smiled.

"BILLY JOE, I want you to meet Parker Davidson. He was quite a football player in his day," Peewee said, stressing *in his day*. Then he saw his Chip at the door. "Come on in here, boy," Peewee said, and added with pride, "These are my sons."

Billy Joe gave Parker a sullen look and stared down at his shoes. Chip smirked.

"Where are your manners?" Peewee asked. "Don't you all know how to shake hands?"

Chip glanced at his father. He gave Parker his hand and a nasty smile. "I already met Mr. Parker, Daddy,"

In the kitchen, Sissy was reaching for a dish towel to wipe up the floor.

"Remember?" Chip asked.

Sissy had to catch herself before she slipped on the grease.

"I remember," said Parker and his tone dared the teenager to say another word.

He didn't.

Billy Joe left the room. His father called after him, threatening, but Parker said, "Let him go. He's just being a kid. You remember what it was like."

Sissy came back in with Marilee, who crawled onto Peewee's lap. Parker looked at Peewee surrounded by his family, surrounded by Sissy's children. "Thou shalt not covet," the Bible said, but it didn't say how that was possible.

Sissy had hardly sat down when Peewee drunkenly ordered her back into the kitchen for another beer. When she came out with it, he wanted some pickled watermelon rinds.

"You should taste Sissy's pickled watermelon rinds," Peewee said to the benighted bachelor. "They're the best in the parish."

Sissy came back and slammed the jar on the table in front of her husband.

"She puts them up with her own hands," Peewee said, taunting him.

Parker fished out a watermelon rind and sucked on it, looking at Sissy. "Sure is good."

Peewee saw her eyes flash in what looked like anger, but it couldn't be. Then he saw Parker smile. Peewee shifted uncomfortably in his seat. He looked at their glasses. They hadn't drunk all that much. The truth of their relationship almost penetrated his dulled defenses before he banished it with "How about some dinner, woman?"

Sissy returned to the kitchen and took the fried chicken out of the skillet. *Who does he think he is, ordering me around like that?* She threw the chicken toward an old silver platter Clara had spent a good hour rubbing until it shined. *I'm his wife, not his servant.* She picked a breast off the floor and was brushing it off when the realization hit her. *If I were his servant, I could go home. I'm lower than his servant: I'm his wife.*

The silhouette of Parker waving to Clara came back unbidden, along with the memory of Clara caressing his leg. *Did they make a date for later? Of course they did. I'll bet he's picking her up as soon as he's finished eating my supper!*

Just then she smelled smoke. Opening the oven she pulled out Clara's biscuits, black and hard. She threw them into the garbage.

She could see the men sitting under the ceiling fan, telling jokes. The testosterone was so thick in the air they could hardly see or hear one another now. They were flying on the autopilot of their hormones.

Sissy walked toward her bedroom thinking about lesbians and wondering where she could find herself one.

"There she is," said the long-suffering husband. "Dinner finally ready?"

"It's on the kitchen table. Dish it up yourself."

"Hold it," ordered Peewee. He took her arm and pulled her aside. His breath was sour. "What the hell's going on with this family tonight?" he whispered. "Can't you even bestir yourself to serve up some dinner?"

"I have a splitting headache." She waved away his sour breath and said in a loud, firm voice, "I am going to lie down."

"Wait a minute . . ." Peewee said. "Now you wait just one dad-blamed minute, woman. Don't you start getting headaches on me."

But Sissy wrenched away from him, slammed into the bedroom, and locked the door on both of them.

Peewee stepped toward the door and rattled the knob. She'd locked him out! Son of a bitch!

He returned to the living room, put a drunken arm on Parker's shoulder, and slurred, "Come on, boy, let's get us something to eat."

Parker watched him stumble toward the kitchen. Now that he had seen them together, he was resolved. He had to rescue his princess from this toad.

Chapter 10

THE NEXT MORNING, Sissy didn't get up for breakfast. After
their fight the night before, she had unlocked the door for Peewee.
Gentry wisdom stated, "Any girl who locks her husband out of the
bedroom is asking for it." But she refused to talk to him. He circled
and sniffed at her like a strange dog, and then slunk off, leaving her
in possession of the bed. He slept on the living room couch.

She pretended to be asleep when he came for his clothes in the
morning and then she stayed in bed smoking. Marilee crawled into
the bed and snuggled up next to her until they heard Peewee leave
for work.

"Clara," Sissy called when she emerged barefooted from the bedroom, her arm around her daughter's shoulder.

Sissy wanted to find out if Clara had met Parker for a late date. If
not, they'd go over in rich and sarcastic detail all the horrors of the
dinner party from *The Black Lagoon*. But Clara wasn't there. And
to make matters worse the dining room looked like a prime candidate for International Disaster Relief.

"Clara!" Sissy yelled again. It was after nine. She sent Marilee into her bedroom to get dressed and went into the boys' room. They hadn't seen Clara all morning.

Damn. Did she and Parker have such a wild night that she couldn't make it to work? Sissy felt betrayed by the first girlfriend she'd had since high school. An emptiness opened in the pit of her stomach. She thought they'd shared something.

She dialed Clara's number, drumming her fingers on the table next to the couch. Nobody answered. Damn her!

Sissy went back into her room and slipped into her shorts and halter. Was Clara still at Parker's? Maybe they were going at it right now. Well, she certainly wasn't going to lower herself by calling him.

Furious at both of them, Sissy began stacking dishes and silverware together with a great clatter. I don't know why you're so surprised, the nagging voice in her head chided her. That's how you met her. You found them together.

Part of her couldn't believe Clara would be any real competition. She's just a teenager, a colored teenager. And she'll be gone soon. All I have to do is give Parker a chance.

Clara's available now, the nagging voice reminded her, and she has a tiny waist just like you *used to* have. And she has beautiful smooth young skin.

Sissy grabbed up a load of dirty dishes. Maybe Clara was so pissed at the way we treated her last night, she's not coming back at all, she thought. Or maybe after her night of passion, she can't face me.

Sissy slammed through the swinging door, dirty dishes teetering in her arms, and found the kitchen was under a siege of cockroaches.

"Good riddance!" she yelled, depositing the dishes in the sink and smashing a little brown sucker with a gym shoe Billy Joe had left under the round kitchen table. But the disgusting creatures were everywhere, swarming over the stove, feeding on the congealed egg yolks and setting up camp in the spilled grits.

It was Peewee's revenge. Ever since hiring Clara, Peewee seemed to delight in leaving every room as if it had been in the direct path of a cyclone. And when Sissy complained, he'd say, "Let the girl do it, that's why I'm paying her."

"Gotcha!" A flying cockroach dropped from the wall onto the University of Chicago catalog. Sissy leaned down and blew off the crumpled body and with it the Chicago Fantasy. A deep sense of loss, almost mourning, overcame her. She reached into her pocket for a cigarette, but she had trouble getting it out of the pack and even more trouble lighting it.

You're really pathetic, Sissy told herself, living vicariously through that girl. But a competing voice reminded her, living vicariously is better than not living at all.

It didn't matter anyway, pretty soon Clara would be off having a real life, having adventures with Yankees.

And then Sissy pictured what passed for her own life in Gentry, as it stretched into the future, gnawed on by the maggots of minutiae until she was hobbling on a cane like her grandmother. "What am I going to do?" she asked out loud. "What am I going to do?" At that moment a cockroach ran over her bare foot and Sissy screamed.

She staged a massive assault to still her grieving. Wielding the sneaker of death, she slashed through the roach infantry, decimating their numbers and forcing the rest into a desperate retreat. Then she hoisted herself onto the kitchen counter to attack their air force with chemical weapons. Balanced on one bare foot, she searched the top shelf for the insect spray, when she heard the screen door slam. Sissy froze. How should she handle this? She ought to give Clara unadulterated hell for being so late and not even calling. In her mind, Peewee's voice came in loud and clear. "Give them an inch and they'll take a mile. You watch, once she knows she can bamboozle you, she'll come in later and later. Pretty soon you'll be working for her."

Yes, she had to give Clara a piece of her mind, but before Sissy could turn around on the narrow counter, she heard a sharp pounding. She slid right down to the linoleum and onto a cockroach making his last foray.

"I did not chain myself to lampposts to see my granddaughter dusting the top of her kitchen cabinets. Don't you have anything more important to do?"

Sissy's grandmother, Belle Cantrell, had arrived.

As far as Sissy knew, Belle had never actually chained herself to a lamppost or anything else. She remembered her mother telling her about the time, in 1916, when Belle had taken her to Baton Rouge to attend a women's suffrage rally. Although her grandmother loved politics, Sissy suspected she'd really gone to that rally to stir things up at home. Sissy's grandfather, Claude Cantrell, a big, melancholy dairy farmer, had expressly forbidden his wife to go. He claimed she became impossible after associating with those uppity suffragettes. They put all kinds of ideas into her head. He was right about the ideas, but Sissy believed her grandmother had always been impossible.

Sissy had grown up hearing about Belle's impassioned letters to public officials and how she'd tried to organize the Gentry Women's Suffrage Committee before the good people of the town put an end to it. Still, they did get the vote. For all the good it did them, Belle would sniff. They never got around to voting for each other. The only thing women today are interested in is how to get rid of old wax buildup.

Sissy knew her grandmother yearned for the days before they'd won the right to vote. Days of optimism and enthusiasm, when their slogan was "Failure is impossible." They genuinely believed the world was about to open up for them. Belle was able to stir things up and do good at the same time.

So what if she'd begun to exaggerate her own role in the movement into one of civil insurrection. Belle was fond of saying,

"Dammit, when you get to be my age you should be able to remember your life the way you want to, even if it didn't unfurl quite that way."

Scraping the squashed cockroach off her bare foot and being careful not to step on any more, Sissy crossed the kitchen and kissed her grandmother.

"I brought the children some figs," the septuagenarian said, setting down a large paper bag and shaking a cigarette out of the open pack she found on the counter. A cockroach jumped out. Belle brushed it away with an imperial sweep of the pack and said sanguinely, "You know, dear, you ought to hire some help."

Sissy started to say something, but Belle cut her off. "I know, I know, you're going to tell me that Peewee can't afford it, but don't you let him chain you to your kitchen. A woman's freedom is more important than money." Sissy knew she'd have said more, much more, but Marilee came running into the house. "Mama, Mama! Come look! Hey, Gram, you gotta come too!"

"Marilee," her mother protested.

"You gotta! You gotta!" the little girl said as she flew out to the front porch.

The two women followed. Belle majestically pushed the scampering cockroaches out of the way with her ebony cane.

She'd been a great beauty in her youth and Sissy knew she'd used her looks to get what she wanted. Now she used her age and its privileges. She wore her gray hair swept up around her head. Her body was stout and imposing, and she always dressed in somber colors and old-fashioned dresses, as befitted a woman her age. But there was a twinkle in her eye and an eagerness for life that belonged to a teenager.

Out on the front porch a large brown puppy with enormous paws was tied to one of the posts. Billy Joe was scratching its head and Marilee lay on her stomach letting it lick her face. The children were in love.

Sissy knelt down next to her daughter. "Honey, I wouldn't get my heart set on this puppy. We don't know who it belongs to."

"Yes, we do," said Billy Joe, grinning. He held up a note tied to its collar. The note was made out to Marilee: "A dog of your own." There was no signature.

"Who left it here?" Sissy asked.

"Who do you think?" said Chip, standing under a tree.

In spite of herself, Sissy was overcome with a feeling of relief. Maybe Parker hadn't come to see Clara after all. At least he wasn't still in bed with her. He'd had to get out early to find this puppy for Marilee. Things were looking up.

"We've got to get him some water," said Billy Joe, untying the dog and opening the door. The puppy sprinted in ahead of him into the living room.

"You going to let them keep it?" Belle asked.

"Of course she is, Gram!" Billy Joe was appalled at the very idea. "It was given to Marilee. It's hers, right, Mama?" When Sissy didn't say anything, he became upset. "Right?"

Sissy looked at the puppy, looked at its paws. It was going to be enormous. She slapped her pockets, but her cigarettes were still in the kitchen collecting roaches. If she let them keep the dog, Peewee would have a fit. If she didn't, she'd be the ogre. "We'll see what your father says." But her words were drowned out by Marilee's delighted yelps.

"Look, Mama, look!" The puppy rolled over on the oriental rug and became entangled in the phone cord. Billy Joe knelt down and disentangled it. Marilee knelt down with her big brother. Chip observed the scene from the doorway. He was keeping a scientific distance.

The puppy rolled to its feet, ran around in a circle, sniffed, and clearly delighted to have found the toilet at last, squatted on the rug.

"Oh my God," said Sissy, leaping for the animal, knocking the phone off the table just as it began to ring.

"No, no, bad dog!" cried Billy Joe and Marilee in a cheerful chorus.

Belle grabbed the still squatting puppy and rushed it out to the yard, followed by the screaming, giggling children. Sissy picked up the phone.

"Sissy?"

"Listen, you SOB, where do you get off giving my children a dog without asking me?"

"Cute little thing, isn't he?"

"I should hang up on you, right now." But she didn't. She could feel his voice resonate in her chest and it made her weak. She leaned against the couch as pictures of him in his shrink-to-fit jeans filled her head.

When Belle came back into the house, she found Sissy with the phone pressed to her ear, straddling the soft arm of the couch, swinging one bare foot back and forth. A small, happy laugh bubbled out of her. And then she saw her grandmother. "I have to go."

Belle stood in the door, her hands crossed over her cane.

"Have you taken a lover?"

"Grandma!"

"Oh, don't use that tone of voice to me. What else is there for a woman to do around here on a hot summer afternoon, except clerk in the dime store?"

"I've been thinking about it. Taking a lover, I mean."

"Whoop-de-doo, everybody thinks about it." It was said that after taking care of voting rights, Belle had become a champion of free love, but about that, Sissy had heard only rumors. Belle had never believed it prudent to kiss and tell, especially in Gentry.

Sissy went into the kitchen to get a cup of much-needed coffee and a cigarette. Belle followed. "You've got to do more than think. You've got to take your life into your own hands, girl." In the yard, the puppy let out a couple of shrill barks.

"I guess," said Sissy, looking into the cigarette pack to see if anything moved.

Belle caught her hand and held it. "Honey, listen to me. I've been seventeen years old all my life. Then one day I woke up and my joints hurt. The next day I looked into the mirror and I saw this hunch-backed old crone." She looked down at their hands—Sissy's long and smooth; her own, gnarled and wrinkled—and dropped them. "And now, all I can do is think about it." She held out an open palm for a cigarette.

Sissy struck a kitchen match, lighting them both up. "Besides, if you don't take your life into your own hands, someone else will take it in theirs. Whose hands you going to trust your life to?" A hundred unanswered questions mixed with the smoke and filled Sissy's head. But before she could put them into words, Marilee rushed back into the kitchen. This time she was weeping hysterically.

"What's wrong?" Belle asked, sitting down on the Victorian kitchen chair. But the little girl was too upset to tell her. Both women pored over the child looking for cuts, bruises, or bites. Finally she hiccuped something about her dog.

"Chip!" screamed Sissy. When she received no answer she ran out to the yard. There was no sign of him or the dog. Billy Joe stood in the corner of the driveway, looking nervously toward the house.

"Billy Joe, where's your brother?"

The boy said nothing. He was being stretched between two loyalties.

"I know I always taught you not to tell on one another. But you've got to forget about that and tell me."

Sissy saw a stricken look in his eyes. Then he averted his head and drew a circle in the dust with his bare toe.

She went to him and took his head in her hands. "Billy Joe, where's your brother?"

He ducked and looked down as if examining the circle he'd just drawn. Then he mumbled, "He's in our room. He's experimenting on Marilee's dog."

*   *   *

SISSY FLUNG OPEN the door to the room the boys shared. Chip was sitting calmly at his desk, making notes in his lab book. "Can't you read?" he said, pointing to a sign with a skull and crossbones and the words "Danger" and "Keep Out."

"Where's Marilee's dog?"

Chip didn't even bother to answer. He calmly looked at the clock and made an entry.

"Chip, I'm talking to you." Sissy bent down and looked under the beds. But she didn't find the puppy. She whistled, "Come on, boy, come on, come here."

A frantic scratching and desperate whine came from the closet. "Jesus, Chip, how could you shut up a little puppy like that?"

"I'm conducting an experiment."

Sissy turned the knob and pulled on the closet door. It was locked. A long time ago, she'd had the wisdom to dismantle the lock on the boys' door, but she'd left the closet alone, so they would have some sense of privacy. An acrid smell wafted through the cracks. She heard her daughter crying in the kitchen. Sissy ran her hand on top of the doorsill. She came away with dust. "Give me the key."

"I can't. I'm in the middle of an experiment."

"Chip!" There was a warning in her voice.

"I have to test my invention. Scientists have to test their inventions, you know," Chip said.

"What invention?" She yanked on the door. The puppy responded, but this time its response was strangely subdued. Again that acrid smell. A terrible thought crept into Sissy's head. "Chip, what invention are you testing?" He didn't answer; instead he made another entry in his book. "Chip, I'm talking to you. What is this invention?"

"A new nerve gas." His voice was quiet, but he couldn't keep out the note of pride.

"Are you crazy? Open the door!" The dog's scratches were getting weaker, and each one felt like it was made across her heart. "The puppy could die. Don't you care?" She heard her voice. It was shrill now.

Chip closed his lab book. "He's just a dumb animal. I don't know why you're making such a fuss. Scientists experiment on animals all the time." He stood and put his lab book into its place in the bookcase.

Sissy jerked him around. "You are not a scientist. Pretending to be one doesn't give you any right to torture animals. Now, give me the key to the closet."

Sissy heard the puppy whimper and cough and felt her own throat constrict. She smashed into the door with her shoulder, but it was cypress and built for the ages. "Don't you have any feelings?"

He moved to the desk. Sissy rubbed her shoulder and watched him. Was he going for the key? He carefully put his sharpened pencil into its coffee can holder.

Sissy was shaking, screaming now, "Give me the key." But she knew her screams made Chip more confident. He knew who was in control. She calmed down and said, "You want me to tell your daddy about your scientific invention?"

"You won't tell on me, Mama. You wouldn't dare."

The dog was choking. She couldn't let her son kill it. She wouldn't. For his sake as well as the dog's, she had to call his bluff. "Now listen up, boy, and listen good. You want to end your parents' marriage? Do it. Go ahead. Tell your daddy everything you saw. In fact why stop with the truth? You're creative; make up stuff. You don't even have to wait for him to come home for dinner. Get on your bike. He's working in the office today. Go on. Just give me the key."

Sissy saw Chip wasn't ready for this. He'd counted on his blackmail working forever. But instead of giving it up as she expected, she saw him making calculations. Didn't he get it? Didn't he get what would happen to them all? Did she have to spell it out? "I'll be all right, I'm the mother, so I'll get the house and the children. Only I can't handle you." She didn't enjoy being cruel but the puppy was gasping for air. "I expect you'll have to live in some dinky apartment with your father or, if he can't handle you, in a foster home or at the state orphanage. Is that what you want? You think they'll let you keep your chemistry set at the orphanage?"

That at least seemed to shake him up, but he said, "Pawpaw'll take me."

"You want to live with Bourrée and Miss Lily? Is that it? I'll call them right now." She started for the living room. "Of course a couple of months with them and you'll be begging for the orphanage. Hell, you'll settle for a reformatory." She glanced back at him.

He was still at his desk, nervously rolling a pencil in his hand. She picked up the phone. The pencil was in his mouth, but he still didn't move. She began to dial . . .

"Wait."

Sissy's heart started pounding. She went back into the boys' room. Chip had the key in the lock and was opening the door. She took it away from him. "Go stand out on the porch," she said.

When he was safely out of the room, she held her breath and flung open the door.

THE PUPPY LAY still on the grass. "Is he dead?" Marilee asked, her voice filled with tears.

Sissy, kneeling over the animal, shook her head, but she was worried. She didn't have any experience with sick animals and the vet was still out on his morning rounds of the farms. She stroked the puppy's head and covered him with a towel. He didn't respond.

"Don't let him die, Mommy," Marilee pleaded.

Billy Joe put his arm around his little sister's shoulders.

A cane clicked on the cement. Belle arrived with a dish of water.

She splashed some on the puppy's face. Nothing. She poured it on its nose. It sneezed and very weakly tried to shake off the water. "Good, he's a fighter." Bending down with some difficulty, Belle took the dog in her arms and walked it like a baby, patting its back, its head nuzzled against her shoulder. "Used to do this with sick calves," she said, striding up and down, her cane crooked over her arm. "The movement reminds them to breathe." And Sissy wondered, not for the first time, if her grandmother needed that cane, or if after seeing an Ethel Barrymore film last year, she simply used it for effect.

"I'll take him, Gram," said Billy Joe, unburdening her, stroking the puppy as he walked him up and down the backyard. Marilee walked with him, talking to the little animal.

Belle eased herself into a redwood chair in the shade of the old live oak near the back bedroom. Sissy dropped to the grass at her grandmother's feet. She saw Chip moving around in his room, where he had orders to clean it up and air it out. She called to him to open all the windows and use the fan. Then she pulled up a weed that had sprouted in the little garden in the roots of the live oak tree. "Where'd I go wrong? Do you think he suspects?"

"Oh, for Lord's sake," said Belle. "Don't take that on. You were what, seventeen, when you had him? You were still a child yourself."

"I always tried to make him feel wanted, in spite of everything."

"Sissy, look at me," said the old woman. "In my generation they worshiped mothers. We couldn't do anything wrong as long as we stayed home and took care of the kids and didn't worry about politics. Now that you all have chosen to stay home and raise your kids without even the help we had, you can't do anything right. Everything's Mother's fault. They just want to get us. The truth is, that child's a throwback. He inherited a mean streak from Bourrée. When Lily Moffat said she was going to marry that Cajun I warned her."

"Let's not start on the Cajuns." Sissy leaned against the arm of her grandmother's chair, too worn out to move and it wasn't even lunchtime.

"Why, Sissy, you know I'm not prejudiced. I've known many fine, upstanding Cajuns in my time. And Bourrée LeBlanc is not one of them. That man will charm the birds right out of the trees and then shoot them."

"What's wrong with Chip isn't Bourrée's fault."

"Don't be too sure," said the old lady. "The boy's losing his conscience. They have some scientific word for it now, psycho-something, I can't remember, but what it all boils down to is he doesn't care about what happens to anybody else as long as he gets what he wants."

"Maybe it's a stage," Sissy said.

Belle looked at her granddaughter and her look was filled with compassion. "No. I don't think so. I've seen it before. I don't know why it happens. Bad blood, bad genes. There are all kinds of theories, but it happens to boys mostly and it happens to them about the time they start noticing girls."

"He's a teenager, not a leftover from *The Invasion of the Body Snatchers*."

"Sissy, I'm serious."

"So am I. Breaking away from us is his job," she said quoting the latest magazine article she'd read. "What we object to is, he has a real aptitude for it."

Belle studied her. "It's always hardest on the mothers."

"Oh, for God's sake." Sissy turned away.

But Belle pressed on. "I've seen more than one boy like Chip tear his family apart and go on preying on his mother year after year. I've seen those same mothers give their sons everything they had and then, when they were all but bankrupt, feel guilty they couldn't give them more. Don't let it happen to you, honey."

Sissy shook her head as if trying to wipe away her grandmother's prediction. "Chip's not like that. You talk like he's crazy or something. He's not. He's just going through a stage."

The old woman saw the dark figure press himself against the screen and then move back into the shadows. "Let's hope," was all she could say.

Never put off your education. The world is lying in wait to

come between a girl and her ambition.

Rule Number Thirty-one

THE SOUTHERN BELLE'S HANDBOOK

Chapter 11

SISSY DROVE THE younger children and the revived dog home from Flannigan's Animal Clinic, but not before making a sizable contribution to the vet's new house, the education of his children, and the welfare of his drug suppliers. Peewee's going to have a conniption fit when he finds out we have a dog, Sissy thought. But Marilee's dog was there to stay no matter what he said. Southern Belle's Handbook, Rule Number Twenty-six: *A smart woman picks her fights*. So when she fights, she wins.

Puppies are naturally seductive. She suspected they had the power of mental telepathy, and this one was beaming "love me, love me" as he bounced around panting. Telepathy or not, Ed Sullivan (Marilee's name) had won her over. But she sure wasn't looking forward to Peewee's learning how much she'd shelled out for its medical services.

She turned the corner and found Clara sitting on the back steps, where she'd spread out a white lace handkerchief to protect her navy skirt. Sissy was flooded with relief. And then sarcasm began making its rounds of her brain, picking up words here and there, accepting some, rejecting others, searching for the really biting phrase. But a second look at the girl stopped sarcasm's progress. Clara, who was usually so bright, looked as if she'd abandoned all hope.

Sissy walked to the back steps as the children and Ed Sullivan rolled over the side of the convertible. But Clara didn't even remark on the dog. "What happened?" Sissy asked, sitting down next to her.

"I'm sorry."

"Don't be silly, everyone is late sometime." Sissy couldn't believe she was saying this at one o'clock in the afternoon. She heard Pee-wee screaming in her brain, "You're letting that girl take advantage of you again. Fire her."

"I mean, I have to quit."

"Now, let's not go through that again." She put her hand on her cousin's arm. "If it's about what happened last night . . ."

Clara shook her head. She'd spent the morning applying for a job as a sweeper for Gulf Chemicals. She'd given Sissy as a reference. "I hope it's okay."

"Are you crazy? What do you want to work at that smelly old place for?"

"A dollar an hour."

"If this is some scheme to get yourself a raise, forget it. I don't have the money." Sissy was still wondering if she should explain the vet bill to Peewee or keep it a secret. Of course if she kept it a secret, she'd have to explain why there was no food on the table for two weeks. She wished she had money of her own, money she didn't have to explain. Still, she felt a need to justify herself to her cousin. "Nobody pays that much for housework."

"I know," Clara said. Misery was radiating from her. Sissy breathed it in and became miserable, too. "Dammit, Clara. Why are you doing this?"

Clara handed her a letter from the University of Chicago, dated

May 10. "Sometimes the mail has trouble finding its way from the post office to Butlertown. This one just found me yesterday."

"I don't understand," said Sissy, looking up from the letter. "I thought you had a full scholarship."

"Me, too. But it was just full tuition. It didn't cover room and board. They want a thousand dollars."

"That's crazy. Nobody can afford that!" Sissy had never seen a thousand dollars in her whole life.

"I talked to the admissions lady this morning. She said the size of my scholarship had been decided by a committee and it was too late now to change it. Then she gave me a lecture on how I should expect to make some contribution to my own education. She said if it was free . . . I mean were free, I wouldn't appreciate it."

Sissy was pissed. She knew the world wasn't fair, but she always hated getting proof of it. "Even at a dollar an hour, you can't make that much before September."

Clara sighed and nodded. "I know, but I'll be that much closer."

"Well, damn," said Sissy.

The two cousins sat side by side on the porch. "There are always the colored colleges around here," Sissy said.

"No!" said Clara. She was silent for a few moments. "I guess I could work for a year and apply again next spring."

"No!" said Sissy, and made up Rule Thirty-one on the spot. "The Southern Belle's Handbook says, *Never put off your education. The world is lying in wait to come between a girl and her ambition.*"

"Yeah, well, does your Southern Belle's Handbook say how I'm going to find the money?"

They were silent for a while. And then Sissy asked, "Have you talked to Uncle Tibor?"

"He hasn't wanted to have anything to do with us since my mama got married."

"Then it's high time you made up with him." Clara shook her head. "He's your daddy." Clara didn't say anything. "Don't worry, he's loaded. My daddy says he only prosecutes the innocent, the guilty pay him off." But her witticism was lost on Clara, who was staring at the Spanish moss hanging from the branches of the live oak. Then Sissy saw the girl's lip quiver. She kept forgetting how young she was. "I'll bet he'd be real proud of you, if he knew. Hell, those boys of his and Aunt Ida May's are never gonna win a scholarship. Together they don't have the IQ of spinach."

"He won't be proud." Clara was rigid.

"Okay, maybe the Great White Hope won't take out an ad in the paper, but I'll bet inside he'll be tickled as he can be." Clara was having a silent debate. "Give him a call." Clara shook her head. "What have you got to lose?"

"I hate him."

"Well, get over it. *There are some principles a poor girl just can't afford.* Rule Number Twenty-seven, Southern Belle's Handbook."

Clara hesitated. Sissy could see she was having a silent battle with herself. "What is it?" But Clara didn't answer. "Haven't you figured it out yet? You can trust me." Still Clara didn't say anything. "What is it? What did he do to you?"

Finally Clara spoke. "I was only six, Marilee's age, and I was dying to see what went on in that big brick house with all those white columns. I figured I was half white and I ought to know. I was too young to understand half don't mean shit around here," Clara said, falling back into the black vernacular she usually kept out of her conversations with her white cousin. "Anyway, the night before, I'd gone to see this movie with my brothers and they had this detective on a stakeout. So after my mama went to work, I snuck out of Butlertown and climbed up into that big magnolia tree in front of his house and watched them through the leaves. But nothing happened. You know how hours dissolve into seconds in the movies? Well, in real life, seconds turn into hours. Pretty soon I fell asleep and out of the tree.

"That's when Miss Ida May came running out of the house with her cook and insisted on bringing me inside. I was so thrilled I could hardly stand it. She sat me down in the living room. I can still remember that big velvet couch, with those maroon cushions. Do they still have it?" Sissy nodded. "I'd never felt anything so soft in my life.

"Anyway, the cook, Miss Virginia, I knew her from church, put ice on my bruises while Miss Ida May sat down next to me and asked me about my people. Well, I'd been warned not to tell anyone who my father was, but I felt so close to this nice white lady and she *was* married to him, so I thought it couldn't hurt to tell her.

"But then Miss Virginia shook her head and introduced me as 'Denise Conners's girl.' Miss Ida May got all excited about that, because my mama had worked for her.

"Anyway, after they'd cleaned me up and painted me orange with Mercurochrome, we all went into the kitchen, and Miss Virginia gave me some chocolate ice cream. I'd had a fight with my mama that morning, and I thought I'd go live with my daddy for a while and eat ice cream every day.

"That night he came to our house and I said, 'Daddy!' and ran and hugged his knees, just like I always did. But before I could tell him I wanted to live with him, he'd picked me up and was shaking me and yelling that I was never even to walk down his street again. I was crying and Mama was trying to pull him off and then the last thing I remember was him chucking me against the wall. I was just a little bitty thing. But he smashed me so hard he cracked the plaster."

"Good God!" Sissy had never had much use for her uncle, but she'd never imagined the self-proclaimed "protector of the family" had sunk to abusing a six-year-old girl, and his own daughter to boot. "What happened then?"

"I'm not sure. When I came around my face was all puffed up and throbbing and I'd lost a tooth, but I was afraid to cry. Mama was trying to calm him down, you know, listening and nodding sympathetically, making all those soft little moves she made around him. It took her a real long time. I thought she ought to chase him out of the house with the shotgun. But she said she didn't know how to do that and stay in Gentry. He was too powerful."

Clara stopped for a moment.

"But now I think, in spite of everything, she kept letting him come back because she was used to him and because she was afraid of being alone."

"So he kept coming around?" Sissy asked.

"Oh, yeah. He even tried to make up with me. Once he brought me a big baby doll, you know with blue eyes that opened and shut and blond hair. 'Rubinstein's best,' he said, smiling that politician smile of his." Clara grimaced. "And my mama made me walk up to his chair and let him give me one of his wet kisses."

And then Clara's eyes blazed. "But she couldn't make me thank him. Not then. Not ever. Or call him Daddy. You know what I did after that? When I went to school, we had those hand-me-down readers you all had at the white school. Remember?" Sissy nodded. "Well, I still couldn't forget that I was half white. So I used to pretend I was living with my white daddy, only I'd pretend he was Dick and Jane's daddy. We all lived together and had chocolate ice cream every day. I'd play with Dick and Jane and Baby Sally all afternoon after school and then at night Father would come home. And he was always especially nice to me and read me stories. You know, the way fathers are supposed to be." She paused and then added, "It was my favorite pretend."

Sissy thought she understood what Clara saw in Parker, but she didn't say it. What she said was "I wish we didn't always have to wait around for handouts from men."

"Why do you think I want to go to college? I don't want to ever have to take nothin' from nobody."

And then Sissy had an idea. She'd always hated do-gooders. They smacked of Amy Lou Hopper and her Christmas baskets for the poor. But this was something else. This girl ought to have a chance. "What you need is a scholarship fund."

"Uh-huh," said Clara. "Who's gonna give me one of those?"

"You wait here," said Sissy. "In fact, you can clean up the kitchen while I'm gone." She didn't want to ruin her reputation by doing something completely unselfish. So she opened the door to the disaster area.

AN HOUR LATER, Clara had finally gotten the kitchen cleaned up and the children fed when Sissy emerged from her bath, smelling all sweet and flowery. She had pulled on her most ladylike dress, the one she'd bought for her rare appearances at the Episcopal church.

"Keep an eye on the children, will you?"

"Where in the world are you going?" Clara asked.

"To see about your scholarship fund."

Clara watched her pull away from the curb and the words of her grandmother, Beulah May Conners, echoed in her head: "Some white womens just loves to pretend they is the savior of the colored. It gives them something high-minded to do, but the truth is they don't have the attention span of a gnat. Soon as it gets a little bothersome, or somebody calls her a nigger lover, she's gonna become the savior to the puppies and the kitties. You just watch."

SISSY PULLED UP in front of the converted cottage that housed *The Weekly Avenger* downstairs and where her father, Hugh Thompson, lived upstairs. He had chosen this name for his newspaper in the days of his youth, before his passions had been ground down by the endless compromises he had to make to support his family and to keep his business solvent in a town that had stopped growing at twenty-five hundred opinionated souls.

It was still called *The Weekly Avenger*, but *The Weekly Absolver* would be more like it, at least in the opinion of some of the town's darker-complexioned citizens. But they didn't subscribe. And his subscribers felt that, with its extensive high school football coverage and weekly recipes, *The Avenger* was all that a small-town newspaper should be.

"Let me get this straight," said Hugh. "You want me to take up a collection for your maid?"

"Not a collection, Daddy, a scholarship fund! My goodness, considering the education they get up at the colored high school, it's amazing she can write her own name, let alone get some Yankee college to give her tuition. I think it's a very worthy cause."

Hugh looked searchingly at his daughter perched on the edge of his desk. "What do you think, Sam?"

Sam Carter, the *Avenger*'s advertising manager and space salesman, mopped up the sweat from the creases on his neck with his big white handkerchief. He'd been intent on watching Sissy uncross her legs under her tight blue skirt. "Hell, yes, it's a worthy cause." He jumped up from his desk and lit her cigarette.

Sissy awarded him a dazzling smile. "I'm so glad you think so, Sam."

Rita Sue Mullins, *The Weekly Avenger*'s sole reporter, looked up from the file cabinet she was searching through and shook her head. Twenty-five years before, she'd pioneered as the first female to study journalism at LSU and dreamed of a career as a foreign correspondent. Now her beat was the high school awards dinners, wedding receptions, and choosing the cook of the week.

"I remember you raised, I don't know how much, last year when May Cuttler's baby needed that operation and Daddy said you increased circulation to boot." Sissy was on a roll.

"We sure did," Sam said. "And it made us real proud to help that little boy. Of course, we can't lose sight of the fact that our advertisers may hold to a different opinion about this here, er . . . scholarship fund."

"What do you mean?"

"He means May and her baby were white," said Rita Sue from the file cabinet.

Sam glared at Rita Sue. "Now, don't get me wrong, Sissy," Sam said. "I mean, I'm all for it. But you know since the Supreme Court decision and all that agitation over in Montgomery about who sits where on the buses, the white trash around here have got themselves all worked up. Some fools have even organized a Klan chapter again, not that any of us would get involved with it, of course, but I don't think this is exactly the time to be taking up a collection to send some nigra to a white college. Even a worthy nigra," Sam hastened to add, mopping his forehead. "You understand?"

"Didn't her father go to jail for drugs?" asked Rita Sue.

"Her father . . ." Sissy began, but Hugh cut her off.

"She means her stepfather, honey. Reuben Johnson. I believe he's in the state penitentiary, serving five to life. I can't remember, was it heroin or marijuana he had in his possession?"

Rita Sue shrugged. "Whichever."

"She never told me." Sissy felt betrayed.

"The family's a real upstanding representative of their race," said Rita Sue, lighting her own cigarette.

Defeated, Sissy slid off the edge of the desk. And she really hated defeat. She flicked an ash over the paste-up Sam had been working on most of the afternoon. "Oh, Sam, I'm *so* sorry."

She would have bumped into Rita Sue, accidentally of course, pushing her headfirst into that file drawer, if her father hadn't taken her elbow and walked her to the door. "She didn't tell you about her stepfather?"

"I think she mentioned him."

"But not his current address?"

"No."

"Well, don't let it throw you. I'm sure she's a fine young woman." Sissy nodded abstractedly as her father opened the door and a wave of heat hit her in the face from the shimmering sidewalk. "If you want to put your public spirit to use, I suggest you join the garden club," he said in a loud voice. Then he closed the door behind them and spoke softly, "Sissy, I can't take up a collection for my niece!"

"You knew?" she asked. What other family secrets was he keeping from her?

"Tibor's my brother. He's been catting around Butlertown since we were kids."

The candidate's face smiled benignly down at them from a billboard covering the side of the building. "Tibor Thompson, Protecting the American Family."

"But he's claiming to be the Great White Hope!"

"That's a laugh, isn't it?" Hugh said.

Sissy nodded and glanced at the huge photograph, but when she turned back to her father she saw him looking startled as if there were something he thought she already knew. "What?"

"Nothing."

Sissy let it pass. "How does he get away with it?"

"Politicians and preachers can get away with damn near anything as long as they say what the riffraff wants to hear."

"But if they find out, won't they turn against him?"

"How're they going do that?" Hugh asked.

Sissy smiled a slow, rebellious smile. "I'd think the newspapers would be in hog heaven to get a scandal like this."

"Sissy, look at me. If you have any notions of using this against your uncle, forget it. Besides, he's too smart. He knows nobody'd print it."

"But . . ."

"It's not news who a man sleeps with. Hell, if we wanted to dig up that kind of dirt on our politicians, every journalist in the country would have black fingernails."

"Wouldn't it sell newspapers?"

"Maybe. But you can't invade a man's private life. Who'd run for public office? Now of course, if he comes to the attention of the readers some other way, a divorce or an inheritance, then his peccadillos are fair game. But the first paper to print this kind of unsubstantiated rumor would be hit with a million-dollar libel suit. No reputable paper wants that kind of trouble for some cheap gossip."

"It's not right. He's her father! Can you imagine what it was like for her all these years?" Sissy was working herself up. "The least he can do is pay for her education. He's got plenty of money—you told me yourself he takes bribes from half the parish."

"Sissy, now listen to me, don't you mess with Tibor." She didn't say anything. She was staring up at the Protector of the American Family. Hugh took her chin and turned her face toward him. "I mean it. He's crazy when it comes to revenge. Clara's stepfather wasn't on drugs. I knew Reuben. He was hardworking and sober."

"So why's he in the jail?"

"He had the audacity to marry Tibor's woman."

"But Uncle Tibor couldn't marry her."

"That doesn't mean he'd allow someone else to. Don't mess with him."

"Oh, Daddy, what can he do to me?"

Hugh was silent for a long moment and then said softly, "You don't want to find out."

SISSY WASN'T READY to give up. Before she went home she drove across the tracks and turned up Grand and parked in front of Hopper's drugstore. She cornered Amy Lou, who was consuming a Baby Ruth with quick little bites like a rabbit gnawing away on a carrot.

"Are you talking about that piece of high yeller trash I saw hanging around your yard?" Amy Lou asked, delicately wiping her mouth on a Kleenex.

"She won a scholarship to the University of Chicago, which is more than I can say for either of us!" Sissy said.

Amy Lou threw her Kleenex into a wastebasket beneath the counter and said, "The Ladies Auxiliary of the Methodist Church has about as much charitable work as we can handle. But if you love the negras so much, why don't you help with our Christmas baskets for the poor? You'll find it so gratifying to do the Lord's work."

Sissy slammed out of the drugstore, furious at herself for giving Amy Lou such pleasure.

She switched on the ignition. What had started as a unpremeditated effort to get Clara away from Parker had become Sissy's personal quest. Rule Number Twenty-six had taken over. She had picked this fight. And she was going to win it come hell or high water.

In the weeks to come she prodded Peewee into talking to the Kiwanis and sicced Belle on various organizations that performed "good works." But regardless of how their views differed, in the matter of their charitable enterprises they all agreed that sending Clara to the University of Chicago was not going to be one of them.

PARKER DAVIDSON, HIS arms filled with groceries, kicked at the screen door until it bounced. He hooked his foot around it and knocked it open. From inside the kitchen he heard Sid barking with excitement. Shifting the groceries to the crook of his arm, he freed his right hand and turned the key in the lock. Tonight was going to be different. The grocery bags were full of real food, lettuce, tomatoes, milk, eggs, and a man-sized sirloin steak. He was going to start taking care of himself.

Sid hunkered down as he watched the door open and, then with an explosion of pure animal joy, leaped up to lick his master's face. His tail wagged in full circles behind him and his sharp claws slashed right through the brown-paper grocery bags. Parker yelled as eggs, milk, meat, lettuce, tomatoes, and cans of dog food crashed to the kitchen floor.

The dog cowered in confusion. Why the yelling and the noise? He was just trying to be a good dog, just trying to show his master how much he loved him. Then he smelled the delicious aromas wafting up around him and Sid knew he was a good dog after all. His master was giving him a treat.

He skidded through the broken eggs and pushed the lettuce into the spilled milk. Man and dog raced for the steak. Dog won. Stepping on a tomato for leverage, Sid sunk his teeth through the butcher paper into the meat. He tore the package apart, covering steak, paper, and string with dog drool. This was the very first time his food had ever come gift-wrapped.

Parker watched his dinner turn into doggy delight and seriously considered killing the beast. Instead he slowly bent his large frame over and picked through what was now garbage to retrieve the fucking cans of dog food. He threw them into the sink, where they dripped a dirty mixture of eggs, milk, and tomato. He opened the kitchen cabinet. He still had to make dinner for himself and the grocery store had closed. He found two cans of corned-beef hash.

He slumped into a chair at the kitchen table. The setting sun beamed its last rays through the screen and the beveled-glass door straight at him. The dog was making gleeful noises on the floor. Parker covered his eyes with his hands.

At first he thought the knocking was just more of the dog's enthusiasm. But when he looked up, dazzled by the glare, he saw Sissy silhouetted against the glass. Her shape glowed against the red sky.

Parker jumped up. The puppy did it. She'd come back to him. Barreling into Sid, who made a low threatening sound over his food, Parker opened the door.

But Clara was standing on the welcome mat. Parker's smile wavered a little and then widened. He stepped aside for her. "Hey, girl, come on in."

"Something wrong with your front doorbell?"

"I don't think anyone's ever used it."

Sid's low, threatening sound turned into a bona fide growl at the entrance of the interloper. When she stepped near his food, the dog hunched back ready to spring. "Sid!" Parker yelled.

Clara shrank back.

Parker pushed Sid aside, so instead of lunging, the dog slid through the slippery mix of egg and squashed tomatoes into the kitchen cabinets. "I was just making supper."

"And it looks delicious," Clara said, carefully picking her way to the other side of the kitchen, as far from the big dog as possible.

"I guess that means you don't want any."

"You white folks sure do know how to make a mess."

"We sure do," Parker said as he tracked through his ruined supper. He grabbed a couple of Dixies out of the icebox and, with one arm around the girl, propelled her into the living room.

"Good to see you again."

"Good to see you." Her voice was warm. She settled down into his couch and knocked back the bottle of beer as her free hand sought his knee.

"I got a new job today," she said.

"You quit Sissy?" His heart leaped. He'd have a free shot at her now.

Then Clara told him about the letter from the university and how excited she'd been at Sissy's mission, a scholarship drive for her and in the newspaper. "I should have known they weren't gonna take up a collection for a colored girl." Misery leaked out of her voice and spilled over to Parker.

He took her in his arms and held her as she talked. He thought about all the schools that had waved scholarships at him. All the schools he'd run out on.

"I was worried I wasn't gonna have enough for bus fare and warm clothes and all. But now I've got to come up with a thousand dollars and I've only got two months." Parker stroked her back until she was comforted a little. "How'm I gonna do it, Parker?"

"Shhh." He felt her nuzzle into him and kiss his neck. But when he offered her money, she stiffened. "Hey, I'm not paying for services rendered." He cupped her chin in his hand. "Heck, girl, don't you know, I couldn't afford you."

But she didn't want to be beholden to him or any man for money. "My mama never had any kind of a life once she started down that road."

He pulled her to him and murmured with his face in her hair, "I want you to get your chance, that's all. I want you to have a real life."

"Let's see where I am next month, okay?" Her voice was hoarse.

He held her to him. She unbuttoned his shirt and ran her fingers through the curling brown hair. Then she slipped her hand into his jeans. But it went in too easily. There was no straining against the fabric. She looked up at him, startled.

"I told you I wasn't paying for your services," he said, taking the hand out of his pants and kissing her carefully manicured fingertips.

She looked down at his crotch and quickly looked away. "I just wanted to be with you." There was a wail in her voice. "I was feeling low-down and blue about having to work at that smelly chemical plant and all."

"I know," he said and kissed her hair.

She smiled up at him like a soldier marching into battle and unbuttoned her white blouse.

He ran his hands lightly over her chest, but tonight, for the first time, he felt nothing. Her bra was pink nylon. It molded her flesh into torpedo points, covered with cheap machine-made lace. He reached around and undid the hooks, freeing her breasts to fall into a human shape. He held them, one in each hand, as if weighing cantaloupes, pretty beige cantaloupes. Sissy's were smaller, more the size of grapefruits, oranges even. He remembered how small and lost they looked in her black-lace push-up bra. He watched Clara's nipples bounce, her dark brown nipples.

"What are you doing?" Clara asked.

He snapped out of his reverie and laughed. "This doesn't turn you on? How about this?" He ran his thumb over her nipple and watched the shiver go through her body. He reached under her skirt and began to stroke her thighs and then between her thighs. She lay back and moaned. Parker wondered why he felt nothing. With his fingertips he reached into her panties. Matching pink lace, he guessed. Clara was always careful to match everything. But he didn't bother to look, didn't even bother to pull up her skirt. She was moving her body up and down, her eyes shut tight.

She reached for him as wave after wave of feeling made her tremble. "Don't stop," she moaned and grabbed the metal buttons on his jeans. Her eyes still closed, she began unbuttoning those tight metal buttons, but tonight they weren't tight at all.

Clara sat up and opened her eyes. "What's the matter?"

He shrugged and tried to smile, but how could he smile? "I don't know." Nothing like this had ever happened to him before. Christ! What had these women done to him? He pulled away from her.

"You feeling all right?" She put her hand to his head.

He took her hand and held it. "These things happen to men, you know." But not to me! Not to me! He wanted to scream at her, shake her, tell her it was her fault. Make her see. What?

Clara pulled her hand away and put it in her lap. She looked at him like a frightened bird. He felt sick to his stomach, but he didn't want her to know.

"You've had other men, haven't you?" He tried to keep his voice kind, neutral.

She didn't say anything.

"I'm not the first?"

She shook her head. Parker felt relieved.

"He was a boy in my school," she said, looking into her hands.

"Oh, high school boys. They're always horny."

A little smile played around her lips. With her head still bowed she said, "For the first couple of months, I thought an erection was a man's natural state."

Gee, thanks for telling me that, Parker thought. That's just what I needed to hear. "What happened to him?"

"I was afraid if I kept on with him, I'd never get out of here. Besides, he just wanted to show me off."

They sat in silence for a long time. Then Clara adjusted her panties and Parker hooked up her bra for her. They both concentrated on being very, very nice to one another. Very thoughtful. Very polite. Parker could see how hurt she was. But goddammit, he was hurting too.

"I'll drive you home."

"You don't have to," she said, waiting for him to protest.

"It's okay. I don't mind." He was looking at his Most Valuable Player award.

"Don't mind! Don't mind!" Parker had never heard her raise her voice before. Suddenly her face was flooded with insight. "You thought I was Sissy, didn't you?"

He looked up at her without saying anything.

"Tonight, when I came in."

He didn't say anything.

"Answer me, Parker."

"No." And then, "I don't know, maybe. What difference does it make?"

"What difference? Oh, sweet Jesus." He saw her eyes fill with tears. "I thought you cared about me. Me. But it was always Sissy, wasn't it? That's why you picked me up, because I looked like her?"

Parker shook his head, but he was afraid she was right. He was also afraid that after finding Sissy again, holding her, he just wasn't interested in anybody else. He was shocked that a girl as pretty as Clara could come over to his house and start taking off her clothes, and he didn't care. It was a hell of a thing for a man who'd always been wild and free. He wondered if he'd ever be wild and free again.

Clara wiped her eyes and stood up. "All that time, I was just subbing for Sissy, wasn't I? Well, school's out, Parker. The substitute teacher's done quit." She walked to the front door, her head held high. Parker remembered the night Sissy had walked the same way to the same door. Clara must have remembered it too, because she turned at the door and said, "To hell with you, Parker Davidson. To hell with you both."

She slammed out of the front door, ran across the porch, and out into the night.

Chapter 12

AS THE MUGGY days of July dripped into one another, Sissy felt as if she were swimming upstream in a warm river of unrequited lust whose source was Parker's endless phone calls.

With Clara gone, Sissy was a hostage to her children and the simplest errand became a fight. Before she could go anywhere, she had to find, wash, and dress Marilee and Billy Joe and load them and Ed Sullivan—or Chip, she didn't trust him and the dog alone together—into the car and rush through whatever she was doing before one or all of them began to whine, make a mess, or chew large chunks out of the car's upholstery.

So Sissy stopped going out. She had the groceries delivered and hung around the house with only the tenuous line of the phone linking her with the outside world. That suited Parker. He called her every time he climbed a telephone pole.

He called when the sun beat down on him, sticking his shirt to his back and shrinking his jeans right on his legs. He called when the air was thick and the sky heavy with dense, gray clouds. He

called when the rain pelted him and lightning flashed across the sky
and the thunder cracked around his head. He loved to talk to her
when he was suspended between earth and sky. They were like
teenagers again, taking up where they'd left off in high school.

At first they caught up on each other's lives. Parker told her fabulous tales of adventures. He described the night they were caught
in a typhoon on the South China Sea and he had to lash himself to
the side of an open boat. He told her about the rigors of monastic
life. "One morning I was dragging my butt out of bed to cover a
bunch of statues with gold cloth, and I asked myself, 'What in the
world is a nice Jewish boy from Gentry, Louisiana, doing with all
these monks?' "

Sissy laughed. She knew exactly what a nice Jewish boy was doing.
He was running away from responsibility. She couldn't say she
blamed him.

Finally he ran out of fabulous tales. He confided in her how he'd
lost his business in Bangkok.

"You couldn't help that. Your partner stole your money."

"There were signs," he said. And she heard the dry echo of
despair in his voice. "There are always signs. You just have to know
how to read them."

"So you're going to spend the rest of your life beating up on yourself, because you weren't . . . what do they call it? Clairvoyant?"

"A man has to take care of his debts." There was an ugly harsh-
ness in his voice, which hurt Sissy, even though she knew he had
turned it on himself. "I was an American in a foreign country. I had
an obligation to set a good example." Sissy knew these were his
father's words, but they sounded as if they had been torn out of
Parker's throat.

They made her throat hurt too, but she couldn't let him know
that, so she laughed and said, "Somehow, I think the United States
of America will survive." There was silence on the other end of the
line. "Oh, come on, sugar, look what you achieved. You started a
business in a country where your men couldn't even speak English.

You built schools and offices and places for people to live. Are the buildings still standing?"

"I made sure the construction was first rate. They wanted me to cut corners, but I never did."

"So people are living and working in buildings you built."

"I guess so. Sure."

"Well, that's a lot more than any other man I know has accomplished." She kept on talking that way, building him up until she heard that old note of confidence, which had been Parker's hallmark when he was winning all those ball games. Rule Number Thirty-three: *The surest way to a man's heart is to become his cheerleader.* She kept up the flattery and the banter until he laughed and said, "Enough, woman. Let's hear about you."

Since she'd been nowhere and seen nothing, she had to fall back on her teasing ways. She never talked of love or even sex, but her conversation was so full of innuendo that her words hung between them like hot nuggets burning up the phone lines. When her teasing really worked and turned Parker to molten metal and steam, it worked on her, too.

She would straddle the fat round slipcovered arm of the couch, throw back her auburn hair, and play with her buttons. Sometimes when his voice became warm and tempting, she'd grip the sides of the sofa arm with her naked thighs and rub them up and down across the nubby fabric. Then she'd laugh a hoarse, throaty laugh that would make him tremble and hold on to the telephone pole for his life.

Sissy knew that *a woman's greatest power came not from love, but from unrequited lust.* Rule Number Thirty-five, Southern Belle's Handbook.

When the children ran in from the yard she had to be careful about what she said. She was always afraid of what Chip would overhear and kept an eye on him when she talked. But Chip had changed. This summer, to Sissy's great relief, he finally made some friends. Almost every day a small band of boys would troop through the house or crawl into his window and sit around his room for hours talking, laughing, or fooling with his chemistry set.

Once, following Parker's instructions, she checked the phone line for taps, but found none. Chip had other things on his mind, she decided, and then smiled to herself. He's growing up. But even if he had tapped the phone, Sissy couldn't have stopped talking to Parker. He made her feel desirable again. She wasn't just Peewee's wife—or that flirt men had dirty thoughts about (although that was better than nothing)—but for the first time in years, since high school maybe, Sissy felt somebody wanted her and was willing to spend hours just talking about it.

Of course Parker wanted to do more than talk. He begged her to come to him or let him come to her. But how could she with the children running around and the Methodists peering at her from across the street and Sister Betty Ruth Bodine keeping watch on his house?

After dark, he suggested. By then Betty Ruth doesn't know what she's seeing.

"What am I going to do with Peewee?" she asked.

"Peewee. Always Peewee."

"He's my husband."

"I remember," Parker said. His voice was dark.

THEN ONE MONDAY afternoon, when the storm the weather forecasters were so excited about kept threatening, but refused to hit and cool everybody down, Parker asked what Sissy was wearing.

Her mother-in-law's old torn chenille bathrobe covered in dog hairs was the truth, but she couldn't tell him that. She described an outfit she'd seen in a Rita Hayworth movie. The next day he asked again.

"Black lace."

"Over what?"

"Over me, sugar, what do you think?"

She heard an intake of air. "Can you see through it?"

"You can if you look."

The iron ring he was holding slowly burned a hole though his glove, but he didn't even feel it. "Is that all?"

"Of course not. What kind of a girl do you think I am?" A long pause. "I'm also wearing perfume." She heard a groan that turned into a high-pitched moan. And when she asked, "You want to know where I smell the best?" the groan was silently echoed up the line, because Calvin Merkin had tapped in to listen.

At first Calvin just told one of the other linemen. But he told a friend who told a friend and by Thursday even the operators knew about it.

Parker called at irregular times, but as soon as he did the word went out and it became impossible to raise directory assistance or make a long distance call. The Sissy and Parker Show became the telephone company's favorite soap opera.

WHEN PEEWEE WENT to the Paradise for a beer after work, he thought people were looking at him funny, talking behind his back. But since he'd done nothing and Sissy seemed to always be home, he decided he was imagining things.

Then on Monday, July 23, things came to a head. The countryside was bursting with life. Morning glories and honeysuckle fought for dominance over old fences and decaying shacks. Water lilies spread themselves over lazy ponds. And Parker hooked into a line.

"Hey, Parker," Sissy purred, and across the parish the signal went out. "It was a long weekend without hearing from you."

Parker swallowed hard. This girl could do it to him every time. "I found us a hotel in the French Quarter I think you're gonna like. It's got great big four-poster beds and armoires, and heavy old brocade curtains to cut out the light, and best of all, icy cold air conditioning." He tried to imagine her body laid out on that big bed, her nipples blue with the cold. He saw himself reflected in the mirror from the armoire, bending over her, warming those nipples, kissing them.

"I never said anything about needing a hotel in the French Quarter."

He laughed. "I guess you just forgot." He thought he was rescuing her from the toad. But what Parker didn't realize was he was looking for some kind of home. Even a temporary home. Even a hotel room for the afternoon.

"Parker Davidson, you know I can't spend the night in the French Quarter with you," Sissy said.

"You can spend the afternoon."

"Is that where you take all your women?" He could hear Sissy was stalling.

"What women?"

"Oh, come on, Parker, you told me you never took a vow of chastity." Her voice was soft and teasing. "What did you all do in that big four-poster bed? You can tell me."

His voice was deep, sincere, and anything but convincing. "I've never been there with anybody else."

"Um-hum," she said.

Parker was too smart to beg Sissy to believe him. Instead he said he'd be glad to tell her what he'd do to her in that big four-poster bed and found a part of his anatomy was standing up parallel to the telephone pole.

"I don't see how I could get away."

"Come on, Sissy, you can find a way if you try."

"Try," echoed the linemen throughout the parish, but of course Sissy and Parker couldn't hear them.

"I'm going to take me a cooling bath," Sissy said, holding her hair away from her neck.

"Aww, don't get naked alone!" moaned Calvin.

"That girl needs to cool off," said one of the operators to Rowena

Weaver, her supervisor and the relief organist at the Methodist church.

"I know you want me as much as I want you," said Parker with a low chuckle, "so why don't you put both of us out of our misery and say yes?"

"Say yes!" Came a chorus of unseen and unheard male voices.

"Don't you do it," said the operator.

"Trash is trash!" declared Rowena, adjusting her headphone for clearer reception.

"I'll think about it," said Sissy.

"That's the trouble with women," said Calvin, taking his cigar out of his mouth as he climbed down the telephone pole. "They all think they can think."

Sissy called Clara and asked her to drop by after her shift at the chemical plant. Clara felt funny about seeing Sissy again, after that awful evening with Parker. But Sissy had persistently tried to set up a scholarship fund for her, so Clara knew she owed her. Besides, Clara missed her older cousin.

They sat in the darkened living room with coffee cups on their knees and Clara couldn't help noticing the floors didn't shine much anymore and she'd bet the wainscoting was covered in dust. She felt uncomfortable as a guest in the house where she'd worked as a servant, especially since Sissy kept pressing her about Parker.

"I don't like to talk about things like that," Clara said.

"Oh, come on, you can tell me. It's important."

Finally Clara admitted, "Well, he can be a real sweet lover."

"I've never had me a sweet lover," said Sissy. Her voice sounded wistful.

"Are you in love with him?" Clara asked. It would be easier to step aside for love.

But Sissy just snorted. "Love's a myth invented by men to get into our pants."

"You don't believe that!"

"More than I believe in love. But I don't want Peewee to have to watch the kids while I'm cheating on him. It doesn't seem right." And then she laughed a deep, throaty laugh. "I still have some standards."

Clara wondered if she wanted a role abetting a sin specifically forbidden in the Ten Commandments, twice. She took her commandments seriously, especially since she was going to church regularly now and praying for a miracle that would get her out of Gentry and into the University of Chicago. It was only seven weeks until Labor Day. All Sissy's attempts to find her a scholarship had led nowhere. "What did I tell you," crackled Clara's grandmother. "These high-minded white womens got the attention span of a gnat."

Clara had received a generous offer of help from Parker, but that was one offer she didn't want to accept. She was desperately searching for any alternative.

"Please say you'll stay with the kids. My grandmother is at some kind of convention on the Gulf Coast and I don't trust anyone else," Sissy said.

"I don't know . . ." Clara's voice trailed off.

"Please." Sissy was begging now. "I need you."

"Well, I could sure use the money." And in spite of everything, Clara couldn't help feeling proud that she could be so useful to her white cousin.

Sissy hugged her. "Then you'll do it!"

"I guess." Silently Clara prayed to God to forgive her. If white folks want to sin, you know there's no way I can stop them, she told the Lord.

THAT NIGHT IN bed, Sissy had second thoughts. Was she really going through with this? Rule Thirty-five came back to her. Did she really want to give up the power of unrequited lust? Suppose it was a disappointment. Suppose it didn't work out. Suppose Clara was lying and Parker got his kicks knocking women around. Or couldn't get his kicks at all! What would she do with the rest of her life? What would she ever have to look forward to again?

Lying next to Peewee in the dark, listening to him grind his teeth, smelling him sweat, she thought about that old hotel. She imagined the cool, dry air, the big bed, the clean sheets, and Parker all over her. Naked and hairy and all over her. That's when Sissy decided to amend Rule Thirty-five to *Unrequited lust can get real old*.

SISSY'S CAR WAS parked in the Maison Blanche garage. The school clothes she'd bought as an excuse for her trip were packed away in the trunk. She still had half an hour before she met Parker. She walked over to Bourbon Street, enjoying the way the damp, hot air felt on her face and arms. Enjoying the looks she got from the men as she swung down the street in her green linen dress and white straw hat.

She walked past Galatoire's, where a crowd was lined up on the sidewalk waiting to eat oysters Rockefeller and trout almondine with crisp loaves of French bread. She passed the Paddock Lounge, open and beckoning the serious drinkers, while a recording of a local jazz band was piped over the sound system and into the street. She stopped and looked at a display of lacy underwear with the nipples cut out of brassieres and slits cut into the bottom of panties. A boisterous group of tourists in Bermuda shorts stumbled out of the Famous Door, carrying their beer and hurricanes in glasses as they made their way to the next watering hole. *"Laissez les bons temps rouler!"* one of them yelled. New Orleans. Disneyland for alcoholics.

"Hey, sweet thing, get a look at this," said a doorman as he beckoned her into a club advertising the Naughty Lass and her Submarine Strip. Sissy was never one to miss a free peek, but all she saw was white skin writhing around behind a hot pink spot.

She remembered the time in high school when she and Betty Ruth, not yet Bodine, had played hooky. They'd gotten hold of Betty Ruth's father's old one-eyed Buick and driven to New Orleans, where they made their way down Bourbon Street from club to club. They reveled in their power to attract attention until Betty Ruth passed out (she'd consumed almost all the drink minimums) and had to be carried back to the car by a couple of very willing sailors. Then, of course, Sissy had to fight them off and drive that big old boat with its one dim headlight through the dark perils of the old Swamp Road only to catch holy hell when they got back to Gentry. It had been their big adventure. It had been glorious. It had been another life.

"Come on in, sweet thing, we'll waive the cover charge for you," the doorman said. Sissy shook her head and moved on.

The next club featured a redheaded stripper with tassels pasted to her nipples. The billboard said she could twirl them in opposite circles while performing indecent acts. Sissy stared at the poster, and turning her back to the street, squeezed her pectoral muscles to see if she could make her boobs swing around in circles. If she could, she'd give Parker a real treat. She chuckled at the thought. There were shops right on Bourbon Street that sold tassels, but all she could manage was a little bounce. She pressed her hands together and bounced some more, trying to make them clap, when she saw her father-in-law come out of a side street holding the elbow of an elegantly dressed woman with blue-gray hair, dripping in pearls. Sissy dropped her arms to her sides and stood up straight.

Bourrée kissed the lady on the cheek, put her in a taxi, and charged over to where his daughter-in-law was standing.

"What you doing, chère? Looking for work?"

"Now, there's an idea, Bourrée. Why didn't I think of that? What were you doing? Pearl diving?"

He squinted his eyes and lit a cigar. "That's Estelle Perkins; I manage her timberland."

She dropped her voice and stepped in real close. "I've heard it said that you manage the widows and rape the land. Or is it the other way round? I never can keep it straight." She knew in this heat he could smell her perfume. He didn't move back.

"You meeting somebody, Sissy?"

Her heart pounded and she felt it beat between her legs. "What gave you that idea?"

Bourrée looked her over. "Don't tell me it's just you and me alone in the big city."

"Could be," she said, not knowing what to do about the pounding of her heart. It sounded so loud she was afraid he could hear it. "What do you have in mind?"

"No reason why kinfolk like us can't have a drink somewhere," he said, blowing cigar smoke in her face. "I mean, New Orleans can get real lonely if you're all alone."

"Just a drink?" Sissy asked and held her breath. The moment she'd waited for all these years was coming.

"You look old enough." He smiled a mean little smile. Then he moved in on her, and said softly, one conspirator to another, "Course, I wouldn't want to take a lady to a bar. But I do keep an apartment over on Royal Street." Two women in street clothes and heavy makeup came out of the strip joint. Sissy felt the cold, clammy air hit her skin.

He raised his cigar hand up to his mouth, brushing her breast in a proprietary manner. Then clamping his cigar between his teeth he brought his hand down and gave her nipple a quick pinch. "For old times' sake."

She jumped back, her body reeling from the invasion.

He twirled the cigar between his lips. "What do you say, chère? I'll be there at two o'clock."

"Sounds good," Sissy said and repeated it so she could feel the sensuousness of the words forming in her mouth. "Sounds real good."

"The address is 428 Royal." He licked his cigar. "And, Sissy, you know I don't like to be kept waiting."

"I know that, Bourrée," she said as the Hallelujah chorus went off in her head.

"Champagne cocktail," Sissy said to the maître d', who'd led her to a table against the back wall. Yellowed pictures of dead Mardi Gras queens lined the dark panels and smiled down on her.

Sissy smiled back, and when the waiter arrived with her drink, she raised her glass to them. She'd spent the last fourteen years of her life waiting for this moment. Waiting for him to ask her.

She knocked a cigarette out of her pack, and when the waiter bowed over her to light it, she ordered another champagne.

She looked at her gold watch with the black suede band. One-fifteen. She tried to concentrate on Parker and what he was doing at this moment. Parker Davidson, the man who'd driven all the way to New Orleans to find a hotel for them to be alone in. Her first love.

The waiter brought her drink. She inhaled the sharp, fruity smell and rolled the champagne around in her mouth, feeling the sparkles prick her tongue in a hundred places. She drank slowly, thinking about Parker, but she couldn't keep the memories of Bourrée from crashing the gates of her mind. She looked up at the dead Mardi Gras queens and mused on all those lovers' trysts they must have witnessed and wondered if any of them had happy endings.

PART II

1941
The
Fall

Watch out for men who are on speaking terms with the Almighty.

Rule Number Thirty-four
THE SOUTHERN BELLE'S HANDBOOK

Chapter 13

SISSY STOOD IN her short cheerleading outfit, looking down at the yellow and brown sycamore leaves strewn over her brother Norman's grave. It was the autumn of 1941. The afternoon sun shone through the thinning branches above her and made dappled patterns on the ground.

She tried to envision her brother's face in the scatter of sunlight and shadow. The way he'd looked this summer, when he'd come home from LSU in his torn Levi's, his red hair long and flying around because he hadn't had time to get it cut during finals.

He'd done real well on those finals. Three As and a B. But he never knew it. They got the news two days after he'd drowned in the gravel pit.

Sissy felt the pang of guilt she always felt when she thought of that afternoon. Maybe if she'd gone to the gravel pit with him, maybe if she hadn't been so busy working on a surprise party for Parker (a party that, in the end, she never gave), maybe she could have stopped Norman from diving into water he hadn't tested since the summer before.

Instead he'd gone alone, eager to wash away the summer heat. He'd hit his head on a submerged log.

She kicked the dead leaves from his grave. They crumbled and crunched under her white tennis shoe. Then she bent down and swept the rest away with her hands. She touched the name on the tombstone. Norman, Norman Thompson. Her big brother.

She remembered the day he'd taught her to swing out over the creek on a rope tied to a tree and splash into the water without hitting the roots. And the afternoon of her first real date with a boy, when Norm patiently watched her try on every outfit in her closet. Afterward, he'd sat her down on the front porch and told her how to intercept a pass without making the boy angry. How to make him respect you instead.

They'd always shared their problems with each other, except she couldn't any more, and she needed him. She needed to talk to him about Parker.

She and Parker had started going out the previous fall. Norm had known Parker the way an upperclassman knows an underclassman who's making a name for himself on the football field. But when she announced they were going steady, Norm had taken the bus home from LSU. He wanted to be sure Parker was straight and would treat his little sister right. The two boys had hit it off right away.

Parker had said he'd always wanted a brother like Norman. And Norm had kissed Sissy on the forehead, giving Parker his stamp of approval as he boarded the bus back to school.

Sissy tried to conjure up the three of them, walking arm in arm to the bus station, but when she closed her eyes, she saw Norman's face, blue and lifeless, staring up at her from the edge of the gravel pit where she and Parker had found him. She opened her eyes and shook her head.

The autumn smell of burning leaves floated into the cemetery, over the vine-covered wall, with its peeling white paint and its crumbling masonry. Her comfortable life had fallen apart this summer. First Norman. And now her mother was set to join him.

All spring her mother had complained about a pain in her stomach. The first doctor had diagnosed it as chronic indigestion and put her on a diet. Then when the pains increased during the summer, a second doctor, this one in New Orleans, had said it was distress over the loss of her son. But it turned out to be a cancer the size of a Ping-Pong ball. There had been operations and optimism, but Sissy could see her mother disappearing every day and taking her daddy with her.

The optimism was still there. But it was like the grin pasted on the face of a monster.

Home had become a place she hated to go.

Sometimes her father was okay. Just like he used to be. Explaining the economic causes of the war in Europe. Throwing a tizzy fit when Sissy didn't pick up her room. But mostly he was preoccupied and she couldn't blame him exactly, but she couldn't count on him either. The only person in the world she'd been able to count on was Parker. Until now.

Half an hour ago, they'd swept into Hopper's Drugs like a triumphal procession, led by the star captain of the football team and the head cheerleader.

It's funny, she thought, how she felt entitled to the attention: everyone wanting to sit next to them, across from them, cramming into the dark wooden booth, hanging over it and bringing up chairs.

Even Peewee LeBlanc had looked up from the magazine rack when Sissy walked by, but as soon as she stopped and turned around to say hello, he grabbed a magazine and buried his head in it. She said, "Hey, Peewee," anyway and watched his ears get red. She knew from the way his eyes followed her in the halls that he had a crush on her. But she also knew he'd never have the courage to tell her so.

Sissy had always been in the town crowd, the "in" crowd, thanks to her mother's admonitions and her grandmother's exhortations. At first she'd simply internalized their advice like everyone else. But three years ago, in ninth grade, she'd read *Gone With the Wind*. In that book Scarlett O'Hara's mother along with Mammy taught her the secrets of being attractive to men and it worked so well that Scarlett became the belle of five counties. Sissy had pored over the novel, reading it and rereading it, but Margaret Mitchell never revealed exactly what these secrets were. Sissy was very disappointed.

She decided to pay attention to what her mother and grandmother said and discover for herself what worked and what didn't. Boys squirm when you look at them over your shoulder and half close your eyes. The best way to make a boy like you is to ask him to do something and then thank him sweetly. Finally she began numbering the rules and the Southern Belle's Handbook was born, although the title had been conceived at a garden party when she was twelve.

One of Norman's friends had taken her shoe. He and Sissy were running through the guests, shrieking with laughter, when her mother pulled her aside and told her to act like a lady and stop chasing the boys. "But he's got my shoe," Sissy had wailed.

"Well, you just sit right down and wait for him to bring it back."

"Why?" That didn't sound like much fun.

"So you'll be admired."

Sissy with all the sophistication of her twelve years said, "What's that, the Southern Belle's Handbook?" Then she jerked out of her mother's grasp and took off after her oppressor.

By the time she was thirteen, she'd decided being admired was a very good thing indeed. Over the years she changed and renumbered the rules, but many of her early discoveries proved to be pure gold, such as *Boys find themselves fascinating*. And her mother's advice: *A lady shouldn't have to fight to get what she wants*. Still, even with her dedication to the arts and graces of being admired, she'd never felt quite so special until she and Parker started seeing each other. *A successful man gives a lady a position in society*, her mother was fond of saying. Sissy figured that should be way back in the handbook. She made that Rule Number Seventy-nine.

Of course, she and Parker weren't supposed to be seeing each other anymore. Not since the night after the game when they'd stolen the sheriff's car and driven it all over town with the siren blaring and Sissy waving a banner that said, "Go Gentry!"

Her daddy was furious that he'd had to pick up his daughter at the parish jail, and to make it worse, the sheriff had given *him* a lecture. But he'd only grounded her for a week until that witch, Betsy Davidson, Parker's mother, had called and said Sissy was a bad influence and was corrupting her son.

That really ticked off her daddy. He told Mrs. Davidson to keep her damned son away from his daughter or he'd go to court and get a restraining order.

Mrs. Davidson had said that wouldn't be necessary. Parker was going to win an appointment to the Naval Academy and couldn't afford to associate with juvenile delinquents.

That's how it had stood for over two whole weeks. No more bicycle rides into the country. No more hot kisses at the drive-in. No more long talks, telling each other their secret dreams and plans in the front seat of his father's car. Now, the only time they could see one another was in school or in a crowd like this afternoon. Even Mrs. Davidson couldn't stop her son from going out for a soda with the football team. And she could hardly expect the football team to go anywhere without the cheerleading squad.

But this morning, Doreen McAlister had taken Sissy aside and told her she'd seen Parker in New Orleans Saturday night with his arm around some girl. Parker had admitted it when Sissy caught him between classes, but had said that the girl was a cousin.

"A kissing cousin?" Sissy asked. She knew Parker couldn't stand to be without female companionship for long.

He just laughed it off and told her he was saving himself for her.

But this afternoon, at Hopper's Drugs, when he pulled out his wallet to pay for her soda, a condom fell out. He slipped it back into his pocket, but everyone saw it. And everyone had laughed. He tried to brush it aside, as though it wasn't important.

Harlan Ratliff, Parker's most reliable receiver on the football team, had said, "Sissy, you have to understand, a man's gotta be prepared for any eventuality." He nodded to Parker and Parker had the nerve to nod back, as if they were both men of the world.

So Sissy slapped Parker and walked out. Rule Number Eleven: *The best way to get a boy to follow you is to walk out on him.* It had always worked before and it did this time too, until his mother, the wicked witch of the South, came charging out of the shoe store on her broomstick and started yelling at Sissy and bawling out her son in front of everybody.

Sissy ran across the railroad tracks and up Progress Street, hating the old witch, hating Parker, hating everybody. She banged her tennis shoes on the sidewalk and jumped in front of cars until she came to the cemetery and stood beside Norman's grave. She'd had the idea she could talk to her brother if something really important came up.

But when she brushed away all the leaves and looked at the bare earth over the grave, she had that terrible moment of realization: Norman was truly and permanently dead. Gone from this world. Forever. No matter how much she needed him, he could never help her again. A sadness welled up in her too deep for tears.

She walked back into town, to the newspaper office. Her mother and grandmother were in New Orleans for yet another treatment that never seemed to work. She wanted her daddy. Not that she could talk to him about Parker, since she wasn't even supposed to have anything to do with Parker. But she needed to see him right now. Just to be with him. He didn't usually disappear into himself at work.

Besides, deep down, she didn't think he'd really mind. He was still writing about Parker, predicting a great future, bringing in sportswriters from as far away as New Orleans to see him play.

Parker had been wonderful when Norm died. And she knew how much her whole family had appreciated it. He'd been over all the time, running errands. Nothing was too much for him to do. He'd even driven her mother to New Orleans for a doctor's appointment when that awful pain in her stomach got worse.

Sissy remembered how her daddy had stuck up for Parker after the funeral. Aunt Ida May, Tibor's wife, had taken Sissy aside and said in her most concerned voice, "Sugar, I just don't understand why a girl as attractive as you would want to be seen with that boy. I mean, I know, he's a football player and all, but my dear, he *is* Jewish." Sissy responded in her own most concerned voice that Jesus was Jewish and so was his whole family. "I don't think Our Lord would appreciate your insulting His Mother, do you?"

Her daddy had put his arm around her and said, "Well, Ida May, it looks like our Sissy is a natural theologian."

Aunt Ida May just pursed her lips. "You know this has nothing to do with theology, Hugh, and you'd better watch your daughter."

Sissy was thinking about how only her daddy understood her when she walked into the newspaper office. The press was making a terrible racket. She hated to be here when it was going. She put her hands over her ears and looked around for her father. He was in his glassed-off office with Buster Rubinstein, going over an advertising layout for his store.

They looked up when she opened the door. "Not now, Sissy," her father yelled over the noise of the press. "Can't you see we're working?"

"I'm sorry." Sissy stood in the open door for a moment, without moving.

"It's not important, is it?" her father asked.

Sissy shook her head and turned on her heel.

"Close the door," her father called after her.

SISSY STOOD ON the sidewalk alone, berating herself. She should have known better than to interrupt her daddy when he was selling advertising. It wasn't important. She just wanted to see him. His car was at the curb. The keys would be behind the visor. She got in.

Soon she was bouncing high and fast up over the ruts and chuck-holes in the dirt road that wound out to the creek. She wondered if she'd get into trouble for taking the car. Well, things couldn't get much worse.

She parked next to a field of goldenrod. She ran through it. The tall, flame-colored flowers came up to her chest. Then she whirled around, stirring up the pollen until it flew into the air. From a distance she thought she must look like she was swimming in the Lake of Fire the Holy Rollers were so concerned about.

She walked through the woods to the creek with the bright golden pollen still stuck to her clothes and hair. The scent of pine comforted her and brought up memories of feelings. Happy feelings. It was too cold to wade in the water, so she sat down on a pile of leaves under the spreading branches of the live oak with the rope swing tied to one of its broad, heavy limbs. Gray strands of Spanish moss hung down through the leaves.

The afternoon sun slanted under the tree, warming her body in her short purple and gold cheerleading outfit. She leaned back on the nubby gray bark and held her face up to feel the heat. When she opened her eyes she saw a flight of wild ducks sailing in formation above the creek.

Sissy wished she could go with them, "wintering" in the tropics like movie stars and spending the sweaty Louisiana summers in Canada surrounded by polar bears.

She was thinking about polar bears lounging around in the summer sun as she pulled up her gold cheerleading sweater. Her tan would be gone pretty soon. She looked down at her freckled tummy and imagined it covered with white polar-bear hair. She thought about unhooking her bra, too. But she'd never be able to explain her brown breasts in the girl's locker room. Amy Lou Hopper would be sure to call her a nigger and tell everybody "Sissy's been painted with the tar brush."

It was funny how the very people who called themselves Christians and carried on all the time about how we should love our neighbors, as soon as they wanted to insult you, called you a nigger-lover. Maybe that's why the coloreds had to live over in Butlertown, so they didn't count as neighbors. Sissy chuckled. Norman would have loved that.

She wished she had someone to talk to, someone who saw things the way they really were, instead of the way everybody said they were. She thought about Parker. He'd been so convincing. She'd really thought he was straight. Oh, to hell with him, the two-timing louse. She wondered what he'd done with his "cousin."

She stroked her chest and ran her hand underneath her bra. She pinched and rubbed her nipples. They said it would give you acne. She decided she'd risk it, but only this once.

She closed her eyes and rubbed the smooth skin on her stomach with her right hand. She thought about Parker again. She remembered those nights at the drive-in, when he'd slip his hand, covered with butter and salt from the popcorn, into her blouse. But he'd never touched her below the waist. He'd never even tried.

Had he really gone "all the way" with some girl in New Orleans? Or just hoped to?

Sissy wondered what was wrong with her as she reached under her short purple skirt and spanned her flat tummy with her hand. Was she too scrawny? Sometimes the boys called her skinny. Maybe Parker's "cousin" was voluptuous, with big bosoms and soft hips. She touched her right hipbone with the heel of her hand and her left hip with her fingertips, spanning her flat tummy. Her little finger strayed and reached under the elastic of her white cotton panties. She wished her mama would let her buy black lace. When she was on her own, she'd have drawers full of black lace panties, slips, and nightgowns, just like Rita Hayworth.

Her finger touched the coarse hair growing under her underpants. Was she really going to hell? The Catholics had to confess all this stuff. She rubbed the hairs with the palm of her hand. Funny they were so coarse. She'd hate to have to tell some priest what she was doing. She wondered if priests did it, too. How else could they stand their lives? Of course, she hadn't seen many priests with pimples. Actually, she hadn't seen many priests.

Her fingers began to curl down to the place she didn't have any real words for. She shut her eyes tight and gave way to the sensations when she heard:

"Hey, girl, a pretty little thing like you shouldn't have to do that all by herself."

The first thing Sissy saw was his gun and then the dogs.

She shot up in the air and was off. She pulled her gold sweater down with one hand and pulled her white panties up with the other as she ran across the sand.

The dog pack barked and nipped at her heels, running alongside of her, crisscrossing in front of her, making her stumble. The hunter yelled for her to stop, but she'd be darned if she was going to, even though a stitch was burning into her left side. He yelled at her again. Sissy ran into the wet sand, trying to make it around the bend in the creek. Suddenly a gun blasted through the air. She froze.

The hunter came up to where she was standing and looked her over. Then he held up a big paw and said, "I'm Bourrée LeBlanc."

Sissy was stunned. "Peewee's father?"

"Yeah, he's one of mine." She'd heard of him, of course. Bourrée had a reputation even among the children, although they had a hard time pinning down exactly what it was he'd done to deserve it. They'd hear his name in connection with mumblings such as "It serves her right for marrying a Cajun." But when they'd ask what he did that was so bad, the grownups would become very vague and say things like "You'll find out when you're old enough." Sissy wondered if she were old enough yet.

She cautiously gave him her hand. He patted it and his eyes sparkled dangerously in his dark Cajun face and his white teeth gleamed. "Now, you listen to me, chère," he said. "Don't you let nobody make you feel ashamed for what you was doing."

She pulled her hand away and straightened her sweater. She could feel her face getting hot.

"It's what makes us human. Look at this bitch." He gestured toward the black-and-gray dog trying to lick his hand. "She can only have sex when she's in rut. Then sure as shooting she'll drop a litter and have to spend all her time taking care of her pups. But God in His Infinite Wisdom wanted us to be different. He wanted our women to *enjoy* sex, all the time, with a partner, with a whole lot of partners, or by herself, making never-no-mind whether anything comes of it or not. What I can't understand is why the preachers want us to ignore God's plan and act like animals."

He bent down and patted the head of the black-and-gray dog bouncing around next to him. "This bitch here, she don't try to mess with the Almighty's design."

Sissy was stunned. She'd hardly ever heard a grown-up talk sense before. Never about religion and certainly not about sex! She figured she'd finally met someone who could teach her how things really were. So when he said, "Come on," she followed him to the edge of the woods, to the makeshift duck blind.

He sat down on top of a patch of wild black-eyed Susans, breaking their stems and knocking them to the ground, and pulled a flask out of his pack. "How old are you, girl?"

"Sixteen." No sense lying, Peewee was in her class. He'd tell.

"Well, hell, you're old enough." He handed her the flask. Sissy swallowed the sharp, amber liquid and was surprised at the kick. She felt hot. He laughed. "That your first taste of moonshine?" She nodded and handed it back to him. She felt dizzy. He tipped the flask up and passed it back. "Nothing like it in the stores. It's a hundred proof. I was making it myself by the time I was your age."

"Did people say you corrupted your classmates?"

He paused for a moment. "I did my best." He gave her another drink. Sissy savored his saying "I did my best." It made her feel like her part in corrupting Parker wasn't so shameful after all. It was simply wicked and wonderful.

"You ever killed anything?" he asked.

She shook her head. "No, sir."

"There's no thrill like it!"

She was close to him now. Close enough to smell the warm liquor on his breath, close enough to see the skin sagging on his cheeks and the creases in his neck. She usually hated old people, because of their wrinkles and sags, but Bourrée was different or he seemed different after all the moonshine. She thought his face was dissipated and interesting, etched by experience. She shivered in her skimpy skirt and cotton sweater, and saw mischief sparkle in his steel-blue eyes.

Bourrée took off his jacket and wrapped it and his arms around her. She leaned unsteadily into him. He squeezed her shoulders and she felt a forbidden thrill.

She watched him load his gun. The sun hung on the treetops and the woods grew cold. The crickets came out and the frogs sang to them. Bourrée took off the safety.

At the place where the creek turned north he spotted a flight of ducks. They soared in formation over the treetops. Then they dipped down low, skimming close to the water. Bourrée cradled the shotgun in his arms, took his time fixing his sights, and when his prey was right where he wanted it, he squeezed the trigger and blew a duck out of the sky. Sissy saw it fall away from the flock and drop into the creek. She felt a surge of excitement she had never known.

Bourrée released the dogs. Joyously they leaped, yipping and crashing through the icy water, racing each other to get at the fallen bird. The black-and-gray bitch pushed her way through the pack and swam back to lay the kill at Bourrée's feet. She wagged her tail proudly. Bourrée threw the dead bird into his game bag and said to Sissy, "Your turn."

For a moment she didn't understand. Was he going to shoot her? Then he handed her the shotgun. She took it with reverence, cradling it in her arms just as he'd done. He reached around her and loaded it and stood in back of her, cradling her in his arms, his hands under hers, until they spotted the next flight. She felt his body come alive as he sighted with her, but she was stiff and frightened. She'd never killed anything.

"Pull the trigger, girl."

The explosion rocked her body, and the birds seemed to laugh as they flew away, leaving her with a terrible sense of loss.

"That's all right, you've got one more shot. Just relax and remember, pick your bird, follow it, and don't let it out of your sight, not for a second."

As they waited together, little by little, she abandoned herself to his arms, so that when they spotted the next flight, they were one. He turned her, following the dark silhouettes as they dipped down toward the creek. This time she was ready for the explosion. And when she saw the bird drop straight into the creek, Sissy knew what power was.

She turned to him, her face shining. "I did it. I did it, didn't I?" He smiled a tight little smile and took the shotgun from her. She was hugging him now. He dropped the gun and took her face in his hand. "We did it!" she corrected herself breathlessly.

He kissed her lips. He was old. Over forty. Nobody this old had ever kissed her before, not like this. She could taste liquor and tobacco on his lips. They tasted wicked and grown-up. Still, she pushed him away. "I don't think you should have done that, Mr. LeBlanc. It just isn't right."

"Call me Bourrée, sugar." He stroked her cheek and offered her another drink from his flask. "Everybody calls me Bourrée." And when he kissed her again, after she'd had a long drink, Sissy felt a new kind of excitement. Deep and sinful.

He laid her down on a bed of fragrant pine needles in the duck blind.

As her hair touched the sand, her head started to spin from the moonshine. The black-and-gray bitch was panting in her face. Sissy's dead duck was in her mouth.

Bourrée flipped the bird into his game bag next to his other kills and pushed the bitch away. Then he turned back to Sissy and pulled up her sweater. As her white cotton bra came into view, Bourrée said, "I already seen this." He reached around in back of her and snapped off her bra. "But not these."

Sissy knew she should stop him, and she had started to protest when suddenly a deep pleasure pulsed through her body and she didn't want to stop him anymore. Bourrée was licking her nipples with his tongue. Sissy wondered if Parker had licked his cousin's breasts. And then when Bourrée started sucking, a shiver shot through her, lodging between her legs. Sissy stopped thinking about Parker. She stopped thinking about anything. She moaned and lifted her hips. Bourrée pulled up her cheerleading skirt and slipped his hand into her panties.

"Oh my God," said Sissy, sitting up. "We can't. You've got to stop, Mr. LeBlanc."

"Bourrée," he said, stroking her with his fingertips. She tried to pull his hand away, but he was too strong. He rotated his thumb under her panties and she couldn't stop a moan. "You're gonna have a real good time, you hear. I told you, the Almighty set this whole thing up for you to enjoy yourself. So just put yourself in His hands."

But it wasn't the Almighty's hands that Sissy was concentrating on when Bourrée opened her up and entered her, pushing her down into the sand covered with pine needles and tufts of grass, pushing her into the earth. She wanted to rise and fall with him and tried to meet him with her hips, but she couldn't keep up. He was pounding on her, beating on her. She knew her hair was caked with sand, she could feel the little twigs and pine needles making welts in her back and she still never wanted him to stop.

Suddenly, he let out a cry like a wild animal and fell on top of her, smothering her with his big body. Sissy tried to breathe under his heavy chest and wondered, is this *it*? Is this what all the fuss is about? The black-and-gray bitch circled them, sniffing and licking Bourrée's face. He knocked the bitch away and pulled out.

Sissy started to get up, to cover herself, disappointed and confused. But Bourrée stopped her. "I'm not through with you yet, little sugar."

He pushed her back down into the grass and sand and began kissing and biting her breasts. Leaning on one elbow, he pinched her nipples until she began to moan. He rubbed her chest, and when he came to her nipple again, she couldn't help arching her hips up toward him. Slowly, he brought his hand down over her body and into those crevices Sissy had no name for. She twisted and pushed against his slow hand.

She moaned. She felt like the next flick of his finger would make her crazy, and she wanted to be driven crazy more than anything else in the world; at that very moment, he took his hand away. She arched again, her eyes squeezed tight, trying to find him with her body.

But he wouldn't give her what she wanted. He rubbed her stomach and her thighs and played all around the spot until she was moving with his hand to the left and right, up and down. She opened her eyes and saw him grin as he watched her dancing to the rhythms he set. When she was ready to burst, he eased up to a light tickle. She grabbed for him. He bore down finally, sending deep shudders through her body. She lay back, panting, but he wouldn't let her relax.

She reached for him, kissing him, and felt him playing with her body until she came again and again. He wouldn't let her rest until *he* decided it was time.

When he was finished, Sissy knew she'd had *it*. That was definitely something to carry on about.

"Don't you ever let some young boy get away without finishing you off, you hear?" He was caressing her cheek. She saw the tips of his fingers were stained with her blood. She wasn't a virgin anymore.

He led her down to the creek and washed her off in the icy water. She let him do anything he wanted. She kissed the back of his neck as he leaned over her, loving its weathered creases. She ran her hand through his black hair and decided it was beautiful. And when he held her head in his hands and she looked into those pale eyes in that dark Cajun face, she knew she'd never meet a more beautiful man.

Only when he took back his jacket did she feel cold. She hugged the black-and-gray bitch and watched Bourrée gather up his shotgun, ammunition, and game bag. He whistled for the dogs and the bitch left her for her master.

Sissy stood on the running board and kissed Bourrée's rough cheek as the sky darkened and it began to drizzle. He turned and kissed her, surprising her with his force, and told her to come back. "I'll give you another lesson in duck hunting." Then he switched on the ignition. The old truck bucked. Sissy had to jump off.

She stayed in the woods until his taillights disappeared. This is the most important day of my life, she thought as she made her way up the embankment. "I'm a woman," she said out loud, testing how it sounded in the air. "A woman."

She opened the door of the car and found herself thinking about Parker. But she hadn't done anything he hadn't done, had she? He had it coming to him. She slid into the car and slammed the door.

Bourrée pulled on his crotch as he bounced over the dirt road. He'd sure bagged his limit today. He grinned as he thought about the cute little girl in her cheerleading outfit. Let one of those horny kids try to satisfy her now. Just let him try to poke that little girl and run. She'd never forget old Bourrée LeBlanc. As he turned onto the blacktop and headed into town, he couldn't remember if she'd ever told him her first name.

THE NEXT DAY, Bourrée was loading his shotgun when he saw Sissy in her saddle shoes and plaid skirt walking toward him through the pine trees. She must have come straight from school. Left all those young bucks behind. He licked his lips. "Hey, little girl. I was afraid you was giving me a one-day special."

She blushed and said, "It was special to me." The wind was blowing her hair around. She brushed it out of her face. "You said you'd teach me some more about duck hunting. I'll bet you know all the ins and outs."

Bourrée whooped and unbuttoned his plaid hunting jacket. "Nobody knows the ins and outs better than I do, little girl."

"That's what I figured."

They were standing a couple of feet apart. A red dog was trying to sniff under her skirt. She pulled it tight around her legs. Bourrée hated to see any animal sniffing around a woman, especially his woman. "Come here!" he ordered. But the girl came right along with the dog. She stepped right up to him, just like one of his dogs. The blood was pumping through his body now.

He looked around. No car. She must have hoofed it all the way from town. Just to be with him. He wondered how he'd got so lucky.

"You think you can teach me how to shoot?" She brushed her hair away and looked at him out of the corner of her eye.

He pulled on the collar of his shirt. "That depends on how bad you want it."

"I want it," she assured him, delighted that Rule Number Five worked on men as well as boys. All she had to do was toss her head, look at him out of the corner of her eye. How about that!

Since yesterday, she'd been haunted by him. She didn't feel happy, the way she had when Parker gave her his class ring. This was entirely different. The attraction was dark, but insistent. It was as if he'd followed her home. Slept with her in her bed. Tied a golden cord around her most private part and was gently pulling on it. There hadn't been a second when she didn't feel its pressure.

Bourrée carefully laid down the gun and carelessly laid the girl. The autumn sun was still warm when he unbuttoned her blouse and pulled down her skirt and pulled up her slip. He spread her out naked on the sand with its tufts of grass. He'd forgotten the pleasures of tight young skin and a willing, indefatigable body. He'd forgotten, but he remembered fast when she wrapped those long cheerleader legs around him.

HE BEGAN PICKING her up after school. Every day after cheerleading practice she'd wait for him in the cemetery. Everyone thought she was going there to visit her brother's grave, so they respected her need to be alone. Sissy felt guilty about using Norman's memory like that. She knew he wouldn't have liked it if he'd ever caught his little sister with a man like Bourrée. Well, he can't catch me, she reminded herself as she waited among the dead for her lover.

Bourrée began bringing a few comforts out to the woods with them. An old red wool blanket to spread over the rocky ground and a heavy leather jacket to wrap her up in afterward when her teeth began to chatter.

Bourrée unbuttoned his jeans but he always kept them on. He didn't want to get naked in front of that smooth young body. Besides, it had turned cold. He marveled that the little girl was still so amenable to letting him take off all her clothes. She'd sit on top of him, working that round little butt, grinding it into him, naked to the wind and the world. A bitch in heat will do anything, he thought.

He always brought along a flask of dark, warm moonshine, which they'd drink after having sex, before he took up his shotgun. Because in spite of the pleasures Sissy afforded him, Bourrée was not one to let a mere girl interfere with duck-hunting season. It was too short. And he always had a fresh supply of condoms. As many as it took. He felt they had lucked out the first time and he had no intention of getting a sixteen-year-old girl in trouble. Although if he did, he doubted that father of hers, Hugh Thompson, would have the guts to come after him. Still, Bourrée hated scenes. He had enough trouble at home, with Peewee whining at him all the time.

"But it's my turn! Senior year, you always take the boys duck hunting."

"Not this year," said Bourrée, pouring himself a cup of coffee, wishing his wife weren't so dead set against liquor in the house.

"But I'm a senior. Last year you took Tommy Lee and two years before that you took Bert."

"This year's different."

"Why?" But Peewee already knew. He was different. His father had never paid attention to him. He wasn't big like Tommy Lee or smart like Bert. He was always just Peewee. Hand-me-downs were good enough for Peewee, the runt of the litter.

He'd thought things would change once they were out in the woods together, man to man. He'd show his daddy what he was made of. He'd secretly taught himself how to load a gun and he was sure he'd shoot more ducks than either of his brothers. He'd make his daddy proud of him.

"You'll just have to wait, that's all."

"But I might not be here next year! What with the war in Europe and all!"

"Oh, for heaven's sakes," said Miss Lily, cutting herself a third helping of yellow cake with chocolate icing. "Have pity on the boy, Bourrée. Take him hunting."

Peewee saw his father looking at her. Saw his father's lip curl. "I don't want pity, Mama! If Daddy doesn't want to teach me to shoot, then he doesn't. I can learn without him." Peewee was fighting tears.

Bourrée pushed away from the table. "Jesus H. Christ! Can't a man get some peace and quiet in his own home!"

"Bourrée, you know I will not have the Lord profaned in my house."

Bourrée grunted, "Don't worry, woman. I won't bother you or the Almighty in this house again tonight." He grabbed his coat and stormed toward the front room, wishing he'd listened to his parents and married a Catholic. But he'd wanted to escape the strictures of his upbringing. Lily Moffat, fat and sassy and just seventeen, looked like a great escape.

But a couple of years of marriage had driven her to religion. And when she took Jesus Christ into her heart, she threw her husband's liquor out the door.

"And just where do you think you're going?" Lily called after him.

"Out!" he yelled, slamming the door.

Miss Lily pursed her lips and all her chins trembled into her ruffled shirtwaist. She turned to Peewee. "See what you've done now? See what happens when you get your daddy all upset."

"Yes, ma'am," said Peewee. "I see."

He never said another word about hunting, but every afternoon he'd see his father coming home with his guns and his dogs and his game bags not nearly as full as in previous years. That's because he's hunting alone, thought Peewee. If I was with him, we'd fill those game bags. He pretended to be immersed in the short-wave radio he was building. He'd show his father yet. But inside something that had been warm and eager just shriveled up.

BOURRÉE COULDN'T STAND to see his son's mute suffering. Its very presence began to interfere with his daily pleasure in Sissy's young body. Besides as the novelty wore off, she was taking up less and less of his thoughts and energy. He wanted to spend more of his precious time in the woods hunting, especially now the birds were thinning out. But Sissy was always there, every damn day, waiting for him with those adoring puppy eyes, eager as a dog and just as demanding. Bourrée was getting real tired of teenagers.

Boys are easy.

Rule Number Forty-one

THE SOUTHERN BELLE'S HANDBOOK

Chapter 14

SISSY LOOKED AT her watch. Ten more minutes and cheerleading practice would be over. Twenty more minutes and she'd be sitting next to Bourrée bouncing out to the creek with his fingers sliding under her skirt. She felt the pull of that golden cord. Mondays were always the best. She hadn't seen him since Friday. It was going to be so exquisitely hard to wait until they got to the woods, especially now that hunting season was officially over and they wouldn't have any other distractions.

It was too cold to make love outside on the ground, but they could fool around in the cab of his truck. There was plenty of room.

She'd been seeing Bourrée five days a week for a month. It seemed like her whole life. She was besotted with him. Her limbs felt languid. She was so marvelously sated.

Her notebooks were covered with Parker's initials in big fluid script. But underneath she'd drawn BLB in a tortured cryptic code that seemed to fit their relationship. Parker was sunlight. Bourrée was shade. Parker was bright and healthy. Bourrée was like a sinful addiction.

She imagined herself straddling him in the truck, right in the cemetery, her back pressing into the horn. Pushing herself into him as her back arched and the horn honked and a crowd came out to see what was going on.

"Sissy, will you please face the squad!" said Miss Robbie. "I should think you—especially—would want to get this right."

"Yes, ma'am," said Sissy.

Parker had run ninety-five yards for the winning touchdown in the game against Hammond last week. Now Coach wanted a special cheer to spur him on to further victories. And he wanted it ready for the next week's game. It wasn't enough that Sissy jump up in the air, throw her legs apart, and come down in the splits. She'd worked on that for weeks last spring and it almost killed her. But then it seemed so much more important to make Parker proud of her. Before he'd found solace in his "cousins."

Now Coach wanted the girls to do a series of squats and leaps, waving their pompoms around and yelling, "Go, Davidson, go!" while Sissy did back flips front of them.

But Sissy was voted head cheerleader because she was popular, not because she was a tumbling champ. And when her first back flip turned into a back flop, she refused to try again.

"You'll get the hang of it," insisted Miss Robbie.

"No, I won't," Sissy assured her and then suggested they let Betty Ruth do her Twirl of Fire. Everyone was horrified.

"You can't do that, Sissy!" said Doreen McAlister. It was the head cheerleader's privilege to stand in front of the squad. No one had ever heard of a head voluntarily giving up that privilege. "Beside, what would Parker think?" Sissy didn't know. The only time she'd seen him in the last six weeks was at school. And she'd heard there had been a series of "cousins."

Coach was pissed. The girl wouldn't even do a simple back flip when his boys were breaking their arms and legs for the team. But she was adamant. He suggested she start with a graceful back bend and finish with a nice slow kick-over. But Miss Robbie pointed out that Sissy might still be upside down while Parker completed a touchdown, and no one would see him, because every man and boy in the stadium would be straining to peek up Sissy's pants.

Sissy said she was willing to do a series of quick cartwheels. Coach didn't think that would look so good.

"It would look a heck of a lot better than me back flopping in front of the whole school."

Coach left shaking his head.

"Just watch the other girls and count," said Miss Robbie.

Sissy watched as the girls squatted, twisted, jumped, and screamed, "Go, Davidson, go," and then dissolved into giggles as she found herself hanging upside down and backward over Parker's shoulders.

"Parker Davidson, you put me down, right now." He had tackled her from behind, and was holding on to her by her ankles, her knees draped over his shoulders. Sissy yelled and tried to beat on his back from the indignity of her position.

"Coach said you wanted to learn to do a back flip." He was careful to keep his hands on her knees and not on some indecent place on her thighs.

"Parker, you put me down now, or say your prayers!"

"Ow-wee," said Parker, laughing to the other girls. "This gal's tough." He set her back on the ground and touched her shoulder. Sissy jerked away from him, but Parker just laughed again.

Miss Robbie announced the end of practice. It was beginning to rain.

Parker put his arm around Sissy protectively as they walked over to their coats. "Harlan's parents are in Baton Rouge today, so a bunch of us are going over to his house and listen to records. What do you say?" He leaned into her as if to tell her a secret and kissed her hair. A shiver went through her. "Our parents won't know."

A biting, wet wind hit her in the face. Sissy imagined herself in

Harlan's knotty-pine living room with a fire in the fireplace, horsing around and dancing to Coleman Hawkins and Duke Ellington. She could almost smell the fresh popcorn and cocoa. "I wish I could." A longing swept through her. It would be like old times.

"Well, if you're real nice to me, I'll see if I can swing an invitation."

"I have to go to the cemetery," she said, and for the first time, she almost wished she didn't have to.

"Dammit, Sissy." And then, recovering himself, Parker apologized. "I'm sorry, babe, I didn't mean to swear, but I hate to see you standing out there in the rain. I know what Norman meant to you. He meant a lot to all of us, but he wouldn't want you to catch pneumonia at his graveside. What do you say? We haven't been together in weeks."

"I know, but I can't. Not today."

"But these afternoons are all we have. Don't you miss me?"

"What do you think?" Sissy asked. She did miss him. She still wanted to be Parker's girl.

Parker cast around for an alternative. "Okay, if visiting Norm is so important to you, I'll have Harlan give us a lift and we'll wait for you in the cemetery."

"No!"

Parker looked mystified. He put his hands on her shoulders. "Hey, we don't have to go to Harlan's if you don't want to."

A shiver went through her. She'd always loved it when Parker touched her. But now she was in love with Bourrée, so Parker's touch couldn't mean as much. It would be immoral if it did. She would be immoral. She was so confused.

She hadn't thought Parker wanted her anymore. Not with all his "cousins."

She had to put Parker out of her mind. She'd made her choice the afternoon she'd first made love to Bourrée. It was a hard choice. And she couldn't go on making it day after day, not and keep her sanity. She pulled away from Parker.

"What if I borrowed Harlan's car and we go out to the creek, just the two of us?"

"No! Parker, I can't. Not today." She saw the hurt spread over his face. Oh, this was terrible.

"When?" he asked, his voice soft and even.

"I don't know."

"Tomorrow after school?"

She shook her head.

"Wednesday?"

"I don't know. I don't think so."

He dug his hands into his jacket. "I get it." And without another word he walked off to the parking lot.

"Parker, don't be like that!" Southern Belle's Handbook, Rule Number Eight: *A girl who lets a boy go away mad risks letting him go for good.* "Parker!" she called. She wanted to run after him, to tell him not to be mad at her, tease him out of it, but there just wasn't time. She didn't know what would happen if she were late. Bourrée wasn't the type to wait around.

So there she was, standing in the cemetery with the icy rain beating on her and mud oozing up around her tennis shoes. She'd been there over an hour, but Bourrée was nowhere in sight.

Bourrée was warming his hands in front of the gas heater. When the bone-chilling rain started, he'd let his tree-cutting crew go and retreated to the office of the sawmill in which he was a part owner.

Maurice DeStephano, the mill's manager, was pouring them shots of whiskey and recounting a fight that had broken out at the mill the day before. "So then this big, fat mammy comes to the door and she yells, 'LeRoy!' and course LeRoy hides, 'cause she's gotta outweigh him by a good hundred pounds." Maurice cracked up as he handed Bourrée the drink. "But where does that dumb nigger hide? Over the rotary saw!" Now Maurice was laughing so hard he was choking as he tried to describe the ensuing fight. Bourrée smiled his hard, mean smile and walked over to one of the windows. He made a circle in the steam and looked out. Then he grabbed his coat. "Wait! Wait, you ain't heard the best part." But Bourrée banged out the door without waiting to hear whose flesh they'd picked out of the saw's teeth. He'd seen Sissy emerging through the drizzle.

He caught up with her in the parking lot and pulled her behind his truck, where they were hidden from the office and from the men carrying logs into the mill. "What the hell are you doing here?" He gripped her arm hard.

"I waited for you in the cemetery as long as I could." Her hair was plastered to her head, and her legs under her short skirt were chapped and gray with goose bumps. She slid her hand into his sleeve, searching for warmth. She didn't find it.

He pulled back, exposing her freezing hand to the elements. "Hunting season's over, girl. I told you that last Friday."

"But I didn't think that meant . . . You didn't say anything about . . ." Her teeth were chattering now, and tears mixed with the rain slid down her cheeks. She wiped her eyes and left streaks of mud on her nose. "I didn't think we were over, too."

"All good things must come to an end." His voice softened. He wiped her nose with his thumb.

His touch warmed her. He continued talking, but Sissy couldn't concentrate on what Bourrée said when he was touching her. She put his hard hand to her lips and kissed it. Then she stepped in close and slipped her hand between his legs. "Don't you *want* me anymore?"

A mill hand came out of the Colored Only washroom and caught sight of them. His teeth flashed through the gloom, and Sissy heard him chuckle. But she was beyond caring.

Bourrée yanked her hand away. "Stop it!" he growled, jerking her back into the shadows.

She was stunned by his anger. "I just want to be with you." It was so simple, why didn't he see it?

"Where? Where you gonna be with me in a little town like this? You tell me!"

He'd always talked so brave, like he didn't care what anybody thought. Now he sounded like everyone else. She was swamped with grief. It was the same feeling of sudden abandonment she'd felt when they put Norman in the ground. "No!" she cried, tears streaming down her cheeks.

But instead of taking her in his arms, he moved away from her. No! She stepped forward, shaking her head. But he kept backing away! She had to stop him. She had to make him see they belonged together. She threw her arms around him, still sobbing. "I'll find us a place. I'll find a place where we can be together."

It was five and the mill hands were leaving. They averted their eyes, but Sissy heard the whispers. "Mr. Bourrée's got him some young meat." "Umm-hummm!" And she saw the grins they couldn't hide.

He held her stiffly at arm's length and hissed, "Cut it out, girl. I've got a family."

"Why'd you take up with me, then, if you knew all along you were going to dump me?"

Bourrée dropped his arms and shrugged. "You looked lonely lying there, your skirt pulled up, playing with yourself."

Sissy hit him as hard as she could. Bourrée was primed to hit her back, but she saw him check himself. His men were watching them, chuckling, saying, "Man ought to be ashamed of hisself, carrying on like that."

Bourrée broke away. "When you get older, Sissy, you'll learn to take your fun where you find it," he said and walked past her toward the office.

She called after him, her voice raspy and hard. "This isn't fun for me, Bourrée!"

"Life's uneven," he said as he opened the office door and went inside.

Maurice was closing up. He gave Bourrée a peculiar look and started to say something. Then he thought better of it. "You still gonna be able to give me a lift?"

"Sure am," Bourrée said, finishing his whiskey, pouring himself another, and then pouring another for Maurice. He was waiting for the girl to leave.

IT WAS DARK when they finally emerged. But Sissy was still there, waiting for him in the rain, next to his truck, hidden on the driver's side. Her head was bowed. He had to push her aside to open the door.

Sissy swung up onto the running board. Her hair was wet and wild and falling in her face. No matter what, she couldn't stand the thought of him abandoning her, too. "Bourrée, don't go! I'm sorry. It was just . . ."

Bourrée gave her a look that would freeze a whore. Then he turned to his partner and said, "Maurice, this here's Hugh Thompson's girl. She's been seeing my son."

Maurice said something polite that made Sissy want to scream, but she didn't. She just stared at Bourrée with fading hope. He spoke to her as if to a small child. "I'll talk to Peewee, sugar. I'll tell him how upset you are. But you're gonna have to let go of the truck, you hear?"

He started the engine. The truck lurched and Sissy fell backward into the mud. An old colored mill hand walked up and bent over her. "You hurt?"

Sissy nodded yes, but denied it with her words: "I'm fine, thank you, just fine." He helped her up gently. And then after a few more words of concern and advice and an offer to give her a lift, he piled into an old, rickety truck with some other men. Sissy was left alone in the dark.

The icy rain beat down on her, but she didn't move. Her fingers turned blue and still she didn't move. Bourrée's words were playing over and over in her mind: "This here's Hugh Thompson's girl. She's been seeing my son." Finally a bitter smile spread over her face and Sissy knew how to take her revenge.

PEEWEE WAS HUNCHED over his notebook drawing the circuitry of an imaginary radio when a girl in a tight red skirt placed her butt right on top of his hand! A deep blush spread up from his collar over his neck and face and landed in his ears. He heard giggles and looked up.

It was Sissy Thompson. Sissy! The popular kids were always picking on him, but Sissy never had. She'd always been real nice, saying hello and everything. Maybe she was on some kind of dare. He pulled his hand out from under her, feeling the soft flesh move as he did. Oh man! But he said only, "You're on my paper."

She smiled down at him and said, "Oh, I'm so sorry," and sort of slithered off his desk. Then she turned and leaned over. He had to duck his eyes or he'd be looking right into her blouse! "What you got there?" she asked.

Should he snatch up the paper and hide it? She was smiling at him as if she meant it, but they always sucked you in like that. Of course she'd smiled at him just the other day in the hall. And she'd said hello that afternoon in Hopper's Drugs.

Before he could make up his mind what to do, he was saved by the arrival of Miss Rose, their European history teacher.

Sissy went back to her desk, rubbing her behind where his fingers had been. She looked at him over her shoulder and whispered, "You've got real nice hands." Then she hid her face in her book.

Jeeze! What did she mean by that?

"Turn to page eighty-four," said Miss Rose. Peewee opened the book, but he was looking at his hands. Nice? They were stubby and broad like his father's. What was nice about them? He looked around the room.

"The only way we can understand the war in Europe today is to understand the past." Miss Rose pulled down a historical map of Europe. Everybody was hunched over their notebooks taking furious notes. Miss Rose pointed to the middle of the map and started talking about the Holy Roman Empire. Peewee put the hand that had been under Sissy up to his nose and inhaled. He didn't smell anything special, so he sniffed the paper.

He was leaning over it when Sissy turned around. He whipped it away and hid it under the desk.

She smiled and bit her lips.

He was in for it now. He didn't know what that smile meant, but it couldn't mean anything good.

When the bell rang, he took his time packing up his books. He figured if he dawdled just long enough, they'd have to go to their next class and he'd still have time to make his.

But when he walked into the hall, she was there, surrounded by what looked like the whole cheerleading squad. He tried to make a dash for it, but she detached herself from the group and hurried after him.

"Hey, Peewee, wait up."

"I gotta go to class." He kept his head down and his books clutched to his body. She had to run after him.

She couldn't believe it. She was running down the hall after Peewee LeBlanc! "Now, you just stop it!" she called and was gratified to have him stop. Boys were sure a lot easier than men. She ought to make that a rule, but she forgot all about the Southern Belle's Handbook when he turned and she looked right into Bourrée's eyes. The swamp of misery she'd sunk into and tried to banish with her outrageous flirting was everywhere. A lump grew in her throat that made her voice sound all husky and hesitant. "I just wanted to ask you to come over to the house tonight and study with me."

"I don't think so."

Peewee LeBlanc turning down Sissy Thompson! She couldn't let that happen. "Please, you've just got to help me."

"Why me?"

She gazed into those pale blue eyes and said, "Because I think you're really smart." He looked at her as if she were crazy, so she went on very fast. "I know you've always been real quiet in class, but that's 'cause you're shy." No boy she knew could resist flattery like that. "Come on, say you will. I'm going to flunk the test if I don't get some help."

He looked like a rabbit sniffing a trap. "I don't think I can."

"Peewee!" A look of annoyance crossed her face. The boy was a real drip. But then she quickly bent her head and looked up at him through her lashes. "I'll tell you what. I'll be home studying at seven-thirty with a whole pot of coffee. And if you don't come, I'll be forced to drink it all by myself and by ten I'll have a tizzy fit and it'll be your fault."

"Well . . ." he said as the second bell rang.

"Say you'll come."

"I gotta go." He sped off to his next class.

"I'll be waiting, seven-thirty," she called after him.

Sissy turned and saw Amy Lou Hopper giving her a look. Don't worry, Sissy thought. I'll send him back to you when I'm done with him, and he'll be as good as new. Better. He may even have the nerve to ask you out.

DOREEN AND BETTY Ruth came up to Sissy in home ec class while she was stirring her slime stew. Miss Loretta, their teacher, had gotten it into her head to teach the girls to cook what she called in her high-pitched, fluttery voice "indigenous foods." And then some fool farmer had donated okra. Well, she'd cook it, thought Sissy, but she wouldn't eat it.

Doreen stuck her head near the pot. "Owww, your slime smells even worse than my slime."

"If the way to a man's heart is through his stomach, who do you think we're gonna catch with this?" asked Betty Ruth.

"I'll bet old Peewee LeBlanc would eat it if Sissy fed it to him," said Doreen, giggling.

"What you doing with him, anyway?" Betty Ruth asked.

"I'm gonna save him," said Sissy, throwing a shake of Tabasco into the pot for Miss Loretta's benefit, so they'd look like they were doing something.

"Uh-huh," said Doreen. "That'll be the day."

"He's not so bad. He's just shy and doesn't know how to dress, that's all." She thought of his hands, those short, stubby hands. "I could help him."

"What suddenly gave you the urge to take up missionary work?" Betty Ruth wanted to know.

"I don't know, I'm just full of urges," said Sissy. The girls broke up at that and Miss Loretta told them to mind their own pots.

"What's really going on? You can tell us," whispered Doreen across the stove.

"Nothing!" Sissy said innocently. "Can't a girl do a good deed?"

"Yeah, well, if you want to do a real good deed, just send Parker to me and I'll satisfy a whole *lot* of urges," said Betty Ruth.

Doreen giggled and Sissy said, "You better keep your painted fingernails off Parker, you hear?"

"Girls!" said Miss Loretta, clapping her hands. "That's enough."

Doreen watched Sissy dreamily stir and burn her stew. She turned to Betty Ruth and whispered, "What do you think she wants with Peewee?"

"I don't know, but whatever it is, Peewee better watch out."

PEEWEE WALKED OUT onto the football field as if he owned it. He was taking an article to the head cheerleader. He adjusted his glasses proudly. He'd been over to her house every night this week.

He hadn't actually gotten up the nerve to talk about much beside European history yet, but he would as soon as he thought she was ready.

Of course, he knew she was going steady with Parker Davidson and he respected that. Especially since they hadn't gone out for almost two months and Sissy explained that while Parker was a great football star, he wasn't so much fun to study with. Peewee took a deep breath. Fun to study with! That's me. Fun. Sissy said so.

He saw Parker out on the field with Doreen McAlister and veered over to the sideline.

Doreen's face was alive with the drama and the sadness of her revelation. "I hate to be the one to tell you, because I've always considered Sissy my very best friend, but she's been with him every night this week."

"Come off it, Doreen," Parker said with the easy grace of confidence.

"Have you tried to call her?"

"Yeah, every night. And she was always there."

"Have any long conversations?"

That stopped him. Then he said, "This whole thing's crazy. If Sissy's been with Peewee LeBlanc, she must have had a good reason. Maybe she was helping him with an assignment."

"Maybe, but I don't want to see you get hurt." Doreen pushed back her long blond hair and looked ever-so-sympathetic, but at the same time she stood so he could see her breasts protruding from beneath her cheerleader sweater. He knew Doreen was proud of her large breasts.

Parker took her by the arm and turned her around so she could see Peewee strutting across the football field, clutching his books to him. "You telling me that's my competition?" Doreen had to giggle. "The day I have to worry about Peewee LeBlanc is the day I'm gonna give up on girls."

"Well, I do hope that day never comes," she said, twisting a strand of golden hair around her finger, "because I'm sure if you and Sissy ever really broke up, half the girls in the school would be standing in line to console you."

He laughed. He was too happy to worry about gossip, even though he'd been hearing about Peewee all week. Parker was going out with Sissy that very night. Officially. Their separation was over. The coach blew his whistle. Parker started to run onto the field and then turned back to Doreen. "You want some brotherly advice?"

She hesitated a moment and then said bright and hard, "Of course. I always want to improve myself."

"Stop bad-mouthing your very best friend," he said, and trotted out onto the field as Doreen ran to the sidelines, her face red with humiliation.

SISSY WAS LYING on the ground in front of the stadium. Miss Robbie and the coach had just about practiced her to death. They'd wanted to see if their head cheerleader could travel the length of the football field doing cartwheels. They found out.

She couldn't.

And she didn't care. Sissy lay there with her eyes shut until the ground stopped whirling around her. When she opened them and lifted her head, she saw Bourrée swaggering across the rotating football field. The swamp of misery began to dry up. She sat up, smoothing down her hair. But then the stadium stopped turning, and she saw it was only Peewee.

She gave him her hand. He held it for a moment, as if he didn't know what he was supposed to do with it. So she said, "You just gonna leave me on the ground or what?"

He blushed and apologized and pulled her up. "I brought that science article, the one I told you about." He shuffled through his books and papers until he found a copy of *Popular Mechanics*.

"That was so *sweet* of you! You came all the way out here to give me this!" She said it as if she meant it, enjoying the effect she had on him.

Peewee took a deep breath and grinned. "I was proud to do it. Do you want to study tonight?"

She put on her best look of regret. "Oh, Peewee, I can't." The Letter Club was holding its Awards Dinner that evening.

Parker had given his parents an ultimatum: he was taking Sissy or he wasn't going. They gave in. They had to. Refusing his awards would be an insult to the town. They had a business to run.

Sissy's parents gave in, too. They thought seven weeks was long enough. Besides, Hugh was covering the dinner for the paper.

Sissy was excited about her date with Parker, and was looking forward to all the attention they'd get when she walked into the banquet on his arm. The whistles and the catcalls and the applause.

But she was uneasy, too. When they'd gone out before she had been a girl. Now she was a woman. A fallen woman. Would Parker be able to tell? Boys all claimed they could. And Parker had such high standards. She wasn't sure she could live up to them anymore. Sissy felt her heart racing. She didn't want Parker to abandon her, too.

"I guess you have a date with Parker."

Sissy nodded and saw his face fall. Saw him slump down into himself. She didn't know why, but she hated to see this boy suffer. It was like watching one of these birds Bourrée shot but hadn't quite killed.

She glanced out onto the field. The first string was all piled up on top of each other. Parker was on the bottom and couldn't see her. She took Peewee's fallen face into her hands. "I'm sorry." Those light blue eyes of Bourrée's stared at her, but so sadly. She kissed Peewee gently on the lips, just to make him feel better.

Peewee felt a shock go straight through him. He squeezed his eyes shut and threw his arms around her. He heard whistles blow. He felt how soft her body was, felt her breasts pushing right into his chest. He tilted his pelvis to touch her, just to feel her against him, but instead felt her step back and try to push away. Of course she was trying to push away, his brothers had told him good girls had to pretend not to like it. But he held on, just like they told him to. He felt her long fingers on his shoulders, pushing. But he wasn't ready to let go.

Suddenly, Peewee was flying. His feet weren't even touching the ground.

Parker Davidson had him by the collar. "Get your cotton-picking hands off her!" Parker yelled, shaking him like wet laundry.

"Put him down," Sissy said.

Parker glared at Sissy. One fist twisted Peewee's collar, the other was poised to slam into his flesh.

"Parker, you stop it this minute, you hear!" She stamped her foot.

Peewee couldn't hide his delight as he kicked Parker Davidson in the shin, jerked out of his grasp, and dropped to the ground. "You heard the lady," Peewee gloated.

Parker pulled back and slugged the ugly, puffed-out toad in the belly. He felt him fold up over his hand. He brought his right up fast and felt his bare knuckles connect with the toad's cheekbone. He heard the crack as he knocked him to the ground, crushing his glasses. But it was over way too fast. The toad was too easy. He didn't put up a fair fight. Parker stood over the curled, quivering body and felt his foot ache to connect with the round toad head. He pulled back his cleated boot.

Sissy jumped between them; her eyes blazed a deep green. "For God's sake, Parker, you want to kill him?"

Parker knew he'd never wanted anything so much in his life. His foot ached to connect and squash this cowering, gelatinous mass. But Sissy stood in front of him and stared him down.

Suddenly, Parker was horrified at what he'd almost done. Sissy! He was awed and nauseated by the power she had over him. He stood very still, shaking, trying to control himself, not knowing what to do with his hands.

"Now you just calm down," she said, but she was proud as she could be. She'd always had plenty of boys after her, but they'd never fought over her before. Not that Peewee was much of a fighter. "My goodness, you didn't have to half kill the poor boy, we were just . . ."

But Parker didn't let her finish. "I saw what you were doing, Sissy. You think I'm stupid?"

"Of course not, sugar," she said, going toward him, putting her hands on his shoulders. He threw them off. "You don't think there's anything between Peewee and me, do you?" She was incredulous. The thought was ridiculous.

Parker didn't answer. Instead he grabbed his class ring, which she wore on a chain, and snapped it right off her neck.

"Parker!" she called. But he turned and ran back onto the football field.

She put her hand to her throat and rubbed it. She hadn't wanted to break up with Parker. She tried to think of a way around it. But a feeling of numbness was setting in. Everyone she cared about was abandoning her. She couldn't deal with so much loss. She welcomed numbness.

She saw Parker hurl himself into two of Gentry's biggest tackles as in a dream. She figured she might as well enter a convent as far as her social life was concerned. None of the boys would want to take out Parker's girl, even if he didn't want her anymore, not after she'd humiliated him. Especially not after she'd humiliated him with Peewee LeBlanc.

Peewee rolled onto his feet, holding his stomach. He was very shaky, but there was pride in his voice. "You broke up with Parker Davidson for me?"

"I guess," Sissy said, not paying him much attention. Memories of the fun she and Parker had had together flooded her senses. She thought about how sweet he'd been the night Norm had died. A lump began to grow in her throat. But even that was getting numb.

"Wanta go steady?"

That brought her up short. Sissy Thompson going steady with Peewee LeBlanc? The idea was ludicrous. All she'd ever wanted was for his father to find out about them. No, she'd wanted Bourrée to see them together, so she could have the delicious pleasure of watching him squirm as she took his son's hand and kissed him on the cheek. That's all she'd thought about since the day at the sawmill. She'd tried for a week to get Peewee to ask her to study at his house, but so far he'd resisted. There was always some stupid reason why he couldn't take her over there.

"What do you say?" His face was turning the color of eggplant destined for the garbage. Sissy reminded herself that his face had gotten that color fighting over her, so it was incumbent on her to find some way to let him down easy. She put on her saddest face and then she saw Bourrée's pale blue eyes looking at her above all that bruised and swollen flesh. "I guess that was a pretty dumb idea, huh?"

"It wasn't dumb, Peewee. I don't want you to think that." Her voice was soft, comforting. Why did this boy's suffering touch her so?

"You mean you might!"

She shrugged. He waited, holding his breath. The left side of his face was puffing up.

"We'd better find some ice for you right away."

"Sissy, say you will. Please."

He was begging her. She'd never had a boy beg her before. It was not an unpleasant experience.

She saw Parker slam himself into the defensive line and run over three tackles. She'd never get him back. It was hopeless. The lump was gone. She was completely numb.

"What do you say, Sissy?"

It didn't have to be forever, she thought. "You really want to go steady with me, Peewee?"

"You know it!"

"Would you introduce me to your parents?"

*   *   *

BOURRÉE AND MAURICE liked to celebrate the end of the work week at the Paradise. This Friday, an old-time Negro band was playing the songs of their youth. The bar was warm and crowded. On the dance floor, everyone was making the most of the Golden Rule and doing unto others what they would have done unto them. So Bourrée found leaving wasn't the easiest thing in the world.

He lurched out of his truck onto his driveway, humming a song from his youth about the right key, but the wrong keyhole. He was late for supper, but he didn't care. He wasn't in the mood to care about much of anything until he walked in his front door and saw Sissy sitting on the couch in deep conversation with his wife. He grabbed the door frame and hung on for balance. He was glad he was already drunk.

Miss Lily, her plump cheeks trembling, asked, "You have trouble finding your way home?"

Bourrée looked from his wife to Sissy with poker eyes.

Finally, Miss Lily said, "You know Hugh and Cady Thompson's girl?"

Bourrée made a sound that neither admitted nor denied anything.

Sissy stood up politely, held out her hand, and said how much she'd been looking forward to this meeting. His touch sent a jolt of electricity through her and shut her up. Miss Lily chattered on about the rug and static electricity. Bourrée smiled a tight, mean smile. "You just happen to drop by?" he asked as Peewee came into the living room with a tray of Cokes. The boy faltered and the glasses tottered and clicked together when he saw his father.

"I invited her, Daddy." Bourrée heard the eagerness in his son's voice and that note of pride. Pathetic.

"Peewee asked Sissy to go steady with him. Isn't that sweet?" Miss Lily said.

Bourrée stumbled and sat down hard in Miss Lily's antique chair. He turned to his son and kept his voice low. "You what?"

Sissy went to help Peewee with the tray. "Peewee popped the question this afternoon." She displayed her green-sweatered chest with Peewee's service pin hooked over her left nipple. Bourrée examined her chest and saw the color rise in her face. She was looking at him like an alcoholic who's taken the pledge and then sees a bottle of whiskey. This little girl was going to be more trouble to get rid of than he'd ever thought. Not that he'd ever given it much thought, especially when she was sitting on top of him, naked to the world, grinding her little butt into him. But he had to think about it now.

He watched Sissy sit on the couch and pull Peewee down next to her. And saw that fool boy beam. "You knew I was seeing your son, didn't you, Mr. LeBlanc?"

Bourrée's lip curled. "Now how was I supposed to know that?"

"Why, Peewee," Sissy teased. "You bad boy. You've been keeping me a secret." And then in a confidential tone to Miss Lily, she said, "He's so sly. He's been over to my house every night this week. Since Tuesday, anyway." Rule Number Twenty-two: *A man always wants a girl another man has.* That's why God made up His rule against coveting your neighbor's wife. He knew men could hardly stop themselves.

Bourrée growled softly.

"Now, Bourrée," Miss Lily said, "you may be drunk as a dog, but that doesn't give you any call to act like one. I'm sure you're as happy as I am that Peewee found himself such a nice girl." She patted Sissy's knee.

"Is that true, Mr. LeBlanc?" Sissy asked, and he knew she wanted to see him squirm.

"I don't know. Are you a nice girl?" He looked her in the eye and his lips curled.

Peewee was mortified. "Daddy!" he wailed.

Miss Lily shook her head in disgust. "Well, I'd better go see about my roast." She hefted herself off the sofa slowly and with some difficulty.

"Oh, let me help," said Sissy as she left the room behind the older woman.

Bourrée watched Sissy sashay out of the room in her modest gray-flannel skirt. But he wasn't thinking modest. He was thinking how it cupped her ass. His nostrils flared.

Peewee rubbed his palms on his pants and said, "Bert brought girls home all the time, and you were always nice to them. Real nice."

"This one isn't for you, son."

Peewee's voice broke. "What's wrong with her? You think she's too pretty for me. Is that it?" He was fighting tears.

Oh, Christ, Bourrée thought, the boy's suffering again! Teenagers just aren't fit to associate with the rest of humanity. There ought to be some kind of pen you could lock them up in when they turn thirteen and hold them there until they reach twenty. Then he thought about Sissy swinging her hips around in the kitchen. He imagined her bending over to get some onions. Maybe he'd just lock up the boys. Let the girls out when you had a use for them. "You been fighting over her?"

Peewee touched his swollen face and grinned proudly. "I took on Parker Davidson. He's the captain of the football team."

"Then you're a bigger fool than even I thought. That girl's nothing but trouble."

"How would you know?" Peewee's voice was sullen.

"Trust me on this one." Bourrée wasn't even aware of the smug tone in his voice. "Just dump her. With a girl like that, you don't have to worry about letting her down easy. Just let her down."

"You go to hell!" yelled Peewee.

Bourrée came back loud and clear. "Don't you use that tone of voice to me, boy!"

And Peewee crumbled. Bourrée had won.

But when Miss Lily told Sissy to call the men in for dinner, she caught Peewee by the hand and said, "I'm having such a good time!" Then she kissed him on the cheek, and turning her deep green eyes on Bourrée, added, "Miss Lily asked me to come for dinner every Friday night."

PEEWEE WAS KISSING her good night. He'd been at it for what seemed like forever, although it had actually been less than a minute. Sissy tried to pull out of the embrace, but he wouldn't let go. His lips were wet and soft and he was holding her tight in his skinny arms, rubbing up against her. The image of a weasel popped into Sissy's head. Peewee slipped his hand under her green sweater. She tried to push him away gently, so as not to hurt his feelings, but he held her tight. She put her hand over his and shoved it down, but his hand immediately crawled back up over her slip. His insistent fingers endeavored to get inside her bra. Touch her skin. She shuddered and tried to pull his hand out, but he grabbed her nipple. That's when she hit his chin with the heel of her hand, ungluing his lips from hers.

"Stop it!"

"But we're going steady," he said, rubbing his sore chin. "I thought . . ."

"I don't care what you thought, I'm not that kind of girl!"

"I know that, but if you love somebody . . ."

Sissy groaned. "Peewee!"

Over his shoulder she spotted a man moving in the dark, stepping out from behind a white oleander bush. Peewee nattered on about respecting her and a man's natural desires. A car pulled out of a driveway, swinging its headlights over the yard, and she saw the silhouette of a short powerful body in a hunting jacket step back into the shadows.

"I've got to go inside." She quickly unlocked the door.

"But . . ."

"My daddy's real strict."

"Just five more minutes," he begged.

"If I don't go in now, he may not let me go out with you again. And I'd just *hate* that."

As she hoped, Peewee was too flattered to protest. Behind him, she made out Bourrée watching her. Well, she'd give him something to watch. She grabbed Peewee and kissed him, and for a brief moment even slid her hand down his back, patting his jeans as a parting gift. Then she shut the door firmly in his face.

She straightened her clothes with a mild feeling of disgust and tiptoed through the house, turning off the lights. Her parents' door was open.

"Sissy," she heard her mother call to her from the dark. Her voice was weak.

"I'm real tired, Mama. You go on to sleep." Sissy stood in the doorway, threw her mother a kiss, then sprinted down the hall into her own room and locked the door.

She switched on her bedside lamp. The silk lampshade turned the room amber. She put Coleman Hawkins on the phonograph. She'd make Bourrée sorry he threw her over. She'd make him beg her to take him back. She could do it. She knew she could. And then she'd have someone again.

She pulled up the shade and searched the darkness until she saw the light of a cigarette moving into the backyard. Bourrée had come back to her! Just like she knew he would.

She pulled out the bobby pins and fluffed out her curls. Turning completely around she lifted the green sweater slowly over her head, showing off her long, lean torso in her pink lace slip. Then she twisted agilely to the side, unzipped a zipper, and stepped out of her gray skirt. Next she pulled up the pink lace slip, slowly, slowly, hesitating: showing tantalizing glimpses of her thighs and panties, and then dropping the slip. Would she? Wouldn't she? Finally she ripped it off and threw it on the bed.

In the yard, Bourrée tipped a flask of whiskey to his lips and watched Sissy, lit by the amber glow of the bedside lamp, take off her pink bra one strap at a time, finally reaching around, unhooking it and exposing her young, firm breasts to the eyes of the night. The girl was trouble, pure and simple. He rubbed himself as he watched.

COLEMAN HAWKINS MADE his tenor sax wail, as Sissy, wearing her pink panties, bent over to take off her socks. Finally, she stood up and slowly rolled down her underpants. She turned away from the window and admired herself in the full-length mirror on her armoire. Lightly cradling her breasts, drawing a circle around her red pubic hairs, sliding her hands sensuously over her flat belly. Then she turned and stood right in front of the window.

"Sissy," her father said.

She jumped. Her father knocked on the door.

"Just a minute." She hurriedly slipped into a short, frilly night-gown, pulled down the window shade, and opened the door.

Her father stood in his pajamas in the hall. He tied his plaid wool bathrobe around him and said, "Your mother told me you broke up with Parker today." Sissy groaned silently. "You okay?"

Sissy nodded. "I'm fine, Daddy. I guess seven weeks was just too long." She hoped he wouldn't tell her about the banquet. She couldn't stand it.

"You think it would help to talk about it?"

Sissy shook her head. "No."

Her father shifted awkwardly in his leather slippers. He ran his fingers through his hair as if he were trying to figure out what to say. Finally he managed: "I wouldn't let it get you down, honey. You know these breakups don't usually last."

She looked into his gentle face with hope in her eyes. "Thanks."

"Sissy . . ." he began, but she quickly cut him off.

"I just can't talk about it. I don't want to think about Parker. Not tonight. Okay, Daddy?"

He nodded, and after a few more words of encouragement, kissed her on the forehead and went back to his bedroom in the front of the house. Sissy took a deep breath and locked the door after him. When his footsteps died out, she turned off the light and pulled up the window shade. The cigarette was still glowing in the dark. Bourrée must be leaning against the big live oak tree in the backyard. Waiting. For her. She turned the light back on, opened her window, and unlatched the screen. Then she went to her bed and arranged herself in a Lana Turner–type pose. Waiting for him. But he didn't move. What did he want? An engraved invitation?

Finally, when she couldn't stand the suspense any longer, she buttoned her new royal-blue coat over her nightgown, turned off her light, and slipped barefooted out of the window.

"Bourrée," she hissed. "You better get out of here, or I'm gonna call the sheriff and tell him there's a peeping Tom in my yard."

He snorted. "You talking about that show you just put on? Hell, girl, I didn't need to peep. You were exposing yourself to God and country."

"You think the sheriff is gonna believe that when he catches you in my yard?"

He grabbed her and pushed her into the old live oak. "Stay away from my family, you hear."

She could almost taste the tobacco and alcohol on his breath. She tossed her head. "How you gonna make me? You gonna tell Peewee what you did to me in the woods? How you took my virginity and . . ." But she didn't have a chance to finish.

He stuffed his tongue into her mouth, shutting her up, choking her. She tried to turn away but he had her against the tree. She felt the jagged bark pressing through her hair, but she wasn't sure she really wanted him to stop. If he'd just quit choking her. Finally he let her up for air.

"Come on, Bourrée," she begged, "don't be like that. Be sweet."

"What do you want?" His voice was as cold and damp as the night air.

Sissy shivered. "I just want us to be like we were. That's all."

His pale eyes flickered over her as if he were appraising a pile of lumber. Just a hint of a snicker escaped the edges of his mouth before he grabbed her coat, ripping off the buttons, rending the material.

"Don't! You'll ruin it!"

But he didn't pay any attention. He yanked the coat, tearing it from her body.

"Bourrée, for God's sake . . ."

"Shut up," he growled, throwing the coat to the ground, leaving her exposed and shivering. He pushed her back against the tree, and pinning her there with one hard hand to her breast, he pulled up her short nightgown with the other. But where he was gentle before, he was rough now, and fumbling. "Is this what you want?" he snarled as he unzipped his fly and rammed himself into her. She tried to scream, but he slammed her head into the tree and silenced her with the heel of his heavy hand, pressing on her windpipe. Sissy felt the gnarly trunk make welts in her back as she twisted and shoved trying to get away. "Is this what you want?" he repeated. She was so dry, she felt her skin tear. She was beating on him now, trying to force him away. But he increased the pressure on her windpipe as he ground his body into hers, thrusting and jabbing and pressing harder and harder on her throat so that screaming was out of the question. She had to struggle to breathe. Then he made a quick grunt and pulled out, dripping along her leg and over her fallen coat.

"Is that what you want, little girl? You want me to come over every now and again to service you?" Sissy shook her head. "Then stay away from me and mine, you hear?" He pinched her cheek hard between his fingers and, baring his teeth, kissed her off.

Beware of other people's plans for your own good.

—Belle Cantrell, Sissy's grandmother

Unnumbered Rule, The Southern Belle's Handbook

Chapter 15

SISSY STAYED AWAY. She stayed away from the whole family and nursed her hatred. She'd never hated before, but Bourrée had taught her how. She felt defiled. Peewee had been upset, of course, when she told him she had to give him back his pin. She tried to push him in Amy Lou Hopper's direction, sang Amy Lou's praises, but he wouldn't budge. After going out with the head cheerleader, Amy Lou must have seemed too low rent for him. Instead, his pale blue eyes, filled with the silent reproach of a wounded bird, followed Sissy in class and around school until she thought she was going to scream.

"Who wants to translate the first two lines?" asked Miss Martine, pacing around the class.

Sissy kept her head down, avoiding all eye contact. In the front row Amy Lou's and Doreen's hands shot up. Doreen had already grabbed Parker and was clinging to him like ivy.

For the first couple of weeks, he hadn't dated anyone else, but he wouldn't have anything to do with Sissy, either. She'd tried all the wiles in the Southern Belle's Handbook, and made up new ones, but none of them worked with Parker.

Then Doreen moved in. She managed to be there all the time now, hanging on to his arm, wearing his letter sweater. And he was so attentive. He seemed to adore her. Sissy figured it was her own fault for being such a fool. She tried to make up some rule that would cover her foolishness and warn her in the future, but all she could think of was: don't give up a good man for a bad one, although that seemed pretty obvious.

She wondered if he "respected" Doreen. She sure hoped so. She couldn't stand the thought of Parker making love to someone else. Especially not someone whose face she knew.

Miss Martine ignored the upraised arms and called, "Betty Ruth."

"Huh?" Betty Ruth looked up very carefully so as not to disturb the steel mallets of her hangover.

"You did prepare this lesson, didn't you?"

"Oh yes, ma'am." All around the class there were titters. Rumor had it that Betty Ruth had stayed on at the football field after practice and had taken on the team. That hadn't happened, of course, but she had lured five of the players over to her house. What had happened there nobody knew. *Boys are such liars.* That should sure go somewhere in the Southern Belle's Handbook as a warning. Sissy decided to make it Rule Number Fifteen. Coach had declared Betty Ruth off-limits for the rest of the season and was pressuring Miss Robbie to kick her off the cheerleading squad.

"Page seventy-two, read the first two lines."

Betty Ruth bent to her task, sounding out each syllable of "Au Clair de la Lune," in a language resembling nothing spoken on this planet.

Sissy flipped to the calendar in the front of her notebook. She was due over two weeks ago.

She studied the calendar. She'd missed two months last summer after her brother died. Her mother had said that was normal, not to worry. But in June it couldn't have meant anything unless someone spotted a star in the East. And it was unlikely that the Lord, even if He wanted to beget a Second Coming, would pick the Virgin Sissy. Of course, she reminded herself, she wasn't exactly eligible for that title anymore.

But she and Bourrée had always been careful. After the first time, he'd always worn a rubber. She remembered how it looked when he rolled it on over his red . . . Sissy brought herself up sharply.

She checked the calendar again, counting backward. The last time— up against the oak tree—was the night of the Awards Dinner, which was, oh my God, four weeks ago. She didn't want to think about that time. She felt raped, except you couldn't call it rape if you'd been having sex with the man, could you? Besides, he'd say, she'd asked for it, and she knew she had, but she hadn't asked for that! Not that! She tried to remember if he'd worn anything or not. Oh, Jesus, she couldn't have gotten pregnant from that! It was too awful.

She was probably just upset like last summer. But last summer her breasts didn't hurt all the time and she wasn't so sleepy.

"Sissy."

Sissy jerked her head up. "Ma'am?"

"Translate the next two lines."

Sissy looked at her book.

"Page seventy-two."

"Yes, ma'am. I know." The class was watching. She didn't want to look like a dope, but she couldn't figure out what was she doing sitting here in neat rows with her whole life crumbling in front of her. French words like black bugs scuttled across the page.

"Start with '*Ma chandelle est morte* . . . ' Do you know what that means?"

"My candle is dead?"

Miss Martine winced. "My candle has gone out. Now read."

"*Ma chandelle est morte* . . ." Sissy parroted and then slowly . . . " '*Je n'ai plus de feu* . . . ' I don't have any more light." What did this stupid French song about dead candles have to do with her? Things were happening to her own body. She was having trouble buttoning the waists of her skirts, she felt like a big old balloon and she had to sit still and read this crap.

Miss Martine walked over to Sissy's desk and closed her book. "That's quite enough. Sissy and Betty Ruth, I want to see you both after class. Now, *mes enfants,* 'Au Clair de la Lune' wasn't written to torture us, it's a beautiful French folk song. Can anyone sing it?"

Amy Lou's hand shot up. "I can, Miss Martine."

Who cares? thought Sissy. Who gives a flying fart? She tried to ignore the growth that might be forming inside her, pushing out her stomach. This tiny growth with Bourrée's face growing inside of her.

God wouldn't let this happen to her. Okay, so she hadn't obeyed *all* His commandments. She ticked them off as best she could remember them. She hadn't killed anybody, and she didn't steal. Well, hardly ever, except that time when she copped the orange lipstick at Rubinstein's, but she'd dropped the price into the collection plate at church the following Sunday. And there was the time she borrowed Norman's penknife, but that didn't count. Okay, it counted. Honor thy father and mother, don't use the Lord's name in vain, keep the Sabbath holy, don't covet, don't bear false witness, adultery . . . okay, she'd broken most of them, but she'd never killed anyone. She'd kept the most important one. And she'd never had another God before Him. She hadn't even been tempted to break that one. She couldn't believe she'd been really bad. Not bad enough for this, Lord.

She was supposed to go to college in the fall. Her parents had been saving up for it her whole life. She'd be the first girl in the whole family on both sides to go. Her grandmother had been talking about it since she was in diapers.

"Ma chandelle est morte, je n'ai plus de feu/Ouvre moi la porte pour l'amour de Dieu." Amy Lou sang out in pure, clear notes.

*   *   *

SISSY WAS SITTING in her bedroom, staring at the clothes drying in the yard, when the sound of the phone made her leap. She headed for the door. "Honey, it's Peewee," said her mother. Sissy slumped back down on her bed. She'd been waiting for the phone, but she hadn't been waiting for Peewee.

Her mother's gaunt figure in her flowered dress appeared in the doorway. The dress was too big for her now. She asked in her gentle voice, "Aren't you going to talk to him?"

Sissy shook her head. "Tell him . . . tell him I've run away to Hollywood. If he wants to contact me, he'll have to get in touch with . . . Clark Gable." She made a grand gesture she'd seen in some movie, but faltered in the middle.

"What's wrong, baby?"

"Nothing's wrong." Sissy turned back and watched the sheets flap in the wind. The clothesline was strung up in front of the live oak tree.

Cady sat down next to her daughter, exhausted. Belle had named her after Elizabeth Cady Stanton, but it hadn't worked. Sissy knew all her mother wanted, all she'd ever wanted, was to be a good wife and mother.

Sissy felt her thin hand on her shoulder. It was all she could do not to shrink back. "Why do you always think there's something wrong with me! There's nothing wrong with me! *I'm* fine."

The New Orleans surgeon who'd removed Cady's cancer in August was still optimistic, but Sissy thought her mother looked terrible.

Pain spread across Cady's face, but she didn't raise her voice. "What do you want me to tell the boy?"

Sissy had stopped and talked to Peewee at school that afternoon. All she'd wanted was for him to quit looking at her like that. She hadn't meant for him to call. She wondered what would happen if she abandoned the Southern Belle's Handbook and told the truth for a change. It would feel so good. "Just tell him he makes me want to puke."

Cady sighed and went back to the phone. Sissy heard her trying to make up an excuse to save Peewee's feelings without actually telling a lie. For God's sake, either tell him I think he's vomitous or lie creatively, Sissy willed. Don't just shilly-shally somewhere in between, feeling all virtuous about yourself. Sissy didn't feel virtuous about herself at all.

She went to the mirror. If only she had X-ray vision. She stared at her stomach and concentrated, trying to divine what was going on. Had her own body, like her mother's, betrayed her? Were cells floating toward one another and sticking, massing together, growing some alien being inside her?

Friday after French class, she'd taken the car, driven to Amite all by herself, and found a doctor who didn't know her family. Now she had to wait around to find out what happened to some rabbit she'd never see. She was unclear what her urine would do to it, but she wished it well. It was funny to think that her life and the life of a rabbit hung by the same chemical thread. On the theory that God didn't like you to pray for yourself, she considered praying for the rabbit. But she thought better of it. Any God stupid enough to believe her motives were pure bunny love wasn't worth praying to.

Sissy switched on the radio, but instead of music, the one clear station was filled with news of Germans and Englishmen slaughtering each other over in some unpronounceable place in Africa. She switched it off.

Shadows were filling up the silent room, but she didn't bother to turn on the lights. She just sat there, waiting in the dark.

"ARE YOU SURE?" Bourrée had asked over the phone.

"I'm sure."

There was a long pause, then: "Now, don't you worry about a thing, little girl, I'll take care of you."

So here she was waiting for him again, in the rain. This time she was standing in front of the library in the dark, her raincoat buttoned up to her chin, burdened down with a stack of library books she'd chosen to give herself an alibi. Where was he? He said he'd be here right after supper. She remembered their last meeting under the live oak and she felt nauseous. But he wouldn't be like that tonight. That time was her fault. She'd scared him by going over to his house like that. Tonight would be different. Wouldn't it? She took a series of deep breaths, but the nausea wouldn't go away.

The rain fell on her cheeks and dripped over her nose. She wiped her face with the back of her hand. Where was he?

She walked back and forth under the awning. No matter what other options she played around with in her head, since the first day she'd missed her period, she knew she would have to have an abortion. She was going to college next year.

But how? Girls died. Girls died in childbirth, too.

A year ago Sissy never thought about death and now it was all around her. Images from her favorite childhood story, "The Water Babies," had invaded her dreams. Except these babies were floating faceup. Dead. Her brother Norman. Her mother. The rest of the dead babies were wearing her face.

Betty Ruth said she knew someone who went to a clinic in Mexico. But, my God, the whole country's Catholic, and besides it isn't even safe to drink the water down there.

Maybe he can fix it with some doctor around here. She'd heard about doctors who did abortions at night right in their offices. But it was supposed to be awful. She imagined the shades down, the lights dim, the doctor's hands shaking, and everybody scared of getting caught, scared of what would happen if his hand slipped.

But Bourrée was connected. He could put a fix in at some hospital in New Orleans or Baton Rouge. Her grandmother had told her about doctors certifying it was for some kind of female problem. And it was all perfectly legal. All you had to do was find the right doctor. Bourrée would know the one, if anybody would. They called it a "c and d" or a "d and c" or something.

Finally he pulled over in his old pickup. He reached across the seat and opened the door for her. "You look like a cat that just crawled out of a ditch."

"Thanks for the compliment," she said, climbing up into the truck. "It was nice of you to show up."

"What's a matter, sugar? Don't you think ole Bourrée's gonna take care of you?"

"Are you?" she asked hoarsely.

"I surely am," he said as he drove through town. Sissy started to ask where they were going and then realized he was heading toward the creek. *Is he taking me back there to ask me what I want to do? Or to talk me into an abortion?* The memory of the night in her yard came back to her. *He wouldn't try to do that again. Not when I'm like this.* She slid away from him and pressed herself against the door. But he didn't seem to notice. Then he drove right past the Big Creek cutoff and turned onto a two-lane blacktop.

"Where're we going?"

"To get rid of your little problem, sugar."

"Tonight!"

"What'd you think?"

"I thought we were going to talk about it. Agree on a plan."

"No sense pussyfooting around. The sooner you take care of it, the better. Besides, you don't want that thing festering inside you any longer than absolutely necessary."

"Where are we going?"

"Now, why don't you just leave that to me."

They drove past a Negro bar. Sissy could hear the band playing as if nothing at all important were happening.

Bourrée turned off the blacktop and onto a dirt road.

"There aren't any doctors out here!" she screamed as the truck bounced and bucked over the ruts and potholes. He didn't say anything. He just squinted through the rain at what was left of the road. An edge of hysteria was creeping into her voice, and a tic was making her leg jump. "You've got to take me back. I can't do it tonight! My parents expect me to sleep at home."

"Where else you gonna sleep? In the fields?" He saw her staring at him, her green eyes wide with fright. "It don't take that long, sugar."

"But with the anesthetics and all . . . ?"

Bourrée laughed and patted her bouncing knee. "A young thing like you don't need anesthetics. Just grit your teeth."

He pulled up to an unpainted shotgun cottage in the middle of some fields. Sissy stared in horror at the rusting tin roof and the sagging porch with dangerous, decaying stairs. An old Model A Ford missing a fender and a couple of wheels was stuck in the mud. A cracked sink was lying in a junk pile next to it.

"I'm not going in there."

"Course you are," he said, cutting the lights.

"I thought you were taking me to a doctor."

"What doctor?"

"My grandmother says there are doctors and hospitals, too, where a girl can go and they'll certify you were just having a female operation."

"Belle tell you the name of any of those brave hospitals or their intrepid doctors?"

Sissy shook her head feeling stupid, "No, but . . ."

"Well, I don't know 'em, neither." Bourrée had dropped the speech he used around town and, as he often did in times of stress, had fallen into the raw vernacular of his youth. "Now, don't you worry none about a doctor. Abortion's a fact of nature. Girls have been getting rid of their little bundles since before there was doctors."

"Girls have been dying . . ." Her voice caught on the word.

He laughed, mocking her. "Aunt Sarah's not gonna kill you,

Sissy. Hell, she's been in business for years and years and never lost a girl that I've heard of. So come on, get out. You'll be fine."

Bourrée got out of the truck, walked all the way around in the mud and opened her door. The rain was coming down in sheets. "Get out, girl."

Sissy sat looking straight ahead.

"Dammit, Sissy, get out, I'm getting mired down in all this mud." Sissy didn't move.

He grabbed her arm and jerked her out. "Act sensible, girl, 'cause there ain't nothing else you can do." And he led her up the rotting stairs.

"Aunt Sarah." His voice boomed as he pushed Sissy into the house. The screen door banged behind them. The rain was making a racket on the tin roof, so he called again.

Sissy tried to pull out of his grip when a stout Negro in a white uniform came out of a back room, wiping her hands on a bloody apron. She was in her late fifties. She squinted at them as she walked through the kitchen. And then a big smile spread across her face. "Mr. Bourrée, I haven't seen you in a while."

"How you been keeping yourself, Sarah?"

"Busy, real busy."

"This here little girl went and got herself in trouble," he said, pushing Sissy toward her. "Think you can help her out?"

"I always got time for one of your gals, Mr. Bourrée, you know that, but," she said, turning to Sissy, "I'm afraid you're gonna have to wait. I'm working on a little gal right now."

Sissy smelled liquor on her breath and wondered how many of Bourrée's "gals" Aunt Sarah had worked on.

"That's okay. Take your time," Bourrée said expansively.

Sissy shook her head. "Maybe we better come back tomorrow. My parents think I'm at the library, and they'll worry if I come home too late."

Bourrée laughed and tightened his grip. "Oh, you'll come up

with a story for your parents. I have faith in you." He winked at Sarah.

"You all sit down and make yourselves comfortable. I'll be with you in just a little while." Sarah went back through the kitchen.

When she opened the door, Sissy caught a glimpse of a skinny brown leg, tied with a rope to a table covered in old newspapers. Her heart began to race. "I'm not staying here."

"Now don't you worry," Bourrée said in a calming voice. "If anyone knows what she's doing, Aunt Sarah does." He squeezed Sissy's shoulder reassuringly as he took her raincoat and hung it on the coat rack by the door. He pointed to a chair and said, "Sit down, chère. A girl in your condition shouldn't be on her feet."

Sissy sat down on the edge of an old wooden rocking chair. Bourrée leaned over and patted her on the knee. "Good girl, I'll be back for you around midnight."

Sissy jumped up. "What!"

"Don't worry. I'm not gonna leave you here forever." He opened the front door.

"Aren't you gonna wait and make sure I'm all right?" It didn't look like it. She heard herself pleading, "Bourrée, please don't leave me alone. I can't stand it."

"Now, honey, I've got business to attend to. Besides, what am I gonna do around here while you're getting yourself fixed?"

She grabbed the back of his hunting jacket. He turned and took her shoulders in his hands. His voice was harsh. "Be sensible, girl, you don't have no choice." And with that, he twisted out of her grip. The screen door banged behind him.

For a moment she was too stunned to move; then she ran outside, only to see him climb in the truck and slam it into gear. She ran, stumbling, through the front yard. The truck leaped forward and splattered her with mud.

Sissy went back inside. There wasn't much furniture in the front room: a couch with a Bleeding Heart of Jesus hanging above it, a couple of chairs with the stuffing coming out, and a scratched coffee table. "At least it's swept out and clean," she said aloud, trying to cheer herself up. She sat back down on the old wooden rocking chair, but as soon as she took the pressure off, her leg began to jerk. She had to rock back and forth, back and forth.

Then the screams began. The terror of the girl tied to the table behind the kitchen called out to her and Sissy answered with silent screams of her own. Her mouth became so dry, her tongue stuck to it.

She got up and went into the kitchen, where she took a glass out of the drainer. It was coated with a thin film of buttermilk. Behind the curtains, beneath the sink, the trash can was overflowing. Newspapers clotted with blood were hanging from the edge and falling out. Sissy looked down and saw the blood from a balled-up newspaper drip onto her shoe. She screamed out loud.

Her scream was drowned out by louder ones behind the door. The fear coming from the back room had turned to searing pain. Aunt Sarah sharply ordered the girl to hush up. What was that woman doing? Sissy had no idea how abortions were performed. She'd heard of girls using coat hangers on themselves. The image of a serrated kitchen spoon dripping with blood and buttermilk came unbidden into her mind. "You don't have no choice." She wiped her shoe on the sink curtains. When she stood up, a tall boy—a year or two older than she—was standing over her, weaving.

"Well, well, look who's come to call. You waiting for my mama?"

Sissy nodded and tried to say yes, but she couldn't make any words come.

"Then I guess I knows what you been doing." The boy was drunk and thought he was hilarious. He slapped his leg at his own joke.

Sissy tried to edge out of his way. But as she edged to the left, he followed her, putting up his right arm to cut her off. He leaned over her. She could smell his fetid breath. "Where's your boyfriend? He take off so he won't have to partake in the consequences in case my mama's hand slips?"

Sissy edged to the right. He almost let her go, but when her back was to the wall he took her by the arm. "You ever try dark meat?"

Sissy pulled herself up and, in her best imitation of her grandmother doing her high and mighty act, said, "Would you please move aside and let me pass."

But the drunken boy was not about to be intimidated. All the constraints that protected white women and kept them safe in colored neighborhoods were inoperative here. Sissy was about to break the law. No white woman could even admit to being at Aunt Sarah's. To accuse a colored boy of doing something to her there was unthinkable. This boy knew it. "A girl like you ain't got no cause to get your neck all poked out. It ain't like you was a good girl." He smiled. His gold tooth glinted in the dangling kitchen light. "You is more a good time girl."

She had to think. But how could she with the rain beating on the tin roof and the screams coming from the other room and her heart racing and her head pounding? "Come on, girl, I'll do you real fast." He grabbed her wrist. Sissy pulled back. "Hey, sweetmeat, don't you know it's your last chance? Once my mama gets through with you, you ain't gonna want it for some time to come," he said, toying with her hair.

"Leave me alone!" She tried to wrench out of his hold, but she couldn't.

He smiled and licked his lips, running his eyes over her body. "You ain't never felt nothing like my gemstones." Still holding her wrist, he jerked her hand to his fly. Sissy pushed him backward. But before she knew what hit her, she was on the floor. The drain board from the sink came with her, spewing silverware all around her. She screamed. She tried to kick, but only managed to hit the trash can, scattering the bloody newspaper.

He had her pinned down, his hands on her wrists, straddling her thighs. Maybe she could shame him. Filling her voice with contempt she said, "Let me up, you fool. Are you so pitiful, the only way you can get a girl is to rape her?"

He was laughing, reveling in his power. "It's not the only way, sweetmeat, but it's a good way, a mighty good way!" He rubbed himself against her and pushed up her skirt. Then beneath the laughter and the screams still coming from the back room, Sissy heard her true voice, calm and sure, telling her what she had to do.

Kicking and flailing, she reached around under the sink. When it was clear there was no way she could buck him off, she let go, her muscles became soft, no longer fighting him. As soon as he felt that he said, "That's right, girl, relax. You gonna enjoy yourself tonight, for sure." He took his hand off her wrist to unzip his fly and then, fondling her breast, said, "If I'm lying, I'm dying."

In a flash, Sissy had the butcher knife in his crotch, poking his bare skin. "Get up, boy, if you take any stock in those gemstones of yours. Get up!" she screamed.

She knew he could probably take the knife away from her, he might even use it to kill her, but she was prepared to give as good as she got. With that sure knowledge shining in her face, he just shriveled up and jumped away from her.

"Hey, gal, all you had to say was no. I don't want nothing you don't want to give." He was zipping up his pants when Sarah stepped out of the back room, her hands dripping with blood. She threw the boy up against the wall, screaming at him about being crazy and ruining her business and getting himself lynched. Then she called for Sissy.

But Sissy didn't turn back. She was running through the rain, her coat and purse left behind, her oxfords caked with mud. The butcher knife was still in her hand. Belle Cantrell's words were pounding away with each step. "You've got to take your life in your own hands."

She came to the Negro bar and pushed her way inside. The warmth and the music calmed her, comforted her. But the music and dancing stopped abruptly and was replaced by tension as everybody watched this white girl with a bloodstained butcher knife. The crowd parted and let her through.

A waitress in a tight red dress stepped in front of her. "You looking for somebody?"

"Just a telephone."

"You don't need that in here."

Sissy looked down and saw the butcher knife was still in her hand. She hesitated for a moment and then decided she wasn't giving it up. Not yet. She dropped the knife by her side, but held on to it. "You got a phone?"

The waitress pointed to the far side of the bar. The band struck up again, playing slow and soft. The piano sounded like the rain outside, the snare drums followed. But nobody danced. The bartender came out from behind the bar and stood in back of her, a towel wrapped around his arm. He eyed her knife. Sissy asked him for a nickel.

She fingered the hilt of the knife, enjoying the power it conferred upon her as she dialed the LeBlanc residence. She prayed for Bourrée to pick up. She didn't know what she'd say to Miss Lily. But a male voice answered.

"Oh, thank God. You've got to come get me right away."

"Sissy, is that you?"

"Peewee?" He sounded just like his father.

"It is you. Oh, my gosh!" He was so nervous he began to babble. "Boy, oh boy, this is my lucky night. Guess what, I got a B on my history test? I was afraid I'd flunked it. It must have been all the studying we did together that did it. I remembered a whole bunch of stuff I never thought I'd remember."

He went on and on like that until Sissy screamed, "Peewee!"

He quieted down then and asked her why she called.

"I'm in trouble. I need you to come and get me."

Once a girl says yes, it's almost impossible to go back and say

no. Boys who respected your wishes before become hard

of hearing.

Rule Number Nine

THE SOUTHERN BELLE'S HANDBOOK

Chapter 16

SISSY DIDN'T SET out to trap Peewee and make him think the baby she was carrying was his. At least that's what she told herself. But when he parked Miss Lily's Buick on the side of Highway 10 and lunged at her, she welcomed his attention. At first. She needed someone to hold her and Peewee wanted her so much. It felt nice. Then when things heated up, she tried to stop him, but he wouldn't stop like normal boys would when she pulled his hand away. He just kept on. She knew she could fight him off and he'd respect her for it, but Sissy just wasn't up to a fight. So she lay back on the long front seat, her head and shoulders against the door, and just let him kiss her and stroke her and tell her he loved her. It wasn't so bad. It wasn't so good either.

She told herself she got the idea for the deceit the next day, when she heard Peewee bragging about his exploits to Newton Carruthers. She was on her way to cheerleading practice, trying to figure out what to do next, when she heard them talking about her as she rounded the corner of the cement bleachers where they had ducked out of sight behind the equipment shed. She heard Peewee say, "Then she let me go all the way."

Sissy quickly stepped back and listened as Newton said, "You are such a liar, boy."

"I am not." Then Peewee went into such smutty detail that Sissy was furious. How could he tell those things about her! She was just about to give him a piece of her mind when he said, "And she didn't even make me use a rubber."

"Are you crazy! What if you get her in trouble?"

There was a hesitation and then Peewee said, "Well, hell, I'd make an honest woman out of her. I bet you wouldn't kick Sissy Thompson out of your bed."

"You're stuck on her, aren't you?" There was wonder in Newton's voice. "Aren't you?"

Sissy imagined Peewee's ears getting red and then she heard him say belligerently, "What if I am?"

That's when Sissy's inner voice spoke up and said her choices were hard, but she had them.

She hadn't much wanted to repeat the experience with Peewee, after the first time, but she found it was hard to tell him no and make it stick. Peewee wanted to make love all the time, if what they did in the backseats of cars could be called lovemaking. At first she thought she could teach him. And Peewee was a very willing student.

Bourrée had shown her all kinds of things she could do to give a man pleasure, so every time they went out Peewee was always eager to "mess around." But the night she tried to show him what he could do for her, he was genuinely shocked. "Sissy, nice girls aren't supposed to like it. A girl does it for a man because she loves him."

She tried to do it just for him, but all too often when they parked out by the cemetery, the image of a weasel slipped in between them, grabbing her with skinny arms, sticking his weasel hand between her legs. Only those pale blue Bourrée eyes could banish the disgusting beast.

She remembered a Sunday school teacher telling her that companionship and shared interests were what made a good marriage. Sex took up only a small percentage of the time. Sissy hoped she was right. She and Peewee got along fine. He was so happy picking her up after practice, so proud to walk through the halls holding her hand. It was always flattering to be adored, Sissy thought. And she sure wasn't looking for love.

It probably didn't exist anyway. Just lies they put in songs. Unless what she had with Bourrée was love, and if it was, she didn't ever want any more. She still thought about Parker a lot, but that was so confusing. She'd felt happy, really happy with him. But was that love? She'd always heard love was about suffering and singing the blues. She decided to forget about everything else and concentrate on companionship with Peewee.

Then one afternoon after school, she saw Bourrée's truck parked down the street from her house. Her heart started racing and her knees didn't want to bend.

But it was at that moment she finally understood all those rules her mother and grandmother had laid down for her. They weren't just to kill her fun. Good girls have a kind of power. Holding her head straight and concentrating on her posture, she walked right by him. He called her name. She pretended to be deaf. A deaf girl with the posture of a queen.

And there was nothing he could do! He couldn't jump out and grab her, force her screaming into his truck, force her to go with him back to Aunt Sarah's. Not on a street filled with houses and children and bicycles.

Yes, a girl has power, if she's prepared to take it. And a girl who obeys all the rules, or pretends to, is safe. Even the rules on proper behavior didn't seem so ridiculous. They were her mother's and her grandmother's way of helping her keep her self-respect. That's when Sissy realized the Southern Belle's Handbook did more than help her attract men—it was her survival manual.

She started accepting Peewee's invitations to Sunday dinner with the family. It was the main thing she had to look forward to now— sitting there, her hair shining, dressed like a princess, watching Bourrée squirm.

She had missed the homecoming prom. It would have been too humiliating to stand in the back of the gym and watch them crown Parker king and Doreen his queen. But when the American Legion threw a Christmas party for the young people, she decided to go. She knew it would be her last dance.

Peewee was thrilled to escort her in her beautiful green taffeta evening dress, which Sissy had let out in home ec. Earlier that week, she'd confided in him that she'd missed her period, but they'd have to wait another couple of weeks before she could take the rabbit test. She told him it must have happened the first time they were together and that proved how incredibly potent he was. Rule Number Eighteen: *Flattery works.*

Of course he was scared, but he was proud, too. He wouldn't mind word getting around that he was the boy who knocked up Sissy Thompson. His plans for the future were vague, but he'd always expected he'd marry sometime. Nothing wrong with now. In his heart he knew he'd never get another shot at a girl like Sissy.

Peewee had never been much of a dancer. He simply didn't hear the beat. But tonight he wanted to dance every dance with her, to show the other guys.

For Sissy, who loved to dance, dancing with Peewee was torture. Toward the end of the evening, Parker cut in, and when he took Sissy in his arms and held her against him in perfect time to the music, she remembered what slow dancing could be like.

"How you doing?" he asked. She felt pain radiating out through his clothes, caressing her. He still cared for her! It gave her an unexpected thrill. For the first time she realized she didn't have to marry Peewee, she had other choices. All they'd have to do was sneak off now. They could do it in the parking lot. She counted the weeks. It was still within the realm of possibility, almost. The thought of finally going all the way with Parker was exciting. She moved in closer and felt he was excited, too. But he was too honorable to leave Doreen stranded.

Okay, she'd get him to make a late date with her. Tonight. Two A.M. She'd climb out the window and meet him at the corner. And maybe when he kissed her and touched her skin, it wouldn't be so bad. Maybe the image of the weasel wouldn't slip in between them, but she suspected Peewee had embedded it in her brain for all time. She wondered if Parker thought nice girls aren't supposed to like it. Maybe all the boys did. Maybe they were right and she wasn't a nice girl. She looked up at him. He smiled and pressed her gently to him, his lips on her hair.

It wouldn't be fair. With his grades and his football record, he was sure to get the appointment to the Naval Academy he had worked so hard for. He had a big future ahead of him. Her daddy said so. Everyone said so. Would he still have a future with a wife and child dragging him down?

"Can I come over tomorrow? We need to talk." His voice rumbled through her and Sissy felt a throb down there. She stroked the hair on the back of his neck. Tomorrow would be as good as tonight. They could park somewhere in the woods. Even go to Manchac and rent a boat, do it in the swamps. He kissed the top of her head and Sissy was caught up in the romance of gliding through those misty waters in a pirogue with Parker.

But if the boys talked, and she knew how boys talked, neither one would want to marry her! And even if Parker did want to, the Naval Academy wouldn't take him if he was married. She wondered if any college would. In the movies, football players went on dates with sorority girls. Did they let married men play football? Did they give scholarships to fathers? The child she was carrying wouldn't even look like him.

The music stopped. "What do you say?"

Sissy hesitated, but just for a moment. "I can't. I'm going steady with Peewee."

*   *   *

"I DID NOT save up all those years so my sixteen-year-old grand-daughter could drop out of high school to marry the spawn of Bourrée LeBlanc!" yelled Belle Cantrell as she stormed through the door. It was a week before Christmas. Bowers of mistletoe and holly decked the living room. A large pine tree stood in the corner. The creche Belle's husband had carved for Cady stood watch over the family from the mantelpiece.

"I'm almost seventeen," said Sissy, but she was glad her grand-mother was making such a fuss.

"I suppose that makes it all right for you to give up your educa-tion to wash that boy's socks! Dammit, Sissy, I've put every dime I could scrape up into your college fund."

"She's pregnant, Belle," said Hugh.

"Of course she's pregnant, why else would a woman with any sense get married?"

"Mama," objected Cady, propped up on the couch, looking gray. The cancer they'd all feared had come back. The doctors were talk-ing about another operation, but nobody was optimistic this time. Sissy, sitting on the floor at Cady's feet, covered her mother's lap with a shawl.

"I know you did it for love," Belle said to her own daughter. "But I said a woman with sense. Now, Sissy's got sense, but she's still a girl. What are you going to do if that boy decides to up and leave you? You won't even have a high school education." Belle lowered herself into a wing chair. In her late fifties, she was still a handsome woman, with auburn hair swept up on her head and fastened with an art deco comb. She wore a broad-shouldered rust-colored jacket with a pinched waist over a straight skirt. She had a red camellia pinned to her shoulder in an effort to look festive, but it was obvi-ous Belle didn't feel festive.

"What about you?" Sissy asked. "You eloped with Grandpa when you were just sixteen."

Belle paused. Sissy remembered stories about how wild her grandmother had been to marry her big, taciturn dairy farmer. "I've had to live with that decision for forty years. Don't do it, baby, life's too long."

"What do you all want me to do?" Sissy asked.

"You're not some country girl who has to get married just because she got caught," Hugh said, trying to warm himself in front of the fire.

"How pregnant are you?" Belle wanted to know.

"About two months, I guess. My last period was ten weeks ago."

"Good! We'll get you an abortion and afterward, we'll get you fitted for a diaphragm," said Belle firmly, her tone brooking no objections. "Then you can screw like a rabbit, if that's what you want."

"Mother!" Cady protested. "Now you just stop it."

But Belle was flying. "She's not a breeding machine, who has to drop a baby just because she's able to conceive one." She turned to Sissy. "I found someone who'll do it." Sissy's green eyes lit up, her heart was pounding with relief. Was it still possible? But Belle didn't look happy. "There's a woman out by Big Creek who's supposed to be reliable."

"No!" Sissy screamed.

"Now, hush, Sissy, her name is Sarah Miller. She's been doing it for years, apparently."

"Tibor told me about her. The police let her operate as a kind of safety valve. Does mostly colored . . ." Hugh's voice trailed off. He shook his head as if to get rid of his thoughts.

"What about those hospitals you told me about, Grandma? With doctors?"

Hugh, Belle, and Cady looked from one to another, embarrassed. "I told you I'd heard about them, honey. I didn't say I actually knew of any around here."

"I checked," said her father. "There's a doctor in New Orleans who used to do them, but he's under indictment."

Sissy screamed, "Shit!" No one told her not to swear. She reached for her mother. "Please, Mama, don't make me." And for the first time since she'd found out, Sissy let herself go and cried. All the fear and grief and anger she'd held back came out in terrible, soul-wrenching sobs. "Don't let them kill me."

Cady stoked her daughter's hair and squared her frail shoulders. "Nobody's going to make you do anything," she said, glaring at her husband and mother. "Nobody, you hear? I'm not risking my daughter's life on some backwoods abortionist."

Belle suddenly looked much older than her years. "I'll talk to your cousin Loreen over in Little Rock. Maybe you can stay there until the baby's born."

Sissy sat up. "That mealymouthed hypocrite! She'd spend the whole time lecturing me about being a fallen woman. I'd rather die!"

"Look at it this way," Hugh said. "When it's over, you can get on with your life. You can finish high school and go to college. You'll just be a year behind."

"Just a year?" Sissy said sarcastically. "What do you know about it? I'm sick every morning. I'm swelling up like some kind of horrible watermelon. Even my legs are all pumped up. You can't make me go through nine months of . . . of . . . manufacturing this baby and then tell me to give it away! By then, don't you understand, it'll be *my* baby!"

"It won't seem so bad after it's over," said Belle without conviction.

"Oh, come on, Grandma, even suffragettes don't give their babies away."

Hugh was fed up. "Stop being so dramatic, Sissy. Girls do it all the time."

"No grown woman would."

"A grown woman can take care of a baby," he shot back.

"So can I! Peewee'll get a job. I'll be an inspiration to him." In the face of what she felt was her father's insensitivity, Sissy was digging in. Even Peewee seemed better than throwing a helpless baby out into the world and never knowing what happened to it.

There was more. A lot more. Hugh talked about the importance of an education, about having a family when she was ready for one.

Sissy didn't see what difference it made when she had a family. It would all come out the same anyway. Especially since she wasn't looking for love. She'd be stuck in a house somewhere with a bunch of kids. At least Peewee adored her.

And then she thought about Bourrée. Carrying his baby to term would make him nuts. They'd live at Sissy's until Peewee graduated. But they'd still have dinner at the LeBlancs' every week. And every week Bourrée would see her getting bigger and bigger and there'd be nothing he could do about it. Revenge was so much more satisfying than love.

Finally, she stormed out of the house, announcing she was going to get married and they had two choices: give her a wedding or watch her elope.

"What does she know about taking care of babies?" Hugh raged.

"What did any of us know?" asked Cady.

"Belle, you talk to her. She listens to you."

But Belle was watching her own daughter. Her face had become a mask of pain. "Cady?"

Cady reached for her mother. Belle moved to the couch, took her daughter in her arms, and rocked her.

When the spasm passed Hugh said, "Dammit, I won't let her ruin her life. If she doesn't want to go to Loreen's, I'll find one of those homes for unwed mothers. I heard about one in Baton Rouge, I'll check it out myself. I'll make her go."

Cady closed her eyes. "I hate to think that my only grandchild is going to be given away to strangers. God knows what they'll do to it." A second spasm racked her body. When it passed, she said, "It would be nice to have a baby in the house, wouldn't it, Mama."

"It would," Belle agreed.

"Are you all crazy! She's ruining her life and that boy's and all you can talk about are babies!"

"She's set on having it," Cady said, reaching for her husband, who was pacing the room now. "Remember how sweet you were to me when I was pregnant? I don't want Sissy to go through it alone in some home in Baton Rouge."

"You think you can hang on until the baby gets here?" Belle asked. Cady's face clouded over. "You'd want to hold it in your arms."

"I'm gonna try, Mama. I'm gonna try." And that's when Hugh knew he was beaten.

Sissy and Peewee were married in a simple but tasteful ceremony the second weekend in January. The bride wore white. Newton Carruthers was Peewee's best man.

The same afternoon Gentry won the state football championship. A representative from Annapolis was on the fifty-yard line. College scouts came from as far away as Notre Dame. Parker broke the state record for passing and running. And he broke the national record for most points made by a single player. As the sportswriters were to say the next day, when Davidson gets his hands on the ball the other team might as well leave the field. But after the game, when the sportswriters and the scouts converged on the locker room, Parker wasn't there.

The Japanese had bombed Pearl Harbor the month before. And at six o'clock, while the minister was asking Peewee to take this woman, Parker joined the Marines.

PART III

1956
The
River
of
Desire

Fourteen years of foreplay are enough for any girl.

Rule Number Forty-five

THE SOUTHERN BELLE'S HANDBOOK

Chapter 17

PARKER OPENED THE front door of the Guest House and walked across the steamy French Quarter street. He'd been there since ten o'clock that morning, driving the staff crazy. He'd changed rooms three times. When he was finally satisfied, he sent the bellboy out to buy some flowers. "Anything but roses." Roses would have been too obvious. He wanted it to look as if he'd gone to no special trouble. He wanted everything perfect.

He spotted Sissy as soon as he opened the door to the restaurant. The maître d' came oiling up to him, but Parker waved him off. He wanted to see her fresh.

She was sitting next to a cream-colored wall with dark wainscoting. Yellowing Mardi Gras photos hung overhead. She was wearing a white straw hat and a green dress that hugged her every curve. Her cigarette made smoke signals in the air.

He sat down across from her and felt the pressure of her knees. He could smell her, even though the kitchen was sending out the aromas of fresh bread, sautéed garlic, and chicory coffee. She leaned toward him. She was wearing perfume, but under that was the deep scent of something much more exciting.

He picked up a menu. "Did you order?"

"No."

"Have you figured out what you want?"

Sissy checked her watch.

"It's quarter of two. We're both early."

She put her hand on his, closing his menu. "Parker, do you know what it means to be a grown-up?"

"You don't have to clean your plate before you can have dessert?"

She ground out her cigarette with her long, freckled fingers. Then she stood and said, "Come on. *Fourteen years of foreplay is enough for any girl.*"

AS SHE LEFT the restaurant, she wondered if Bourrée was already in his apartment on Royal Street waiting for her. Eat your heart out, you old coot, she thought as she took Parker's arm. And then she didn't think of Bourrée any more for the rest of the afternoon.

As soon as Parker opened the door, Sissy felt her heart racing. She stepped into the room and was greeted by a huge bouquet of white flowers on a polished rosewood table in front of the cypress armoire with its full-length mirror. The honeyed scent of jasmine hung in the air.

She saw his reflection close the door and walk over to the white canopied bed. It was a beautiful old bed. High and wide. She wondered if she'd made a terrible mistake.

She turned and looked at him straight on. He smiled. It would be terrible form to get him all this way and change your mind, she told herself. She had to go through with it. But unlike that afternoon in the kitchen, all her fantasies had abandoned her. In that delicate moment before the first touch, she wondered if she knew this man at all.

Why had she been so brash in the restaurant? They could be eating oysters and sipping champagne, right now. Telling jokes, talking. Anything!

She went over to the air conditioner and fiddled with the dials. She turned up the fan so high the white organdy curtains floated up in the air. She opened the armoire door and took out a couple of fat pillows, when she felt Parker slip his arms around her. As he pressed her to him, she realized he was ready. Right now. Ready. Oh God, she wasn't. She tossed the pillows on the bed.

His calloused fingers were gentle as he unzipped her green linen dress, letting it fall to the floor. She wondered if she could force herself to go through with it. Of course she could. He ran his hands over the satin lace that sheathed her body and stepped back. "Walk around."

"What?"

"Walk around. I like to see a woman wearing a slip."

"Parker . . ."

"It looks like home."

She walked across the room, relieved to get away, and watched him warily. He unbuttoned his shirt. As the fabric came apart, she saw his chest was rippled with muscles and covered with scars and those same soft brown curls she'd remembered. But she kept her distance.

He slid his pants over his thighs. Then he slipped out of his shorts. She saw his penis standing up, hard and red against his body. She didn't know it could do that. Straight up.

She was surprised how completely at ease he was in his nakedness, how confidently he moved in his body. She wondered what he wanted her to do. Men were so peculiar about sex. They had rules. Bourrée wouldn't undress. Peewee wouldn't let her move too much or make any noise.

Suddenly, he scooped her up in his arms. She let out a little squeal and found she naturally wrapped her legs around his naked waist. And pressed herself to him. She was beginning to wake up.

He laid her on the bed and caressed her body, still covered in satin and lace. And then as he began to kiss her, she thought maybe she wouldn't have to force herself after all. He kissed her all over until every inch of her shivered, and Sissy decided she definitely wouldn't have to force herself. But the kisses went on and on, until she began to feel uneasy.

Peewee and even Bourrée had always zeroed right in on a couple of obvious targets, eager to get the job done. But Parker was taking such a long time, she wondered if something was wrong. He ran his work-hardened fingers slowly over her back until it tingled. Then he peeled off her slip and kissed her flat stomach, her ribs. He reached around her to take off her bra and licked the creases under her breasts. Working his way over her breasts, both nipples between his rough fingers, he kissed her neck so softly she thought she could feel its pulse beating in and out. Then he ran his hands down her arms, kissing her breasts and tickling her skin until the inside of her elbows became erogenous zones. Sissy shivered deep inside herself. If this was wrong, she never wanted to do it right again.

He knelt down and rolled off her lace panties. She arched and waited for him to enter her. But Parker just stood over her. He seemed to be drinking in her nakedness. Then he kissed her.

Down there! Sissy had heard about men doing that, of course. Women, too. But she thought they only did it in New York.

All her upbringing told her they were going straight to hell. She pushed against him, trying to push him off her. But he sucked on her and she began moaning in spite of herself and then as he held her thighs, flames shot up through her body and she started to scream. He didn't even try to hush her. He just laughed and began licking her and flicking his tongue back and forth! That's when Sissy decided hell was okay with her, especially if it took a real long time getting there.

He entered her finally and filled her up, pushing her knees over his shoulders, rubbing places she'd never felt before, turning them to yearnings as he moved back and forth, back and forth, and exploded inside of her.

And just as she found herself wishing he could have lasted a little longer, he wanted to do it again. And this time as she caressed him with her fingers and wrapped herself around him, there was no question of forcing herself. No question at all.

Afterward, they lay with their legs entwined, his hand cupping her breast. "Why didn't you do this fourteen years ago?"

"I don't know, I must have respected you."

"Shit, Parker, why'd you have to do a thing like that?"

"You know why I love you, Sissy? You talk just like my buddies in the Marines." They laughed, but beneath the laughter, Sissy grieved for all those years and what could have been.

He ran a bath for her in the big claw-footed tub and washed her breasts and the inside of her legs until she pulled him in with her. As they were splashing water all over the tiles, trying to get his big body to fit, Sissy wondered how long he planned to stay in Gentry.

"Are we just some kind of pit stop for you, Parker?" She heard a lonely wind blowing through her voice and tried to hush it. "I don't want to pressure you or anything."

He laughed and slid his knees around her hips, bobsled fashion. "You trying to get rid of me, girl?"

"No! I mean, I just . . ." How did she get herself into this? "Everybody expected you to be a big success. You know, my daddy wrote all those articles. And you had an international business. Don't you want that anymore?"

Parker shrugged. " 'Desire is the root of all suffering,' " he quoted.

Sissy froze. "Who says?"

"The Buddhists."

It was a good thing he couldn't see her face. She thought of the years she'd spent in Gentry before he'd come back. All those years without desire. All those years of nothing much. "Well, let me tell you something, Parker Davidson, and you can tell those Buddhists of yours, *Desire is the root of . . .*" She paused, casting around for the right word. "*Life! And if you ain't got that, you ain't got nothing.*"

Parker laughed again. "That the Word According to Sissy?"

"You can quote me." She thought about adding that to the Southern Belle's Handbook. Rule Number . . .

But before she could assign it a number, Parker said, "Let's just see what kind of desire we can stir up right here." He slid his hands under her buttocks and moved her around until she found out it was possible to stir up quite a bit even in a tub filled with hot water. Parker taught her a lot of possibilities that afternoon.

When they left the bathroom, it was already dark. "Oh my God, Peewee's expecting me home by now!"

"Stay." Parker was sitting on the bed. He held out his hand to her. "Stay the night."

"I can't. You know that."

He took her hand. "I don't want you to go. It's too soon. I've waited too long."

"You think I want to?" She pulled away from him and started to dress. "Don't worry, this is not a one-night stand."

He didn't say anything, but watched her intently as if trying to make up his mind about something. He helped her hook up her bra. She pulled her slip over her head and with one leg on the bed, attached her stocking to her garter belt. But when she started to put on her panties, he took them from her. "Just put on the rest of your clothes. I want to see you in your dress and know that part's still open and ready for me!"

"Parker, you're a pervert!" she said, but the thought excited her, too. He stood up and took her over to the mirror. She looked at his big, naked body and wondered how she'd be able to stand Peewee now. He slid his arm around her shoulder and slipped his hand into her bra. She slapped at him. "I've got to go."

He bent over and kissed her ear and pinched her nipple. She remembered hot nights in the drive-in when they were kids, and she pressed her body against his. But when he started pulling up her slip she pushed away from him. "I can't stay. I want to, but I can't."

She stepped into her green dress, zipping it up behind her. He picked up the phone and asked the operator for her number. Sissy tried to grab the phone, but he held it away from her until a voice on the other end said, "Hello."

"Say you'll be late."

"Hello," the voice said again.

"Clara?" Sissy asked.

"Where are you? Mr. Peewee's been expecting you for over an hour."

"Tell him . . ." Parker reached his hand up under Sissy's dress, feeling along the top of her stocking. She tried to push him away. "Tell him . . ." Parker's fingertips gently stroked her pubic hair. "Tell him I'll be . . ." He touched her skin, rubbed, and brought up the wetness . . . "staying . . . here . . . all night."

"You can't!" The voice over the wire was shocked.

A feeling of wild abandon swept over her. After fourteen years Sissy was busting loose. "Oh, yes I can!"

"Oh, Lord, what am I supposed to tell your husband?" Clara asked. Sissy could hear the envy in her voice.

That's when Sissy experienced another first. As Parker pulled her onto his lap, she didn't want to lie. She didn't even want to think one up. "Tell him . . . tell him anything you want."

AROUND 2 A.M. THEY were famished and went out to an oyster bar where the night people of Bourbon Street and the jazz all came in through the open door. Sissy had been to New Orleans many times, but she'd never slept there. Peewee didn't see the sense in putting out good money for a hotel room, when he could sleep in his own bed just two hours away. She couldn't get over the way the city was alive all night long. People went out for supper whenever the mood struck them. She was all eyes as the musicians, the strippers, and the society crowd stood around the oyster bar calling to one another, passing the catsup and horseradish like family. A saxophone player helped her mix her oyster sauce. A man in a tuxedo drunkenly, but gallantly, presented her with the carnation from his lapel. She squeezed Parker's hand, and his heart soared at how young and alive she looked. She felt like a princess who'd been freed from enchantment. Cinderella out of the cinders, on the arm of her prince.

When they were seated at a table, a lone clarinetist wandered in and sat down next to them and began to play softly. Sissy kissed Parker on the cheek. She thanked him for giving her this perfect evening and told him how she loved their hotel. The Guest House. She'd always wanted to stay at a place like that. On the few trips she'd taken with Peewee and the kids to the Gulf Coast, they'd always stayed in cement block motels with broken air conditioners and dingy sheets. Parker smiled, proud he could make her so happy, but when she added: "A cheap motel would make what we're doing feel sort of, well, you know . . . cheap," he shifted uncomfortably on the wooden chair.

"I thought we might meet out on the Airline Highway, next time."

She laughed. "Sure."

"You wouldn't mind?"

Sissy had an uneasy feeling he was serious. "You figure once you've had your way with me, you don't have to go to any special trouble? Concrete walls and dirty sheets are good enough for me now?" she said as lightly as she could manage, which wasn't very light at all.

"I just thought it might make a nice change."

She leaned toward him and said softly, "I don't want to change nothing." She made a little kiss at him.

Parker shifted again. He didn't seem able to get comfortable in his skin. Finally he admitted, "I don't think I can swing the Guest

House again for a while. At least not as often as I want to see you."
He reached for her hand.

She pulled away. "I thought money wasn't important to you."
What was going on? she wondered. Parker made a decent salary
and he didn't have any dependents, at least not any she'd heard
about.

Finally, with great reluctance, he told her he was giving Clara a
little help.

"We're all giving Clara a little help." Sissy had gotten Peewee to
chip in an extra twenty-five dollars.

It turned out that Parker had promised her a monthly stipend. A
large monthly stipend, one that would take a big chunk out of his
paycheck. "What else was I going to do with the money? You kept
turning me down." He seemed uncomfortable. Sissy suspected
there were things he wasn't telling. "I just wanted to help her.
There's no way she's going to make enough at Gulf Chemicals."

"In other words, you'll be keeping her in Chicago." She didn't
feel much like a princess anymore.

"It's nothing like that," he said, hastening to assure her everything was over between them. He spoke with such conviction and
sincerity that Sissy believed him. But she knew as long as he was
supporting Clara their romance could rekindle at a moment's
notice, fanned by those two carnal emotions so difficult to resist,
emotions that were the basis of most marriages: gratitude and enti-
tlement.

"It's temporary. Just until she gets settled and finds a part-time
job."

"Parker, have you lost your mind? No girl getting that much
money is ever going to find a part-time job."

The waitress brought their food.

The band at the Paddock Lounge around the corner on Bourbon
Street was playing "When the Saints Come Marching In." Next to
them, the solitary clarinetist played counterpoint. Parker picked up
his oyster po' boy. "Sissy, it's her big chance to do something with

her life. Everybody needs a chance." Through the music they heard the empty echoes of their own lives.

"Her father should take care of her," Sissy said stubbornly.

"Right. This is just until he gets around to it," he said.

Sissy made up Rule Number Thirty-six on the spot. *A man will believe anything as long as it's convenient for him.* She pushed her plate away. She was feeling sick.

"Come on, babe, don't be like that. I'll find us a place with clean sheets. Okay?"

It was meant as a joke, but she didn't smile. The man in the tuxedo lifted his glass and made a silent toast to her. Suddenly, Sissy felt her eyes fill up with tears. She tried to tell herself it really wasn't important who Parker was keeping in Chicago or what it was costing him. Except it was further proof that nothing ever worked out. And she wanted, she wanted . . . something. Something whole and beautiful and hers. Not just bits and pieces and a few leftover crumbs. The worst part was, she didn't have any right to demand it. None. After all, she was married. *Marriage. The root of all suffering.* Rule Number Thirty-seven. She wiped her eyes with her napkin and came away with black smudges. Her mascara must be all over her face. She threw down the napkin and ran out of the restaurant. Parker tossed some bills on the table and ran after her.

He caught up with her on Bourbon Street just as a band came out of a bar and marched around them, still playing "When the Saints Come Marching In." He had to yell over the music. "I'll take a second job."

Sissy swung around. "Dammit, Parker, don't you dare to be a martyr. I hate martyrs." She started to storm off again, but he held her arm. Black rivulets ran down her cheeks.

"So what do we do?"

She looked down at the sidewalk and saw an abandoned sequined pump. "I don't know."

"I'll tell you one thing, not seeing you next Saturday is not an option."

The band marched down the street. A warm wave passed over her. Suddenly she knew with her deepest voice, that she wasn't going to give up the first adventure she'd had in her life because of a change in motels or because of what he might do one day with Clara. So in spite of everything the Southern Belle's Handbook said on the subject, and it said plenty about what no self-respecting lady ought to do, she decided to take the crumbs he offered her and make the best of them. She moved into the protection of his body and said, "I guess I'm being a selfish bitch, huh?"

He nodded. "But then I can't stand a sweet-tempered woman. Wouldn't want to waste my time trifling with one." He ran his knuckles over her smudged cheek. "We're going to be all right, you'll see."

She managed a nod and a smile. But she wasn't sure about anything anymore.

They walked in silence until he asked, "What was that you said about desire?"

Sissy shrugged. "I don't remember."

"Well," he said, steering her toward the Guest House, "maybe it'll come back to you." He slipped his arm around her waist.

BOURRÉE OPENED THE door of the bar where the stripper famous for twirling her tassels worked. He had his arm slung around her shoulder and his fingers were reaching for one of her famous tassels, when he saw something across the street. He pushed the stripper back into the bar.

"Bourrée, you bastard, what the hell do you think you're doing?"

He didn't bother to answer. He watched Sissy sashay down the sidewalk wrapped around that worn-out football player. So that's why the bitch stood him up. Bourrée's pale eyes narrowed. Spit formed at the cracked corner of his mouth. He always hated to see another man moving in on his property—past, present, or future.

*   *   *

THE NEXT MORNING the bellboy brought Sissy and Parker the Sunday *Times-Picayune* on a tray with their rolls and coffee. They read it naked in bed, their legs entwined in the crumpled sheets and each other. "This feels like home," he said.

"Not my home," said Sissy. Then on one of the back pages, she spotted something that just might be the answer to getting Clara that scholarship she'd promised her and getting Parker off the hook. She considered sharing it with him, but decided against it. Parker could be awfully high-minded. Rule Number Thirty-eight. *A smart girl never disillusions a high-minded man.* Besides, at that very moment he had an inspiration all his own, an inspiration that took Sissy's breath away and her mind off everything else.

SHE STOPPED IN Butlertown on her way home. If Clara's mother had been there she might have been able to talk some sense into the two young women. But she wasn't.

Sissy remembered Clara bragging about her grades in English. She inquired into Clara's essay writing skills, and upon learning she'd won every prize, Sissy showed her a contest she'd seen in back of the *Times-Picayune.* Clara was all for it. She would finally get back at her father for all those years of neglect. And when Sissy explained how they could use it to collect the money she needed for college, a dangerous light shone in Clara's eyes. "Is blackmail part of your Southern Belle's Handbook?"

"Why no," said Sissy, "but I'm sure I could make up a rule for a situation like this, when it's for a really good cause."

Clara assured Sissy she could have the essay ready by Labor Day, the official kickoff of Tibor's congressional campaign. Sissy suggested she also check out something her father had let slip about the lineage of the Great White Hope.

In the coming weeks, the parish librarian wondered why a colored girl would take such an interest in genealogy, but she was glad to help. She believed it was her Christian duty to eradicate ignorance wherever she found it. Besides, she liked Clara, a smart, sensible teenager and a credit to her race. When she heard the girl had won a big scholarship to a Yankee college, she took it on herself to break the rules and allowed her checkout privileges.

While Clara was following these intellectual pursuits, Sissy was following others, not nearly so mental, but much more pleasurable. Except for her alibi.

She'd always been terrified of dentists and needles and hadn't so much as had a checkup since her marriage. Now, to get out of the house every Saturday, she found herself forced to expiate the sin of adultery with long-overdue dental appointments. She had to show up, because Peewee paid attention to the bills.

Every Saturday morning, after checking Clara's progress with her research, she'd drive to New Orleans and creep into Dr. Cohen's big black dental chair and let him torture her. Then she'd drive out to the Airline Highway and meet Parker, who'd make her moan and writhe all afternoon. For Sissy, affairs of the heart were never easy.

Someone once said that the depth of love can only be measured by the sacrifices you're willing to make for it. Sissy was willing to make great sacrifices in pain, but she wasn't willing to admit it was for love. For her, love was standing in the rain on the running board of a truck and getting thrown into the mud.

She told Parker as much one afternoon, when he asked if she loved him. "I don't believe in it," she said. "What we have is an acute case of raging hormones. Pure and simple."

She would have shown him how acute, but he said, "You're probably right." Then he got up and went into the bathroom.

But in spite of her protestations, she lived for those Saturdays. All week she was in a frenzy of desire. She wallowed in it, reveled in it like New Year's confetti and Mardi Gras all rolled into one.

She discovered their cheap motel with its cement block walls lent a certain romantic squalor to their affair. She lightened her hair to red and picked up a set of trashy, black-lace underwear in the French Quarter that encouraged wild abandon in Parker and heightened her own sense of sin. Sin, Sissy believed, was hardly worth committing if it didn't produce a rush of naughty, wicked feelings.

But deep down, Sissy's true voice admitted it wasn't just the coming together of their bodies she cherished. It was the way he cared for her. The way he treated her, making her feel that she, Sissy, the high school dropout, might not be disposable after all. She might not be just a piece of trash that men wanted to paw over.

That's when she realized she hadn't thought about the Southern Belle's Handbook in a long time. She didn't need it with Parker. That she could be with a man and trust him to be good to her without having to manage or manipulate him was a whole new world for her.

One afternoon in late August, as she lay naked on those perspiration-soaked sheets, under Parker's big, hairy legs, she caught him looking at her, searching her face for the answer to what seemed like the most important question in the world. When she asked him about it, he just shook his head.

The next day, however, he began to make phone calls. As the summer rushed toward Labor Day, Parker discussed his future with old friends and Marine buddies all over the country. And when a man he'd fought side by side with in the Pacific told him he was building a subdivision outside of Boston, Parker told him, "Let me know if I can do anything for you." And then he said, after a long hesitation, "No, I've got nothing to keep me down here. Nothing at all."

Letting go is the best revenge. It frees your heart for much

more satisfying pursuits.

Rule Number One Hundred

THE SOUTHERN BELLE'S HANDBOOK

Chapter 18

LABOR DAY IN Gentry was usually celebrated with the same indifference as in the rest of the country, offering the men an excuse to get drunk with their buddies and offering their exhausted wives real hope that the long summer was ending and school would actually begin. But this year, since Gentry was the parish seat and their own D.A. was running for U.S. Congress, the Committee to Elect Tibor Thompson had turned the annual picnic into a virtual orgy of politicking, praying, and carnival rides.

Belle Cantrell sat in a folding chair in the shade high up on the riverbank, where the septuagenarian could oversee all the festivities. In the 1930s during one of her many spurts of self-improvement, she'd taken a WPA course in art history. The scene spread out before her reminded her of something. All these half-naked people, jumping around, pleasuring themselves, awakened a wavering recollection of a famous painting, but for the life of her, she couldn't remember which one.

On one side of the fairgrounds a traveling carnival was raking it in. Peewee sat Marilee on a giant bird and mounted a fish as children and parents scrambled onto gay ponies and camels before the calliope screamed and the merry-go-round began to turn.

Next to the carousel, teenagers clutched each other in libidinous delirium as they whirled around and around in fruit-colored spheres.

Belle searched her brain as she watched young men and women float up into the sky and back down in the colorful hanging baskets of the Ferris wheel. The painter was . . . God, she hated old age. She never used to forget anything.

An Irish marching band, wearing green suits and leprechaun hats, danced along the riverbank blowing their horns. Labor Day was almost as good an excuse as St. Pat's to get drunk and noisy. One of the marchers spotted Belle and stopped to share his flask with her.

Going the other way, dressed in maroon robes verging on red and singing "Onward Christian Soldiers," was Brother Junior Bodine's choir led by Sister Betty Ruth in virginal white. They were drumming up business for his tent show and revival meeting downriver. Sister Betty Ruth's singing faltered when she saw Belle take a swig from the flask. She licked her parched lips and for an instant wished she were an old lady sharing a drink with a friend instead of the Holy Willie she'd become. The instant passed. She renewed her hymn with added fervor, hoping God didn't read her heart continuously, but just tuned in from time to time.

In the river itself, half-naked people were swimming, splashing, and fondling one another. Miss Lucy, looking like an enormous peach in her salmon-colored bathing suit with its modest pleated skirt, waved merrily from the inner tube of a truck tire as she floated downstream. A towheaded boy tried to ride a swimming dog, who was growling and snapping to get him off his back. The painter had naked people carousing in giant fruit, floating in bubbles. His name was . . . on the tip of her tongue.

Then she saw Bourrée LeBlanc with a crew of Cajuns carrying

bundles of dried sticks and reeds and banners proclaiming A FREE AMERICA DEPENDS ON TIBOR THOMPSON. America's in deep shit, thought the old lady as Bourrée stopped to pay his respects. "Bour-rée, what in the world are you and those Cajuns up to?"

"Just helping out a friend, chère."

"You building bonfires in September?"

"Tibor's getting TV coverage all the way from Baton Rouge. Gotta give them something to cover."

"That a fact?" she asked. He nodded. "You two never did have the sense the good Lord gave oysters."

"If I was you, Belle, I'd climb on his bandwagon before it's too late." In back of him a bevy of Thompsonettes, in white shorts and skimpy T-shirts adorned with giant Ts, were tacking up signs, KEEP THE AMERICAN FAMILY PURE, VOTE FOR TIBOR.

"I'm not all that partial to his music," said the aging suffragist.

Bourrée laughed, and for a moment he remembered how fine she'd been all those years ago when he'd first hit Gentry, young and horny, and she was "the fascinating older woman."

Belle remembered, too. Eleven years hadn't seemed like much then. But time, that infernal sorcerer, had changed her from the beautiful lady into the old hag with a cane. Suddenly she remembered the painter and the painting: Hieronymus Bosch, *The Garden of Earthly Delights*. We're in the hell part, she thought as Sissy came up to them.

Sissy hadn't seen Bourrée since she stood him up in the French Quarter. She saw his lips turn into a sneer. Gotcha, she thought, but was surprised that she didn't feel much of anything. The thrill of revenge was gone.

"You all seen Uncle Tibor?"

"He'll be along tonight in time for his speech," Bourrée said. He appraised her freckled legs stretching out under her shorts and adjusted himself in his khakis.

Belle's eyes darted from one to the other. That dirty old man!

"Not till tonight?" Sissy was clearly disappointed.

"Why? You want to volunteer for something, chère?"

"I just might," Sissy said.

"Don't you dare," Belle said to both of them.

CHIP DROPPED SILENTLY from a tree onto the roof of the girl's bathhouse. He saw Sally Reinhold and Mary Beth O'Brien walk right in through the swinging doors, whispering to each other. He licked his lips. This is gonna be so neat! They were the prettiest girls in his class, especially Sally, with her mass of black curls. But where the hell was his brother? If he didn't get his ass in gear, it was gonna be too late.

Chip lifted his army-surplus field pack out of the tree and methodically laid out his equipment on the roof: rubber gloves so he wouldn't leave any fingerprints, a piece of garden hose, his chemistry funnel, a pickle jar half filled with ferrous sulfide, and two clothespins. He heard the girls giggling below him. He slipped on his rubber gloves. But where was Billy Joe? He had to get there before the girls left the bathhouse. He just had to!

Chip leaned over the back of the roof and pried open the louvers of the ventilation window. He couldn't see the girls. Good. They couldn't see him, either. Quietly, carefully, with a scientist's concentration, he stuck one end of the hose through the louvers into a dark corner of the window. And missed seeing his mother and Marilee enter the bathhouse.

He spotted Billy Joe running across the fairgrounds, a paper bag banging against his bare leg. He willed him to be careful! If the lid wasn't screwed on tight, the jar would fall right through the bag.

Inside the bathhouse, Sissy and Marilee stepped into a changing booth. Sissy leaned over to unbutton Marilee's jumper when she heard a loud thump on the roof. She looked up at the ceiling.

"Shhh!" Chip ordered Billy Joe, who had dropped from the tree limb. The boys froze and waited.

Inside, Sissy listened for a moment. Hearing nothing more, she slipped out of her blouse and shorts.

In the next booth, Sally and Mary Beth were trying on each other's bathing suits.

"Did you get it?" Chip whispered.

Billy Joe nodded and pulled a mayonnaise jar out of the paper bag. It contained a blue liquid. "It was in the toolshed in back of the pool, just like you said."

Chip grabbed it, unscrewed the lid, and sniffed. "This is gonna be so neat!"

"Nobody saw me." But Billy Joe looked worried.

Chip recognized the look. "They'll never miss this little bit. It's not like stealing."

Billy Joe nodded. "What's it like?"

"You're such a drag," said Chip. He poured the swimming pool acid into the pickle jar and shook it up.

Billy Joe hesitated. He didn't want to be a drag, but he just had to ask. "We can't hurt them, can we? I mean this stuff isn't dangerous, is it?"

"Billy Joe!" the big brother said in a threatening voice so the younger boy shut up. Chip couldn't be bothered with reading all that warning crap. "They'll be fine, as long as they get out fast enough."

INSIDE THE BATHHOUSE, Sissy was trying to shimmy into her tight green bathing suit, yanking up one side and then the other, as Marilee stepped into hers backward.

Chip poured the contents of the pickle jar into the funnel attached to the hose. And waited. He didn't have to wait long. The wooden bathhouse seemed to tremble and then naked and half-naked ladies poured out.

Billy Joe, hidden by a tree limb, peeked over the edge of the roof.

"This is so neat! This is really neat!" Then he turned back to his brother and said in an anxious voice, "They're coughing and wheezing!"

"Stop worrying," Chip said, handing him a clothespin and attaching another to his own nose as the putrid smell of rotten eggs drifted toward them.

Then he saw his twelve-year-old brother rock back and forth with excitement. "Look!" Billy Joe said, and his voice was almost reverent. Chip leaned over and saw Sally's beautiful buns sticking straight up in the air! She had run out with Mary Beth's bathing suit around her knees and was furiously pulling it up. Mary Beth ran out next wearing only the bottom of Sally's new bikini. Billy Joe grabbed his brother's arm. "Oh, my gosh. Mary Beth's boobs. Look at 'um! They aren't like torpedoes at all. They're squishy!" He lay on the roof and rolled on his back. "They bounce!"

Chip watched all that naked protoplasm jumping and jiggling and marveled that mere protein and fat would give him an erection. He touched his hand to it, purely in the interest of science, of course.

A scientist's job is to observe and measure. He made a mental note to find out the minimum number of naked girls he'd need to produce the same effect. Hidden in the tree, he touched it again, to assess its measurement. Big.

Then he saw his mother run out of the bathhouse, holding Marilee in her arms.

Sissy had her bathing suit on, but Marilee was completely naked, choking and crying hysterically. Belle arrived with a beach towel. She covered her weeping great-granddaughter and took her down to the river to wash her off as Sissy searched the bathhouse roof.

She couldn't see the faces peering out among the leaves, but she knew. "Chip!" she growled. "You get down here this minute!"

Two boy figures rolled off the other side of the roof and ran toward the carnival.

Oh, God, he's got Billy Joe. I should have known. "Your next stop is reform school, you all hear?" she called after them. But the boys weren't stopping.

BOURRÉE STOOD NEAR the side of the bathhouse, where he had the privileged view of the naked girls running out the front and the two boys rolling off the back. That boy of mine is a pistol, he thought with pride. Then he caught sight of Sissy and sauntered up to her.

Competition always excited him and Gentry's greatest, failed football star was the kind of competition he liked. He decided to invite Sissy for a drive in the woods, but when he approached, said, "Ouwee, woman, you smell just like a skunk in heat."

"Only you would know its mating scent," she said.

But Bourrée also knew Sissy would never allow herself to smell like a skunk, mating or otherwise. He watched her make a quick run to the top of the high bank and dive into the deep, dark waters of the river.

He picked up one of the inner tubes piled up on the bank and threw it to her. "Here you go, chère. See if you can swim downwind of the rest of us."

She made a quick obscene gesture.

He chuckled as he watched her float downstream, cradling the inner tube in her arms. Her cheek rested on the black rubber. Her red hair was spread out around her. He saw the river water lapping at her round butt in its green bathing suit, and he couldn't remember why he'd denied himself her favors all these years, especially since she'd always been so handy.

Sissy felt Bourrée's eyes on her and then forgot all about him as she floated down the warm, rolling waters of the swollen river. Aunt Ida May's Chihuahuas, Thunder and Lightning, raced along the bank, pulling tiny carts announcing the time of Tibor's speech.

The yipping dogs excited a great deal of attention. But Sissy knew if anyone was stupid enough to pet them, they'd bite.

Near her, a man had lashed up two inner tubes, one for himself and one for a case filled with beer, which he drank as quickly as he could, one after another. Empty beer cans followed him downstream like ducklings in the current. They bore silent tribute to his major accomplishment in this world, the ability to hold prodigious amounts of alcohol and live.

Sissy climbed into her inner tube and floated on her back. Overhead, graceful strands of Spanish moss waved to her. She closed her eyes and held her face to the sun. As she drifted along, she gave herself up to the dark water. It played gently with her hair and licked the soles of her feet.

She didn't see Bourrée's black Cadillac parked next to the bridge spanning the river. Nor did she see Bourrée standing on that bridge, waiting for her. She felt the shiver of a cold shadow only as she drifted under it.

"SISSY!" SHE FELT a hand hook her inner tube and jerk her toward the shore.

She opened her eyes. Bourrée was silhouetted upside down against the bright sky. For a brief moment, she saw him as she'd seen him all those years ago. He was in an inlet, hidden by bushes and moss-covered cypress trees from the rest of the river.

"What do you want?" she asked warily.

He turned her around, brushing her knee. He had kicked off his sandals and waded into the water. He was still wearing his green-and-red Hawaiian shirt printed with parrots. The river water darkened the material and stuck the parrots to his belly, but he still didn't take it off.

"You're smelling better."

"Not like a skunk in heat anymore?"

She lay before him as if on a platter, knees and chest in the air. He whispered, "Not like a skunk. We'll find out about the rest, won't we?" He ran his hand over her cold thigh.

"Cut it out, Bourrée." She pushed him away.

But he pulled her inner tube closer. "I'm giving you another chance, chère."

Sissy laughed. "You're what?"

"I'm giving you your last chance."

"Don't be ridiculous."

Bourrée's face became purple. He growled. "What's the matter, that clipped-dick football player of yours keeping you plugged up?" He clutched her thigh with one hand and drove his other hand up inside the crotch of her bathing suit.

"Stop it, damn you!" she yelled, and kicked him in his big stomach.

Bourrée grunted. His eyes went cold. He jerked her out of her inner tube. He was still a lot stronger than she was. "I'm getting tired of this, Sissy. You get your hot little butt into that car."

Sissy was incredulous. "Just like that?" She started to laugh again.

Bourrée seethed with rage. "Just like that." He squeezed and cut off the circulation in one of her arms.

"Let go of me, Bourrée, or I'll scream so loud those widows and orphans you've been stealing from all these years are going to hear me."

He grabbed her hair and pulled her against him. She could feel he was hard as he pressed his cold, wet belly against her. "You know you want it. You've been angling for it for years."

Sissy screamed and screamed again.

Picnickers deserted their fried chicken and potato salad and ran through the woods. Swimmers pressed against the current and floaters abandoned their inner tubes and converged on their inlet.

But all they saw was Sissy and Bourrée standing waist-deep in the river glaring at each other.

"False alarm, folks," Bourrée said in a jovial voice that barely masked his rage. "This little girl here thought she saw a water moccasin."

"I was wrong," said Sissy, not taking her eyes off him. "It was just your garden variety snake."

As Sissy floated downriver, away from the man who'd taken her innocence, the Hallelujah chorus went off in her head. She felt like a spellbound princess who'd finally broken free. Turning the tables on all those fairy tales, she'd shattered the enchantment by refusing to kiss the frog. Said, Don't be ridiculous. That was all it took: the courage to say no. Suddenly she had a giddy thought. Maybe those fairy tales were simply propaganda put out by aging frogs because princesses, real princesses, wouldn't have anything to do with them.

Sissy realized she'd wasted half her life on resentment and dreams of revenge—and, she had to admit, a mixed-up, crazy kind of longing for something she never really had. Real freedom comes from no longer caring.

Maybe that was what the religious people meant when they talked about forgiveness. Sissy had always thought they meant loving thy fellow bastard again. But now, she realized, it could mean just letting go. She turned that over in her mind.

Letting go is the best revenge. It frees your heart for much more satisfying pursuits.

Bourrée was neither wizard nor warlock nor tempting Satan. He wasn't even the incarnation of all that was wicked and wonderful. He was just a small-town philanderer, hiding his spreading girth beneath a ridiculous Hawaiian shirt, preying on the loneliness of women and the innocence of young girls.

She'd been gripping the inner tube, but now she let her hand trail in the water. She closed her eyes and drifted.

A hand touched hers. "Thinking about me?" Parker was swimming next to her.

"You're so stuck up, Parker Davidson," she said, looking at him from the corner of her eye. "What makes you think I was thinking of you?"

"You were smiling."

They floated downstream side by side, not touching, but she felt his nearness in the ebb and flow of the water. As the current carried them away from the fairgrounds, the river became deserted and the sounds of celebration died out. They listened to the lapping of the water and the music of the birds frolicking in the branches above them.

"Let him kiss me with kisses of his mouth, For his love is better than wine . . ." Betty Ruth's voice, sweet and clear, reached them as they drifted toward Brother Junior's tent.

Parker pulled up under the bridge that led to the revival meeting. "Come on, we have to talk."

He helped her out of her inner tube and guided her up the bank, deep into the pine, sycamore, and swamp maples.

"I sat under his shadow with great delight, and his fruit was sweet to my taste," sang Betty Ruth.

Parker led Sissy to a leafy sanctuary, lit by dappled gold and green sunlight. The dark scent of wildflowers rose around them from the mossy ground. The music from the revival meeting hushed. "No one will disturb us here," he said, taking her chin in his hand. He was studying her face as if trying to memorize it.

"What?" Sissy asked. Instead of answering he kissed her gently.

She checked out the overhanging branches and dense underbrush. Reassured they were sheltered from the eyes of anyone who might happen to be standing around the revival tent or crossing the bridge, Sissy slid her wet arms around Parker's cold back and traced a scar that crossed his shoulder to his heart. She'd never felt such tenderness for him before.

The only way they could be seen was through a small gap between the foliage and the bridge. And then only by someone walking along the path on the deserted side of the river. However, that's where Amy Lou Hopper happened to be.

A smile of pure malicious pleasure spread over her face. She'd been waiting for this all summer. She didn't pause to see what would happen next. With the tails of her man's shirt flapping over her blue jeans, she strode up the riverbank to find Peewee.

SISSY KISSED A broad scar on Parker's wet chest and again felt the lightness. Now that she was no longer nurturing revenge, all sorts of possibilities began to unfold in the hitherto obscure recesses of her heart. "What did you want to tell me?"

"I have to leave town."

AMY LOU FOUND Peewee with a couple of buddies, building one of the giant bonfires scheduled to be lit along the river that evening to kick off Tibor's campaign for Congress.

"I've got something to show you." She made her voice sound mournful, but she was licking her lips.

"What?" asked Peewee, who'd been tossing down Dixies and wondering how long Sissy's "headaches" were going to last. He wasn't all that anxious to give up the comfort of his buddies and the ice chest filled with beer.

"You'll see." Amy Lou pulled him up and hooked his arm in hers. He offered no more resistance because she squeezed his bare arm right up against her magnificent prow.

SISSY EXTRACTED HERSELF from Parker. Now that he'd "had his way with her," as the Southern Belle's Handbook would say, he was leaving! She shivered in the soft breeze.

She wasn't listening when he told her about a Marine buddy who was building a large subdivision outside of Boston. "He thinks his foreman is stealing from him. He's gonna try to convince his partners to let me take over, run the whole job. He knows I can handle it." But all she heard was he was leaving her. She knew he'd never wanted to get tied down, so she should have expected it. She was just a pit stop on the racetrack of his life, after all.

"It's a great opportunity and there's nothing for me here."

"Go, by all means," Sissy said, but she couldn't hide the bitterness in her voice. "You'd be a fool to hang around here another minute. You're right. There's nothing for you here."

PEEWEE STUMBLED. IT wasn't easy to keep up with Amy Lou. He thought about how comforting it would be to sit down right here and lay his head on that pillowed breast. "What's the rush?"

"You'll see," she said as she forged ahead.

PARKER TRIED TO explain. "I can't spend my life playing 'the other man' to Peewee LeBlanc. How do you think it makes me feel, only *allowed* to see you on Saturday afternoons?"

Sissy loved those afternoons. They were completely outside of reality, pure and unsullied by the drudgery of life. They should be perfect for a man who doesn't want to be tied down. Oh, what the hell, you can't hold a man who doesn't want to be held. That sounded like a rule for the handbook. Well, he won't catch me begging. "I guess it's time for you to move on. Things were getting pretty boring, weren't they?"

He shuddered as if he'd received a blow, but he kept his voice casual. "Think you'll find someone else to stimulate—what did you call it—your raging hormones?"

"I guess," she said, leaning wearily against a cypress tree. And suddenly she was sick of pretending. "But I never did before."

"No kidding?"

She shrugged, too tired to answer.

"You mean you never cheated on Peewee?"

"You're the first, Parker." Her voice was flat. "I didn't tell you because I didn't want to scare you off."

He chuckled and the sound had none of the meanness of Bourrée's tight little snickers. It was soft and good to hear. He put his arm on the tree and leaned over her. "I think you love me, girl." She shook her head. But he persisted. "I think you loved me all the time, but about fourteen years ago, you just got distracted."

A glow rose up through her. She began to understand the lightness she'd felt. Her voice was weak and shaky. "It's possible, I guess."

He looked as if he wanted to dance and cheer and take her in his arms. Instead, something caught his eye. He stood back, and with a meaningful glance at Sissy, gave a nonchalant wave. Sissy turned as casually as she could and saw her husband and Amy Lou Hopper staring at her from across the river.

"Oh, Lord." She nodded and smiled weakly. And then to Parker: "I'd better go."

"Meet me somewhere. I won't know for sure about the job until about eight tonight."

"What?" He didn't know? And then she wondered if the whole job thing was just a ruse to make her admit her feelings. She wouldn't put it past him. Men!

"In back of the bandstand," she said, stepping onto the bridge. "And, Parker, I lied. I was never bored."

"Me neither," he said as he dove into the river.

AMY LOU COULD barely hide her disappointment at not catching them in the act. "Looks like you and Parker were having a real serious discussion."

"You have a problem with that, Amy Lou?" Sissy asked.

"Oh, my goodness no, I don't have a problem. Why should *I* have a problem?" Amy Lou eyed Peewee.

Peewee wished he were somewhere else. Anywhere else. It was bad enough that he had to find Sissy in the bushes with Parker, but it was humiliating to have Amy Lou carry on like this about it. Now if he didn't do something she'd think he was a wimp, and she'd never again press him to her wonderful prow. But what was a man supposed to do? He lowered his voice manfully and grabbed his wife by the arm. "What were you all doing?"

Sissy wrenched away from him. "Oh, for goodness sakes, Parker and I went to high school together. Can't I even talk to an old friend?"

"Well, yes," he said uncertainly.

He would have said more, but Sissy said, "Well, good," and strode off down the riverbank. She couldn't help it and it wasn't fair, but Peewee's touch made her skin crawl.

Chapter 19

SISSY CLIMBED UP on the bandstand where Ida May Thompson was overseeing the setting up of the speaker's platform. Even if Parker was chasing Clara, Sissy thought, she wouldn't let that stop her. She was going to do what was right and help that girl, no matter what. She kissed her aunt and asked nonchalantly, "Uncle Tibor here yet?"

"Oh, heavens, no," said Ida May, wiping her forehead with an immaculate lace handkerchief she kept in the breast pocket of her shirtwaist dress. "I don't expect him until it's time for his speech. He's going to make a real dramatic entrance," she confided with a little laugh.

That was not good news. Sissy had Clara's essay in her straw handbag and she wanted to present it to Tibor today, when he was feeling rich after his first full day on the campaign trail. Tibor took good care of his contributors, and he took their contributions in cash.

Then she had an inspired idea. Smiling her best flower-of-Southernwomanhood smile, she said, "I'd be proud to sit up here on the platform."

Ida May blinked. "I didn't think you all saw eye to eye."

"Well, I admit Uncle Tibor and I have had a few *ideological* differences, but family comes first, don't you think?" Ida May looked as if she didn't know what to think, so Sissy rushed on. "Being a Thompson and all, I want to show my support."

Ida May smiled graciously and said, "I think you'd better not, dear."

Sissy looked at her smelly shorts. She pressed down the collar of her white shirt and said, "I'll have plenty of time to run home and change. I'll put on my best Episcopalian dress, okay?" When it didn't look like it was going to be enough, Sissy added she'd wear a hat.

"It's real sweet of you to offer, honey, but we're going to be pretty crowded up here." Ida May handed her a program of the evening's festivities. Then she turned back to the Thompsonettes, who were positioning the American flag over a sign that read, A VOTE FOR THOMPSON IS A VOTE FOR PATRIOTISM.

Disgusted, Sissy left the platform and lit a cigarette. She started to chuck the program when something caught her eye and a tiny smile curled around her lips.

At the refreshment stand, she bought herself an orange Nehi and poured half of it out. Then she went over to where Belle Cantrell was watching Marilee and playing gin rummy with Felicity Fairchild, her oldest living friend. They were talking about the candidate and reminiscing about the old days when they expected that once women got the vote, they would naturally vote for each other. And that would mean an end to war and other assorted ills like inferior education and poor health care, which men seemed to think were not worth serious consideration.

Sissy opened her picnic basket and filled the pop bottle back up with Peewee's vodka. Belle looked up from her cards and wanted to know what she was doing. "Just getting a drink."

"What are you up to, Sissy?"

"Nothing."

"Belle, you sound just like your mother used to," her octogenarian partner said. "Let the girl have a drink."

"Thank you, Miss Felicity," Sissy said, watching her scoop up Belle's discard.

Belle peered at her granddaughter. "Nobody drinks vodka and orange pop."

"I wouldn't say that," said Sissy.

She heard a triumphant "Gin!" from Felicity and Belle's complaints about being taken advantage of. Sissy knew how much Belle hated to lose. She took after her.

SHE WALKED UP to the revival tent and stopped to chat a minute with the choir. Then she opened the tent flap and looked inside. Up at the pulpit Brother Junior was packing up. There was an angry energy in his movements. Betty Ruth stumbled around after him.

"I thought you'd be proud of me! It was my own composition." When she received no response, she continued, tears welling up in her eyes. "I was praising the Lord!"

"Singing filth from the pulpit?"

A tear coursed down Betty Ruth's cheek. "I took the words right out of the Bible. They're the words of the Lord."

"When you're on my pulpit you'll sing the words from this hymnal, you hear!" Brother Junior thumped a worn blue book. "My mission don't need no 'creativity.' " He said the word as if he were saying depravity.

"But those songs are so dull," Betty Ruth wailed.

He slammed the hymnal on the altar. His voice was low. "Are you gonna behave like a preacher's wife or the whore of Gentry High!"

A shocked inhalation of breath and then another wail. "Junior!"

"You're getting hysterical again," he said. Contempt dripped from his lips like molasses.

Betty Ruth reached into her large straw basket purse and pulled out a bottle of pills.

Brother Junior grabbed them out of her hand. "Pull yourself together. I won't have you embarrass me tonight." And with that, he strode out of the tent.

Betty Ruth sat down on the edge of the platform and gave vent to all the rage and shame that were galloping in tight confused circles around the paddock of her mind. She pulled a giant-sized bottle of Hadacol from her bag and began to open it when she saw someone walking down the center of the aisle.

"Here, you want some of this?"

Betty Ruth shrunk back, hiding the Hadacol, squinting through her tears.

"It's me, Sissy." When Betty Ruth still looked confused, she added, "Sissy Thompson."

"Sissy!" Betty Ruth screamed, jumping up, stumbling against her. "Is it really you?" She hugged her. "I haven't seen you in an age."

Sissy didn't correct her, she just offered her the pop bottle. Betty Ruth took a big swig and a look of pleasure deep and fervently desired came over her face. "This is what we used to drink in back of the football stadium during practice!"

"That's right."

And then a look of fear. "Did you put vodka in it?" she whispered.

"Of course."

Panic spread over Betty Ruth's face. "I took the pledge."

"Oh," said Sissy, as if she hadn't heard.

"I swore no liquor would ever pass my lips again."

"Well, God can't blame you if you didn't know." Betty Ruth didn't seem so sure of that, so Sissy continued, "He's not that mean, is He?"

The preacher's wife answered with the passion of a convert. "God is infinite in His grace."

"Well, there you are," said Sissy, and saw the shadow of the old Betty Ruth briefly cross her friend's face as she put the Hadacol back in her purse.

A few minutes later, the two women were splashing their feet in the river and talking over old times. "I never used to cry," Betty Ruth said. "Now, it's like that's all I do."

"Maybe you should go easy on that tonic."

"But I get so nervous." Betty Ruth eyed the Nehi.

"Here." Sissy handed her the bottle.

"I can't! Not now that I know what's in it," Betty Ruth wailed, taking out her Hadacol.

"How much alcohol does that stuff have?" Sissy asked, setting the Nehi down between them.

"That's different. It's a tonic."

Sissy took the Hadacol away from Betty Ruth. "It smells awful."

"Terrible." Betty Ruth giggled. "And it tastes worse, like cough syrup."

Sissy made a face.

Betty Ruth picked up the pop bottle and began to caress it absentmindedly in her hands. Then she held it to her nose and inhaled the smell of vodka. "Oh, Lord, this is tempting."

"I always said, *The good Lord wouldn't have made temptations so attractive if He didn't expect us to give in to them every now and then*." Rule Number Thirty-four, Sissy said to herself.

Betty Ruth giggled and inhaled again. "Junior would have a fit."

"Looks to me like he will anyway, so you might as well get some fun out of it."

"Sissy, you're terrible."

"Oh, come on, Betty Ruth. If you're good all the time, you miss all the drama of repentance and forgiveness."

"That's so true," said Betty Ruth, studying her friend with new interest. "I didn't know you and Peewee was religious."

Sissy held her tongue and watched what happened next. Betty Ruth licked the mouth of the bottle. Then she looked over at the tent, where the volunteers were working in the hot sun.

"They'll never know. Nobody drinks vodka with orange pop."

Betty Ruth bit her lip with anxious excitement. "You won't tell?"

"Did I ever?"

Lights long since extinguished sparkled in Betty Ruth's eyes. She took the bottle of Nehi and vodka and tipped it down her throat.

THE SUN HAD set and the carnival lights were all aglow when Hugh Thompson swung his old Ford into the fairgrounds parking lot for the official kickoff of his brother's campaign for United States Congress.

A poster flapping in the wind proclaimed, TIBOR THOMPSON FOR THE AMERICAN FAMILY. The candidate, white-haired and avuncular, smiled down on the crowd, displaying perfectly matched capped teeth. Hugh shook his head at his brother's cynicism. Why didn't he proclaim himself the Great White Hope and be done with it? But what Hugh hated most was not his brother's ruthless bid for power, nor even his racism, but his own complicity as editor-in-chief of the *Avenger* in not having the courage to point a finger at him and try to pull him down.

But was it cynicism, after all? Maybe Tibor had deluded himself into the belief that he was protecting the family, that he offered them the last bastion of the American way of life as they had known it as boys. It was a long time since the brothers had been able to talk.

Hugh had heard rumors that Tibor's first televised campaign foray was going to be like no other in the history of the parish, perhaps in the history of the country. But as he walked toward the bandstand, he was unprepared for the triumph of kitsch that awaited him.

The Gentry High School Marching Band playing "It's a Grand

Ole Flag" moved through the audience up the center aisle, led by eight drum majorettes in blue-and-white star-spangled T-shirts and little red-and-white-striped skirts, performing a synchronized Twirl of Fire. The audience went wild, especially those seated on the aisle as fingers of flame dropped into their laps.

As the drum majorettes mounted the steps, their flaming batons held in a final salute, Hugh whipped out his camera. He knew he was being manipulated, but he was a newspaperman. As soon as he got his shot the Gentry gymnasts cartwheeled onto the stage and formed a human pyramid between the blazing columns of batons.

Hugh moved in for a better angle.

Then an arc light switched on. He heard a roar in the sky. A twin-engined plane flew over and disgorged a female parachutist in a short cheerleading skirt with TIBOR THOMPSON emblazoned across her bottom.

Newspapermen snapped their shutters as television cameras whirred. Hugh saw that even the photographer for the New Orleans *Times-Picayune* couldn't resist the shot, and his paper was backing Tibor's opponent. The photographer was standing on a chair.

Caught in the arc lights, the plane ejected its passenger too soon, and instead of tracking her descent onto the top of the human pyramid in front of the American flag, the cameramen traced her descent right into the river.

The entire audience leaped to their feet and rushed down to the water's edge. At least half the men jumped in, pushing and shoving and pulling on the silk and cords until the parachutist, who was only in chest-deep water, started thrashing about, gasping for air.

The photographers were having a field day when Ida May pulled victory out of the jaws of debacle. "Make sure you get pictures of all our brave young men," she called, and cajoled until the heroes climbed out of the river to pose along with the parachutist, who had been lucky enough to survive each and every rescue attempt.

Hugh put a fresh roll of film into his camera with a sigh. The "heroes" posing on the riverbank would be so pleased to see their pictures in the paper and so grateful to Tibor for making this happen, they'd vote for him now if he proclaimed himself a Communist and buggered Joe McCarthy on national television.

Once everyone's picture had been taken, Ida May had the Thompsonettes move through the crowd handing out leaflets proclaiming Tibor's support of the embattled white Christian majority. The leaflets implied that only he could keep at bay the Negro Hordes who wanted to sully white schools and take away white rights.

Then the band played a patriotic tune and the audience went back to their seats. Hugh slipped into a folding chair next to Belle and Marilee.

"That was some spectacle," he said, shaking his head. "Where's Sissy?"

"Up to no good, I expect," Belle replied as Brother Junior's choir could be heard marching toward the risers across the back of the stage singing "Onward Christian Soldiers."

They were marching without Sister Betty Ruth. She was out on the riverbank, dancing among the unlit pyres, silhouetted against the moon. She was singing, too. But tonight her songs had nothing to do with the Words of the Lord.

Harlan Ratliff spotted her there. He'd played football with Parker and now owned a filling station out on Highway 51. Harlan didn't think much of politics or preaching, but he'd always thought a lot of Betty Ruth, who'd been kind enough to save him from the ignominy of graduating from Gentry High a virgin. He lent his baritone to her lovely voice and pretty soon the two of them were dancing together along the river's edge. Betty Ruth broke several vows that night, which cheered her up considerably and added whole subplots to the continuing drama of her life with Brother Junior.

*   *   *

"MARCHING AS TO war..." sang the choir as their bowed heads appeared above the risers. Hugh jumped up, camera ready, and then slunk back down into his seat as Marilee screamed with delight. Billy Joe and Chip slid in next to her.

Sissy, in Betty Ruth's hooded robe of virginal white, was leading the choir.

"What the hell's she up to?" Hugh asked Belle.

Belle shrugged. "Damned if I know, but I doubt she suddenly up and caught religion."

Sissy stood in the front of the others, singing just slightly off key. It was her first time in front of a crowd since her cheerleading days, and when she saw all those people looking up at her, she felt she'd finally come home. Unfortunately as she raised "the Cross of Jesus" above her head, she also raised her arms. Her robe, which was too small for her, exposed one long, freckled leg, bare, to the top of her shorts. Photographers sprang into action. The audience poked one another and clicked their tongues. Sissy was at it again. Hugh put his head in his hands. Chip got up to leave, but this time Billy Joe pulled him back. "Wait. You can't leave now." So Chip sat back down to see what would happen next.

As the singing died out, the audience turned to the sound of hoof-beats. The candidate had arrived on a white horse.

He was flanked by Bourrée, Peewee, and a bunch of the boys. They galloped around the crowd yelling and whooping, until Tibor left them and rode his milk-white steed up onto the bandstand to the cheers of the enthusiastic voters, who'd never seen anything like this campaign in their lives and weren't likely to see anything like it again.

The television crews, expecting the usual boring speeches from the usual boring candidates, were ecstatic as the candidate dismounted to the cheers of the multitude. A colorful congressman like Tibor would light up the evening news.

Brother Junior stepped up to the mike and gave a rousing invocation. He managed to link Tibor Thompson and the white race to Jesus Christ, while pointedly ignoring His association with the Jews.

Sissy moved down from the risers and stood in back of the candidate's chair, where she slipped him the essay for the *Times-Picayune* contest, "The Finest Man I've Ever Known."

Tibor, flushed with a day of speeches, applause, and fund-raising, whispered that it was mighty nice of her. He knew all about the contest and wished her luck.

"I didn't write it." Sissy surveyed the audience, nodding to a colored girl in a copy of Sissy's PTA dress. "Your daughter did."

At first Tibor looked confused. "I don't have a daughter, sugar." And then he saw the name on the cover. "It's a damned lie!" he whispered, his jaw clenched.

"Could be," agreed Sissy, smiling out at the crowd, "but she did a real good job of research."

By now Brother Bodine was prayed out and had ceded the mike to Hyram Goode, the president of an organization that presented the Vigilant Patriot Award to right-minded politicians. He was presenting one to Tibor. He began by working up the crowd with the news that the only thing that stood between them and the mongrelization of the races was Tibor Thompson.

As they cheered and applauded, Sissy pointed to the second page, where Clara had found that Tibor's great-grandfather was not the son of a poor but honest French girl, as he'd always claimed, but of his great-great-grandfather's quadroon mistress, who'd died in childbirth, giving the candidate quite a few drops of Negro blood. "Clara found out all about it right in the genealogy section of the Gentry public library. Isn't she amazing?" Sissy whispered. "She's gonna do real well at the University of Chicago, don't you think?"

Tibor accepted the applause of the crowd, but his smile was stuck across his capped teeth and his eyes had become slits. "What do you want?"

"Only that you take care of your daughter's education. She needs money for college," Sissy whispered.

Hyram was working the crowd with pleas to bring back "old-fashioned family values, which are so sadly missing in our fast-paced society."

Tibor looked out over the audience and waved. "How the hell can I do that without your aunt Ida May finding out?"

"Announce you're endowing a scholarship fund. She only needs four thousand dollars."

"Have you lost your mind, girl?"

"You endowed a white scholarship."

"Coloreds don't vote." His voice was gruff and coarse.

"But they write. In fact your daughter seems to have your gift for words."

Tibor was silent for a moment. He turned the essay over in his hands. "I'll see to it."

Sissy reached into her shorts and handed him a counter check from the Gentry Guaranty Bank.

"Don't push me, girl, I said I'd take care of it."

"When?"

"When I'm damned good and ready," he said, stuffing the essay into his pocket. They locked eyes. Combat was declared.

Hyram called for the candidate to come forward and accept the Vigilant Patriot Award. The applause was deafening. Sissy knew if she let the Vigilant Patriot get away, it was all over. So she walked right up behind him and whispered, "I have a carbon."

When the applause died down, Sissy stepped between the two men and reached for the mike. Hyram naturally gave it to her, attired as she was in a choir robe. The candidate smiled to the audience as he tried to wrest it from her, but Sissy held the mike in a death grip. He glared at her, teeth clenched, and jerked the mike. She let him pull her toward him and kissed him on the cheek. She heard a sprinkling of confused applause. She knew he could have her dragged away, but he wasn't likely to do that in front of all these reporters, who were bound to follow her for her story.

"Isn't my uncle Tibor something! Let's hear it for the Vigilant Patriot!" the ex-cheerleader yelled. The audience cheered in response, and the candidate let go of the mike.

She introduced herself as Tibor's niece and said she wanted to tell them about her uncle's newest charity—a scholarship fund for a deserving Negro student.

She glanced out at the audience. Her father had a frozen expression on his face, but next to him Belle was chuckling.

Sissy continued, "It's true my uncle, Tibor Thompson, wants to keep the races separate, but he's not a bigot."

She saw Tibor's eyes flick toward the sheriff, who responded by shifting his hand to his holster and stepping forward. So she quickly added, "My uncle's a good man." She paused for the dutiful applause. "He believes in separate education." More applause, this time with enthusiasm. "But equal education." She looked at him. He nodded stiffly. "And he believes in equality of opportunity. That's why he has personally endowed a four-thousand-dollar scholarship fund . . ." A gasp went up from the audience. ". . . for deserving colored students to help them get a college education."

Sissy paused again for the applause. It was scattered at first and then built and built. She was surprised she wasn't scared. Her cheeks were hot and she felt a wild rush of energy. She was elated. She wondered if she could run for office.

Then she saw her uncle's look and her knuckles turned white as she gripped the mike. "It's my pleasure to announce the winner of the first scholarship, Clara Conners."

The applause this time was perfunctory, hot in spots but most of the audience sat on their hands. It was one thing for the candidate to do a good deed. It was quite another for the colored recipient of his largesse to get up on the stage next to him.

Sissy spotted her family. Billy Joe and Marilee were applauding wildly for their mama. Hugh was applauding his daughter's courage, and Belle Cantrell was applauding a vision of herself as she wished she could have been.

"We did a pretty good job with our Sissy, didn't we?" she said to Hugh.

Chip slid down in his chair, deeply embarrassed. "She's making a damn fool of herself," he muttered, but nobody paid him any attention.

Hugh turned to his mother-in-law with an expression of courage she hadn't seen since he was a young man courting Cady. "What would you say if the *Avenger* ran a series on the genealogy of our leading citizens?"

"Including yours?"

"Starting with mine."

Belle peered at Hugh with new respect and patted him on the arm. "I'd say it's about time."

They turned back to the stage and watched Clara climb the steps. Billy Joe jumped up, clapping and whistling. Marilee jumped up next to him, cheering like mad.

Sissy handed the blank check to Tibor once again. He hesitated. The TV cameras whirled. He scribbled fast and handed it back to her. A television reporter yelled for her to let them get a picture.

Sissy held it high for the cameras. "Uppity women unite!" But of course she didn't say that out loud. And then saw the check was only for a thousand dollars. She'd hoped for four thousand, so she wouldn't have to keep coming back, but this would get Clara started.

Clara took the check and shook hands with the candidate.

"I hear you want to go to school with Yankees," said Tibor at his most avuncular.

"Yes, sir," said Clara, her voice trembling.

"Well, you have a real good time. And don't get too cold up there, you hear?" he said, playing to the audience.

Clara had planned to walk up to him, a tough, brilliant student, accepting no more than her due. While she was writing the essay, she'd run the scene over and over in her head. She'd get back at her father for all those years of abuse and neglect. She'd make him pay. And not just money. She had an acceptance speech written and memorized. It was filled with cutting innuendos, designed to make him squirm, but now that she was actually in his presence, all sorts of old feelings she hadn't felt since she was a little girl came back. And she choked up. All she could think of were three words. These she whispered in his ear.

"Louder," yelled the television soundmen. And, "Give her a mike." But instead the evening news would show a pretty colored girl standing on tiptoes, whispering something into the candidate's ear and then running off the stage.

"What did she say?" asked the *Times-Picayune* reporter. But Tibor just shook his head. The paper would report that whatever it was moved him. The candidate needed several minutes to recover for his speech.

The three words Clara had managed to whisper in Tibor's ear were "Thank you, Daddy."

Chapter 20

TIBOR ASSESSED THE applause as his daughter left the stage. Not so loud as for his Vigilant Patriot Award, but applause strong and clear. He was beginning to see how he could use this. Hell, a thousand dollars to keep the bigot bashers quiet, he could raise that in an afternoon. And it wouldn't hurt that he could tell his cronies that he was sending this smart-ass nigger up North so she could pester the Yankees.

But what he couldn't stand was having Hugh's daughter get the better of him. He scrutinized his niece. If she had the nerve to do this, what would she do next time? He couldn't let her get away with it. He'd spent months planning every detail of his campaign kickoff and the little slut waltzed in and ruined it. He'd get her. The opportunity would present itself. It always did. Nobody got the better of Tibor Thompson. But he couldn't think about that tonight.

Tonight he was off and running. He leaped out of the starting gate protecting the embattled rights of Americans of European descent and rounded the first turn calling on them to relight the Fires of Freedom.

On cue the bonfires all along the riverbank burst into flame. His audience went wild—they stood and cheered.

Bourrée's Cajuns had covered the wooden pyres with the dried detritus of the cane fields, so the flames crackled and sparks shot from the conflagrations like rockets into the hot night air. Just like Christmas when bonfires were lit all along the levee. The audience loved it. And more important, the TV cameras loved it. Tibor knew he was running on a crowded track and he wanted to be sure he got plenty of TV coverage. That's where the voters were nowadays. And nothing looked better on TV than a fire. Might even get national coverage.

Tibor's ambitions were not limited to the U.S. Congress. He had plans to take over the state. Become another Huey Long. And then? He'd confided to his closest advisers, if the niggers keep on agitating, who knows how far a country boy can go.

PARKER, STANDING IN the shadow of the trees in back of the platform, watched Sissy melt into the crowd and then slip down the rickety back stairs, lifting the hem of her choir robe to her knees. Her hair was wild and blowing in the hot wind.

He went to her and brushed it back from her face. "That was a damn fool thing to do."

"You think so?"

"Yeah, and brave as hell." In back of her, sparks were shooting off a crackling bonfire into the night sky. They glittered around her head like a halo. He'd never seen her so beautiful. "I have good news." She was completely still, waiting. "The job in Boston came through."

"You're not going to take it, are you?" He heard a note of desperation in her voice.

"I don't have a choice, honey. I was fired."

"Calvin Merkin fired you!"

"Rowena Weaver and a delegation of church ladies stormed into his office and carried on about moral turpitude. I guess you and I just can't get together without getting into trouble." He saw her face drain of color. She shook her head as if trying to deny what he said. "It doesn't make any difference. I'll be making big money now. I can take care of you."

"Me?"

"I want to take you with me. I thought you knew that."

Sissy stood perfectly still. "How was I supposed to know that? I thought you'd gotten tired of me."

"Girl, I'm not letting you go." He took her arm and led her away from the crowd. He felt the nearness of her body.

When she spoke again, her voice wavered. "What about my children?"

"Bring them. They'll be our children," he said.

"And Peewee?"

He paused for a moment and then said, "Don't bring him."

Sissy didn't smile.

They walked down toward the river where the bonfires leaped and sparked against the night sky. He had to explain, make her understand. But Parker had never been a salesman, he'd never talked anyone into doing anything. He'd never had to. Especially not women. They'd always wanted him. Except Sissy. But Sissy was the only one he wanted, the only one he'd ever wanted. He knew the next few moments would be the most important ones in his life.

For once he wanted to say something romantic, even poetic. As they walked downhill in silence, he tried to rehearse. I want to build a house for you. He did, but he couldn't just say that. Where was the poetry? He had to think of something more persuasive. If a man finds a woman he can love for as many years as I've loved you, it's like he's been given a gift from God. Ugh. He couldn't say that. Suppose she laughed. But he couldn't let her go again. Not back to the toad.

They stood on the edge of a broad beach. Their feet sank into the deep sand. He could smell the soft fragrance of wood smoke as the bonfires blazed in the distance along the riverbank. She turned to him. Her face glowed in the dancing firelight, her red hair tumbled over her forehead, and the wind pushed it over her cheek. It was now or never. "Say yes," he said.

"You want me to just pick up my kids and run off and live in sin with you in Boston?"

"I want to marry you, Sissy. Haven't you figured that out?"

She shook her head. "Marriage is the root of all suffering."

"How do you know? You've never been married to me." And then he began to talk. Sissy listened as words spilled out of his mouth and swirled around them in the wind. He'd be making big money. He'd take care of them all. Build them a house. In a few years they'd be able to travel. Finally he got to the romantic part. He'd never wanted to be tied down to anyone else, because of her. That's why he'd been so wild and free. And Sissy realized he'd come back for her. He loved her. He'd always loved her.

A warmth swept over her. She felt it pulsating though her body. She wanted to bathe in it. Stop it! The Voice of Reason ordered her. Think! You've got to stop feeling and think.

A dark cloud of smoke from the bonfires along the wooded banks whirled up and covered the moon.

Think. She willed herself to go numb with the same numbness she'd experienced when she'd first heard her mother had died. Think. Don't feel. Sissy took refuge inside a crystal dome. She had to get her thoughts together. After a moment, she lifted it a crack to test what was coming at her as Parker talked. A warm excitement enveloped her. She was loved and wanted! He thought she was special. Not some piece of trash, but special. Then she heard the voice of her conscience: you can't do this to Peewee. You tricked him into marrying you. You can't take his kids away from him now. She remembered him jumping into the gravel pit to save Marilee. His pride introducing Billy Joe to Parker as his son. His look of gratitude when she took up for him in front of Bourrée. What would he do without her? She thought about the way Peewee looked at his father's table. His mute suffering, like a rabbit trapped in a hunter's headlight. She couldn't abandon him. She'd taken a vow, for better or for worse. And she'd broken it. She'd been unfaithful, but she hadn't deserted him. She hadn't made him suffer. Not ever. She pulled the dome down firmly. But a tiny echo bounced around in the crystal and whispered, if she didn't go with Parker and he left her, she'd have nothing to get up for in the morning.

"What do you say?" he asked.

Sirens wailed in the distance. She didn't answer.

"They want me to leave tomorrow."

"No!" she heard herself scream. She saw flames from other bonfires shooting up through the trees.

"They need me right away or not at all." He looked into her eyes and came as close to begging as he ever had in his life. "Come with me, Sissy. Dammit, you know I'm the man you should have married."

The dry wind whipped around her. She wanted to go with him. She would go with him, but what about Peewee! The acrid smell of smoke filled her nostrils, choking her. She was in turmoil. How do you make a decision like this? "Call me tomorrow."

"My phone's already turned off." Then he hesitated and added, "And yours is tapped."

"What?" She moved away from him and heard the rattling of dry leaves on her crystal shell.

"They've been listening to us all summer." He grinned. "We're a public disgrace."

Sissy felt smothered. What was she doing in this little town? She had to go with Parker. Then she saw Peewee's face. "I'll tell you tomorrow."

"Where?"

She just shook her head.

Parker cast about for a place to meet. "They're showing my house."

"The Paradise. Nobody'll be there in the morning."

"Ten o'clock. Okay?"

"Okay."

"But, Sissy, if your answer is no, don't . . ." He hesitated. "Don't show up."

"Parker . . ."

He just shook his head. "I'll wait until ten-thirty."

Before she could say anything Harlan and Betty Ruth ran out of the woods straightening their clothes. Harlan was furious. "That damn politician set the forest on fire."

Betty Ruth was happy and more rational than she'd been in years. Harlan had convinced her the fire was in no way retribution for her sins. "It was Tibor Thompson, not the devil," she told Sissy, laughing.

Suddenly, they were surrounded by firemen stringing hoses, distributing buckets and shovels to any able-bodied men they could find. They told Sissy and Betty Ruth to go up to the parking lot with the other women and children. Betty Ruth turned to go, but before Sissy could join her, Peewee and Bourrée, still on horseback, rode up together.

Sissy saw Bourrée squint his cool blue eyes at Parker. She remembered the afternoon he shot a neighbor's dog for sniffing around his breeding stock. He looked the same way now. He watched his son to see what he would do.

But Sissy knew Peewee wouldn't do anything. Pity swept over her. It was bad enough finding her in the woods with Parker again, but finding her here in front of Bourrée meant months, years of humiliation. She had never meant to humiliate him. She saw his lip quiver. His eyes looked at her like the eyes of a whipped puppy. He opened his mouth, but nothing came out. And then Parker came gracefully to his rescue.

"Hey, Peewee, Mr. LeBlanc. Glad you're here. The fire department needs volunteers." He handed Peewee a shovel. "Sissy offered her services, but I've been trying to convince her that a forest fire's no place for a lady."

"He's right. Your place is with Belle and the children," said Peewee. He sounded so grateful to Parker for rescuing him in the eyes of his father.

But Bourrée snorted and curled his lip. "What service was you offering this time, Sissy?"

As he spoke, Sissy heard in his voice the bitterness she'd nursed for him all these years. She'd passed it on to him. A strange sense of elation came over her. A giddiness of power. But she pushed down those feelings. She knew how dangerous he could be. She said with injured innocence of a Southern belle, "Why, Bourrée, whatever are you talking about?"

Parker looked as if he wanted to knock Bourrée off his horse, but he contained himself with throwing him a bucket and hitting him directly in the stomach.

Bourrée's nostrils flared. His horse reared up. Parker stood his ground. The two men had recognized each other. War was declared.

Sissy knew she had to get out of there or hostilities would erupt. She lifted the hem of her choir robe and climbed the railroad ties leading to the parking lot.

She turned at the first landing and saw flames shoot out of the trees. The horses whinnied and reared. Peewee's horse took off before he could get hold of the reins, galloping out of control away from the fire, down the riverbank. Bourrée watched and then with cold resignation pulled his horse around and galloped after him.

Smoke blew out of the woods and engulfed her. At first she couldn't see the river and then she couldn't even see the beach. The birds screamed as they flew madly overhead. The underbrush trembled with scampering, shrieking animals.

Sissy ran up the steps, stumbling on the hem of her robe. The live oaks and pine trees crackled in the heat. A long finger of Spanish moss burst into flame, blocking her path. Burning leaves and moss swirled around her face in the wind.

She turned coughing, gasping for breath. Her eyes burned and teared, blinding her. She ran back down the steps, when suddenly a strand of flaming moss dropped onto her choir robe.

In seconds, she could smell the cheap synthetic fabric ignite. She screamed and tried to pull the choir robe off. But the hook that held the vestment tightly around her neck was stuck. She grasped the collar in both hands and pulled at her throat. She was flailing, tearing at the robe, when she smelled the awful stench of burning hair. Her hair.

She fell to the ground, thrashing about. But the dry pine needles beneath her ignited and Sissy found herself rolling in a bed of flame. Hysteria seized her throat and choked her.

Strong arms reached through the flames. Parker lifted her out of the burning bed of pine needles and ran with her to the sand.

He was coughing as he turned her over onto her stomach. She felt him beat on her back with his bare hands. He ripped through the choir robe and tore the burning garment away from the collar.

His shirt began to smolder, but he ignored it as he rolled her over in the sand, picked her up and ran with her, stumbling across the deep, broad beach until he finally reached the water.

After the first shock, the cold water eased the pain between her shoulders and comforted her. She began to breathe again. She opened his shirt to see if he'd been burned. But his chest was all right. She could feel the sand and ashes float away from her scalp. The river was washing them clean. He held her with the cold water rolling around them. Then she saw his hands. They were black and swollen. He was so worried about her, he hadn't noticed.

"I've got to find my children!"

A fireman told them a first-aid station was set up in the parking lot.

The air was filled with suffocating smoke and the screams of fire trucks arriving from all over the parish.

*   *   *

HUGH HAD RUN down to the river with his camera to cover the fire for the newspaper, but Belle, Marilee, and Billy Joe were waiting together in the parking lot. Chip was standing by the road in deep conversation with an older boy wearing motorcycle boots who had a comb sticking out of the back pocket of his jeans. Sissy's oldest son glanced up to see his mother soaking wet, her hair and clothes burned, appear out of the smoke. Then he quickly turned back to his conversation.

"Mama!" called Billy Joe, running to her, followed by Marilee. "We were so worried!"

"What happened?" the little girl asked, trying to wrap her arms around her mother, but Sissy gently pushed her away and took her hand.

Parker followed Sissy up the path.

Dr. Moore took Sissy into the first-aid tent and told Parker to stick around. He wanted to look at his hands. Parker assured him he wasn't going anywhere.

Billy Joe paced nervously in front of the entrance to the first aid tent, his face shut down, worried. Marilee paced with him. Belle watched them.

Feeling his hands throb, Parker bent down to get some ice out of a cooler. Marilee sat next to him and began talking about her dog. Parker listened attentively, hunkering back on his heels, rubbing ice between his hands, as the little girl spun out a very long-winded story. He told her he was proud that she took such good care of her dog and Marilee just swelled with pride.

Then Hugh came up from the river, blackened by soot and out of breath. The fire had been contained and there were no more injuries. Peewee and Bourrée were fine. They were staying to help the firemen mop up. He told Belle to go home. The smoke wasn't doing her lungs any good. He'd take care of Sissy and the children. Belle said she'd check on her granddaughter in the morning.

As soon as Sissy came out of the first-aid tent, her back bandaged from her shoulders to her waist and a light sheet thrown over her shoulders, Parker went to her.

"I'll drive you and the children home."

"No, I'll be okay. I want him to look at your hands."

"Sissy . . ."

"Parker, I can see you now," Dr. Moore said.

But Parker ignored him. "How do you feel?" he asked her.

"I'll survive. Go on, now."

Parker turned to Dr. Moore, who assured him that Sissy had suffered only first-degree burns thanks to his quick action. "Now let me see those hands."

"Go on," Sissy said.

"Tomorrow?" he asked.

She hesitated and, giving him a noncommittal nod, gathered up her children. Parker watched as Hugh drove them out of the parking lot in Sissy's red convertible before he turned back to the doctor.

SISSY PUT MARILEE to bed and took a pain pill. She told Billy Joe to stop worrying. "The best thing you can do to help me is for you and Chip to go to bed." He kissed her gingerly on the cheek and went into his room, where Chip was carefully setting out his test tubes for the next day. Sissy lay down and fell asleep flat on her stomach as soon as she hit the pillow. She woke up at 2 A.M., her back throbbing. In her head, all of her voices were holding a convention.

She'd had very little experience making big decisions, wrenching her life out of its grove and sending it careening off into the unknown, so she didn't know that her head wouldn't be much use. She had to listen to the quiet wisdom of the heart. But even if she'd known, she couldn't have heard it. The voices of her head were working overtime.

Think! You can't break up your family just because you have

feelings for Parker, her Practical Voice said. You can't take your children out of school, away from their friends, and leave their father over a feeling.

But, sputtered another quieter voice, even if the feeling's love?

And then the Voice of Fear stepped in. For a month you and Parker were wallowing in forbidden love. Forbidden love is easy. So's unrequited love. Intimacy's hard. You think this "love" can survive it? Do you really believe you'll feel the same after months, not to mention years of close contact? Look around and name all the happy couples you know. Sissy couldn't honestly name one. Keep the memory. Cherish it, but stick with Peewee. The Voice of Fear won out. Sissy decided she couldn't risk it.

Besides, added the Voice of Guilt, think about Peewee. Think how he'll suffer. She remembered how his lip had quivered when he saw her with Parker. She didn't have the heart to hurt him.

He'll get along without you. Better. Came a whisper. Stop thinking about his lip and remember how he looked chugging after Amy Lou.

Give me a break! said the Voice of Guilt. You don't believe that.

Sure I do, said the whisper. I'm not be-all and end-all. If I stay, he'll never have a chance to feel really loved. He deserves that chance, doesn't he?

Yes! said Sissy's true voice, at last. And so do I! I can't let Parker leave without me. I'm going to Boston! Having made her decision, Sissy dozed off. Half an hour later she woke up again.

Miss Practicality was screaming, or was it the Voice of Fear? What makes you think Parker will stick around? For the last fourteen years the man's done nothing but run from responsibility. What happens if he leaves you in Boston with three little children after you burn all your bridges? You can't risk it. You've got to think about your children. You don't even have a high school diploma.

As soon as Sissy made up her mind, the chattering would begin and she'd make her mind up all over again. You have a duty, chatter, chatter, chatter. But what about me, don't I count? Chatter, chatter, chatter. What about Peewee? I've already humiliated him. Chatter, chatter, chatter. What about Parker? What about his suffering? How will he feel if I reject him twice? She remembered his face at the Christmas dance when she told him she was going steady with Peewee. She remembered his face when she told him marriage was the root of all suffering and he said, How do you know? You've never been married to me. Maybe happiness was possible, after all. For both of them. Conversations got stuck in her head and replayed again and again, like a broken record.

She finally fell asleep again. Around five, she woke up in screaming pain. Peewee, reeking of beer he'd drunk with the firemen, was climbing over her burned and bandaged back, trying to get inside her. He'd decided the time had come to assert his marital rights.

Never marry a man who makes your skin crawl.

Rule Number One Hundred and Three, a late addition to
THE SOUTHERN BELLE'S HANDBOOK

Chapter 21

"GET OFF ME!" Sissy tried to push him away, but she was on her stomach and vulnerable. He held on like some little animal. "You're hurting me." He didn't seem to care. He rubbed against her. "For God's sake, Peewee, you're pulling off my bandages!" Her skin was raw and burned where he touched her. "Stop it!"

"What's the matter? You'd rather fuck Parker Davidson in the woods?" He was in her now and pumping, his full weight pressing on her back. She was in agony.

"You're going to learn to treat me like a man!"

"Get off, damn you!" She gave him a jab with her elbow. She tried to scratch him, kick him, anything. But he was on top of her back and she was helpless. She tried to roll over, to roll him off her, but he wouldn't let her. She tried to slip out from under him, but he grabbed her by her shoulders. She started to scream. That's when he pushed her head into the down pillow.

"You're going to learn some respect!" he growled.

"It's over, Peewee!" But the words came out muffled as he stuffed another pillow over her head and held it down. Now Sissy was fighting to breathe.

He kept on grunting and rubbing, grunting and rubbing. Then he grunted one final time and came inside her. He gave a contented sigh and rolled over. She crawled out of bed and headed for the bathroom, her bandages flapping.

Sissy stood at the sink looking at herself in the mirror. She felt violated, abused. Hell, she felt raped. Except she knew the law said a woman couldn't be raped by her husband. Well, dammit, she felt raped all the same! She felt the way she'd felt all those years ago when Bourrée had shoved her against the oak tree. Only this was worse, because she was already so bruised. How could he do that to her? What was it with the LeBlanc men? She had to get her sons out of there.

She had to get herself out of there.

She filled a douche bag with water and vinegar. She was not a piece of trash. She was not the kind of girl a man can treat any way he wanted. She would not be the kind of girl a man could abuse. She would clerk in the five-and-dime, she'd wait tables in a diner, but she would never, never let a man treat her like this again.

Peewee hit the door. This time it swung open. "What are you doing?" he asked as if she were merely having a fit of pique over an everyday marital squabble. Then he saw the bandages flapping, pulled off. Saw the red, burned skin in the bathroom light. "You okay?"

Her eyes narrowed. Her face was haunted and determined. "Get out, Peewee. Get the hell out of here!"

Then he realized she was getting ready to wash him out of her. He slammed the door, swearing, threw on his clothes, and left the house without breakfast.

SISSY SAT AT her dressing table in her slip, staring at herself in the mirror. Her back was throbbing. She felt like a piece of raw meat

somebody had used a meat mallet on. It was nine-thirty. Her grandmother should be here any minute to take the children. She had to
get herself ready. She wanted to be at the Paradise at ten o'clock
sharp.

The morning was breathless. The air was so hot and still that
dust kicked up by passing cars hung suspended over the road and
floated through her open window where it clung to her lips. She
reached up and began to take out the bobby pins. What was left of
her hair sprang free like little coiled snakes. But the movement of
her arms intensified the throbbing in her back. She leaned into the
mirror and stared at herself. She took a deep breath and heard her
true voice. *It's not falling in love that makes a girl come of age. Any
snit can fall in love and usually does. What makes you a woman is
working up the courage to take your life into your own hands.* She
thought about that for a moment. *The courage to take your life into
your own hands.* She ran it through the Southern Belle's Handbook,
which was evolving in her mind. She decided it deserved to be Rule
Number One, taking precedent over anything she'd assigned to that
place. And *A smart girl can't just sit on the porch and wait for her
life to start*, would move up to Number Two.

"I've sat around Gentry long enough," she said out loud and
thought about Parker. They'd be together in half an hour. Her
whole life would change today.

The phone rang. Her heart skipped. Parker said he wouldn't call.
Had something happened? Oh God, please don't let him change his
mind now!

She gingerly slipped into a light cotton wrapper, ran into the living room, and grabbed the phone. But it wasn't Parker on the line,
it was Clara thanking her, telling her the check had cleared. She had
the money.

"I'm so glad you called. Are you at the chemical plant?"

"No."

"Thank goodness. I need to talk. Can you come over?"

"Sissy, I . . ." Clara began, but Sissy cut her off.

"I can't talk on the phone. You can spare a couple of minutes, can't you?" Sissy hated to plead, but she didn't have anyone else to talk to.

"I can't," Clara wailed.

Sissy fought the ignoble feeling that Clara was being damned ungrateful. But she told herself you can't give a person something and hold it over her for life. Still, she'd put herself on the line for Clara only last night.

"Uh-oh, Sissy, I have to go. They're loading my bus right now."

"What are you doing at the bus station? I thought you wanted to work for another week."

"I did. But Mama said after what we pulled off last night, I had to get out of town right away. Just a minute!" Clara called to the bus driver. Then she spoke quickly into the phone. "Sissy, be careful. Don't let my daddy get you."

"What can he do to me?"

"I don't know, but, please, take care of yourself."

Sissy hung up with a sense of foreboding of that unnamed fear we all carry around with us. Well, she wouldn't give in to it. She knew her uncle was furious, but he wouldn't do anything to her, would he?

She heard Bill Haley and His Comets singing "Rock Around the Clock." Deafening music had been blasting from the boys' room, all morning.

After the prank with the stink bomb, Peewee had grounded the boys for life. Sissy thought it wasn't quite fair to Billy Joe, but in Chip's case it wasn't nearly long enough.

She heard laughter. How many boys were in there? She checked the clock in the bedroom. Nine forty-five. Already? God, she was running late, but everything takes so much longer when you're in pain. Where was her grandmother? She ought to see if the children were ready.

She went into the hall outside the boys' bedroom and smelled something sweet. She pushed on the door, but the little darlings had blocked it. She started to knock and then changed her mind.

Quietly, barefooted, tying the wrapper around her, she slipped out of the house and around the veranda, where she caught a neighborhood boy, a couple of years older than Chip, wearing motorcycle boots, with a comb sticking out of the back pocket of his jeans, sliding the window open. When he saw her he lit out across the street and down the block. What was he so guilty about?

Sissy hurried up to the long window. The shade was pulled down. Giggles. That smell . . .

Sissy carefully stepped through the window. The room was stifling. Chip was bending over the gas heater, pouring some powders into a bubbling beaker. Marilee and Billy Joe were sprawled out facedown on the bed. One boy was lying on the floor, a second was bending over the beaker greedily inhaling the sweet gas, and a third was sitting next to it with a stupid look on his face and a straw up his nose.

Sissy ran to the bed and shook her children. Billy Joe opened his eyes and braced for trouble. Marilee giggled and lay down again.

Sissy didn't know much about drugs, but she knew what alcohol could do. If this was worse, she'd be damned if she'd let it get a hold on her children. She grabbed Billy Joe's baseball bat, and ignoring the pain in her back, advanced on the heater. Chip shielded it with his body.

"I didn't buy you a chemistry set so you could drug the neighborhood!"

"It's just nitrous oxide," he cried.

Sissy didn't know what that was and she didn't care. She could see the effect it had on the children. Looking like one of the Furies, her hair wild and snaky, she turned to the neighborhood boys and yelled, "Now, git."

The children fell all over each other shoving the dresser away from the door.

Then she turned to her own children. "Go on out to the front porch and wait for Grandma Belle, you hear."

Marilee and Billy Joe nodded, and lit out after the other children.

"I'd advise you go with them," Sissy said to her oldest child. The sweetish smell permeated her nostrils, making her feel giddy.

"To hell with you," Chip said, lunging at her, trying to grab the bat. But she was too fast. Pushing him aside, she shattered the beaker against the wall.

Then turning to Chip's desk, where his chemicals were carefully laid out, she swung the bat back. "Noooo!" Chip shrieked, knocking her against the wall. Suddenly Sissy was swimming in a sea of pain.

A smile formed on Chip's lips. He grabbed at the bat and kicked out, trying to trip her, but she managed to hold on. Chip yelled and slugged his mother twice in the stomach.

Sissy folded. Pain was everywhere. That's when Billy Joe vaulted back into the room and smashed into his brother. "You gone crazy? That's our mama!"

Chip howled like a wild animal and rolled onto the floor under his brother's pummeling. Chip hit, kicked, scratched, anything to get Billy Joe off. But Billy Joe, though smaller, held on.

Sissy choked down her pain and swung the bat. A jumble of colored chemicals streaked the wall. Acid ate into the linoleum as the record exchanger dropped a new record on the turntable and Dean Martin crooned "Memories Are Made of This."

Chip wrenched out of his brother's grasp. He jackknifed up, ran to his desk, and hunched over it, grieving. He turned to his mother, his blue eyes cold as the grave. "Bitch!" he hissed.

"My God, what's going on?" Belle Cantrell stood in the doorway, her arm wrapped protectively around Marilee.

"World War III," said Sissy, not taking her eyes off Chip, the bat held high in case he came at her again.

"Now, sugar, you just calm down, you hear, and put down the baseball bat. Just put it down," Belle said. She wrapped her other arm around Billy Joe. "I understand how they can get to you. But I realized long ago that children are sent to us to be an affliction."

Sissy turned, looked at her grandmother, and let out a little hacking laugh. Still holding the bat, she let it rest on the floor. "Affliction, hell, this kid's a one-man plague."

"Fuck you!"

"Chip!" But he was past listening. He shot out the window. "Chip, you come back. You hear me!"

Chip climbed the old magnolia tree, stepping on the big white flowers his mother loved to float in bowls. He'd get that bitch and make her pay. He didn't care what happened to him as long as she got what was coming to her and got it today.

The heat and the laughing gas made his head pound. Sweat poured off him, but he didn't answer when his mother and his great-grandmother called.

He saw them walking around the yard with Marilee and Billy Joe. Saw Sissy kneel in front of his sister. Belle and the children stayed outside when Sissy went back into the house.

He slipped down the tree and sneaked into the side door of the garage. It was a little cooler in here. Then he heard the bitch walking across the gravel. He slammed down the hood of the convertible and hid.

"Chip!" He saw her silhouette, black, in the open door. Fats, sugar, and proteins, the boy reminded himself, that's all she is, a blob of fats, sugar, and proteins.

"Chip, we have to talk!" the blob said and walked into the garage. "Look at me, son, I'm not your enemy, but I can't let you run wild. And I sure can't let you hit me. Come on out . . ."

He ran past her, forcing her to jump back or he'd have smashed her into the wall. He climbed into the magnolia tree and then crawled along the roof to his eavesdropper's refuge outside his mother's open window and heard her talking. "They say there are no bad children, just bad parents."

His great-grandma scoffed. "You notice, they never seem to give us credit when the boy turns out all right. Just once I'd like to hear them say, there are no great men, only great mothers."

And then he heard his own mother say those terrible words: "I think he knows I didn't want him."

He didn't hear what they said after that. He didn't need to. He didn't want her, either. Didn't need her anymore. He'd be better off without her. His father wouldn't pry into his life, interfere with the progress of science. He thought of his chemistry set shattered on the floor, the chemicals running down the wall. His blue eyes narrowed into Bourrée's icy stare.

He was still hiding when his great-grandma backed out of the driveway with Billy Joe and Marilee on the seat beside her. Ed Sullivan, his head out the back window, was drooling down the side of the car. He saw his mother, all dressed up, lean into the driver's side.

The clock on the dashboard said ten-fifteen. She was late already, but Parker said he'd wait until ten-thirty.

"Would you mind taking them to see Dr. Moore before you go out to the farm?"

"Sugar, there's nothing wrong with these two that a couple of hours of fresh country air won't fix."

Billy Joe was tickling his sister. "Make him stop, Grandma!"

Belle turned around and gave her great-grandson a look Sissy remembered all too well. Without a word, Billy Joe sat up and put his hands under his thighs.

They looked all right. "I'd still feel better if the doctor listened to their chests, just in case," Sissy said.

"Okay, I don't want you to worry. You have enough on your mind. I'll swing by right now."

"I wish I could get Chip over there."

Belle shook her head sympathetically. She knew what it was to be a mother, not that Cally had given her any trouble. "The boy's just like his father. You've got to face it. He's going to do what he wants."

"I don't know what I did that made him that way."

"You didn't do anything. Look at these two perfect people in the back." Billy Joe and Marilee sat up proudly.

"You heard her, Mama, I'm perfect!" said Billy Joe.

Sissy put her head into the back window and gave them both a kiss.

"Now go on," said Belle. "It's after ten. You don't want him to leave without seeing you."

Sissy watched her grandmother turn down Church Street and speed away toward Dr. Moore's office.

Then Chip saw his mother cross to the garage. He heard the convertible door slam and the starter motor complain. And complain again. He smiled Bourrée's tight little smile as he tossed the distributor cap from hand to hand.

Sissy ran inside, pulled out the phone book, and dialed the Paradise. The line was busy. She tried again, drumming her broken fingernails on the pecan table. Then she ran outside.

Chip was still in the tree when his mother came out of the house. He watched her walk quickly down the blistering sidewalk. He saw her ankles wobble in her high-heeled sandals. He hoped the pavement burned her toes. From his vantage point he watched her cross Church Street and head up Hope.

Sissy stepped off the curb with difficulty. Muscles she didn't know she had ached. The Paradise was five and a half long country blocks away. It only took a minute to drive there. She checked her watch. Ten-twenty. She'd make it on foot, if she kept up the pace. But every time her stiletto heel hit the pavement a jolt of pain shot through her back. And the sun was bearing down on her.

She stepped up onto the sidewalk and into the shade of a giant live oak in front of the Rubinsteins' big antebellum house with its white columns and picket fence. Mrs. Rubinstein was playing "*Nessun Dorma*" on the piano. Sissy wanted to stand there and catch her breath, but she didn't have time.

When she was halfway down the block, Chip shot across the street and hid behind the live oak. He was a spy on a mission and the enemy was his mother.

PARKER LOOKED AT the clock over the bar. Ten twenty-two. She'd be there. He was sure of it. She had to be. There was still plenty of time. He'd awakened at four-thirty that morning, worrying about whether he was cut out for a settled life with a ready-made family. What kind of husband would he make day in and day out? What kind of father? Well, he was about to find out. In a few hours he and Sissy and her kids would be together and for the rest of their lives. It was terrifying.

By nine, in spite of the bandages around his palms and on the fingers of his right hand, he was packed and ready to go. He had left Sid in the yard. He'd swing by and pick him up on his way out of town. At nine-thirty he was in front of the Paradise, waiting for the place to open.

"You sure I can't do something for you?" asked Rosalie, polishing the bar. He moved his stool so he could watch the door.

IDA MAY THOMPSON was carefully cutting flowers in the front yard of her pretentious house built of new brick, white trim, and enough Doric columns to hold up the Parthenon in its heyday, when she spotted Sissy all dressed up trotting down the sidewalk in the middle of the morning. Gathering her flowers to her ample breast, Ida May hurried up the stairs and into the house, and banged the door behind her. She was sending a message to that no-account niece of her husband. Sissy didn't get the message. She was too busy concentrating on putting one foot in front of the other as fast as she could, but the pain and the heat were slowing her down.

As she crossed Education Drive, Chip hid behind that same magnolia tree that Clara had crawled into when she was six. Its leaves
were brown and twisted with blight now, but it still provided ample
cover for a spy.

Sissy checked her watch. Ten twenty-four and she had four and a
half more blocks to cover and only six minutes to do it in. Across
the street was the red-brick high school, where she and her girl-
friends had planned their Junior Prom, where she'd been chosen
head cheerleader, and where she'd cheered Parker on to glory. She
began to run as she'd run then, but each jarring step on the broken
pavement sent sharp pains through her feet and legs and into her
back. She had to slow down. She thought she heard someone in tennis shoes running behind her but she didn't look. She couldn't look;
she didn't have time to turn around, not now.

"CAN I GET you something, Parker?" Rosalie asked.

"I'm fine," he replied, but he wasn't fine. She should be here by
now, it was ten twenty-eight.

SISSY WAS PASSING Brother Junior Bodine's white clapboard
Church of Everlasting Redemption. Music spilled out through the
open window, music so jazzy that at first Sissy didn't realize it was
the opening strains of "Nearer My God to Thee." And then she
heard Betty Ruth Bodine's clear voice belting out the words. Betty
Ruth sounded more upbeat and assured than Sissy had heard her in
years. Then the music became all twisted in "Heartbreak Hotel," as
the black hearse filled with teenagers roared by.

As soon as it was past, she hurried across Commerce Street. She
turned around at the corner and thought she saw a shadow dart in
back of the church. Was someone following her?

"Chip, is that you?"

Nothing. It was ten thirty-two. She didn't have time to worry about it. She hastened down the sidewalk lined with little one-story cottages. Her back was burning with pain as her toes in her little strappy sandals hit the searing pavement. Across the street was the old parish cemetery where her brother Norman was buried, next to her mother. The crape myrtle shading their graves spread its pink blossoms over them. She felt a pang of guilt. She hadn't visited them all summer. She promised herself she'd take the children there before she left with Parker. If Parker hadn't left already. She looked at her watch. It was ten thirty-three. Oh God, let him stay a little longer. Please let him wait for me.

CHIP FOLLOWED HIS mother along the street, hopping fences, hiding behind the wash flapping on the lines. He watched her go into a fit of coughing and slow down. He noted with satisfaction the dark circles spreading under her arms.

She began to wheeze. A stitch of pain dug into her side. What if he's gone already? He wouldn't leave before I got there, said her Voice of Hope. But what if he does? He'd said he had to leave today. If he thought I'd stood him up, he'd be gone and I'd have no way of reaching him. Then a thought, like a cloud she was trying to banish, hung over her no matter how fast she walked. If he's gone, what do I do with my life?

THE PARADISE WAS cool but Parker wasn't. He checked the clock. Ten-forty. A bottle of JAX was going flat in front of him. Untouched. A sick feeling spread over him. Sissy had suckered him. Again. She was staying with the toad.

"Something wrong with your beer, Parker?" Rosalie asked.

He raised the bottle to his lips. The liquor tasted sour. The minute hand on the wall clock clicked over to ten forty-one. Sissy wasn't coming. Okay, he could handle that. He was out of here.

But first, he'd give her a call at home. Maybe her burns were worse than the doctor thought. Maybe she couldn't leave the house.

RED ROSES CLIMBED over a picket fence, filling the street with their fragrance. As Sissy neared the open gate the roses shivered and dropped their pedals. A chicken stumbled out onto the sidewalk. It gyrated in front of her, blocking her way, spraying some kind of dark liquid. Sissy jumped back and saw the chicken's head was cut off. The dark liquid was its own blood.

A Negro cook ran out of the yard. "I hope you didn't git no blood on that pretty green dress of yours," she said, catching the bird. "Lemme have a look."

But Sissy had already started to run around the corner into Progress Street. She still had two and a half blocks to go. Her heels made clicking and scraping noises on the burning cement.

Parker put down the phone and went back to the bar. "Sure I can't get you something else?" Rosalie asked.

"No, thanks." He threw her a dollar. Before she could make change he was out the door.

The sunlight blinded him.

BUT NOT CHIP, who caught sight of Parker, a block and a half away, leaving the bar, turning away from them, and heading for his car. Then Chip saw his mother pick up speed, run out into Commerce Street, dodging trucks and cars and Gentry's lone taxi as Parker opened the door of his MG. He saw the big man get into the convertible and start the engine.

"Parker!"

Chip knew the man couldn't hear his mother over the roar of the engine. He saw Parker turn and start to back up and then jam on the brakes. Saw him leave his car half out in the street, vault out of the MG, and run to her. And he saw them go into the bar together. Chip smiled. Knowledge is power, all right.

He dashed back to the house and into his room, where he snaked under the bed and pulled out a box. On the outside was a picture of his chemistry set, on the inside was the yellow sundress with the creosote handprint that his mother had thrown in the trash at the beginning of the summer. The dress he had sneaked outside in the middle of the night to collect for just such a target of opportunity.

PARKER HELD HER chair. The bar was dark. The aroma of bourbon and Coke filled her nostrils. The air conditioner beat a soft drum solo. They were both strangely shy. She had already asked him about his hands. He had already inquired about her back.

"I must look a sight," she said, raising a fluttering hand to her hair.

"Yeah." He pulled up a chair so close their thighs touched.

CHIP PEDALED AT top speed. The box with the dress was in his basket. He dropped his bike in front of the old brick courthouse that filled a whole block on Grand Street between Church and Education. He went inside, looking for his father.

PARKER LEANED TOWARD Sissy and touched her hair. His heart was pounding in time with the air conditioner. "I was afraid you wouldn't come," he said.

"I'm not fool enough to let you get away from me again," she said. Her eyes shone and caressed him.

Parker touched Sissy's cheek with his fingertip. "You're sure, now?"

"I'm sure," said Sissy, surprised at how sure she was. She took a deep breath and all the chains that had wrapped up her existence burst. She was finally free. "It's time I had a life. And I want to spend it with you."

Parker let out a whoop and opened his arms. Sissy moved toward them. They were her home.

Parker, careful of her bandaged back, pulled her onto his lap, just as Peewee came through the door.

OUTSIDE, CHIP LEANED against the wall, under the wooden overhang. He'd tried to squeeze in behind his father, but Peewee had pushed him out. Sharp fumes of bourbon and Coca-Cola filtered through the door.

He felt anxious. What if his daddy didn't do anything? It would be just like him. The boy paced back and forth in the shadows. He thought about his chemicals running down the wall. He needed someone on his side. Someone with some gumption.

He ran around the corner to Grand Street looking for his grandfather and found him, just as he thought he would, at Thompson Campaign Headquarters with the candidate, watching the Thompsonettes paint campaign signs.

The candidate took him into his private office, where Chip told Tibor and Bourrée everything. And as his mother had predicted, he saw no reason to stick to the truth. "They was fucking right there in the kitchen, Pawpaw, standing up!" Chip saw his grandfather's eyes become slits. "This is where he was feeling her up!" The boy held up the yellow sundress. He gave it to the men so they could touch the creosote handprint.

"In front of her children," said the future congressman and defender of the family.

"When?" asked Bourrée. His voice sounded constricted.

"Just about every morning. Soon as Daddy left for work, they'd be going at it."

"Corrupting the morals of her own children," said the candidate, shaking his head.

Bourrée's face shut down. That's why she stood him up in New Orleans and humiliated him in the river yesterday. "A woman like that don't deserve to live."

When Peewee entered the Paradise, the blast of sunlight from the open door burned into Sissy's vision. All she saw was Peewee's shadow. She jumped up and felt Parker stand up behind her.

Her heart was loud in her ears. She was afraid Peewee would find some way to stop her. And then she saw his chin tremble. "Peewee . . ." Even after what he'd done to her the night before, she still hated to see him suffer.

Beads of sweat dripped into Peewee's eyes. He wiped a tar-stained hand across his forehead, and Sissy remembered how many times those dirty hands had touched her and her skin crawled at the memory.

"We were gonna tell you, Peewee," Parker said.

Peewee looked like he wanted to jump the bigger man, knock him down, but he checked himself and made an ugly sound that had a *k* and a *y* in it.

Rosalie, behind the bar, handed him a drink. "On the house, Peewee." He picked it up and looked straight into Parker's picture in his high school football uniform, framed above the bar. Peewee gulped the bourbon and Coke and slammed down the glass. It slid across the bar out of control. Without another word or even looking back at them, he walked out the door.

"Oh God, Parker, I didn't mean for it to happen like that," Sissy said.

"I know."

And then she thought about Peewee grabbing her shoulders, stuffing a pillow over her face as he crawled over her tender back, bruising her skin, rutting and grunting. "But I can't go back to him."

* * *

PEEWEE CAREENED OUT of the darkness into the sunlight.

Chip was waiting for him in front of a neon sign that said PARA-DISE LOST and DIXIE BEER. "You see 'em?" he asked with the excitement of a boy who knows the right answer. But Peewee just stared at his feet and shook his head. The blacktop, hot and bubbling, rose to his throat. It bubbled up out of his mouth and boiled in his stomach. He was drowning in it. He wondered why he bothered to go to work in the morning.

"It's like I told you, right? Am I right?" Chip asked, hopping.

Hot tears of shame trickled from Peewee's eyes. He heard a mean little snort. He raised his head and saw Chip had Bourrée with him.

Tibor had been waylaid by some voters at the corner of Grand and Progress. He slapped one on the shoulder and shook hands with another, but he was keeping his eye on Bourrée and Peewee in front of the bar on Progress Street.

Bourrée looked at this sniveling son of his, and something mean rose up inside him. It was like with a cockroach. It don't bite, but you stepped on it all the same. People said they spread disease. But in his entire life, Bourrée had never heard of anybody catching cockroach fever. No. He knew better. You stepped on a cockroach to hear the shell crackle under your boot. "Stop blubbering, boy. For once in your life act like a man."

"She cheated on me, Daddy."

"Pitiful," Bourrée said under his breath. "What'd you expect? You married the town pump."

"You take that back!" Peewee's voice was high and out of control. "Before we got married, she swore to me she'd never slept with Parker Davidson. And she never went with anybody else before me. Not steady. And her daddy was real strict." His voice trailed off. The pavement quivered with mirages.

Bourrée eyed his son with contempt. It was time the boy faced facts. He reached into his pocket, pulled out a quarter, and gave it to Chip. "Run around the corner and get me a newspaper."

"Awww, Pawpaw!" Chip whined.

Bourrée knew the boy didn't want to miss a minute of the drama he'd launched. "You do as I say." And then he leaned down as if to a conspirator. "I don't expect no change."

The teenager sped off, passing Tibor, heading toward the bar.

When Bourrée figured Chip was out of earshot, he turned back to Peewee. "Fine boy," he said.

"Do you know something about my wife that I ought to know?" Peewee strained to make his voice strong and manly, but it quivered like the sidewalk.

"Only that you sure as hell wasn't the first."

Tibor came up behind Peewee and laid a comforting hand on his shoulder.

Bourrée savored the moment. It had always stuck in his craw that another man claimed to be the father of one of his sons. Of course, he'd realized how convenient it was at the time. But times change. "Now, I don't know about these other kids of yours, but I was the one that stuck that first baby into her belly."

"You goddamn liar!" Peewee screamed, and tried to punch his father in the stomach, but Tibor grabbed his arms from behind and held them.

"Now, you just calm down, you hear me!" the D.A. said.

Bourrée breathed into his son's face. "What do you think I was doing out in the woods that year you was whining to go duck hunting? Playing with my dogs? When did you start diddling her? Count the months, boy."

Peewee let out a sharp cry and began to shake. "Chip was premature!"

Bourrée and Tibor exchanged amused looks. "Mighty big preemie," Bourrée said. Peewee looked like he wanted to kill his father.

Bourrée just stared his son down until he crumpled and Tibor let him go.

Bourrée adjusted his white shirt, remembering how Sissy looked lying there in her short, little cheerleader skirt, her legs covered with goose bumps, her panties pulled halfway down. And how she felt all young and tight when he crawled on top of her. "Now she's giving it away to that clipped-dick in the bar." He should have drowned the bitch yesterday.

Bourrée saw the rings spread under his son's arms. He could smell the sour sweat of rage. Bourrée remembered the bucket Parker had thrown at him. Total war. "At least you could take care of that mutt that's sniffing around under her skirt."

"Do what you have to, Peewee. No jury in the parish would convict a man for standing up for his rights," the district attorney said. "Hell, I don't believe you'd even be indicted."

Bourrée watched the D.A. take Peewee aside and walk him down the street. He saw him pat the younger man on the back and send him across the tracks to Rubinstein's.

SISSY GRABBED HER purse and tossed in her cigarettes. "Let's get out of here," she said. But as she headed for the door her ankles wobbled in her high-heeled sandals and she stumbled against a scarred wooden table.

Parker helped her to a chair. "I'm okay," she protested, "really." But she didn't try to get up. The nervous energy that had propelled her through her pain all morning had deserted her. She looked up at Parker and said, "Give me a minute, okay?"

Parker smiled until the corners of his brown eyes crinkled. "You can have the rest of my life." He brought her a bourbon and Coke over a glass filled with cracked ice.

*   *   *

PEEWEE WALKED PAST Rubinstein's windows jammed with pressure cookers and lawn mowers. A rifle hung on a rack in the back of the display. But all Peewee saw was his own reflection.

He walked into the sporting goods department, where Buster was standing around, talking to the salesclerks. He pulled up his belt, which had slipped below his belly, and said, "Hey, Peewee, gonna do some duck hunting this year?"

"I expect so," said Peewee.

"How can I help you?" Buster stepped behind the oak display case and took out a key. He helped Peewee to a Smith and Wesson .38 Chief's Special and a box of cartridges. He put the sale on Peewee's bill.

Peewee loaded the pistol and stepped out into the street. The heat suffocated him. The bourbon beat a tom-tom in his brain. She'd stolen everything. Even his own father. His heart pounded in his temples and his feet felt heavy, but the excitement of a loaded gun in his hand drove him on.

OUT IN THE country, the *Panama Limited* hurtled down the Illinois Central tracks, heading for Chicago.

Sissy heard its early rumblings in the bar and tried to stand. Rosalie made an ice pack and wrapped it in a bar towel. Parker held it to Sissy's burning neck.

"Rest for a minute," he said. "You've had a hell of a time."

RED LIGHTS FLASHED and the railroad warning bell clanged. Peewee stepped onto the tracks anyway. He felt them tremble, heard the train coming in, but he didn't pay any attention. His glasses were so fogged up he couldn't see. He took them off with his left hand and rubbed them on his shirt. He thought about his wife sitting on that clipped-dick's lap and his face twisted at the memory.

"We were gonna tell you, Peewee." He picked up his step. The railroad gates closed behind him. The *Panama Limited* shot through the intersection and screamed.

Sissy felt the cold water from the towel filled with cracked ice drip down her back, wetting her bandage as Parker rubbed it over her neck, under her hairline. "I want you and the children out of there, today."

"Oh, Parker . . ." she began.

"I'll pack you all up."

Sissy sighed. She was so exhausted.

"There's nothing left for you there except to torture one another. How many more days of your life you gonna devote to that project?"

She reached for his hand. "Thank you."

"You mean it?" His voice was eager.

"I can't sleep there another night," she said, stroking the fingers of his right hand.

He bent over and gently kissed her hair. "I love you, you know."

Sissy looked up at him. "I know." She took the ice pack away. She thought about sleeping all night next to Parker, waking up with their legs entwined. She thought about them traveling together, seeing all those places he'd told her about. She wouldn't let him feel worthless or doubt himself ever again. She'd help him build whatever life he wanted, in Boston or Timbuktu.

He sat across from her and brushed her cheek. "Say it."

She shook her head. She'd never told any man she loved him.

"You can say it, Sissy."

She looked into those deep brown eyes and a shiver of excitement went through her. She realized she was finally a woman. She was taking her life into her own hands.

"Say it," he whispered.

But she never did, because at that moment Peewee came back into the bar with a half-cocked revolver in his hand.

Parker jumped up, knocking over his chair.

"Size don't count for nothing now, you fucking Jew!" Peewee raised the gun.

Sissy saw Rosalie duck behind the bar.

Parker tried to push Sissy behind him, but she was fed up with men fighting over her.

"Now, just stay cool, sugar, I'll handle this," she said. Her heart was pounding as she faced down that greasy black pistol. She knew it was Peewee's first real hold on power, but she placed her body between the two of them anyway and held out her hand to her husband. "Give me the gun, Peewee. You don't want to shoot anybody."

There was an urgency in her voice and fear, but Peewee didn't hear. The blood was pumping in his ears. He hadn't heard a word she'd said since she'd called Parker sugar.

He saw that long freckled hand and thought about all she'd taken from him, all she'd done to him. He wiped his left hand on his pants, but he couldn't wipe his right and it was sweating so badly he could hardly hold the pistol. He looked at his wife cool and pretty and aimed at her face.

A blast of hot air hit him.

Bourrée stepped through the door behind the lovers. He couldn't resist checking out what was going on. He smelled his son's sweat from across the room. Saw his hand tremble. Pitiful.

Peewee glanced up as his father moved past the targets. Their eyes met. The air conditioner pounded.

Bourrée's nostrils flared with contempt. The master puppeteer willed his son to get on with it.

And Peewee obeyed.

The shot ripped a hole though the rest of their lives.

> *You can't change the past, but a smart girl won't let that*
>
> *stop her.*
>
> Rule Number One Hundred and One
>
> THE SOUTHERN BELLE'S HANDBOOK

Epilogue

MARILEE TRIED TO help her mother down the stairs. "You don't have to treat me like a cripple," Sissy said, pulling away from her briskly.

"You were faking, weren't you?" Marilee asked. "You just wanted a chance to sit on your old porch for a while, didn't you?"

"I told you. When you get to be my age, doing what you want is the only thing you have time for. Now, hurry up. We don't want to be late for the senator."

MARILEE TURNED THE corner onto Hope Street. The Rubinsteins' big antebellum house had been torn down. A stucco apartment block with aluminum-clad windows took up most of the lot. Tibor's pretentious brick monstrosity with all its Doric columns was still standing, but the big magnolia tree where Clara had once hidden was gone. The old high school was gone too, with its pilasters and curlicues and engraving of "*Mens sana in corpore sano.*" In its place was a two-story glass and cement building that would be at home in any suburb of Los Angeles. Sissy sort of missed the old school, which had housed so many of her memories, but was sure that the students she saw with their backpacks and baggy clothes pouring out of the classrooms, released early for the victory celebration, undoubtedly preferred air conditioning.

Brother Junior Bodine's white clapboard Church of Everlasting Redemption had been replaced by a glass and stucco structure with a soaring roof and a huge cross that caught the sun as it reached to the heavens. "Looks like a lot of people have been real successful finding Everlasting Redemption," Sissy said.

Marilee didn't say anything. She was still pissed at her mother and concentrated on getting them to the fairgrounds.

Sissy looked to her right at the cemetery. She could see the crape myrtle tree over the graves of her mother, father, brother, and grandmother. "Honey . . ." she started.

"We don't have time to visit dead people, Mama. The live ones need us right now."

Sissy laughed. "Sometimes you sound just like me."

Marilee couldn't suppress a smile. "Sometimes you drive me crazy."

"I know, sugar, that's a mother's job."

Marilee laughed and, shaking her head, picked up her cell phone.

THE SENATOR WAS late.

Sissy, standing by the side of the stage, looked around at the fairgrounds and thought about how it had changed over the years. The river had cut into it and a lot of the trees were gone to make way for "improvements."

Where Belle Cantrell had set up a folding chair in the shade was now a sun-bleached Little League field. A cement slab had been poured in front of the stage, with metal chairs set into it. They made clacking noises as people scrambled to find a seat, because there were not nearly enough to accommodate all those who had come to celebrate one of their own in the United States Senate.

No one was swimming in the river on this crisp autumn day. And there were no Irish marching bands in leprechaun hats nor maroon-robed choirs singing "Onward Christian Soldiers," but there was a piano onstage and the high school band was setting up next to it, scraping chairs and making anticipatory toots. Sissy looked at those shiny-faced boys and girls in their purple and gold uniforms and suddenly it came over her that at least half of them were black, as were the voters sitting in the metal chairs and standing behind them.

Then she saw him, coming from the parking lot. He waved as he hurried toward her. Sissy felt that little leap in her heart that she always felt when they'd been apart for a few days. She watched him move stiffly around the crowd. The easy grace he'd once had was gone and the dark brown hair was now gray, but he had the same strong features, high cheekbones, and prominent nose. In a couple of minutes he was with her.

"I was afraid I wouldn't make it in time," Parker said, bending over her to give her a kiss.

WHEN PEEWEE GLANCED up and saw his father enter the Paradise, he saw Bourrée's nostrils flare, saw that familiar look of contempt, and at that moment, he must have realized that killing Sissy and Parker wouldn't be enough. Not nearly enough. Sissy hadn't made his whole life a misery. And Parker was an afterthought.

It was his father who'd raised him in the sink of humiliation and laughed about it. Peewee's hand shook as he pressed his finger against the trigger. The squeeze was such a little thing. Just the fleeting pressure of the forefinger of his right hand was all it took.

Bourrée was thrown back into the wall. His head cracked the knotty pine paneling. The holes in the wood dripped blood as he slid to the floor. A roar rolled out of his mouth and his breath became shallow.

Peewee traced his fall with the barrel of his revolver. "It's all your fault!" he screamed and this time his hand didn't shake.

Parker pushed Sissy to the floor and rushed Peewee. If he'd had a knife or a broken bottle or a blunt instrument, Parker could have taken it from him. Easy. But Peewee had a.38 Chief's Special, and he got off a second shot that hit Parker, but didn't stop him. His third shot hit the ceiling as the ex–football player tackled him, knocking the revolver out of his sweat-slick hand. It scuttled across the floor into a table as Parker slammed Peewee into the bar and knocked him to the floor. Sissy heard the crack of a bone breaking and heard Peewee scream.

She grabbed the gun and, as Bourrée had taught her all those years ago, quickly emptied out the chambers. There'd be no more shooting today, she vowed, pocketing the shells.

She heard Rosalie calling for an ambulance. Then she saw Bourrée groaning on the floor. She thought about going to him. Instead she reached for Parker, who was crossing the room to see if she'd been shot.

"I'm okay," she said, but her voice was shaky. Parker helped her to her feet, keeping his eye on Peewee.

That's when she saw the blood seeping through Parker's shirt. "My God, you've been shot!"

Parker looked down. "I guess so." He tried to smile to reassure her, but she saw he was sweating. Her heart hammered in her ears as she opened his shirt. But the bullet had only grazed his side. She felt her whole body flood with relief. She picked up the ice pack to stop the bleeding. But Parker never took his eyes off Peewee, who was pulling himself up with his right hand.

Peewee stumbled over to the man who'd belittled him his whole life and so casually betrayed him. He held his throbbing left arm in his right as he stood triumphantly over him.

"Who taught you to shoot, boy?" Bourrée whispered.

Suddenly Peewee's expression changed. Was that a note of admiration in his father's voice? Peewee couldn't be sure. He'd never heard it before. He dropped to his knees. Bourrée's hands fluttered and jerked.

WHEN THE SHERIFF arrived, Peewee was sitting on the worn plank floor, holding Bourrée in his arms, desperately trying to stop the bleeding with his good right hand.

Outside an ambulance wailed. Peewee wailed too, but it was too late.

He had killed his own father.

Hugh wrote his daughter a firsthand account of the funeral. Widows from all over the South came and wept copious tears. In fact, the only dry-eyed woman in that crowd of wailing mourners was Miss Lily. She had a kind of relieved look on her face as they lowered Bourrée's coffin into the ground.

The trial was a sensation. Juries understand about a man shooting his wife. It was only natural. But killing his own father—and the D.A.'s campaign manager to boot—that was something else.

For the first time in his life, Peewee saw his picture in the paper and in the New Orleans and Baton Rouge papers too. He was secretly glad no one believed he was insane, even temporarily. He was sentenced to seven years in the state penitentiary for manslaughter, with time off for good behavior. He got out in four. His behavior had always been very, very good.

Amy Lou Hopper took it as her mission to save his immortal soul. She visited him every Sunday, bringing him baskets of baked goods. And when she raised her voice in prayer, thrusting her fervent prow right up against the visitor's screen where Peewee's hand was pressed, he had his first vision of heaven.

AT FIRST SISSY enjoyed "living in sin" up in Boston. But Parker didn't like it and the kids hated it. So Sissy gave in, filed for divorce, and married Parker.

He was true to his word. He made big money in the construction business and built them a house first outside of Boston and then in Alexandria, Virginia, where Sissy and Clara got together again. The younger woman was going to law school, marching for civil rights, and discovering that black is beautiful. She introduced her cousin to a whole new world. By now Clara was in love with a black activist. Sissy let them—no, encouraged them—to organize civil rights protests out of their new house in Alexandria.

But before they moved to Virginia, back in Boston, Sissy told Chip that Bourrée was his biological father and the boy decided to make her and Parker pay for the tragedy. He almost succeeded. Until with Hugh's and Belle's help, they shipped him off to a Southern military academy where distraught parents sent their delinquent sons to keep them out of jail. Chip loved it. He won all the medals on the shooting range and wrote an honors paper on the strategic benefits of poison gas. The school commander predicted a brilliant future.

Chip joined the army right after graduation, when they promised to assign him to a chemical warfare unit, and he rose through the ranks. Sissy suspected he'd personally made the decision to deploy Agent Orange, but she never had any solid information on that subject. The army sent him to college and he stayed in until his retirement in 1980, when he went to work for a chemical company no one had ever heard of, doing top-secret research somewhere in the Middle East. He never married, never wanted to have anything to do with his family, but Sissy never gave up trying.

Billy Joe got a football scholarship to Northwestern in 1961 and discovered acting. He studied Shakespeare, Chekhov, and Ibsen in college and then went to New York. He had his mother's charm, which served him well on the stage and in his many love affairs, as he knocked around in regional theater. When he was thirty he fell in love with a woman very much like Sissy, who was smart enough to let him think he was chasing her. They married the next year, soon had two children, and moved to Southern California. He played numerous roles in forgettable films and then after years of classical stage training he found fame, at last, on a TV sitcom. He and his family vacationed with his mother and Parker whenever his schedule permitted, and his burgeoning celebrity lent a real air of excitement when he was able to campaign in southern Louisiana towns.

The stage was filling up with dignitaries. A woman with a lot of teased blond hair sat down at the piano and belted out "America the Beautiful" in a clear bluesy voice. It took Sissy a few minutes to recognize Betty Ruth under all that hair. After her drunken foray in the woods with Harlan, Betty Ruth wrote Sissy that she'd joined Alcoholics Anonymous and had taken her own first step—by divorcing Brother Junior Bodine. She'd played the piano and sung in dives all over the South and in her later years had become a revered figure in the New Orleans jazz scene.

Then the mayor announced the senator had arrived. The band played "The Star-Spangled Banner" and the crowd stood and cheered for their new United States senator, Gentry's own Clara Conners.

Parker took Sissy's hand, which was covered in age spots now, but then so was his. He kissed her hand gently as Clara, with her hair turning gray and her figure thickening, walked onto the stage. Sissy thought how far they had come together.

Once Clara had enlisted her into the civil rights movement, Sissy found she had a real talent for fund-raising. The Southern Belle's Handbook was a big help when it came to talking rich businessmen into giving money to worthy causes. And later when Clara began running for office, there was no cause Sissy felt more passionate about than the rising political career of her cousin. A political career Clara strengthened by her own judicious use of certain rules in the Southern Belle's Handbook. She also used it to great advantage when she decided to marry the black activist she had loved for so long. He was a handful, but she managed to keep him faithful and supportive until his sudden death from a heart attack shortly before her run for the Senate.

Clara thanked the political establishment, her supporters, and then said, "There's one person I owe everything to, without whom I'd never be standing on this stage today. Sissy Davidson, get up here, girl."

Sissy hadn't expected this. She turned to Parker.

"Go on, honey, you deserve it."

"Come on, Sissy," the senator said. And the crowd cheered, "Sissy! Sissy!"

Sissy mounted the stage as Clara talked about all that Sissy had done for her. How she never would have had an education without her, never would have had the funds to stand there before them. Sissy's cheeks were burning, but she felt that same wild rush of energy she'd felt so many years before, when she stood on this same stage and spoke to a very different crowd on Clara's behalf.

Without letting her leave the stage, Clara told the crowd what she intended to do up there in Washington, for Gentry, for the state, and for the country. Sissy had heard it all before, when she'd helped Clara write it. She looked out over the audience and saw Marilee and the other campaign workers, those black-suited sisters in mourning, hovering together at the edge of the stage. Sissy knew most of them well. They were attractive, some of them even beautiful, all of them intelligent and well educated, and most of them miserable. Most of them lived alone.

For the first time in years, Sissy thought she just might take the advice Clara had given her in her kitchen back in 1956 and write the Southern Belle's Handbook. God knows, these poor benighted Yankee girls needed it. She'd seen the way they cut men down, not even trying to make them feel good about themselves. Sissy had long ago discarded Rule Thirty-seven, *Marriage is the root of all suffering*. Her new Rule Thirty-seven said, *Marriage can be the root of great happiness, when you marry the right man*.

She knew these bright, resourceful young women starved themselves diligently and worked out their bodies relentlessly, but they had little real grace or understanding of courtesy. She'd comforted

them as they wept hot tears when the humiliated men in their lives
left them, or worse, stayed and treated them badly. She had to write
the Southern Belle's Handbook for them, to help them attract a
good man and keep him in line, because Sissy knew even the best of
men needed a little managing. And if the other women took up the
handbook, maybe Marilee would too. Then maybe, just maybe, her
daughter would be able to find happiness, and not just empty bus-
tle, in her life.

The high school band struck up her old school march, and Clara
slipped her arm around her cousin's waist. The two old ladies
waved as the crowd cheered.

But how could she write the handbook? She'd never written anything except thank-you letters. Of course she'd helped with the
speeches and put together fund-raising proposals, but that wasn't
really writing.

As the band played and the crowd sang "Onward, onward to victory!" Clara took Sissy's hand in hers and held it up in a victory
salute. The crowd went wild. Parker and Marilee applauded loudly,
beaming with pride.

Suddenly Sissy knew she'd never succeed unless she tried. She
had to take that first step. She'd write down what she remembered.
The rest would come. Hell, she was only seventy-six. She had time.

ACKNOWLEDGMENTS

THERE ARE SO many people who helped me give birth to this novel. I am indebted first and foremost to my agent, Robert Tabian, who kept the faith and never let me down, and to my editor, Claire Wachtel, a woman of great taste and perspicacity. I also want to thank Jennifer Pooley at William Morrow/HarperCollins for her guidance and hand-holding, and Sharyn Rosenblum for her brilliant support. Sissy was born in Deena Metzger's workshop, and without her prodding, Sissy and her eccentric family might never have kept me awake at night and invaded my dreams. I am indebted to Mollie Gregory, Johnna Levine, and especially Sarah Timberman for their careful reading of the manuscript and their enthusiasm for it in its earliest stages and to Patricia Eskovitz and Dr. Ernest Scheuer, who proofed it at the end. Carolyn Kolb in New Orleans supplemented my childhood memories with her own recollections of small-town life in Louisiana. My father-in-law, Dr. Chesmore Eastlake, researched illegal abortions in the 1940s for me. The accuracies are theirs; any mistakes are all my own. I wish to acknowledge Dianne Dixon, who with unbridled enthusiasm urged me on. (Easy for you, Dianne.) And I am eternally grateful to my fellow writers, who have inspired me and who go daily into solitary rooms, sit in front of relentlessly whirring computers, and attempt to commit literature. I appreciate my son, David Despres Mulholland, for his unswerving belief that I could do anything. Finally, for my peculiar worldview I am beholden to the memories of two great southern belles—my grandmother Dora Stern and my aunt Francis Stern Schwarz—and to the memory of my mother, Doris Stern Despres, who never let the bastards get the better of her. This book could not have been written without any of them.